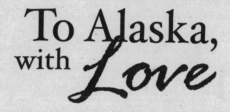

To Alaska,
with *Love*

LORI WILDE

To Alaska, with *Love*

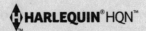

ISBN-13: 978-0-373-77927-7

TO ALASKA, WITH LOVE

Copyright © 2014 by Harlequin Books S.A.

The publisher acknowledges the copyright holder of the individual works as follows:

A TOUCH OF SILK
Copyright © 2002 by Laurie Vanzura

A THRILL TO REMEMBER
Copyright © 2002 by Laurie Vanzura

Recycling programs for this product may not exist in your area.

This edition published by arrangement with Harlequin Books S.A.

For questions and comments about the quality of this book, please contact us at CustomerService@Harlequin.com.

Printed in U.S.A.

CONTENTS

A TOUCH OF SILK

To Birgit Davis-Todd,
who gave me the chance to write about
my wild, sexy Alaskans. And to my inspiration—
the great state of Alaska.

CHAPTER ONE

THE PANTY HOSE were killing him. Cutting his gut clean in two. Whoever invented the torturous things should be strangled outright. No mercy shown.

Sheer, black, tight. They clung like second skin to the most exquisitely shaped pair of legs he'd ever seen. Narrow ankles, smooth rounded calves, supple knees and firm thighs.

She crossed her legs and the panty hose murmured a soft whisper. *Swish.*

And what about that dark seam running up the back? Simply *sin*-sational!

Lord have mercy on an Alaskan man's soul. He'd never witnessed such sights in his hometown of Bear Creek. For a second there Quinn Scofield thought he would have to ask the flight attendant for an oxygen mask.

Boldly he peered over the top of his *Wilderness Guide Monthly* at the blond, sleek-haired, Charlize Theron look-alike. She sat in first-class seat 1B, one diagonal row up from his position in 2C. She and her dynamite hosiery, presumably on their way to JFK, had boarded the plane during the layover at O'Hare, but not once had she glanced behind her. Instead, she had been studiously typing into her laptop computer for the past thirty minutes.

This one was too cool for school and she knew it.

Polished, classy, undeniably an urbanite, she was definitely not the kind of woman he was searching for. But man, did she ever rev his engines. Without the slightest provocation, he could easily imagine those fine, gorgeous limbs wrapped around his midsection or slung over his shoulders in the throes of serious sex.

"Real hottie, isn't she?" his seatmate, a paunchy, middle-aged businessman who'd had one too many whiskey sours, slurred, and nodded at the woman.

"She's very attractive, yes," Quinn agreed, but kept his voice low so she wouldn't overhear.

Unfortunately the other man's volume control had been affected by his alcohol intake. He leaned close in a confidential manner, nudged Quinn in the ribs and winked boldly. "I'd do her in a New York minute. Know what I mean?"

Slowly Charlize turned and pinned them both with an icy glare. Quick, like a little boy chastised, the businessman looked away. But Quinn didn't flinch. He'd been dying for a glimpse of those eyes, and he wasn't going to let his seatmate's bad manners deprive him of the thrill.

Their gazes met.

And he wasn't disappointed. Her eyes were as compelling as the rest of her. Sharp, slightly almond-shaped, the color of dark chocolate.

His heart did a triple axel, then dropped, *ker-plunk*, into his stomach. He'd always had a weakness for brown-eyed blondes. Quinn smiled, giving her his best George-Clooney-on-the-make imitation.

Charlize didn't return the favor.

"Hi," he greeted her boldly. "How you doin'?"

For a minute there he thought she might speak.

Her lips parted. Her eyes widened. A hint of a smile hovered.

Come on, sweetheart, give it up.

His hopes lodged in his throat. Suddenly his imagination transported him back to the fifth grade. He remembered sneaking off during recess to play spin the bottle with his classmates in the basement of Seward Middle School with the singular hope of kissing Mindy Lou Johnson.

But then Charlize cruelly shattered his dreams. Without a word, she flicked her gaze away, as if he was of no more significance than a pesky fly, and went back to her laptop.

Snubbed! Okay, that's what he got for daring to speak to the Queen of Cool.

Quinn tried to focus on his magazine, but he couldn't concentrate. Eventually, his gaze found its way back to those legs. Eighteen months without the comforts of female companionship was a far stretch to go.

That's how long it had been since his ex-girlfriend Heather had turned down his marriage proposal. She'd told him that no matter how much she might love him, she could never be more than a fair weather Alaskan. The winters were just too harsh.

Heather begged him to move to Cleveland, but Quinn figured he must not have loved her as much as he thought. He had not yet met the woman who could convince him to leave his home. Alaska was in his blood, his heart, his soul. But man alive, sometimes those long, dark winter nights got really lonely.

Some of his friends had told him he was too stubborn, letting his love of Alaska overrule his heart. They said if he didn't learn to compromise, he'd never find true love. But others had congratulated him on sticking to his guns. He was an Alaskan man, and only a woman willing to become an Alaskan wife could make him happy.

At thirty-two Quinn was ready for a family of his own, but he knew it would take a very special lady to make her home in Bear Creek. Elegant thing like Charlize Theron there, with her fancy panty hose and her hundred-dollar haircut, would be crushed by the regal brutality of the Alaskan landscape. Nope, pretty she might be, but he needed someone tough and strong and resilient. Someone like his younger sister, Meggie. Or at least how Meggie used to be before she married Jesse Drummond and moved off to Seattle to fulfill her dream of becoming a city girl. Trouble was, in Bear Creek, men outnumbered women ten to one.

In the meantime he wasn't opposed to studying Charlize for sheer enjoyment. He tried to imagine her in Alaska and had to smile. No Broadway theater. No champagne-and-black-tie charity events for cultural enrichment. In Bear Creek if you wanted to raise money for, say, the volunteer fire department, you threw a salmon bake, got a keg of beer, slapped some hard-driving music on your CD player and let it go at that.

From where he sat, Quinn could only see her profile and those elegant hands tapping away at the keyboard. Her nose was perfectly shaped. Exquisite, in fact. Not too big, not too small. Not too sharp, not too soft.

Her cheekbones—Quinn could see just one, but he knew the other matched—were as high and sculpted as any fashion model's. Her firm but feminine chin was an artist's dream. And that mouth! Full, but not overblown like those Hollywood actresses who had their lips shot full of collagen. Lips currently adorned with lipstick the same russet shade as an Alaskan summer sunset.

Oh, this one was a fascinating combination of fire and ice, all right. Her regal demeanor shouted "You're never gonna get it," but those panty hose and spike-heeled shoes gave totally conflicting messages. Deep down she was a sensual woman aching to shake off that repressed disposition.

She closed her laptop and settled it under her seat. Her pencil dropped to the floor, unnoticed.

Quinn, never one to let good sense hold him back from something he wanted, seized the opportunity. Leaning forward, he tapped her gently on the shoulder.

"Miss?"

She jerked her head around and stabbed him with a hard, what-do-you-want-from-me-wilderness-boy expression. No doubt she was accustomed to strange men making passes at her, and she'd perfected that "hands off" look to quell even the most ardent admirer in his tracks. A necessary skill for a woman who dressed like that.

"You dropped your pencil." He pointed.

Her expression softened when she realized he wasn't hitting on her—even though he was working up to that. The corners of her lips edged upward and she silently mouthed, "Thank you."

Argh! Her simple thank-you struck like an arrow through the heart.

Yo, Mama, I think I'm in big-time lust.

When she leaned down to retrieve the pencil, she shifted her legs and her skirt rode up higher on her thigh. Quinn almost choked.

He spied the hint of something black and lacy. She straightened, pencil in hand, and reached to tug her skirt down.

But it was too late. He already knew her secret.

She turned her head, met his eyes again and sent him a Mona Lisa smile.

Those were no panty hose.

The audacious woman was wearing a garter and stockings!

KAY FREEMONT CASUALLY TOOK a compact from her purse.

Okay, maybe it wasn't so casually. Maybe she wanted another peek at Paul Bunyon back there without turning around and giving him the satisfaction of knowing she was interested.

Not interested in a serious way, of course. She was trying to untangle herself from an unsatisfactory relationship, not get into a new one. She merely wanted to confirm that the broad-shouldered man clad in flannel and denim was indeed as ruggedly cute as she thought.

Kay might have worried her bottom lip with her teeth, so curious was she about this man, but many years of her mother's nagging stopped her. Mustn't smear one's lipstick. Freemonts had a certain image to maintain.

She feigned using the compact mirror to pat her unmussed hair into place, but she angled it so she could see him. Secretly she'd always been sexually attracted to burly, outdoorsy men. Strong, physical men who played contact sports and repaired their own cars. Men who chopped wood and roasted raw meat over fire pits. Men who'd fight to the death to protect their women.

The fact that her boyfriend Lloyd was a slender, brainy, pacifistic vegetarian who didn't even own a car, much less know how to work on one, did not escape her. But just because she daydreamed about extremely manly men didn't mean she coveted a relationship with one. It was simply a sexual fantasy.

Besides some things were more important than sex. Companionship, for instance.

And Lloyd is such a great companion? He works eighty-hour weeks. And when was the last time he made love to you? Seven, eight weeks ago?

That wasn't fair. She couldn't lay blame solely at his feet. She was as busy as Lloyd.

And is it your fault that Lloyd has never satisfied you in bed?

Maybe it *was* her fault. Even though she spent a lot of time researching and writing how-to-improve-your-sex-life articles like "How to Achieve Multiple Orgasms" and "Tantric Sex, The New Revolution in Intimacy," for the hottest women's magazine in the country, Kay had yet to experience such lofty sensations herself.

Yes, she read and she read and she read. From classics like *The Hite Report* and *The Story of O* to the most up-to-date literature on the subject, she knew them all by heart. Kay understood the mechanics of sex, and she kept thinking that if she just gathered enough knowledge on the subject, one day she'd be able to scale her way to the stars.

Maybe she should see a counselor, instead.

Or maybe you should just have a wild, uninhibited fling. I bet Paul Bunyon's got what it takes to please a woman. Did you get a load of those hands? If it's true what they say about the size of a man's hands and the size of his...

Kay tilted the mirror to the right to get a better look.

Paul Bunyon's upper arms were as big as her thighs. For some illogical reason, this thought made her shiver. He was so very large and seemed to be constructed of pure steel. He was tall and muscular and solid. She imagined he could toss her over his shoulder more easily than she could pick up a tea bag. He possessed hair the color of aged whiskey and sultry gray eyes that snapped with surprising intelligence.

His shirt was a comforting shade of blue, and he had the sleeves rolled up a quarter turn, giving her a peek of sexy forearms offset by a thick, leather-banded watch. Nice. Very nice. Just the right amount of hair. Kay had a weakness for sexy forearms.

She licked her lips, forgetting all about smearing her lipstick. A weighted feeling settled over her and made her blood flow hot and sluggish as the erotic sensation drifted down to wedge heavily between her legs. She wondered what would happen if she stood up and walked toward him. What would he do if she bent down to his ear and with a seductive whisper invited him to become a member of the mile-high club with her? Tingles dove down her spine.

If she pivoted on her heel and sashayed to the lavatory, would he follow?

She swallowed hard past the lump in her throat. What a tight fit! The two of them crammed into an airplane lavatory. It would require some maneuvering. Kay stared so hard into the mirror of her compact that her vision blurred and she was transported.

He lifts her up on the counter; his eyes fill with heated desire. He takes one of those big hands and, starting at her right ankle, he oh-so-slowly moves it up her leg, past the curve of her calf, to the bend of her knee. She gasps at his touch. His callused fingertips snag her stockings, tearing them until she resembles a lady of the evening after a long night of selling pleasure.

Then his other hand starts its journey up her left leg. He moves closer, and she wraps her legs around his waist. The top of her head is resting against the rest-

room mirror, and her back is arched. He stares into her eyes, captivated. Clearly he thinks she is the most exquisite creature on the face of the earth.

His right hand goes farther. Moving up her knee inch by inch. Her skirt hikes high. The sensations are incredible. His rough fingers sliding over her bare skin, the cold sink beneath her bottom, the feel of his hard waist against the inside of her legs. She feels a million things at once, and they are all good.

He's still looking at her, but not saying a single word. He smells delicious, like Christmas trees and woodsmoke and leather. She feels herself moisten with desire. She wants him like a lion wants a lamb.

"Kiss me," she commands him in a bossy voice.

He dips his head. His hands are on her thighs, palms splayed. He's so close, but he doesn't lower his lips to hers. He's teasing. There's a naughty gleam in his eye.

"What will you give me for a kiss?" he asks.

His voice is heart-stoppingly sexy. A resonant sound that fills her ears like the loveliest bass instrument. Her pulse throbs at her throat. She's hot all over. Hot and wet and desperate.

"I'll give you whatever you want," she whimpers.

"I want you to touch me," he says. "Here."

And then he takes her hand and guides it to the bulge straining against the zipper of his blue jeans. She eases down the zipper, slips her hand inside. He's going commando, no underwear. She touches him.

It's so big. So hard. So hot. Scalding. He smells of musky male, and her excitement escalates. He groans and closes his eyes.

At the same time as she's touching him, his hand is busy snaking up her thigh to hook a finger around the waistband of her panties.

She moans. He crushes his mouth to hers.

He tastes too good to be true. Not the finest caviar in her mother's pantry, not even the most expensive bottle of French champagne in her father's cellar can compete with his flavor.

Her palm is pressed hard against his erection, which seems to keep growing and growing and growing. His tongue is a menace, dazzling her with moves she never thought possible.

"I want you inside me."

"No. Not yet. First, I'm going to make you beg."

She whimpers again.

"That's right." He nods. "This has been a long time coming."

Her nipples tighten. She wriggles her hips. Her panties are whisked off.

"What are you doing?"

"Hush, woman," he growls. "Hush and enjoy. You deserve everything I'm going to give you and so much more. You drive me wild."

She glows at his words. Men have told her she's beautiful before, but no one has ever told her she drives him wild. He's telling her exactly what she needs to hear, and she loves him for it. She feels incredibly powerful that she's controlling such a big man with her sexuality.

Then he goes to work with his fingers.

He's stroking her inner thigh, and then he trails his fingertips inward. He's doing something that makes her eyes roll back in her head with sheer ecstasy.

Oh, gawd, what that intoxicating hand is doing at the apex of her womanhood!

She writhes against him, clutches his shoulders with

both hands, digs her fingers into his flesh through the soft flannel of his shirt.

His movements are gentle but firm. The pressure builds. No man has ever caressed her in quite this way. It's as if he knows exactly how to make her cry out for more. She's never been this excited, this desperate, this famished for a man's body.

"Don't stop," she pleads.

He grins. For a moment she fears he'll stop simply to taunt her. But to her relief he keeps going. And going. And going.

She feels as if she's riding a roller coaster. Chugging up, up, up. Breath held in anticipation of the rapturous plunge.

She's close. So very close. Teetering on the verge. One more second. Oh, yes. Yes. She's just about to—

"Miss?" The flight attendant's voice slammed her rudely back to earth.

"Yes," Kay gasped, feeling breathless, edgy and achy.

"Would you care for another beverage?"

She shook her head. The flight attendant moved on down the aisle. Then Kay realized she was still holding the compact. She glanced into the mirror one last time and was horrified to see Paul Bunyon staring right at her.

Their eyes met in the mirror's reflection. Her heart raced. Her mouth went dry. He gave her a cocksure smile as if he knew exactly what she'd been thinking.

Flushed and flustered, Kay snapped the compact closed and dropped it into her purse. She burned weak, shaky, her entire body swamped in heat. This wouldn't do. She had to compose herself. Immediately, if not sooner.

Unbuckling her seat belt, she got up, slipped into the lavatory and locked the door. Bad idea. This was the scene of the fictitious crime, and she couldn't escape her own mind.

She wet a paper towel, pressed it first to the back of her neck, then to the hollow of her throat and took several long, slow, deep breaths. For the past few months she'd been plagued by uncontrollable sexual fantasies. It was quite embarrassing, really. As if she was some kind of X-rated, female Walter Mitty.

Perhaps a fling was in order. Find someone to pop her cork, as it were. Perhaps that would put an end to these persistent flights of sexual fancy.

Kay pinched the bridge of her nose to ward off more blushing. This was simply ridiculous. She had to stop entertaining such unsuitable thoughts about total strangers. She took several more deep breaths, tossed the damp towel into the trash, then ran her fingers through her hair. There. She looked fine. Perfectly normal. Perfectly in control. No one would suspect anything to the contrary.

The plane lurched, jostling her as she unlocked the accordion-style door and tried to shove it open, but the silly thing stuck.

The plane pitched again, throwing Kay forward. She put a hand on the door hinges to brace herself, and the door folded open. She raised her head in alarm.

And found herself tumbling headlong into Paul Bunyon's arms, as if he'd been waiting outside the door just to catch her when she fell.

CHAPTER TWO

"WHY, HELLO." Quinn smiled down into the face of a goddess.

What compelled him to trail her to the lavatory, he couldn't say. Maybe it was that sassy, controlled walk of hers that hypnotized him. Maybe it was her contradictory aura, pushing and pulling him in two different directions. Or maybe it was plain old horniness on his part.

But now he sure was glad he'd followed her. If he hadn't been there to catch her, she would have pitched head first into the bulkhead opposite the lavatory and bruised her pretty face, and that would have been a crying shame.

"Are you all right?" he asked.

"Fine," she whispered.

Her voice surprised him. One more irreconcilable fact that added to her allure. He'd expected her tone would be more cultured, aloof, cool and reserved. Instead, the sexy sound of her had him remembering all those nights during high school and college that he'd spun records of throaty-voiced female blues singers at his family's tiny radio station in Bear Creek.

Unblinking, the goddess met his gaze and held it. The impact slugged him. Her sultry eyes, dark as coffee and surrounded by lashes as impossibly thick as paintbrushes, snagged something deep inside him and refused to let go.

In the brief, endless moment he held her in his arms, he noticed everything about her.

The tiny mole at the left corner of her mouth. The smooth, expertly penciled arch of her brow. The erratic throbbing of her pulse in the hollow of her neck. The slim curve of her waist. Her rich, fresh scent that made him ache to bury his nose in her hair and breathe deeply.

And the unnerving realization that beneath her ultrasoft silk blouse and bra, her nipples were puckered.

It wasn't cold in the plane's cramped confines. In fact, it was very, very hot.

Had her breasts hardened in response to him? Quinn almost groaned aloud at the thought.

Was he reading too much into this casual encounter? Was his desire for one last fiery sexual adventure before he found a wife and settled down for good feeding into his imagination and causing him to misread her reaction?

Her lips parted, and he could see the pink tip of her tongue pressing against her top teeth. She looked as if she might say something to him, but she didn't.

Oh, Lord, he could feel her stockings rub against the leg of his jeans as she shifted in his arms.

So many thoughts raced through his brain it seemed as if eons had passed. But it couldn't have been more than a few seconds since she'd toppled into his embrace.

She raised a hand to her cheek to brush away a strand of golden hair. He tracked her movement, peered into those compelling brown eyes once more.

And stumbled. Literally lost his balance as the plane hit another pocket of turbulence. He tipped backward, taking Charlize with him.

They ended up in the middle of the aisle, a jumble of arms and legs. The fall hadn't knocked the air from his lungs, but nonetheless, he found it hard to breathe with her lying on his chest.

"Are you okay?" There was that breathy whisper again, uncertain, a bit nervous. And unless he missed his guess, tinged with an acute awareness of him as a man.

"Okay," he replied, hating for this moment to end.

"Please take your seats," a flight attendant said sharply as she rushed over. "And buckle yourselves in."

"Let me help you up," Charlize offered, rising to her feet with amazing agility and grace for a woman wearing three-inch heels and a mean pair of stockings.

He almost laughed at the notion of a slender branch like her helping a tree trunk like himself to his feet. But he liked the idea of touching her again, so he put out his hand, which dwarfed hers, and allowed her to tug him.

Quinn pushed against the floor of the plane, and his own momentum brought him to a standing position. The top of her sleek head only came to his armpit. Her hip was level with his upper thigh. She seemed as perfect and delicate as the first butterfly of spring.

Without a doubt she was the most exquisite woman he'd ever met. Her straight blond hair was cut in a polished style and appeared as finely spun as silk. Her complexion was flawless, except for a small scar below her right earlobe. He had an almost overpowering urge to explore that scar with the tip of his tongue.

How he wanted to say something more to her, to do something more with her, but the frowning flight attendant was clucking her tongue and waving at them to take their seats. Charlize scooted past him, her breasts lightly brushing his upper arm, causing a brushfire to leap up his nerve endings, and made her way to her seat.

Kay was practically panting as she clicked the seat belt in place around her waist. Her heart pounded, blood suffused her skin. She couldn't believe what had just happened and her body's heated response to a stranger. Touching him had been far more electric, far more satisfying than her wildest imaginings.

She didn't look up, because she knew he was still standing there staring at her as if he'd been struck with a bolt from the blue. What was the matter with him? Didn't they have women wherever it was he was from?

"You sure you're all right?" He squatted in the aisle beside Kay, defying the angry flight attendant, who looked as if she wanted to tie him into his seat but was too quelled by his size to approach.

"I'm fine, don't worry about me. Please, for your own safety, sit down."

"If you need me, I'm right behind you." He touched her wrist with his massive paw, and her blood slipped through her veins like quicksilver. Intense. So intense. If she closed her eyes, she could see the two of them in a forest. Walking. Alone. On a bed of soft, mossy ground. The sunlight flitting through the trees.

Stop it, stop it, stop it. Don't you dare go into another sexual fantasy, Kathryn Victoria Freemont!

She raised her hand to her face. The hand that had been wrapped in his. She smelled of him. Robust, masculine. Like pine needles, wilderness and soap. A shiver she could not suppress overtook her body. She could easily imagine him back there in his seat watching her with eagle eyes.

What was it about this man that so stirred her blood?

What was it that made her feel giddy and girlish and oh-so-happy to be alive?

Kay was kidding herself, and she knew it. Just because he made her feel desirable didn't mean she was licensed to jump his bones. She didn't even know the guy's name. What he made her feel was simply a reflection of her wishful thinking. She wanted rescuing from her life, and he was a convenient escapist illusion.

Because lately, nothing in her current experiences seemed to satisfy her. Not her relationship with her parents, who were pressuring her to marry Lloyd and produce an heir. Certainly not her romance with Lloyd, if you could even call what they had a romance.

Lloyd had proposed to her by email two days ago in a manner as romantic as a root canal. His exact message had been "Your father says he'll make me partner if we're married by the end of the summer, guess it's time to do the deed."

Whoopee! Sweep a girl right off her feet, why don't you?

She'd ignored Lloyd's email, pretending she hadn't yet seen the missive, because she wasn't ready to deal with it, and surprise, surprise, he hadn't even called her in Chicago to see why she hadn't responded.

And even her job as a reporter for *Metropolitan* magazine no longer fulfilled her as it once had.

"What happened to you?" she whispered to herself, grateful no one was seated next to her. "In college, you dreamed of writing novels and having adventures and taking a lover that was as kind and considerate and understanding as he was good in bed. Where did that girl go?"

It seemed her entire youth had been spent trying to please Mommy and Daddy and striving to be the perfect Freemont. Her one tiny insurrection had been insisting on studying journalism rather than art history, as her mother had wished.

"Lloyd Post comes from blueblood stock, dear, just like you," her mother had told her when she called the day before to see if Kay had gotten Lloyd's emailed proposal. Apparently Lloyd had already discussed it with her parents. Would have been nice if he'd talked things over with her first. "Give his proposition some serious thought. You could do worse than marrying him."

Hmm, what was worse than binding yourself for life to a man who virtually ignored you for weeks on end? What was worse than until death do you part with a man who didn't even care where your G-spot was located? What was worse than spending the next forty years beside a guy with whom you had absolutely nothing in common other than the fact you were both filthy rich with impeccable pedigrees?

Let's see, what was worse than marrying Lloyd Post?

Well, owing money to the Mafia had to be a bummer. Being stranded in the desert with no water wasn't cool. Having oral surgery wasn't a blast. So yes, Mommy, you're absolutely right. There are worse things than marrying Lloyd.

But there were so many better things, too.

Like taking that rugged woodsman to bed?

She tried to picture what would happen if she was to walk into her parents house on Paul Bunyon's arm and announce they were engaged. Laughable! Even she, of the overactive imagination, could not conceive of such an event.

Helplessly she found her head drawn to the right, her eyes peeping surreptitiously over her shoulder.

And there he was, just as she knew he'd be. Staring at her and not a bit ashamed of his unabashed appreciation.

He was pure testosterone in a huge package that proclaimed, "I'll never let any harm come to you." It was a heady promise. Between his protective attitude and his raw animal magnetism, the man oozed an essential sexiness that called to something wild within her. Like a wolf to his mate. Something primal and elemental she hadn't known she possessed until now.

She deserved to be happy. She deserved to be sexually satisfied, and she deserved far better than settling for Lloyd Post. In reality she knew Paul Bunyon did not figure into her future, but regardless, meeting him at this juncture had changed her. It was time she stood up to her parents and started living her own life. It was past time she found out what she'd been missing.

QUINN PLANNED TO WAYLAY her in the jetway, help her with her luggage, hail her a taxi, get her phone number and ask her out to dinner. In fact, he was so excited about the idea that he'd kept shifting restlessly in his seat, unable to think of anything else.

But when the plane landed at JFK, she leaped from her seat the minute the flight attendants opened the door. Quinn got up to follow her, but an elderly lady sitting across the aisle asked him to retrieve her carry-on bag from the overhead bin. What else could he do? By the time he made his way into the terminal, Charlize had vanished as if she'd never existed.

He looked left, then right, but the crowd had swallowed her. How could she have disappeared so quickly?

Damn!

He hadn't mistaken her interest in him, no matter how cool she liked to play it. The attraction had been instant and physical. No denying her raspy breathing when he'd held her in his arms, no hiding her aroused nipples. She'd wanted him, all right.

So why had she run away?

Maybe she was married, the thought occurred to him, but he didn't recall seeing a ring on that delicate third finger of her left hand.

Ah, well. Quinn wasn't the sort to cry over spilt milk. He took a deep breath and headed for the baggage claim. Nothing to be done about it now. He tried to push her from his thoughts.

But despite his best intentions, he couldn't help feeling he'd lost out on something pretty darn terrific.

"KAY, COME HERE, you've got to see this." Her editor, Judy Nessler, stood in the doorway of Kay's office on Monday morning, grinning from ear to ear and crooking a bejeweled finger at her.

Kay frowned and glanced up from the piece she was working on about finding love on the internet. She'd gone to Chicago to interview a couple who'd met in an online chat room, and she had her notes spread out on the desk around her. Included in the pile were copies of the spicy messages the couple had posted to each other during their courtship. Reading the sizzling missives had her feeling oddly cranky.

"What is it, Judy?"

"Ask me no questions and I'll tell you no lies."

She wasn't in the mood for Judy's guessing games. It had been almost twenty-four hours since her plane ride with Paul Bunyon, but she couldn't seem to stop spinning fantasies about him. How could the thought of one man make her ache so badly?

Nor had she been able to locate Lloyd in order to

pin him down for a dinner date to discuss his marriage proposal in person, and he hadn't yet returned the call she had left on his answering machine.

"I'm in the middle of something," Kay said.

"Just come with me."

Sighing, Kay pushed away from her desk and followed Judy down the corridor to the advertising department. As usual, the room was abuzz with activity. But atypically, all the activity seemed concentrated in the middle of room. Centered, in fact, around a skyscraper-size man who had his back to them.

A man clad in red flannel and blue denim. His head was cocked to one side and he was laughing at something one of the blushing assistants had said. Kay's pulse momentarily stuttered to a stop. She raised a hand to her throat.

No. It couldn't be.

Judy leaned in close and whispered, "You don't see guys like him traipsing up Fifth Avenue every day of the week."

Please, don't let it be Paul Bunyon, Kay prayed, but in her heart she knew.

Judy took her by the elbow and dragged her across the room like a reluctant puppy on a leash.

"Quinn," Judy said. "I'd like you to meet Kay Freemont, one of our top writers."

Slowly he pivoted on one booted heel, an insouciant gleam in his eye. Then recognition hit. His brows sprung up on his forehead and the grin went from free and easy to downright seductive.

It was Paul Bunyon! What an awful coincidence.

Of all the magazine offices in Manhattan, he had to walk into mine.

Why was he here? Was this some kind of a sign, him

showing up so unexpectedly? Was the universe trying to tell her something?

"Kay, this is Quinn Scofield from Bear Creek, Alaska."

She stared at him.

He stared back at her.

Neither of them spoke.

The air around them seemed to vibrate with heat and energy and overpowering awareness.

Quinn. From Alaska. The Mighty Quinn. She should have known he would have a macho moniker. The name fit him like the mackinaw he wore.

Puzzled, Judy watched them watching each other. "Have you two already been introduced?"

"Actually, no." Quinn didn't even wait for Kay to offer her hand. He simply took it, and her blood puddled like melted butter in the pit of her stomach. "I'm very honored to make the acquaintance of such a lovely lady."

Pul-leeze. Enough with the flattery. I just saw you flirting with that assistant.

And yet, a small frisson of pleasure spiraled through her body and lodged with stunning acuity in her most feminine parts. If anything, her attraction to him was even stronger than it had been the day before.

Scary.

When Kay finally tore her gaze from his face, she realized that all the single women—and more than a few of the married ones—in the room were looking at her as if she'd snatched a prized morsel of filet mignon from their mouths.

"Quinn's come to New York looking for a wife," Judy said.

A wife? Kay took a step backward.

en there's no time to waste. Kay can do it. She's pretty
ntrepid, aren't you, darling?"

Ten degrees below zero! Kay shivered at the very
dea. "Are you nuts?"

"Come on, where's your spirit of adventure?" Judy
oaded her. "Besides, it's perfect for the article. You can
ell the readers firsthand that being an Alaskan wife is
ot for the faint of heart. Marriage-minded, handsome,
uccessful bachelors do not come without some kind
f price tag."

Kay shook her head. She was not going to Alaska—it
ould give Quinn the wrong idea. He might start think-
g she was interested in becoming his bride. Besides,
e had to settle things with Lloyd. "I'm sorry, I can't
mmit to this project right now—I've got too much
my plate. Why don't you ask Carol? I'm sure she'd
e to go."

Was it her imagination, or did Quinn look disap-
nted? The notion that he wanted her to come to
ska did strange things to Kay's insides.

Don't give me your answer yet," Judy said. "I still
to talk to Hal. Then you can make up your mind.
's that sound?"

All right, but don't tell Hal that I've agreed to sign
t."

Understood. Now why don't you take Quinn to
? In fact, take the rest of the afternoon off. Show
New York. Since you're practically engaged, I
you won't be a threat to his bachelorhood and
him off the market before the ad even has a
e to run."

She jerked a quick glance in Quinn's direction and
saw he was observing her reaction to Judy's news. Oh,
boy, and here she'd been dreaming of having a red-hot
fling with him. Well, certainly not now!

She'd just about decided to give old Lloyd the heave-
ho and to tell her parents she was tired of living her life
to suit them. She was ready to stretch her sexual wings
and fly. She was not getting involved with a man who
was looking for a commitment. No way. No matter how
sexy he might be.

"He wants to place this full-page color ad with us."
Judy took the advertising copy from an assistant and
handed it to Kay.

Full-page color-ad space in *Metropolitan* magazine
didn't come cheap.

"The four of us pitched in," Quinn said, as if reading
Kay's mind. "The bachelors of Bear Creek."

"Doesn't that have a great ring to it?" Judy's eyes
glistened. Clearly she was enamored of Quinn, his buddies and their ad.

Kay stared down at the photograph in her hand and
sucked in her breath. Pictured were four of the most gorgeous men she'd ever laid eyes on, one of them Quinn.
They looked sexier and far more masculine than anything Madison Avenue could have dreamed up. The men
wore blue jeans, devilish grins and nothing else, their
hunky, well-muscled bare chests on prominent display.

In the photo Quinn was lounging on one end of a
black leather couch. He was bigger than she'd even
imagined, with the buffest biceps on the planet. Draped
across the other side of the couch was a coal-haired,
blue-eyed Adonis with a dreamy, angelic air about him.
On the floor, perched atop a bearskin rug, sat a dishy
blond man with more charisma than a movie star, and

another dark-eyed man with a lantern jaw and deep-set brown eyes. All four men were looking straight into the camera as if staring into the eyes of a beautiful woman.

Her gaze went from the one-dimensional, bare-chested Quinn to the fully three-dimensional Quinn standing beside her, and she gulped.

"That's Caleb Greenleaf," he said, leaning over her shoulder and pointing to the Adonis. "He's a naturalist for the state of Alaska. And that's Jake Gerard and Mack McCaulley. Jake runs the local bed-and-breakfast, and Mack's a bush pilot."

But Kay wasn't thinking about Caleb or Jake or Mack, no matter how good-looking they were. She was completely and totally distracted by Quinn's warm breath fanning the hairs on the nape of her neck.

Her gut tripped. She inhaled sharply and caught the arresting scent of his subtle aftershave and heated male flesh. That delicious smell sent her senses reeling.

Shaking her head to dispel the sultry cocoon Quinn had woven around her, Kay returned her attention to the glossy paper in her hand. Beneath the photograph of the four very eligible bachelors was the provocative caption: *Wild Women Wanted!*

"Do you have what it takes to be a wilderness wife?" was the first line of copy.

For absolutely no reason at all, Kay's heart fluttered. That line shouldn't have titillated her. She definitely did not have what it took to be a wilderness wife. She considered eating fast food roughing it. She had a low tolerance for cold weather, and she was scared to death of creatures like wolves and moose and bears.

Of course, if you had a man like Quinn to protect you from the cold and the critters, it might make Alaska a little more palatable. Still, a life without four-star res-

taurants, Broadway shows and department st too dismal to consider.

"I love this whole idea," Judy was chat Quinn. "Sexy bachelors forced to advertise in forty-eight states to find wives. It's romanti chanting. It's a modern-day fairy tale. Our re eat it up. In fact, I'd like to run a feature arti four of you."

"We could hold a contest," Kay volunteered keting instincts kicking in, despite the fact t ally wanted nothing more to do with this bachelor and his wife hunt. "In thirty wo tell us why you'd like to win a free trip to Alaska. That sort of thing."

"Fabulous!" Judy enthused, and patted "You're such a dynamo. I knew you'd ha valuable to say. I love the idea. Simply lo can do a follow-up story on the contest wi knows, if any of the guys find a wife a of the ad, we can do follow-up articles year. I'll have to run this by Hal first, going to adore it, too."

Kay shrugged, playing it cool as a never acted too eager.

"So what do you say, Kay? Ready and spend a couple of weeks in Al

"What?" She shook her head, t question. "Me go to Alaska?"

"Well," Quinn said, "late Fet the best time of year to visit. Wh ten below."

"No kidding?" Judy whistled. want the article to run with yo

CHAPTER THREE

PRACTICALLY ENGAGED.

So that explained why she'd fled from the airplane before he'd had a chance to ask her name. She'd been as attracted to him as he was to her, and very clearly disturbed by that attraction because she was in a serious, committed relationship.

Damn.

And he'd come to New York in person, rather than handling the details of placing the ad over the phone or through the mail, not only because he was considering purchasing new wilderness gear from a sporting goods outfit run by an old friend, but because he'd secretly hoped to have one last sexual adventure before seriously beginning his wife search.

With all his heart and soul, Quinn believed in monogamy. His parents, who'd had a solid, loving marriage for forty years and still counting, provided him with a blueprint. Once he made a commitment to a woman, he'd be hers for life. But until he found her, well, he was a red-blooded male, after all. He had physical needs. Needs that were growing stronger by the minute.

He'd known from the moment he'd watched Kay Freemont board the plane that he wanted her, and then to find her working in the office of *Metropolitan* magazine—unbelievable! He'd taken it as a positive sign that she was supposed to be his passionate last fling.

But now, to discover that she was practically engaged. Where did that leave him? He wasn't the sort of guy who came between a woman and her almost fiancé.

Then again, what the hell did "practically engaged" mean, anyway? Quinn ran a hand through his hair. Where he came from, either you were engaged or you weren't. Maybe it was a New York thing.

"Well." Kay nodded and looked rather uncomfortable with the assignment of baby-sitting him for the rest of the afternoon. "Well."

Had her boss's edict to wine and dine him left her at a loss for words? Or was it something more? Was it meeting him again?

Dream on, Scofield.

And yet, that was exactly what he wanted to do. Dream on and on and on of taking her to bed. Seeing her in her work environment, amid people who obviously admired and respected her, looking so professional and self-possessed in that short-skirted purple business suit made him crave her even more. Did she have any earthly idea what those magnificent legs of hers did to a man? Women who were practically engaged and possessed legs like Thoroughbreds should not be allowed to wear skirts like that! There oughtta be a law.

Damn, but the woman blew him away! Her cocoa-brown eyes simmered with a suppressed sexuality that begged to be brought to a boil. When he had turned and spied her beside Judy Nessler, adrenaline walloped him in the gut.

Now, simply standing here next to her, inhaling her scent—a fetching combination of vanilla ice cream and sharply scented cinnamon sticks—his body came alive.

To the point where he wished for a bucket of ice cubes to chill his throbbing member.

"Your cologne smells nice. What's it called?"

"White Heat."

He angled her a glance. "White Heat, huh? It suits you."

"Pardon?"

He could tell by the way she pursed her lips that he'd unnerved her. "You're like white heat. You've got this cool, outer demeanor, but inside, there's a deep, smoldering flame."

She gulped. He watched her struggle to control her features. She hated giving away her thoughts, he realized, and she'd mastered the art of suppressing her emotions.

How he longed to unsuppress her. To teach her how to open up and say exactly what was on her mind.

"Uh, let me get my bag and coat and change my shoes." She gestured in the direction of what he supposed was her office. "And we can grab some lunch."

She dashed away, leaving him to rein in his hormones, and returned a few minutes later wearing a black leather coat with an oversize purse thrown over her shoulder and a pair of Nikes on her feet. He almost laughed at the sight of her in that glamorous business suit and shod in running shoes, but once they were out on the street, he noticed a lot of the women similarly dressed. He commented on it.

"Try walking twelve blocks in high heels. You'd carry a spare pair of sneakers in your bag, too."

"We don't even have blocks in Bear Creek." He grinned.

She gave him a strange look as if he was speaking Mandarin. And it struck him then how different their lives were. He could survive alone in the Alaskan wilderness for weeks if necessary, but in New York City, he feared being unable to survive something as simple as crossing the street. He couldn't understand how people lived here day in and day out. The pollution, the noise, the crowds. Eventually it had to drive you out of your mind.

Kay stepped off the curb and raised her hand. A taxi glided to a stop at their feet.

How'd she do that? he marveled. When he'd tried to get a taxi to carry him to the magazine office, he'd been ignored. Was he so obviously an out-of-towner? Or did she know some taxi-halting secrets? Then again, if he was a cab driver, he would willingly risk whiplash to jam on the brakes for those legs.

Quinn moved to open the taxi door for her. Kay gave him an odd look, then scooted across the backseat of the cab to make room for him.

"You don't have to do the he-man routine with me."

"What?" He stared at her, puzzled.

Kay could tell he had no clue what she was talking about. "You know. First the door to the building, now the cab. I can open my own doors, you know."

"Oh. Sorry. I didn't mean to offend. It's just habit. My mother drilled good manners into my head. I'll try to stop if you want."

"No. Please forget I mentioned it."

She immediately felt badly for saying anything. She had to remember he was an Alaskan and obviously rather old-fashioned. He probably carried a clean hankie in his shirt pocket at all times in case some damsel burst into tears. Plus, she was accustomed to Lloyd only opening doors for her when they were around other people. Putting on a show to impress his business associates.

Honestly, she'd never met anyone quite like Quinn.

Kay took him to a Cuban restaurant that served to-die-for mahi-mahi with mango chutney, black beans, rice and fried plantains. And as she suspected, he told her that he'd never tasted anything like this exotic fare as the food disappeared from his plate.

He also told her stories about Alaska. About his loyal friends and loving family. Then he asked her questions about New York. He spoke with such open animation, she was helplessly drawn to his enthusiasm. He didn't play games, he didn't pull punches. Her parents would probably have thought him too loud and too eager, but she found his down-to-earth candor refreshing.

"So tell me," he said after he'd polished off the last crumb of key lime pie. "How long have you been 'practically' engaged."

She could tell by the way he said "practically" that he found the notion ridiculous. "Lloyd and I have been dating four years."

"Your guy's commitment-phobic, huh? Hasn't gotten around to popping the question, but you're expecting him to?"

"No, that's not it. I mean, well, actually, he did ask me to marry him a few days ago."

"So you are engaged." His tone was flat. She saw disappointment in his eyes.

"No."

"You turned him down?" Hope flared fresh in his face, and the sight of his renewed optimism confused her.

"No."

He frowned. "I don't understand. You told him you'd think about it?"

"It didn't happen that way. Listen, I really don't feel comfortable discussing my personal life with you."

"Okay." He gave an easy shrug, but she could tell by the look in his eyes that he wanted to dig deeper. What she didn't know was why, but she certainly wasn't going to open up and spill her guts to a stranger.

Not even her closest friends knew what was in her heart. She'd been taught by her father, the cutthroat businessman, that the more people knew about you, the more they could use against you. Once, when she was a little girl, her father took her to work with him. When his secretary asked her if she'd rather be playing in the park, instead of touring a stuffy old building, Kay had responded with an enthusiastic yes. Her father then jerked her into his office and lectured her until her ears burned about expressing her true feelings to underlings. She never forgot that lesson.

Quinn cleared his throat. The waiter refilled their coffee cups.

"I'm sorry about what I said," Kay said. "That sounded bitchy."

"No need to apologize. You're right. It's none of my business. It's just that if I was dating a woman like you, I wouldn't have waited four years to ask you to marry me."

"Which raises the question, if you're not commitment-phobic yourself, how come you've stayed single so long?"

"Not a lot of women to choose from in Bear Creek. And most of the tourists that come to town are looking for a summer fling. And who's to say I've never been married?"

"Have you?" Kay lifted an eyebrow. Although she hated answering personal questions herself, she had no compunction against asking them. Enjoyed it, in fact. Perhaps that's what attracted her to journalism. The opportunity to discover the intimate details of others' lives without revealing any information about her own.

"Came close once."

"What happened?"

"Now I'm the one who's uncomfortable discussing my private life."

"Whoever writes the feature article on you is going to want to know the answer to these questions."

"Then I'll save the interview for that reporter."

Silence.

"So in general, what qualities do you look for in a woman?" She spoke lightly, but every cell in her body stood at attention as she waited for his answer.

"I don't really want a career woman. I know it sounds old-fashioned, but I see myself with a woman who's mainly interested in making a home. I want kids. And I like the idea of providing for the woman in my life."

"Oh, I see. The caveman mentality. Keep 'em barefoot and pregnant."

"I don't mind if she wants to work," he expounded. "But the children and I should be her priority. Just as she and the kids will be my top priority, not work, not a job. Family and friends. That's what counts. Don't look so disapproving. I'm being honest here."

"I'm not disapproving. You're misconstruing my expression. Besides, does it matter what I think?"

The truth was, she'd been thinking that she'd never heard a New York male express such a sentiment or, for that matter, even admit to wanting children. She found it oddly refreshing, even though one side of her wanted to argue that women could have both prosperous careers and happy, well-adjusted children if they learned how to juggle.

His gaze was on her face. He was running his index finger around and around the rim of his coffee mug in a slow, languid motion that made her feel dizzy with desire. "My ideal woman has to be tough. She's got to be hardy enough to brave winters in Alaska."

"What about beauty?"

"Beauty's good, but not really important. I mean, there's got to be sexual chemistry between us, but I'm not looking for perfection. On the contrary, I think a little sass, a little attitude spices things up."

"Really?"

"And even though I'm ready to settle down, I'm not willing to settle. When I get married, it'll be forever. Until then—" he grinned "—I'm up for whatever adventures come my way."

"Oh." At this, Kay took heart. Perhaps he might provide that illicit affair she was yearning for, after all.

"So what do you look for in a man, Kay Freemont?"

She shrugged. "I don't know."

"You don't know? Then how do you know if Mr. Practically Engaged is the right one for you?"

She winced. "Please, I—"

"Oh, right, no personal questions."

"How long are you in town?" She changed the subject and wondered what she was going to do with the information. Wondered why her heart was pounding.

"I fly out at seven-thirty on Wednesday morning. Tomorrow I've got an all-day thing with my friend from Adventure Gear. I'm thinking of switching over to their climbing harnesses, and he's taking me on a climb upstate."

"Ah." Her hopes plummeted. No time for a wild fling.

He reached across the table and lightly grazed her hand with the tips of his fingers. It shouldn't have been an erotic gesture, but it was.

"You could come to Alaska," he said, reading her thoughts as clearly as if they'd been etched on her face. His habit of expressing exactly what was on her mind was uncanny and, frankly, a little disturbing. "Write that article for your editor. We could have a lot of fun together, you and I. Why not consider it?"

Astounded by the sensations that surged through her at his touch, she slipped her hand away. She never did answer his question.

After lunch he wanted to see the Empire State Building, so off they went. Quinn moved through the crowd like a redwood among matchsticks. On more than one occasion, she noticed women's heads turn as they shot him appreciative glances. She felt oddly jealous.

And strangely aroused.

More aroused, in fact, than she'd ever been.

While Quinn admired the view from the top of the Empire State Building, Kay admired Quinn.

She couldn't seem to draw her gaze from the ripple of muscle in his forearm where he'd rolled back the sleeves of his mackinaw. It was as if he knew how much she loved sexy forearms and was simply taunting her with a view of his.

She studied his strong profile, raked her gaze down his shoulders to his back before stopping to blatantly admire his delectable fanny so prominently displayed in snug-fitting blue jeans.

Raising a hand to her throat, she inhaled deeply, hauling in an unsteady breath. Quinn turned from the railing, a wide, boyish grin on his face. Kay smiled back.

"Wow. So many people. So many buildings. So many yellow-checkered cabs."

She nodded.

The wind gusted. Shivering, Kay used a pillar as a windbreak. She crossed her arms over her chest and danced from foot to foot.

"You're cold," he said, and she found it touching that he'd noticed. He stripped off his mackinaw.

"I can't take your jacket. It's freezing up here."

"Honey," he said, and she did not take offense at his easy endearment; rather, she found it kind of charming. "Where I'm from this would be considered a heat wave."

He stepped closer and settled his mackinaw around her shoulders, wrapping her as tenderly as a mother swaddles her baby.

"Thank you." Her voice emerged as a breathless whisper, and she realized they were the only people still on the observation deck. The cold had forced everyone else back inside.

"You're welcome."

Quinn peered down into her face and damned if little Miss Too-Cool-for-School didn't look nervous. The tip of her tongue darted out to wet her upper lip. Was her gesture an unconscious invitation to kiss her? God, he hoped so, because he wanted to do that more than anything in the world.

"Uh—" she took a step backward "—perhaps we should go now."

"Why?" His body was so very aware of hers. "Are you frightened?"

She forced a laugh. "Frightened of what? Heights?"

"Of this."

Then, taking them both by surprise, he caught her upper arms in his hands, raised her to her toes and kissed her the way he'd been longing to kiss her since the moment he'd caught her in his arms on the airplane.

She yielded. Accepted him with ready acquiescence. Complied by parting her lips and letting him slip his tongue in deep to taste the honeyed, warm recesses of her mouth. Languidly his tongue glided against hers.

Lust, swifter, more vehement than anything he'd ever experienced, exploded inside him. And it was just a damned kiss.

His gut clenched hard. He could only imagine how his hardness sliding into her would feel, her slender arms entwined around his neck, her luscious tush cupped in his large palms.

He was not the kind of guy to sit idle on the sidelines. When he saw something he wanted, he went after it. But even he had never moved so fast or wanted anyone so strongly. He had no more control than a moose in rut. That's what this woman did to him.

Had he shocked her with his boldness? Had he indeed moved too quickly?

But no, she moaned softly and leaned into him. Quinn swallowed the sound, tilting her head back, threading his fingers through her hair. The softness of those silken strands was in sharp contrast to the hardness building inside him.

Incredible. Simply incredible.

He forgot that she was practically engaged. He forgot that he didn't steal other men's women. He forgot that she was out of his league. He forgot everything except how wonderful she felt, how good she tasted.

Kay held her breath, dazed and ashamed. Freemonts did not act like this! They didn't kiss strangers in public. They did not lose control. They did not succumb to wanton lust.

Good. Good. Good. Good.

She was no longer behaving like a Freemont, and it was liberating beyond description.

But what was she getting herself into?

Quinn, the Alaskan man who smelled of wilderness and tasted of mangoes and key lime pie, was giving her the most possessive kiss of her life. Branding her with his tongue, searing her with his passion.

She'd never experienced anything like it, certainly not with Lloyd or with that guy from college. Her heart did a triple backflip before taking on a frantic, galloping rhythm of thrill and response.

Up was down, down was up. Nothing made sense anymore, but it felt so right.

Was she indeed supposed to begin her journey of self-discovery with this man? Or was she kidding herself? Using his willingness as an excuse for acting out her long-hidden desires?

Splaying a hand on Quinn's chest, Kay thought to push him away, but instead, she let her hand rest there, feeling his heartbeat and marveling that it pounded as forcefully as her own.

Even through his flannel shirt, she could feel his muscled flesh. In spite of the cold, he felt blisteringly hot and wonderfully solid against her palm. She realized he was coiled as tense as a snake waiting to strike. The comparison alarmed her. Did she really believe he might be dangerous? What was she doing? She didn't know this man.

But that was rigid Freemont thinking, and more than anything she wanted to break free of the constraints of her old thought patterns. She wanted to stop berating herself, wanted to take some risks, inhale the danger, embrace the challenge, not fear it. She wanted to be fully alive. She wanted to replace fantasies with reality.

And Quinn was serving up huge helpings of reality on a silver platter.

Her knees were weak, her breath faint. How could one simple kiss do so many different things to her? Okay, it wasn't such a simple kiss. It was more like an implosion. His mouth caused her insides to topple and collapse in on themselves.

He tugged her close against his body, bringing her in startling contact with his rock-hard erection. One of his hands slipped underneath the hem of her leather coat to caress her behind.

Oh, my!

Everything she was feeling was so new, so exciting, so unbelievable, and precisely like one of her fantasies.

Quinn pulled his mouth from hers at last, his breath coming in jerky gasps. Her lips felt swollen and wet, her body both tight and liquid at the same time. He rubbed his cheek against hers, setting her on fire. She quivered and he pressed his lips to her ear.

"Woman," he whispered hoarsely, "I'm so turned on by you."

In that moment she experienced a unique and exhilarating power. She, cool, poised Kay Freemont, had made this mountain of a man lose control. She wanted more from him, and that was all there was to it.

What would your parents think? What about Lloyd? the nagging voice that made her do all the right things for all the wrong reasons piped up.

To hell with her parents. To hell with Lloyd. She'd been the dutiful daughter for twenty-seven years, and where had it gotten her?

An orgasmless career woman practically engaged to a man who did not even love her.

Marshaling her courage, Kay took Quinn's chin in her palm and looked him square in the eye. She'd never done anything like what she was about to do, and therein lay the thrill of it. She knew he would be a kind and gentle lover and maybe, just maybe, he would be the one to turn the key of her womanhood and lead her to new levels of physical joy.

His smoky-gray eyes met hers with a sheen of raw desire, and he did not look away. He didn't even blink. He stared into her eyes as if he could peer right into the depths of her soul.

"Yes?" he growled. This talent he had for anticipating her thoughts was downright spooky.

"Would you like to go back to my place?" she asked breathlessly.

Quinn couldn't believe his ears. "What? What did you say?"

She cleared her throat. "My place. You. Me. Now."

He shook his head, unable to comprehend his good fortune. "Are you sure?"

"No. I'm not sure of anything, except that for once in my well-ordered, well-behaved life I need to do something irresponsible and unpredictable and capricious. So let's go before I change my mind."

She grabbed his hand and started pulling him toward the elevators.

"Whoa, wait a minute." He dug in his heels and she couldn't budge him. "I don't want to be your biggest regret."

"Well, you should have thought of that before you kissed me."

"A kiss is one thing, Kay. Sex is something else entirely."

"That's what I'm counting on." Her voice was husky, her eyes heavy-lidded.

He shook his head again. What was the matter with him? This was his fantasy. So why was he putting on the brakes? Was he out of his ever-loving mind?

"Please."

Ah, this was killing him.

"You're a beautiful woman, and I want to make love to you so badly I can taste it. But I don't break up couples. And you're practically engaged."

"No. In fact, I was thinking I might break up with him."

"You don't love the guy?"

"I thought I did once. Or what passed for love. But lately I've come to understand that I don't even know what love is," she said. "My parents like Lloyd. They think we're great together. They're the ones pushing for this marriage."

"You let your parents tell you who to date?"

She took a deep breath, waved a dismissive hand. "Let's not talk about them. Let's not talk at all." She angled him a coy glance that almost brought him to his knees.

She looked so damned appealing standing there with the wind whipping his mackinaw around her shoulders, her golden hair falling across one cheek, her full lips pursed in fervid anticipation of his acquiescence, her hands cocked on her slender hips.

Much as he wanted to say yes, as much as he knew

he'd be kicking himself tonight in his lonely hotel room, Quinn knew he had to turn her down.

He heaved in a heavy lungful of chilled air and shook his head. "I'm sorry, Kay, but I've got to say no."

CHAPTER FOUR

OH GOD, SHE'D made a fool of herself. What had she been thinking? Freemont women did not throw themselves at perfect strangers, no matter how sexually appealing they were.

She tossed her head, averted her gaze.

"Don't be embarrassed. I'm flattered. Very flattered. You're one hell of a sexy woman."

His comment, meant to soothe, only served to fluster her more. Was she that transparent?

"I'm not embarrassed," she lied, and gave a casual shrug for good measure. "I asked—you weren't interested. I can handle rejection."

"Lady, you're wrong about that. I'm extremely interested. But you've got something to settle with that boyfriend of yours, and hopping into the sack with me won't solve your problems. I'm sorry." He reached out to take her hand, but she stepped back and shook her head.

Don't touch me. Please. If you do I'll crumble into your arms.

She held only the most tenuous control over her libido. These unstoppable, blazing-hot fantasies, combined with her lack of sexual release, had compelled her to do something she normally would never have done in a million years. And she was ashamed of herself. Best to get away from this man ASAP.

Especially since the hot tingling between her legs had not abated one whit since he'd kissed her.

"Look," she said with her usual crisp efficiency. "You're right. Maybe we should call it a day."

"Yeah," he murmured, and pushed the elevator button. "That'd probably be best."

Quinn gazed at her with such heated desire, with such greedy longing, Kay almost threw her arms around his neck and begged him to reconsider. But she didn't, of course. She was at her core a Freemont, after all.

She drew herself up straight. "Yes. Well, it's been an experience meeting you."

"Will I see you again? Are you coming to Alaska?"

She shook her head.

"I was afraid of that." He smiled wistfully. "Another time, another place."

Her heart hung suspended in her throat, and for some idiotic reason tears hovered behind her eyelids. Kay blinked. The elevator door dinged open.

"Come on," she said. "I'll hail you a cab."

She dropped him off at his hotel in Times Square, but asked the driver to linger a moment at the curb so she could watch him disappear through the revolving glass doors. She was too shaken to return to work. Besides, Judy had given her the rest of the afternoon off, and she'd be irritated to know Kay hadn't spent it squiring Quinn around town.

And besides, there was another matter that demanded her attention. She couldn't go forward with her life until she broke up with Lloyd. No more phone calls or emails. No more evading. This had to be face-to-face. She had a key to his place; she would go to his apartment and confront him. And if he wasn't home, she'd pack up the few things she kept stashed there and wait for him to return.

It was a plan. Taking action made her feel better. She gave the cabby Lloyd's address and leaned back.

Sighing, she wistfully trailed her fingers over the seat where Quinn had been sitting, the vinyl material warm from the heat of his body. She lowered her head, lifted her collar to her nose and breathed deeply of his scent, still clinging to her blouse.

What a masculine man.

Hair as thick and wavy as a Kansas cornfield. Eyes the color of a cold November sky. Warm, inviting lips that promised so much in that short but sizzling kiss they'd shared. Broad shoulders, honed waist, narrow hips.

Kay moaned under her breath, closed her eyes and pictured him with his shirt off.

He's splitting logs with an ax, and he's stripped bare to the waist. It's summer. Midday. Hot for Alaska.

She's watching him from a shelter of thick trees. The scent of pine fills her nostrils. Behind him in the distance rises snowcapped mountain peaks. He doesn't see her. She knows he's had trouble with hunters poaching his land, and he's not friendly toward secretive visitors spying on him from the trees.

She shouldn't be here, but she can't look away. She can't even move. Her eyes are transfixed on his exquisite, tanned torso.

His muscular biceps bunch as he swings the ax down in one long, smooth stroke.

Whack!

The ax strikes home with a metallic, hypnotic ring that echoes strangely in the still forest. Shivers of excitement run up her spine.

She licks her lips.

He pauses in his work. Rests one arm against the ax handle, swipes at his forehead with a blue bandanna pulled from the back pocket of his tight, denim jeans.

The sun glints seductively off the sweat beading his chest. A sultry heat settles low in her belly, then fans out like thick fingers, growing, clutching, pressing down on her, until every part of her body pulsates with awareness of his overt maleness.

She shifts her position, lifts her head higher, hoping for a better look. She startles a squirrel, which begins to chatter at her.

The woodsman jerks his head sharply in her direction.

"Who's there?" he calls out.

Heart racing, she jumps to her feet. She can't be discovered. No telling what he'll do to her if he finds her encroaching on his land.

"Show yourself," he demands.

She whirls around—must get away—and darts through the underbrush.

"Come back here, damn you."

She hears him crashing through the forest as he thunders after her, but she doesn't look behind her.

Something snags her blouse. The silky material splits wide open, exposing her bra. Her skirt, too, gets caught on something sharp. She hears the rip. Her clothes hang in tatters, flapping about her skin.

Thud, thud, thud.

He is coming.

Faster, run faster.

She tries, but it's as if her feet are encased in cement. She's moving in slow motion. She can hear his breathing as he gets closer.

Her hair streaks out behind her, and her legs churn through the thick carpet of pine needles. She zigzags around trees, leaps over downed logs like a doe fleeing a pursuing rutting buck. She's heading for the clearing and freedom. Her pulse is pounding, thumping, thrashing madly in her ears.

He's quick for a big man. So quick. And so very close now. She's not going to make it.

He tackles her. His arms go around her waist. He pulls her atop him as they fall together.

Then she's on her back and he's above her, pinning her arms to the earth with his knees. His breathing is raspy, ragged. There is an angry gleam in his smoldering eyes.

"Who are you?" he commands.

But she can't answer. She's so afraid. Her whole body trembles. What's he going to do to her?

"You were trespassing on my land."

She nods, fear and a strange feeling she's never had before pooling in her belly.

"You must be punished."

She squirms, trying to get free, but his knees hold her fast. She can't move. Can't get away. She is captured. His prisoner. Will he require her to be his love slave?

She catches her breath.

He grabs what's left of her blouse and rips it from her body. Her bra follows, exposing tender breasts. Her chest heaves as she exhales.

His hands, work-roughened and callused, are suddenly gentle as he massages her nipples. "I must teach you a lesson," he whispers. "You must learn never to spy."

She whimpers.

He leans over her, takes one nipple into his mouth, and she gasps. He plunders her with his tongue.

The pleasure is beyond description. She writhes beneath him wanting more punishment, more sweet torture....

"Lady—" the cabby's voice jerked her rudely back to reality "—that'll be seven-fifty."

She thrust a ten at him. Dazed and stuffy-headed from her interrupted fantasy, she stumbled out of the taxi.

The doorman greeted her with a smile, and Kay took the elevator to the penthouse and let herself into Lloyd's apartment. Emotionally exhausted, she dropped her purse on the table in the foyer and kicked off her shoes. This wasn't going to be easy.

That was when she heard the noises coming from the bedroom. She cocked her head, listening.

Giggles. Moans. Oohs. Ahhs. It sounded like someone having sex.

And not just any sex, but wild, uninhibited, swinging-from-the-chandelier monkey sex.

Bed springs squeaked. The headboard banged. *Ka-wham, ka-wham, ka-wham.*

"Oh, baby, yeah, you hot stud. Give me all you've got. That's it. That's right."

Kay froze. Who was in Lloyd's apartment having sex? His maid and her boyfriend?

She tiptoed down the hallway, her stocking feet gliding over the cool, terrazzo floor. She should be upset or offended on Lloyd's behalf; instead, she was weirdly curious. It sounded as if they were having a hell of a time.

His bedroom door stood slightly ajar. Kay pressed her body against the opposite wall of the hallway and angled her head around for a peek. She shouldn't be doing this, she knew, but she wanted to see how other people made love.

Clothing lay strewn across the carpet, a bra—that looked to be nothing short of a D cup—dangled over the shade of a thousand-dollar antique lamp.

"Faster! Harder!" the woman cried.

Kay inched closer, helpless to stop herself from watching. A man, garbed only in black socks, stood with his back to her, his arms supporting the woman bent over in front of him.

She recognized the man at once. No mistaking that bony behind. Shock jolted through her. It took a moment for her to react, but then Kay kicked the door open wide.

Startled, her wannabe-fiancé turned to gape at her, his body still embedded in the flesh of the buxom redhead in his arms.

"Kay!" he cried in a strangled voice. "What on earth are you doing here?"

Two HOURS LATER Kay sat morosely in her darkened kitchen, staring at the crystal salt and pepper shakers that sandwiched a crystal napkin holder and slowly shredding a lace paper doily.

She felt empty inside. Empty, hollow and cold. She hugged herself tightly and clenched her jaw to stay the tears that threatened to roll down her cheeks if she dared let them.

It wasn't so much finding Lloyd with another woman that bothered her. No, what really upset Kay was the cruel words he'd hurled at her as he'd wriggled into his pants.

"I'm glad you caught me, Kay. I've hated sneaking around behind your back. But you gave me no choice.

Do you have any idea how frustrating it is being with a frigid woman?"

Frigid.

The word reverberated in her head. Was she really frigid? She'd suspected for many years she might be, but to have someone say it to her face caused her more pain than she could have imagined.

He blamed his cheating on her.

A sick sensation flipped over in Kay's stomach as she recalled the blissful expression on the red-haired woman's face. She had obviously been having a very good time with Lloyd. If he could satisfy that woman, then apparently his lousy technique wasn't the reason for Kay's lack of sexual arousal. It was true. She was frigid.

She dropped her head into her hands and softly began to cry. In that moment she felt so alone. All those years of struggling to be the perfect daughter, the perfect Freemont, had extracted an extravagant toll. Decades of watching her p's and q's, worrying about what other people thought and putting on a polished facade had resulted in a repressed personality.

In truth she didn't know who she was or what she wanted. If only she could activate her sexuality. If she could come alive in that area of her life, might it not be the gateway to freedom?

But how did she go about liberating her libido?

Then she thought of Quinn. With his heated kissing and his bedroom eyes, he'd obviously desired her. If anyone ever made her feel like a woman, it was him.

And she'd let him get away.

She stroked her lips with fingertips gone salty from her tears and wistfully recalled their kiss and the power of their connection. A shiver passed through her. Could

Quinn light the fire in her that she feared did not even exist?

You're idealizing him, Kay. He's nothing but wish fulfillment. The inner, sensible voice that had guided her actions throughout her life spoke sternly.

Right.

Sighing, she raised her head and straightened her shoulders. Freemonts did not pine for the impossible.

At that moment her door buzzer went off.

Great. Just what she needed. Company. Kay trudged to the door and pressed the intercom. "Yes?"

"Dearest, it's Mommy. I'm coming up."

Oh, no! "Mother, I'm pretty busy."

"Sweetheart, you don't have to pretend with me. Lloyd has been to see your father. I know what happened between you two."

"Then you know I never want to see his two-timing ass again."

"Is that any way for a Freemont to talk?" her mother chided.

More Freemont guilt. "Come on up." She sighed again.

A few minutes later Honoria Freemont rushed into Kay's apartment with her hair freshly coiffed, smelling of expensive French perfume and wearing an impeccably tailored suit. Immediately she took both of Kay's hands in hers and led her to the couch.

"You look terrible, darling. Your eyes are red and puffy."

"I've been crying."

"Do you have any cucumbers? We could make a cold compress."

"Mother, I don't care if my eyes are swollen. I'm in

my own apartment. Don't worry, none of your friends are going to see me."

"Oh, you're in one of those moods."

"Yes, I do believe I am. Not two hours ago I caught my boyfriend in bed with another woman. Under the circumstances I'm entitled to be a little testy, don't you think?"

Her mother shifted, let go of Kay's hands. "You mustn't allow something like this to come between you and Lloyd."

Kay stared at her mother openmouthed. "What?" She wasn't sure she'd heard correctly. Was her mother suggesting she overlook Lloyd's blatant infidelity?

Gently Honoria reached out and pushed Kay's jaw up. "Lloyd is your father's right-hand man. He'd be lost without him."

"What's that got to do with me?"

Her mother would have frowned, but her recent Botox injection ruled that out. Instead, a disapproving look came into her eyes. "It's got everything to do with you, darling. One day Freemont Enterprises will belong to you."

"And I can't inherit without a man at my side?"

"Not just any man. You must have a husband who comes from the right stock. A man who knows how to navigate your world. A man of good breeding."

"Oh, from what I witnessed this afternoon, Lloyd's good at breeding, all right." Kay crossed her arms and glared. How could her own mother side with her father and Lloyd in this matter?

"Don't be crude. It's unbecoming of a Freemont."

If her mother said one more word about being a good Freemont, Kay was going to scream. She rubbed her pounding temples.

"I'm not saying what Lloyd did was right," Honoria went on, "but he's very sorry. He's already apologized to your father, and he desperately wants to apologize to you, but he's afraid you won't speak to him."

"He's right. I never want to see him again."

"You're making a grave mistake. Lloyd comes from a long and illustrious bloodline."

"I'm not a racehorse, Mother."

"You're going to be seeing him at every social function. You know he's got opera-season tickets right next to our box. There's no way to avoid him."

"So I'll stop attending social functions and, news flash, I hate opera."

"You can't avoid him forever."

"Then I'll ignore him."

"Darling, you're old enough to understand this." Her mother patted her knee. "There're certain things a woman must put up with in a marriage. Any marriage. Be it good, bad or indifferent."

"And infidelity is one of those things?"

She simply couldn't believe her mother was saying this to her. Then again, what did she expect? Her mother had chosen to look the other way whenever Kay's father came home with lipstick on his collar or took late-night telephone calls in his den or went on "business" trips several times a month. Well, not her! She'd be damned if she'd live that way. No amount of money or social status was worth that kind of misery.

Kay got to her feet. "Mother, I think it's time for you to go."

Honoria looked startled. "Excuse me?"

"I'm not going to discuss Lloyd Post. I'm not going to marry a man who cheats on me. You might have been willing to settle for a marriage in name only, but not me."

Her mother looked as if she'd been slapped across the face with a broom. "Kathryn Victoria Freemont, I will not allow you to speak that way to me."

"Then if you don't want to hear what I have to say, there's the door."

Flabbergasted, her mother picked up her purse. "I'll talk to you later when you've come to your senses."

"Don't hold your breath," Kay muttered, and locked the door behind Honoria, then collapsed onto the tiled floor and drew her knees to her chest. She rocked back and forth in a vain attempt to comfort herself the way she had as a little girl on Nanny's night off.

Oh, God, she had to get out of the city. Away from Lloyd's humiliating behavior, away from her father's chiding disapproval, away from her mother's terrible advice.

When had her life become such a mess?

From the outside, strangers might be envious of her. She had a plum job at the most successful women's magazine in the country. She had lots of money, got invited to all the right parties. She was thin and young and blond.

But others had no idea what it was like to be Kay Freemont. She was miserable to the core and hadn't a clue how to salvage herself. All her life she'd had this bizarre sensation of being on the inside looking out. While in the midst of prestige, money and privilege, she dreamed of being like other kids, wearing clothes off the rack, cheap sunglasses and colorful, rubber flip-flops.

She'd longed to do simple things like eat cotton candy or ride on a carnival Ferris wheel or lie on her back in the grass and stare up at a canopy of stars.

Instead, she'd been escorted to the planetarium and the museum by bodyguards. She'd been forced to attend boring parties and was kept isolated from ordinary people.

She was sick of it. And she wanted out.

For the longest time she had experienced no passion, no fire, no zest for life. That is, until yesterday when she had met Quinn Scofield.

Something about the man—be it his ruggedly sexy appearance, his independent nature, his engaging smile—stirred dormant emotions deep inside her. For the first time in years she felt excited.

The man was real; he didn't hide behind a facade. He was honest; he spoke what was on his mind, consequences be damned. He had true friends, not leeches who sucked up to him for his power and money. And he had family who loved him for who he was. In other words, he was everything she was not.

Go to Alaska. Write the feature article. Get away. Spend some time with Quinn. Tell him you've broken things off with Lloyd. Find yourself. Find your sexuality. Come home a new woman.

It sounded so good.

Determined, Kay crossed to the telephone in the alcove, picked up the receiver and called Judy to tell her she was taking the assignment. She was going north to Alaska.

CHAPTER FIVE

KAY FREEMONT WAS coming to Bear Creek. Quinn still couldn't quite get his head around the notion. To think, in less than an hour, that cool, sleek beauty would be strolling the streets of his hometown.

The notion was enough to give a man the shakes. He wasn't quite prepared for the reality of her visit, and yet he didn't feel as if he could wait another second, much less sixty minutes or more.

She had already arrived in Anchorage, and Mack had flown out to retrieve her. Quinn could scarcely sit still. He had reserved the best room for her at Jake's B&B and arranged for her to borrow his parents' extra vehicle. Since his mother had slipped on ice and broken her right ankle the week before, she wouldn't need the old Wagoneer, anyway. He'd stocked his refrigerator with supplies, planning to cook a few meals for her. Quinn was proud of his culinary abilities and couldn't wait to show off for her.

And he was hoping against hope that his wildest dreams might come true and they could finish what they started in New York City. He had stopped by Leonard Long Bear's sundries store and picked up a box of condoms, a bottle of massage oil and edible body paints. Bear Creek might be small but because of the cruise ship trade, Long Bear's had to be prepared for every kind of request. Especially those of a confidential nature.

Unfortunately Quinn's private business hadn't remained private for long. By lunchtime at least half a dozen townspeople had kidded him about the naughty thoughts running through his mind.

Fine. Let them talk. He wasn't ashamed of his sexuality. Particularly since he hadn't had sex in more than eighteen months.

He hoped he could keep himself under control. He wanted to please Kay as much as he wanted to be pleasured. That kiss they'd shared atop the Empire State Building told him she was as hungry for physical love as he.

He couldn't wait to taste those lips again, to caress her soft flesh, to run his fingers through her silky hair. For the past week, ever since Judy Nessler had called and told him Kay was on her way, he'd been unable to consider anything else. Although he couldn't help but wonder if she was still "practically engaged" or if she had broken things off with her boyfriend.

Just thinking about Kay stirred him, and he had to breathe deeply and think of ice hockey in order to calm down.

Finally, finally, he heard the sound of Mack's bush plane glide to a stop in the inlet. Bundled in his parka, he threw open his front door and hurried down the walkway that was already covered with a light dusting of fresh flakes, even though he'd shoveled it earlier.

The first of March was an awful time to visit Bear Creek. They wouldn't be able to do much beyond sit by the fire. Kay certainly didn't seem the type to snowshoe or snowmobile or ice-skate. He couldn't see her sitting in the bleachers wrapped in thermal blankets at his hockey games. Ah, but he could visualize her curled up in his bed.

By the time he reached the dock, Mack had already helped her from the plane. Quinn took one look at her and his heart flipped.

She smiled in that cool, controlled way of hers. "Hello, Quinn."

He'd been nervous, not knowing exactly how to proceed, but in that moment instinct took over. He swung her into his arms, lifted her off her feet and hugged her to his chest.

"Welcome to Bear Creek, Kay," he whispered in her ear. "I'm so glad you decided to come."

"Thank you." She stiffened in his arms and he realized that his easy informality made her uncomfortable.

He sat her gently on the ground, wanting to respect her need for distance, and surveyed her with hungry eyes. She looked good, if somewhat out of place, in her virgin-white ski outfit and snowboots. It was probably the only cold-weather gear she owned.

Feeling self-conscious before Quinn's intense perusal, Kay adjusted the knit cap she wore. She loved the way he'd swung her into his arms but she had a hard time relaxing and enjoying his ebullience.

Mack, the bush pilot, busied himself with tying down the plane and pretending he wasn't eavesdropping on their conversation. She had enjoyed talking to the down-to-earth man on the flight over, and she'd been unable to stop herself from pumping him for information on Quinn. Now she feared Mack knew exactly how much she liked Quinn. For a woman who'd spent her life hiding her feelings from the world, this was a disconcerting prospect.

"Well," she said. "Well."

Her heart was galloping a mile a minute. On the long flight to Alaska she had decided once and for all to use that sexy underwear she had stuffed into her suitcase and seduce this bear of a man. One way or the other, she was bound and determined to prove Lloyd wrong. She was not frigid.

But now that she was here, staring into Quinn's mesmerizing gray eyes, an odd sensation of anticipation, excitement and fear gripped her. Her brain short-circuited, issuing two simultaneous but opposing commands.

Run for your life! Get out while you can!

Strap your arms around him and never let go!

Oh, God, she wanted him so badly. Maybe too much. But did she have the guts to go through with this? Were her expectations of this chemistry between them unrealistic?

He looked impressive in his fur-lined parka and allweather boots. A rugged man's man who needed no fancy gym to keep in shape. Life in the Alaskan wilderness was his personal trainer.

Another twinge of anticipation. This time low in her anatomy. Heavens above, she was scared and thrilled.

You don't have to do anything you don't want to do, she reminded herself. *After all, you're here to write an article. Focus on that. Forget the other for now.*

That admonition and a deep breath of frosty winter air calmed her nerves.

Quinn held out his gloved hand to her. Tentatively she accepted it and allowed him to lead her cautiously up the snow-dazzled sidewalk to his rustic log cabin, which was perched on a small hill just above the shoreline.

"Come inside." He ushered her over the threshold,

stopping long enough to stomp the snow off his boots on the welcome mat. Kay followed suit.

"Let me hang up your coat."

Kay started to pull down the zipper, but her fingers, even through her leather gloves, were so cold that she fumbled.

"Allow me." He reached for the zipper. Their hands brushed briefly. They both tried to ignore the contact. She glanced at the moose head mounted over the mantel, while he kept his eyes trained to the floor.

Rubbing her palms together, she gazed around the cabin. It was obvious he'd tidied up. The room smelled of pine cleaner and air freshener. The floor was hardwood and covered with a thick, braided rug. Hockey trophies were displayed in a glass case. In one corner sat a massive fireplace, in the other, a big-screen television with satellite hookup. It was definitely a man's place, painted in dark, masculine colors and decorated with large, sturdy furniture. A brown leather couch, a bold scarlet recliner, a hand-carved rocking chair.

She shrugged out of her ski jacket and stripped off her ski pants. He took the garments from her and hung them on a rack by the door. When she felt confident enough to glance his way again, she apprehended his gaze in a leisurely stroll down her body. He took in her red cashmere sweater, her form-fitting black pants, her fluffy white after-ski boots.

Despite the fact that she was bundled up to the teeth, thermal underwear on from neck to ankles, the way he looked at her made Kay feel like Lady Godiva prancing through the town square in the altogether.

"Nice place," Kay said, trying her best to keep her tone upbeat and lighthearted, as if his perusal didn't affect her one bit. But her breathless, whispery voice gave her away.

"Here," he said eagerly, his voice no steadier than her own. "Stand by the fire, get warm. I'll make us some hot chocolate."

Hot chocolate? Had she stepped back in time to a simpler place, a simpler era? It was nice, very nice, but she felt out of place. A stranger in a strange land.

"That'd be great."

Then an appalling thought occurred to her. Was she supposed to lodge here with him? Not that she didn't want to stay with him. She just didn't want it assumed.

"Quinn?" She watched him move around the kitchen, which was separated from the living area by a waist-high counter. She heard the oven door open, saw him bend over and remove a cookie sheet.

The smell of chocolate-chip cookies filled the air. Handsome and he could cook. A deadly combo.

"Uh-huh." He deposited the cookie sheet on a cooling rack and glanced over at her. His hair had flopped boyishly over his forehead. For no good reason whatsoever her stomach did a backflip.

"Did you…am I…" She cleared her throat and tried again. "Where am I supposed to sleep?"

"At Jake's B&B a quarter mile up the road in the center of town. Mack's already hauling your luggage there."

"Er…that's good."

"You didn't think…I mean…did you want to stay here?" He raised an eyebrow in surprise.

"Oh, no. No. Of course not." Kay groaned inwardly. This was going horribly. They were both so afraid of making a mistake, they were treading on eggshells.

He returned to the living area, balancing two mugs of hot chocolate and a plate of cookies on a tray.

"I really am glad you changed your mind about coming to Alaska." He handed her a mug.

She took a sip of hot chocolate and nibbled on a cookie. The room was silent except for logs crackling in the fireplace.

"Cookies are good," she said as a way to fill the void.

"You can thank the Pillsbury Doughboy. All I did was slice and heat."

"Still, you sliced them very evenly and heated them to the perfect degree of doneness."

"Are you making fun of me?" His eyes teased.

Feeling suddenly shy, she glanced away. Oh, she was getting in way over her head here. Liking this guy too much, when they had no future together.

But she was in no position to ask for anything more from him than sex, nor did she want to. For one thing he was an Alaskan and she was a New Yorker. For another, she was on the rebound, still aching from Lloyd's betrayal. She had a lot of things to sort out before she could ever entertain a relationship that extended beyond the physical. With anyone.

Maybe coming here hadn't been such a great idea, after all.

Disconcerted, she moved away from Quinn and turned her attention to the photographs artfully arranged on the paneled wall on the opposite side of the room.

There was Quinn playing hockey. In another he was standing on the summit of Mount McKinley grinning like a happy kid. In a third he was kayaking. In a fourth he was guiding a group of tourists down white-water rapids in a rubber raft.

One picture caught her eye. It featured six muscular, bare-chested teenagers laughing and lobbing fistfuls of blueberries at each other. She recognized four of the boys from the magazine advertisement.

Quinn hadn't changed much. His hair was darker, his shoulders broader, but he still possessed the same insouciant grin and macho stance.

"That was the summer we all worked in Juneau taking tourists down the Mendenthall." He come up behind her and was standing so near she could almost feel his chin touching the top of her head. "We'd been picking blueberries and things got out of hand. My sister Meggie, the camera buff, sneaked up on us and snapped this photo."

"Who's that?" She pointed to a swarthy, dark-haired boy with straight white teeth.

"That's Jesse, Meggie's husband. They weren't married then, of course. In fact, I believe that was the summer Jesse's father married Caleb's mother."

"And this guy?" She pointed to a lanky, string-bean fellow whom Quinn had in a headlock while he smashed berries into his hair.

"That's Kyle."

"You two look like the best of friends."

"We were."

Something in his voice made Kay turn and look at him. "You're not friends anymore?"

Quinn shrugged. "I don't talk to him much. He met some girl who'd come to Alaska for the summer. Kyle fell head over heels. Moved to California for her. Haven't seen him in twelve years."

"You act like he betrayed you by falling in love."

Quinn cracked an uneasy smile. "It wasn't the falling-in-love part, it was the leaving Alaska. That woman put a ring in his nose, and he let her pull him around by it. Guess that's why I'm so determined to find a wilderness wife."

"Because you're not willing to compromise?"

"Not when it comes to leaving Alaska." He thrust his chest out as if he was proud of his stubbornness. "In fact, that's what happened to my last relationship. I asked Heather to marry me, but she refused to move to Bear Creek. I wasn't about to go to Cleveland where she lived. If a woman wants to love me, she's got to love Alaska, too. It's a package deal." He took a sip of his hot chocolate, then said, "You can quote me in your article."

Kay raised her eyebrows. With such an obstinate attitude the man might be hard-pressed to find his perfect mate. So why did she find his stubbornness attractive? Maybe it was the clear-cut, simple way he said what was on his mind and if people didn't like it, well, too bad. "I'll be sure to note that. Getting your story for the article is the reason I'm here."

"The only reason?" His eyes sought hers.

"No. It's not the only reason."

"No?" He gave her a quirky smile, which struck her the wrong way. As if he was feeling pretty cocky about his ability to attract her all the way across the continent.

"I needed to get out of the city after breaking things off with Lloyd."

"Ah." He grinned all the wider. "So you're no longer practically engaged."

"No, I'm not."

He smirked.

"Stop that."

"Stop what?"

"Looking so smug. My breaking up with Lloyd had nothing to do with you."

"I never said it did."

"Your expression implied it."

Why was she being so sensitive? What was the matter with her? For the past week, while she packed and made travel arrangements, she had been unable to think of anything but seeing Quinn again, and now that she was here, she was experiencing all kinds of conflicting emotions.

"I'm sorry," she said. "That sounded argumentative."

"Hey, I can handle it. If you need to get something off your chest, go right ahead."

Well, that was refreshing. He was ready to let her spew out her emotions. Her mother and her father and Lloyd encouraged her not to express her feelings. To keep things bottled up. Good little girls didn't let their anger show. She was damned tired of being good, and here was Quinn egging her on.

"You sure you're up for this?" She looked into his eyes, saw nothing but sincere interest and acceptance. She leaned forward and set her half-empty mug back on the tray.

"FYI for the article. I don't want a submissive yes-woman for a wife. I want a true partner who speaks her mind, shares her thoughts with me even though I might not agree with her. I'm a firm believer that passionate couples fight. As long as they fight fair. Hell, if you don't fight sometimes, if you agree about everything, where's the spark? Where's the passion?"

Kay gulped. Oh, yes. She had always felt the same way. Just once when her father came home late, she had longed for her mother to confront him, throw a tantrum, demand he stop sleeping with other women. But Honoria had never once expressed her anger or voiced her opinion. Well-bred wives did not behave that way. Civilized-society women simply went shopping, spending extravagantly, consoling themselves with expensive but totally meaningless gewgaws.

And when she had tried to tell Lloyd her feelings or express her displeasure over something, he'd always headed her off, shut her down, closed her out, reminding her she was a Freemont with a certain level of dignity to maintain.

"You got something to tell me, Kay? Blast away, I'm listening."

Quinn gave her his full attention, his eyes on her face, his palms splayed over his thighs. Kay couldn't help but feel that the future Mrs. Scofield was going to be a very lucky woman—just as long as she was willing to move to Alaska.

"All right. It hurt my feelings when you turned down my offer at the Empire State Building. I don't go around inviting men into my bed willy-nilly. I just thought you should know that."

"I never thought you did."

"You thought I was terrible, wanting to cheat on my boyfriend."

"I didn't."

"You did."

He shook a finger. "Now don't go telling me what I thought."

"So what *did* you think about me?"

"I figured there must have been trouble in 'practically engaged' paradise for there to be so much attraction between us."

"And?"

"I thought you were a beautiful, sexy woman who was obviously unhappy with her life and not getting what she needed from her primary relationships."

Boy, he'd hit the nail on the head. Was she that obvious, or was he that observant?

"I think you're frustrated and disappointed and searching for something special."

She ducked her head. This didn't feel very comfortable, having him analyze her and be so accurate.

He reached out and cupped her chin with his palm, raised her face to meet his gaze once more. "I'd like to make you feel special, Kay." His expression was doing her in, causing her to feel hot and cold at the same time.

"Quinn, you're looking for a wife, and the last thing I'm in the market for is a husband."

"Kay, I'm a pretty simple guy. I take life as I find it. I don't put expectations on people."

"Then why did you reject me back in New York?"

"Like I told you then, I don't come between couples. You had to get free from Lloyd first before you could come to me. But you're here now. Officially unattached. Anything can happen."

Anything.

The word reverberated in her head. It was exactly what she wanted to hear. Exactly what she feared most. By coming to Alaska she had set herself on a course of sexual exploration. If a man as virile as Quinn couldn't give her an orgasm, if he couldn't save her from a life of frustrated sexual fantasies, then could anyone?

QUINN DROVE KAY over to Jake's bed-and-breakfast in his parents' Wagoneer and gave her the keys. He'd started to walk her to the door, not wanting her to slip in the gloom and the snow, but she surprised him by announcing she wanted to walk around and check out the town.

"For the article," she explained.

They walked to the end of the half-mile-long board-walk, which ended at the pier where the cruise ships docked in the summer. Most of the shops were closed for the winter, except for Long Bear's sundries and Mac-Kenzie's trading post. He took her over to KCRK, his parents' radio station, and they waved to Liam Kilstrom who was in the control booth. They wandered past the community rec center and the nearby church, where the ladies' auxiliary was having a quilting bee. They strolled by the Happy Puffin bar, where half the town was hanging out, because it was trivia night. The other half of the town was either probably in Jake's huge sitting room or at the adjacent restaurant, Paradise Diner.

He was not quite certain what had passed between them at his house. Had she come to Alaska to have an affair with him or not? She wanted him as badly as he wanted her. He saw the desire reflected in her eyes, noticed her passion in the way she held her body, recognized longing in how she got flustered in his presence. But something was holding her back.

It was all he could do to keep from touching her, brushing a wisp of hair from her cheek, taking her hand to guide her over the icy patches on the road. He wanted to caress her and hold her and never let her go.

He had it bad and he knew that wasn't good. He had to be careful. Kay was not a long-term relationship. He knew that. He didn't want either of them to get hurt. But man, how he wanted to make love to her.

His gut somersaulted and he drew in a deep, steadying breath, unable to remember when one woman had tied him so inextricably into knots. He was afraid of screwing up, of making a wrong move, of letting this one slip through his fingers. He wanted her with a power that shook his normal confidence.

Kay stopped on the wooden promenade, inhaled deeply of the cold air and gazed at the mountains surrounding the town.

"It's so incredibly beautiful here," she murmured. "Breathtaking. Overwhelming. Majestic. Totally wild. Honestly, I had no idea."

"It's just home to me." He grinned.

"I can't believe how different it is from New York. Bear Creek is quaint and clean and charming. No noise, no pollution, no panhandlers. I've got to tell you the truth, all this quiet is a shock to my system. How do you stand it?"

"How do you stand Manhattan?"

She gave a little laugh, and the delicate, feminine sound drilled a corkscrew of awareness straight through his groin. "I suppose it's what you're accustomed to. Although I've got to admit it can be a tough place to live. I've been mugged twice in two years."

"That's awful."

She shrugged. "Builds character."

"I hate the thought of someone accosting you," he said vehemently. "Makes me want to do bodily harm."

"Omigosh!" she exclaimed, and latched on to his arm.

"What is it?"

"There's a moose. Trotting right down Main Street. I was reading a book on Alaska on the flight over, and it said moose are often more dangerous than bears. Is that true?"

"Moose have been known to cause a lot of damage."

"Do they bite?"

Quinn struggled not to laugh. Her gloved fingers dug into his forearm. Her lithe body trembled against his. Ah, at last, here was his opportunity to touch her, even if he had to do something a little underhanded to keep her latched on to him.

"Shh. Hang on to me, Kay. We'll tiptoe past him and hopefully he won't notice us."

"Quinn—" her voice warbled and her eyes grew round as hubcaps "—maybe we should turn around and go back to the pier. Give him the whole street."

The moose snorted and trotted closer.

"Oh! Oh!"

"I'll protect you." He thrust her behind him.

Her arms went around his waist and her sweet-smelling head popped out from under the crook of his arm so she could keep her eyes fixed on the moose.

"He's huge," she whispered. "What if he charges?"

"I'll hold him off while you run away."

"Quinn, I'm scared."

He patted her hand. "It's all right, Kay. I won't let any harm come to you. This isn't New York."

The moose snorted and pawed the ground. Then raised his shaggy head and glared at them.

Kay tightened her grip on his waist.

"We'll just ease on by." Quinn took a tentative step forward.

"No, no." She dug in her heels. "Please don't move."

The moose chose that moment to turn and lope off in the opposite direction. Kay sighed and sagged against his body. "Whew. That was a close call."

Reprobate, his conscience accused. *Tell her the truth.*

"Kay…" he began, but she was no longer next to him. She was sprinting toward Jake's B&B. He had to run to catch up with her.

She wrenched open the door and tumbled headlong into the foyer.

The place was packed with toddy-sipping locals

gathered around a roaring fire, playing chess, swapping tall tales, listening to the weather report on the radio. The minute Kay burst through the entryway, every head turned to stare at her, and he hated the way they gawked.

"Wild moose!" Kay gasped. "Walking down Main Street."

The denizens of Bear Creek, mostly men, all Quinn's neighbors and friends, stared at her as if she was some exotic bird who'd migrated too far north. More than a few mouths dropped open, and even Lulu, Jake's Siberian husky, lifted her head off the rug. A twinge of guilt bit him for having let her believe the moose was dangerous.

"Well," Kay demanded, sinking her hands on her hips and glaring about her, "aren't you guys going to do something about it?"

The room broke into raucous laughter.

Kay blushed and pivoted on her heel to face Quinn. "What's so funny?"

"Quinn got you thinkin' that moose is a killer?" cackled an old fellow seated at a table near the door, a chessboard on the table in front of him.

"Don't let old Gus give you a hard time," soothed a handsome man that Kay recognized from the publicity photo Quinn had shown her in New York. He had sandy hair and a boyish grin that promised lots of fun. "That's just Kong, our resident moose. Caleb bottle-fed him from the time he was a calf. His Momma got hit by an RV during tourist season five years ago. Kong's tamer than a poodle."

"Oh." She felt like fifty different kinds of fool. Why had Quinn let her believe the moose was dangerous?

She glared at him, and he had the good sense to look ashamed of himself.

"I get it, ha, ha, ha. Play a trick on the city girl."

"I'm sorry." Quinn jammed his hands in his pockets.

"It's okay. I can take a joke."

"I'm Jake, by the way. You must be Kay." Quinn's buddy held out his hand. "We've heard a lot about you. Welcome to Bear Creek."

"Thank you, Jake." She shook his hand and smiled graciously, determined to regain her dignity.

"Would you like me to show you to your room?" Jake asked.

"That would be lovely."

"This way."

Jake led her up the wide cedar staircase to a room decorated with rustic charm. Quinn started to trail after them, but Kay turned and planted a palm on his chest. "Excuse me, big man, but I don't recall anyone inviting you up to my room."

CHAPTER SIX

"SHE SURE PUT YOU in your place," Jake teased Quinn when he returned to the B&B three hours after Kay had kicked him out. Lulu lay on the rug at his feet, eyeing Quinn with the same amusement that was evident in her owner's face.

"Oh, shut up."

"Quinn's got a girlfriend."

"Grow up," Quinn growled, and scowled.

He had gone home to give her time to cool off and to prepare a peace offering, and he'd come back to restlessly pace the corridor of the B&B, trying to gather his courage to knock on Kay's door. Since when could one feisty little woman make his knees quake?

He pushed his fingers through his hair and let out a long breath, which did nothing to ease the nervousness and self-reproach squeezing his gut. If he wasn't careful he was going to mess things up royally with Kay.

He had fibbed to her, inadvertently embarrassed her, and that had never been his intent. He had to apologize, get back into her good graces.

Resolutely he knocked on her door.

"Should I go get Meggie?" Jake asked. "Just in case Kay decides to slam-dunk you down the staircase and you need the services of a trained RN?"

"Beat it." Quinn glowered at his friend.

Chuckling to himself, Jake sauntered off, Lulu on his heels.

And Kay answered the door. "Oh. Are you still here?"

"Can we talk?"

She crossed her arms over her chest. "So talk."

"In private." He waved a hand. "Eavesdroppers are rampant around here."

She shook her head and studied him for a long moment. Should she stay mad? He gave her a sad expression. She opened her door wider. "All right."

Quinn scooted over the threshold.

Kay shut the door behind him, then turned to face him. "Did you have fun embarrassing me in front of all your friends?"

"It wasn't like that."

"Wasn't like what? I was terrified of that moose!" She punched him lightly on the shoulder. He arched his eyebrows in surprise. She wasn't given to admitting feelings of weakness, and the fact that she had done so amazed her. But darn it, she had been scared.

"You told me you'd survived two muggings and it was no big deal. Why would a moose scare you?" Quinn looked genuinely puzzled.

"Because it's the unknown. Why did you let me make a fool of myself?"

"I had no idea you were going to rush into Jake's and call everyone to arms against Kong. What can I say? I liked it when you grabbed on to me, when you needed me to protect you."

"Really?" She slanted him a sideways glance. She was flattered and she probably shouldn't be, but truthfully it had made her feel very feminine to know this brawny man could protect her from wild creatures.

"Yeah. I am sorry—I acted like a jerk, Kay."

Her name on his tongue tracked an unstoppable awareness through her. She pressed a hand to her stomach to still the fluttering there. A man who could admit when he was wrong? Unbelievable.

"Forgive me?"

"You're forgiven," she said.

"Forgiven enough so that you'll agree to have dinner with me?"

"All right." She nodded. "Just let me change."

"I'll wait for you in the lobby."

Grinning, Quinn hurried back downstairs. Thank heavens she'd accepted his dinner invitation. He'd gone all out, preparing his famous salmon chowder, putting Coltrane on the CD player, chilling a bottle of champagne. He hoped he wasn't going overboard or pushing too hard.

His stomach took a dive at the thought. He'd never felt so out of his element with a woman. He was used to cocking a seductive grin at the ladies and having them tumble right into his bed. Why this one caused him to doubt himself, he had no idea.

Maybe because he wanted her so badly.

A few minutes later Kay floated down the staircase. Once again every eye in the room was trained on her lithe, graceful form. Even Lulu thumped her tail approvingly from her place by the fire.

Quinn gulped. He could only stare, bug-eyed. She wore a black velvet long-sleeved dress and black high-heeled fashion boots. Not exactly Alaskan wear, but damn, those boots did fine things for her legs.

In that moment he flashed back to the first time he'd seen her on the plane. He recalled the way her legs looked encased in silk stockings. A rampant forest fire suddenly blazed through him, and he was at a loss for words.

The bodice of her dress clung snugly to her full breasts. The skirt swished seductively when she moved.

As she descended the last step, he stood up to greet her.

"Are you going to be warm enough in that outfit?" he asked.

She leaned in close, the hair on the top of her head tickling his nose. "Shh, don't tell anyone. I have on long-handled underwear."

That secret should have killed his libido-fed fantasies about satin and lace covering her silky skin. Instead he found himself even more aroused by the thought of her in cotton flannel. Perspiration beaded his brow.

He was a sick, sick man.

The sky was inky black as they walked to the SUV. This time of year they got only about five hours of daylight. He carried a flashlight and shone it over the parking lot to light their way, while keeping his arm firmly locked around Kay's waist. He wasn't about to let anything happen to her.

"I can't believe how dark it is," she whispered. "No streetlights. No cars on the road. Quiet as a cemetery."

He tried to see Bear Creek from her point of view and failed. He considered the darkness comforting, the vastness of the landscape inspiring.

"Where are we going?" she asked.

"My place."

"Not to a restaurant?" Her voice rose on the question, as if she was nervous about his reply.

"The only restaurant open during the winter months is the Paradise Diner next to the B&B. You'll be sick enough of it by the time you head back to New York."

"Only one restaurant? You've got to be kidding."

"I'm not. Bear Creek's winter population is about fifteen hundred."

"And in the summer?"

"Late May through mid-August the population swells to three, four thousand, double that when the cruise ships are in town."

"Wow."

They arrived at his cabin, and he escorted her inside and took her coat.

"Something smells wonderful!" she exclaimed. "I'm starving."

"Salmon chowder and grilled sourdough bread."

"Sounds delicious."

"Made it myself. The chowder that is, not the bread."

She laughed.

Once in the kitchen, she enthused over the table-cloth, the candles, the champagne just as he'd hoped, and Quinn began to relax. He'd pleased her, which was precisely his intent.

He pulled back her chair for her. She smiled up at him. They ate and talked and ate and talked as if they'd been friends for a thousand years.

Quinn couldn't quit staring at her. Whenever her pink tongue flicked out to take a morsel of food from her spoon, it felt as if she was licking him in a very private place. Several times he had to bite down on his bottom lip to keep from groaning out loud.

Kay was impressed that he'd worked so hard to make such a delicious meal. She admired his impeccable table manners and sent sideways glances at him. The candle-light accented his features. He'd rolled up his sleeves while serving their dinner, exposing those magnificent forearms that drove her wild with desire.

"So, Quinn, for the sake of the readers of *Metropolitan* magazine, what's your idea of the perfect date?" she asked, desperate to get her mind off his extreme sexiness.

"We're back to the article again."

"Yes."

"We're having it."

"What?"

"The perfect date." He reached across the table, laid a hand on hers. "Good food. Great conversation. A pretty woman."

"Oh." Taken aback by the very bold look in his eyes, Kay removed her hand from underneath his.

"There's only one thing that would make it better."

She held her breath.

"Dessert."

He disappeared into the kitchen for a few minutes and then brought out baked Alaska.

"You made this yourself?" she gasped as he set the flaming dessert in front of her.

"It's not as hard as it looks."

"I'm impressed."

"That was my intent."

He nailed her with his steady gaze.

She'd never met a man like Quinn. At once extremely masculine, yet oddly enough quite domestic. He possessed a self-confidence that would attract any woman. He had an intense strength underlying his every action, and hey, the guy could even admit when he was wrong. She wagered that mere weeks after his advertisement ran in the magazine, he'd be well on his way to matrimony with the wild woman of his dreams.

She experienced a strange tug in her belly. Was she actually jealous of that as-yet-nonexistent woman?

You don't have to be jealous. You can have him for now. He's the tonic to soothe your shattered ego. So what if there's no happily-ever-after? What about happily-right-now?

They ate the baked Alaska; then Quinn wiped his mouth with his napkin, checked his watch and shoved back his chair. "It's about time."

"Time for what?"

"Come with me. There's something I'd like to show you." He got to his feet and held out his hand to her. "This way."

He guided her toward the stairs.

Toward the bedroom?

Kay gulped. Was she really ready for this? She had taken the assignment because she wanted to see Quinn again. And because she couldn't stop lusting after him, but when push came to shove, could she go through with it?

"Quinn...I..."

He placed a finger to her lips. "Shh."

His finger tasted slightly salty, the pressure of it against her mouth startlingly arousing. She had the strongest urge to capture that finger with her teeth and suck.

He cocked his head and smiled oh-so-slightly, as if miraculously reading her thoughts. The five-o'clock shading riding his jaw looked rough, exciting, and she wondered what it would feel like rasping against her cheek.

In a split second she was locked in another fantasy. She envisioned him without his clothes on and hiccuped at the image that rose to her mind. He would look gorgeous naked. She just knew it. Golden skin, perfectly defined muscles, firm hiney.

Kay gulped.

"Come," he urged. "Come."

Did she dare?

Maybe, Kay realized, maybe she was afraid of finding out that she really was sexually dysfunctional. But how could she be frigid when she felt so hot and wet and achy deep inside? When her entire body begged for a release she'd dreamed about on a daily basis?

He laced his fingers through hers and, walking backward, slowly pulled her up the first step. "I'm not going to bite," he murmured. "Unless you want me to."

Her heart punched her rib cage as she placed one booted foot on the first hardwood step.

His gaze snagged hers and held on tight. Kay shivered at the purely masculine gleam in his sultry eyes. Even from arm's length, she could feel his body heat radiating outward.

She was coming undone. Something uncoiled in her belly. Something soft and warm and messy.

His breathing, husky with desire, echoed loudly in the confines of the staircase. The erotic sound strummed along her nerve endings, escalating her excitement. She struggled to draw in a steady breath of her own, but ended up panting shallowly, her eyes locked to his.

Up another step and then another.

Scalding hot. It must be 110 degrees in here. Quinn tightened his grip on her fingers. She needed to run outside and roll around in the snow.

"Almost there," he coaxed.

Almost where? His bedroom? At the thought she experienced this incredible, inextricable push-pull. Her nipples tightened in anticipation; she could feel them protruding against the material of her bra. Pressure, sweet, sweet pressure, grew between her legs.

"Here we are," he said at last, and she mounted the last step.

But where he led her was not a bedroom.

Kay blinked.

It was another spacious living area with rafter ceilings, a second fireplace, leather couch, braided rug. A handmade quilt graced the back of the couch. The far corner housed a desk complete with computer, printer, fax, copier and scanner.

Outdoor and rescue equipment hung from pegs mounted along the paneling or were in organized rows on built-in shelves. Harnesses, ropes, pulleys and crampons for mountain climbing. Life vests, oars and wading boots for river rafting. There were fire extinguishers and first-aid kits, a citizens band radio and a huge stash of flashlights. Obviously this was his office.

But what grabbed her attention and held her transfixed was the plate-glass window running along one wall overlooking the bay and the incredible display on view.

Kay's hand rose to her throat as she stared at the brilliant curtain of shimmering green, red and white that fluttered ghostlike across the sky. She had never seen anything so awe-inspiring as those radiant spectral waves.

The shimmers danced and twirled, gauzy curtains of brilliant brightness changing shapes, billowing out like a green genie from a bottle in those old cartoons she had been banned from watching as a child.

"The northern lights," she whispered.

"Yeah." His voice was as husky with awe and respect as her own.

"It's incredible. Resplendent. Superlative. Words can't began to describe it."

"Nature's light show. We see the aurora up to two hundred times a year from early spring to late fall. This year promises to be particularly vibrant because of increased sunspot activity."

"What causes this spectacle?"

"Scientifically speaking," Quinn said, "the northern lights are electrical discharges resulting from the interaction between wind and the earth's magnetic field."

"Oh."

"But the Native Alaskans believe the lights were torches carried by old souls to guide the new souls into the next world."

A carpet of gooseflesh covered her arms, despite her long-handled underwear. She felt shivery inside and not just from the eerie legend, but from her closeness to Quinn.

He'd brought her up here to see this breathtaking display, not to make love to her. She was simultaneously relieved and disappointed.

Kiss me, she thought. *Kiss me now, kiss me hard, kiss me long.*

But she didn't say those things. Instead, she turned to him and smiled softly, belying the inner turmoil raging through her mind. "Thank you, Quinn, for showing this to me."

"You're welcome. Hang on, I'll get us some champagne and we'll toast your arrival and the appearance of the sometimes temperamental aurora. I'd hoped she would come out to play tonight, but you never know for certain."

"She?"

"The aurora is most definitely a feminine force," he said. "Watch the sky. See how the lights flicker and tease? She's fickle. Coming on hot, then shying away.

Coyly fading one minute, flaring boldly the next. Cool yet strangely hot. Oh, Aurora is a woman all right. She's got many moods."

"You're quite the romantic," Kay said.

"So I've been told."

"I still don't understand why you're not married." She shook her head.

"Hopefully your article and our ad will help rectify that."

But I don't want you to get married, a selfish little voice inside her cried. *If you get married, you can't be my boy-toy.*

She watched him amble to the champagne bucket positioned next to the stereo system. He turned on the radio, and the sound of Wilson Pickett's "Midnight Hour" spun out into the room.

"Oh," she said, "I love this song."

"That's KCRK," Quinn told her. "I put together the play list for tonight."

He wrangled with the champagne bottle. She heard the cork pop, watched him fill two flutes with fizzy champagne.

"You went to a lot of trouble for me."

His eyes met hers as he handed her a flute. "You're worth it."

Blinking up at his handsome face, Kay noticed things she hadn't paid attention to before—the way his brown hair, shot through with golden strands, curled slightly over his forehead, the way his eyes went soft and seemed to caress her, the tiny mole an inch above the left side of his mouth.

He raised his glass. "To the moment," he murmured.

She clinked the lip of hers against the lip of his. "To the moment."

They sipped their champagne, eyed each other over the rim of their glasses. Kay felt at once heavy and yet extremely light, like a helium balloon tied to a child's wrist. Weighted but yearning to fly.

Suddenly she burped.

"Oh, my goodness!" she exclaimed, and slapped a hand over her mouth. In her family burping aloud was a sin akin to indecent exposure. "I'm so embarrassed. Please forgive me."

"Lighten up, sweetheart. What's to forgive? So you burped. Actually it makes me feel better. I was beginning to think you were too perfect."

"I'm not perfect. Not by a long shot."

"Well, if burping on champagne is your biggest fault, I won't kick you out of my bed."

Their eyes met, held for a long moment.

"Come sit." He eased down on the couch, patted the cushion next to him.

She sat down beside him. He stretched his arm out over the back of the couch. She was acutely aware of it resting there. She imagined his fingers tangling in her hair, his mouth devouring hers. Briefly she closed her eyes and when she opened them again, she focused on the dancing lights beyond the window.

Quinn studied Kay as she watched the northern lights. Her profile mesmerized him. Her nose was refined, her cheekbones sculpted. Just looking at her made his heart feel crooked, as if it had slipped in his chest.

Her scent teased his nostrils. Warm and rich and compelling, it smelled of something foreign and exotic. Was that what attracted him to her? She was like no other woman of his acquaintance.

Her hair brushed lightly across his skin. He noticed her perfectly manicured fingernails, the delicate shape of her hands, her narrow wrist decorated with a gold tennis bracelet. Even though she was right beside him, she still seemed detached somehow. Her detachment intrigued him just as it had on the airplane.

Her aloofness roused him, made him want to do something drastic to bring her into the fold. She had lived in New York too long, spent too much time disconnected from people, too often kept her feelings to herself. Her two-week stay in Bear Creek would do her a world of good. Help her open up to herself and the world around her. He wondered if he should tell her about his urge to rattle her cage, ruffle her feathers, crack her facade. He ached to tell her exactly how he hoped to liberate her. But Quinn feared that if he spoke these words, it would be a mistake from which he could never recover.

And yet he felt driven, nervous. His heart began a fretful pounding. There were no words for what he wanted to say, and his tongue lay paralyzed on the floor of his mouth. A knot of pressure built inside him. Pressure that urged him to haul her into his arms and show her everything he simply could not say.

He wasn't good with flowery sentiment. He was a man of action, and only action could quiet his restlessness. His body tensed and he leaned in close.

She looked at him then, her pale hair gleaming in the firelight, rivaling the natural phenomena flickering outside the window. Her breathing was shallow, and her brown eyes shone with a fevered effervescence. He'd never seen anything so lovely.

Kay felt his body shift toward her, pressing her deeper into the plush leather couch. His left side was crushed against her right, and he placed a hand on her thigh. Then his mouth was on hers—oh, how she had dreamed of kissing him again—urgent and insistent. She was concurrently both hot and cold. His body was tense, hard, but his lips were soft, inviting.

And his tongue.

Dear Lord, it ought to be illegal to possess such a tongue!

From there everything went wild, flailed totally out of control. He dropped his arm from the back of the couch, wrapped it around her waist and hauled her against his body, forcing her to spread her knees.

She felt his erection through his pants. It throbbed against her belly with a provocative rhythm. They were fused. Lips to lips. Chest to chest. Thigh to thigh. And yet it wasn't nearly close enough. Too much clothing in the way.

Twining her fingers into the warm, thick, whiskey-colored hair at the nape of his neck, she arched her body against his. She opened her mouth wider, encouraging that roving tongue to pepper her with wet, sexual thrusts.

He mimicked her moves, one hand cupping the back of her neck. The fingers of his other hand stroked her jaw, her throat and skimmed lower until he was caressing her breasts through the velvety bodice of her dress. He kneaded the pliant flesh, searing her with triple-digit heat. Oh, she couldn't wait until his hands were on her bare skin.

His thumb flicked across the pebble-hard nipple straining tight against her restrictive clothing. Damn, but she wanted to be naked. She threw back her head and a needy moan escaped her lips.

Putty. She was nothing but putty in his hands. The notion both frightened and exhilarated her.

Feverish desire clawed through her, pulling her

down, drawing her under the power of Quinn's spell. With the aurora borealis whipping gracefully in her peripheral vision, the fireplace embers glowing and Quinn's tongue on its restless pursuit, she felt swept away by some unstoppable, forbidden fantasy.

Except this reality was more titillating than her most taboo dreams.

Too much torture. She simply could not stand this any longer. She wanted him. Now. Crazily, illogically, this very minute. She refused to stub out her urges. Passion pushed all her fears aside. Desire evaporated any shred of common sense she might have possessed. She wrenched her mouth from his.

"Quinn," she gasped. "Before we go any further, there's something I must tell you."

He looked dazed, muzzy with craving. Their breathing mingled in rapid spurts.

"What is it?"

"I'm not…" She paused, not quite certain how to put this. "I'm not like other women."

"You got that right, sweetheart." He couldn't seem to resist dropping a kiss on her jaw. That achingly light pressure threw her completely off-kilter.

She splayed a hand on his chest and pushed him back. She needed a moment to regroup. "No. I don't mean it like that."

He rearranged himself on the couch, shoved a hand through his hair and gave her his complete attention. "I'm listening."

"I've never…" She squirmed uncomfortably. She hated admitting her deficiencies. She'd been raised on the myth that Freemonts never revealed their flaws. So why was she going to tell him her darkest secret? Because she felt as if he was the only one who could help her. "Well…you know…"

"What? Had sex?" He stared at her in disbelief.

"I'm twenty-seven, Quinn. I was almost engaged. Of course I've had sex."

"Oh. What then?" He frowned.

This was so hard. She squirmed, she fidgeted. She tried the words out mentally first, but nothing seemed right. Finally she blurted, "I've never…" Then paused again.

"Never what?"

She dropped her voice to a whisper. "…had an orgasm."

"You're kidding. For real?"

She nodded. "Lloyd says I'm frigid. That it's my fault he had to turn to other women."

"Bullshit!" Quinn spoke with such vehemence, Kay jumped. "Sorry, I didn't mean to scare you. But that ex-boyfriend of yours is a jerk."

His anger at Lloyd flattered her. She knew then that she had done the right thing by coming to Alaska, by revealing to Quinn her hidden shame.

"How he could fool around on such a beautiful, exciting, interesting woman is beyond me. He must have sawdust for brains."

"You think I'm interesting?" She smiled shyly, not meaning to be coy. She wasn't milking him for more compliments, but she was touched beyond measure that he found her interesting, as she'd always thought herself rather dull.

"Interesting, hell." Quinn snorted. "You're downright mysterious. You keep yourself so contained. I ache to know what you're thinking when you get those Mona Lisa smiles on your face. And you're anything but frigid. If you've never been able to come, it's through no fault of your own. You've just been with the wrong men."

Kay gulped. This next part was hard, but she had to say it. "I want to ask a favor of you."

"What is it?" His eyes never left her face.

"Do you think that maybe you could help me…er… achieve sexual fulfillment?"

"Say the word, sweetheart," he encouraged her, lifting a hand to capture a strand of her hair and rub it between his fingers. "Put aside that aristocratic breeding of yours and tell me that you want to come bigger than the state of Alaska."

Pressing her teeth into her bottom lip, she stared straight into his eyes.

And almost lost it completely.

"I want you to make me come," she begged him. "More than anything in the world."

CHAPTER SEVEN

How HAD HE GOTTEN so lucky?

Kay Freemont, rich, successful, cultured and beautiful, wanted to entrust him, a simple Alaskan man, with her sexual awakening.

Stunned, delighted, touched, flattered and horny beyond comprehension. How had he gotten so lucky?

He sent a brief prayer of thanks to the heavens and added a pleading postscript: *Don't let me lose control. Help me to be strong so I can give her what she needs.*

It was going to be hard—pun definitely intended—to rein in his own ravenous desires. He hadn't been with a woman since he and Heather had broken up. He was hanging by a thread.

But he had to dig deep, find a way to put his own needs on hold. Because Kay was giving him the opportunity of a lifetime. She was granting him the privilege of bringing her to the heights of her sexuality.

He was a fortunate SOB and he would not let her down.

She took a long swallow of champagne, then sat her glass on the floor at her feet and shifted her body into his. "I'm ready, Quinn. Make love to me."

Shaking his head, he reached out and tenderly traced her lips with his thumb. She shivered beneath his caress, and the shot of adrenaline that jumped into his gut floored him.

Control, Scofield. Control.

"Oh, no, my sweet, not so fast," Quinn said, when what he wanted to do more than anything in the world was strip that velvet dress over her head, rip off those long johns and make messy, wet, hot love to her.

"What do you mean?" she whispered, her eyes growing wide.

"A proper seduction takes time."

"Oh, yes? How much time?" She seemed alarmed.

"Depends."

"On what?"

He grinned wickedly. "When you're ready."

"I'm ready tonight," she said a bit peevishly. She narrowed her eyes at him and he understood her frustration. If she thought she was frustrated now, she was in for a big shock.

"No, you're not."

"Yes, I am."

"Listen, sweetheart, we're doing this my way or not at all. Got that?"

She glared at him, crossed her arms over her chest, flipped one knee over the other. "I'm not sure I like this."

"Before I make love to you, you'll have to eject that uptight demeanor."

"I'm not uptight."

"Arms crossed, legs crossed. Babe, you're closed up tighter than Glacier Bay in January."

"So you *do* think I'm frigid."

"No! Okay, that was a bad analogy. I do not think you're frigid. But in order for you to get the full sexual experience, you're going to have to relax. And before you can do that, you're going to have to trust me completely."

"And how long will this take?" she asked, purposely uncrossing both her arms and her legs to show she was ready, willing and able to start trusting and relaxing right now.

He lowered his head, his mouth almost on hers. He smelled the fruity scent of champagne on her lips. Right then and there he almost caved. He barely resisted the urge to capture that sassy mouth with his once more.

"Don't worry," he whispered huskily. "You'll know."

EXHAUSTION CLAIMED HER MIND, haunted her body. Kay had spent the rest of the night in her lonely bed at Jake Gerard's B&B pining for a man who was bent on serving up sweet torture.

And in between the tossing and turning, she had been consumed with rampant fantasies about Quinn. In one scenario he was a wild-eyed pirate who kidnapped and savaged her repeatedly in the hold of his ship. In another fantasy she was a domineering amazon who kept him chained in the basement for her pleasure. In yet another vision he was a wounded soldier fighting for the other side, and she was a caring nursemaid who hid him in her father's barn.

Ack!

She was slowly losing her ever-loving mind. She had to stop thinking about Quinn. She had work to do. An article to write. She was going to get dressed, go out on the town and explore Bear Creek. She refused to dwell on the fact that he wouldn't make love to her yet and put her out of her misery.

Groaning, she threw back the covers and crept out of bed, stripping off her nightgown and heading straight for the shower. Standing under the stream of hot water, she kept thinking about what Quinn had said.

You're not ready.

Well, how the hell did he know what she was ready for? He barely knew her. But in a way that was what made this whole venture so exciting. Knowing she would never see him again after her trip to Alaska, having this fabulous memory of her sexual adventure and possessing a wistful fondness for the man who showed her that she was all woman. This knowledge was the only thing that had given her the courage to express her true desires to him. To ask him to become her mentor in love.

So here she was, with her fanny on the line, ready, willing and able for action. And Quinn had been the one to put the brakes on.

She soaped her hair but in an instant she was fantasizing again. She saw Quinn in the shower, massaging the shampoo into her scalp, then rinsing her hair.

Her belly clenched with heated desire as she envisioned his hard body brushing hers, his manhood standing at attention. He would press her against the cool tile while hot water sluiced over their fevered skin. He would claim her mouth with his. Roughly, insistently, pillaging her territory. Then he would change tempo and the kisses would turn long and soft and lazy.

She arches her body into his. Desperate for release. She begs him to enter her. She needs to feel him inside her. Needs to experience the fullness only his large shaft will bring.

His fingers curl into the most private part of her. He rubs her cleft gently at first, then with more pressure.

Her sensitive breasts tighten and swell in response, and he gloats over her hardened nipples, taking credit for her arousal. He dips his head to those perky mounds, taking first one into his mouth and then turning his at-

tention to the other. He flicks his tongue over the pink peak. It's as if there is a string connecting her nipples to her groin. With each seductive lick she feels a deepening ache at her very center.

She bites her bottom lip to keep from crying out, but he urges her to let go.

"Scream if you want," he insists, his mouth against her ear. "Let the world know we're making love."

Then he's nibbling her earlobe, running his silky tongue along the outside of her ear. The shudder that crawls through her rocks her to her core. She wraps her arms around his neck, clings to him....

The hot water gone cold forced her back to reality.

Kay opened her eyes, found her lips were pressed against the wall tile. Chagrined, she hopped backward, slipped and would have crashed to the floor of the tub if she hadn't grasped the soap rack.

Oh, she was pathetic. If Quinn didn't make love to her soon, she would explode into a million pieces. That would go over big on the New York social register—and with her mother!

Shaking her head, Kay turned off the water, eased out of the shower and wrapped a towel around herself.

Okay. No more nonsense. She was going to stop thinking about Quinn. She had work to do.

Twenty minutes later she was in the Paradise Diner enjoying blueberry pancakes and surrounded by a curious contingency of Bear Creek's entertaining citizens.

Kay knew she was a novelty, and they were asking her more questions than she was asking them. Jake Gerard introduced her to Caleb Greenleaf, the only wife-hunting bachelor she hadn't yet met.

Caleb turned out to be a serious man with almost unbelievable good looks. It took a lot of coaxing, but after a while he told her about his job as a naturalist for the state of Alaska. He was quite different from his buddies. Introverted, where the other three were clearly extroverts.

Everyone in Bear Creek was friendly, open, welcoming, so very unlike some of the New Yorkers she knew, who had a tendency to be curt, suspicious and unimpressed. They enthusiastically told her many things about their lives. They were so trusting. Too trusting, to her way of thinking. But that's what she liked most about them.

Her New York life seemed very far away, and she couldn't think of anything she missed.

Later, after she'd already compiled copious notes and recorded more than three hours worth of conversations, an attractive, middle-aged couple, holding hands and grinning at each other as if they shared the secret to long-term romance, came in for lunch.

The woman stepped carefully, slowed by a booted walking cast on her right foot. Her husband solicitously helped her up to the counter. They sat on Kay's left, the man taking the stool Caleb had vacated.

He held out his hand to her and gave her a friendly smile. "Jim Scofield. We just had to come over to meet the reporter our son coaxed to come here all the way from New York City."

"You're Quinn's parents? Thanks so much for letting me use your extra car." Kay ran a hand self-consciously through her hair. She hadn't bothered to blow-dry and style it that morning since she knew she would be wearing a woolen cap much of the day, but now she wished she had. Skimping on her grooming was not normal for her, and she felt exposed and at a disadvantage, even though she had already discovered most of the women in Bear Creek didn't wear makeup or style their hair. Everything from their chunky Gore-Tex boots to their sensible parkas was geared for warmth and comfort. You'd never find a fashion show in Bear Creek.

"Yep." Jim slung his arm over the woman's shoulder. "This is my wife, Linda."

"You did a fine job raising your son," Kay told them as she shook their hands.

"We're pretty proud of him." When Linda smiled, her gray eyes softened into welcoming crinkles, just like Quinn's. "And our daughter, Meggie. She's an emergency-room nurse at a children's hospital in Seattle. She's visiting for a couple of weeks to help me while I'm out of commission." Linda gestured at her cast. "You and Meggie ought to get together. She's a city girl just like you, and I do believe you two are the only single women in town under thirty and over eighteen."

"I'd love to meet her."

Kay felt a tug of sadness in her heart, and she couldn't really say why. Maybe because this couple were so different from her own parents. They wore woolen pants, nylon and flannel, where Honoria and Charles Freemont were never seen in public without being impeccably dressed.

Linda and Jim sent each other private signals with their eyes. Kay's parents rarely even looked each other in the face. The Scofields touched frequently with simple, loving gestures. Her mother and father were rarely even in the same room together.

Without any encouragement, Quinn's parents extolled his virtues.

"Did you know Quinn's on the volunteer fire department?" Linda asked.

"No, I didn't." Kay scribbled on her notepad, *Bet*

he looks good in fire boots and suspenders and noth-ing else.

"He's captain of the local hockey team," Jim bragged.

"Quinn has a bachelor's degree in sports physiol-ogy," Linda said.

"He's owned his own business for ten years and each year he turns a bigger profit." Jim nodded.

"And he still finds time to help us out at the radio station. You couldn't ask for a better son." Linda took a sip of her coffee. "Or better husband material. Write that down." She waved a hand at Kay's notebook. "I'm hoping this advertisement thing pays off for Quinn. I'm ready for grandchildren, and Meggie doesn't seem to be in any hurry to accommodate me."

Jim eyed Kay. "You wouldn't be interested in our boy yourself, would you? You're a beautiful young lady. You two would have the handsomest kids."

"Oh, no." Kay struggled to tamp down the telltale blush she knew was spreading up her neck. "I mean, I like Quinn very much, but I'm a New Yorker. And I just got out of a relationship. I'm not ready for anything seri-ous. Quinn and I are at two different places in our lives."

Immediately she realized she'd given too much in-formation too quickly. Why had she said so much? That certainly wasn't like her, spilling her guts to strangers. Probably she'd spouted off because she didn't want them getting the wrong idea about Quinn and her.

But oddly enough, her nervous revelation seemed to endear her to Quinn's parents. The Scofields smiled at her sweetly and Jim patted her on the shoulder. "No explanation necessary."

"But you do like him," Linda said.

Oh, great. How had she gotten herself into this con-versation?

"Mom, Dad," Quinn boomed from the door of the restaurant, "stop bending Kay's ear."

Relieved, Kay looked up to see him stalk toward them. Her heart gave this strange little thump and she suddenly felt all loose and melty inside. He was even better-looking than she remembered in that hard-edged, masculine way of his.

He stopped beside her stool. "Hey."

"Hey, yourself." Inwardly she cringed. That sounded too flirty.

"Sleep well?" He grinned as if he knew she hadn't slept a wink.

"Considering the circumstances."

"Strange bed and all that."

"And all that," she echoed.

"We better be heading out." Jim Scofield got to his feet, left some money on the counter, then turned to help his wife from her stool. "Linda's got a doctor's appointment in Anchorage at two-thirty, and Mack's waiting to fly us over, so we better get a move on. Nice meeting you, Kay."

"Nice to meet you, too." She wriggled her fingers at them.

"Quinn, you must bring Kay to dinner on Saturday night," Linda insisted. "We're having a little get-together."

"Thank you, Mrs. Scofield. I'd love to come."

Linda whispered something in Quinn's ear and nudged him in the ribs.

"All right, Mom. We'll be there."

"What'd she say?" Kay asked after his parents had left the restaurant. Quinn perched on the stool beside her.

"She said I was supposed to be nice to you."

"Oh, really?"

"She likes you."

"How can you tell?"

"I just know."

"I like her, too. I like both your folks."

Kay couldn't help but think about her own parents again. Honoria and Charles would be as rejecting of Quinn as his parents were accepting of her. The vast differences between them yawned before her. Good thing her relationship with Quinn was purely sexual. They wouldn't have to deal with sticky things like disappointed in-laws. Best leave that to the bachelorettes who would come pouring into Bear Creek with marriage on their minds.

"I dropped by to see if you'd like to come over tomorrow night," Quinn said.

"Tomorrow? Not tonight?"

He smirked at the disappointment in her voice. "I'm playing hockey tonight, but I'd love to have you in the stands rooting for me, if you'd like to come."

"And after the hockey game…?" She let her sentence trail off.

His grin widened. "I'll take you to the B&B."

"Couldn't we go back to your place afterward?"

"No way." He shook his head.

"Why not?"

"Because I'm clearing my calendar on Wednesday night for you. What I've got in mind, sweetheart, is going to take hours and hours and hours." And with that, he winked, chucked her under the chin, pivoted on his heel and strode out of the restaurant.

THE TEN PLAYERS whizzed over the ice in a blur. Hockey sticks clashed loudly in the still night air. Bright stadium lights lit the perimeter of the frozen lake turned outdoor hockey rink. In the bleachers, Kay sat huddled under a blanket with Jim and Linda Scofield, her notebook and pen clutched in her gloved fingers. She had yet to write a word, so caught up was she in watching the game.

The players zipped by them again heading for the opposite team's goal. If Quinn wasn't so tall, Kay would have had trouble following him. He moved with a graceful power, pushing across the ice with smooth, long-limbed strokes. The expression on his face showed fierce concentration. He manned his stick like a gladiator doing battle.

Wow. Did he bring that kind of concentration to the bedroom? Kay shivered at the thought, grateful she had the cold as an excuse for her quivers.

She was so busy eyeing Quinn's amazing bod, she never even noticed when he slammed the puck home until the crowd roared and jumped to their collective feet. Kay followed suit, dropping her notepad and pen into her seat so she could applaud without hindrance. "We Will Rock You" blared from the outdoor speakers mounted on the lampposts.

Because of his goal, the Bear Creek Grizzlies had taken a 2 to 1 lead.

"Quinn, Quinn, Quinn," the crowd chanted.

He turned then and caught Kay's eye.

A chill of excitement shuddered through her.

He put his hand to his mouth and blew her a kiss.

Kay's heart fluttered and her belly went warm against the sudden adrenaline rush. Quinn skated down the middle of the ice alone, his stick raised over his head in victory, accepting his accolades, relishing his accomplishment with unabashed glee.

The man was truly magnificent.

A warrior, self-reliant and strong. He was brave and passionate and not the least bit hesitant about expressing what was going on in his head.

Oh! To be like that, instead of a repressed rich woman so alienated from her emotions she didn't know if she would ever find the approval she needed to release herself from her societal prison.

"Kay, dear, you're shivering, get back under the blanket." Quinn's mother smiled and held up the thick thermal cover, welcoming her beneath it.

Kay sat beside Linda, squashing her notebook and pen beneath her, but she didn't care. Quinn's mom tucked the blanket around her and snuggled close. It felt nice to be wrapped in this warm cocoon, to share body heat with Quinn's family.

In that sweet moment she experienced an amiable sense of kinship she had never felt with her own mother. Linda Scofield, she knew with sudden certainty, would never advise her to marry a man who cheated on her.

Why can't my mother be like this?

But Kay knew it was a ridiculous wish. Wishing her mother was different was like wishing that she was five inches taller or had been born in Bear Creek.

"Here comes Meggie," Linda said. "Let's scoot down."

Kay looked up to see a woman about her own age picking her way through the stands. Unlike everyone else, who were clad in mackinaws, boots and woolen pants, Meggie wore an outfit more like Kay's own stylish attire.

Meggie possessed an open, honest face and an understated but totally natural prettiness that would serve her well into middle age and beyond. Her eyelashes were enhanced with mascara, her cheeks heightened with rouge. Flame-red lipstick adorned her mouth. Her jet-black hair was tucked up under a bright red and orange cap.

Just like Kay, she looked out of place among the locals. City girls in the Arctic wilderness. Kay felt an instant kinship with her.

Meggie greeted her parents, then plunked down beside Kay. "Hi." She slipped off a glove to shake Kay's hand, revealing slender hands with short-trimmed but well-manicured nails. "I'm Meggie Drummond." Her lively green eyes twinkled. "And you must be Kay."

Kay nodded. "Nice to meet you," she said.

"I hear you're from New York City."

"Yes, I am."

"Wow, I've always wanted to go to New York. They practice some of the most cutting-edge medicine in the country."

"That's right, you're in the medical profession."

"Head nurse of the emergency department at Seattle Children's Hospital."

"Aren't you awfully young to be head nurse?"

Meggie grinned. "I live and breathe pediatric medicine."

"How are they managing without you?" Kay asked.

"Probably very happily since I'm not there to keep them in line." Meggie laughed. "I'm known as something of a taskmaster among my crew. I strive to be fair, but I've got high standards when it comes to patient care."

"I can see that about you."

Meggie's eyes sparkled at the compliment. Obviously, she loved her work. "I had lots of vacation time accumulated—in fact my boss was threatening to lock me out of the hospital if I didn't take off—then when

Mom broke her ankle and needed help around the house, I figured now was as good as any time to get away."

The woman was so easy to talk to. Friendly, frank, uninhibited, with definite opinions about the world. Just like Quinn.

"I'm going for hot chocolate," Quinn's dad announced, getting to his feet and taking his wife's hand. "You ladies want anything?"

Meggie, Kay and Linda all said they wanted one, and Jim climbed down the bleachers. When he was gone, Meggie turned back to Kay. "Quinn's been unable to talk about anything but you since he came back from New York."

"Really?"

"You've impressed the hell out of him."

"He's a special guy," Kay replied, surprised at the sudden pressure pushing at her heart like champagne bubbles against a bottle cork.

"Yeah," Meggie murmured, "real special. Can't say I'm too keen on this modern-day mail-order-bride concept he's instigated."

"No?"

"Oh, Meggie," her mother said, "give it a chance. You never know what might happen."

Meggie shook her head. "He's just going to get hurt."

"You think so?" Kay asked.

"Uh-huh. You wouldn't believe it by looking at him, but Quinn's pretty tenderhearted. When he loves, he loves deeply."

"That's true," Linda added.

Don't worry, Kay longed to tell them but couldn't. *This thing between us is purely physical. He won't fall in love with me.*

"He needs an Alaskan wife," Meggie said. "Someone who understands him and his love for this land. I'm afraid that all he's going to get for his advertising dollars is a gaggle of giggling bimbos who'll take him for a ride, then skedaddle out of here at the first sign of winter. Just like Heather did."

"His ex-girlfriend."

"He told you about her?"

"Now, honey, don't judge Heather," Linda interjected. "She just couldn't get used to the quiet of Bear Creek. Besides, isn't criticizing Heather's reluctance to live in Alaska a little bit of the pot calling the kettle black?"

"Hey," Meggie said, "I never pretended to want to stay in Alaska. Even though I happened to be born here, I'm a city girl through and through. I gotta have action."

"Isn't that the truth." Linda rolled her eyes. "I swear you kicked like a mule to get out the entire last trimester of my pregnancy."

"I love the city, too," Kay said, happy to have found a kindred spirit in this land of ice and snow.

"Honey, you are *the* city."

"I don't understand what's so fascinating about people being crammed on top of each other and driving like maniacs. What's the attraction?" Linda shook her head.

"Stimulating conversation," Meggie said.

"Great parties," Kay added.

"Museums," Meggie popped off.

"Shopping!" Kay grinned.

"Symphonies."

"The theater."

"Terrific Chinese takeout delivered right to your door!" they cried in unison, stared in awe at each other, then burst out laughing.

Kay felt instant camaraderie with Meggie, and the

feeling astonished her. She didn't make friends this readily. Ever. But they'd forged a connection. She knew by the merry gleam shining in Meggie's blue-green eyes. She possessed the same irresistible magnetic personality as her older brother.

"My daughter, the cosmopolitan gourmand." Linda smiled indulgently. "Who'd have thought it when she was spitting peas in my face at ten months?"

"Ah, Mom. If you'd just give Seattle a chance, you'd love it."

"Not as much as I love Bear Creek," Linda replied adamantly.

Kay had to admire their affectionate mother-daughter exchange. She felt another twinge of sadness that she and her own mother would never have this kind of relationship.

The crowd roared again. Kay's attention was drawn back to the ice rink. Quinn had scored a second goal.

The referee blew his whistle. Shook his head, made some kind of motion with his hands.

The crowd booed.

Quinn skated over to the ref and shouted in his face. The man shouted back.

"What's happening?" Kay leaned over to whisper to Meggie.

"Ref's claiming the shot was no good. Puck got caught in the crease."

Quinn argued. The ref balked. Quinn gestured at the goal. The ref crossed his arms over his chest, adamantly shook his head.

It was exciting to watch Quinn. He was so ardent in his beliefs, and he didn't avoid conflict. Kay, a confrontation avoider from way back, couldn't help but admire his courage.

"Uh-oh," Meggie said.

"What? What?"

"The referee's going to toss Quinn out if he doesn't let up."

"Will he back down?"

"Not if he thinks he's right."

Nervously Kay raised a hand to her mouth and realized she had been holding her breath. The other players rallied around, tried to get Quinn to accept the verdict. But nothing doing. When Quinn took a stance, he took a stance. There'd be no swaying him from his original position. She found that passionate quality in him both compelling and disturbing.

The ref blew his whistle and pointed for Quinn to leave the rink. Quinn ripped off his helmet and threw it on the ice.

Kay's stomach looped and dived like she was on a roller-coaster ride.

"Yep," said outspoken Meggie. "It's going to take more than some sweet little city girl from the lower forty-eight to corral our Quinn."

CHAPTER EIGHT

"HI THERE, BEAUTIFUL," Quinn said when Kay came over to sit beside him. He was sitting on the sidelines unlacing his skates.

Happy to see her, he raked his gaze over her body. She looked stunning in that white ski-bunny suit with the hood zipped up around her head. To think she was here with him made his heart give this strange little hop.

She'd stood in the stands with his family and friends, looking like a pristine rose in a field of wild, black-eyed Susans, until Meggie had shown up. The appearance of those two city girls in Bear Creek added color to the place. He imagined the streets filled with pretty women, and his heart soared. That was exactly what the town needed to pump some life into it, and even if he personally didn't find a wife, if his ad pulled women into Bear Creek, then it was money well spent.

While he'd been playing hockey, he had tried hard not to look Kay's way too often, because every time he did he got distracted. An unusual occurrence. He found her power over him slightly disturbing.

Just hormones, pal. Don't read more into it than there is.

"Too bad about the ref's call." She nodded at the game still in progress.

"I was robbed." He grinned. "I made that shot fair and square. Where's instant replay when you need it?"

"Does it really matter? Your team is still in the lead."

He stared at her in disbelief. "Of course it matters. I was right."

"Yes, but your stubbornness got you thrown out of the game."

He shook his head. Was this discussion about much more than hockey? "Ah, your politically correct side rears its head."

"What's that supposed to mean?"

"Nothing. Forget I said anything."

"No. I want to know."

"You were raised in a world where you subjugated your beliefs in order to fit in with those around you."

"And you think that's bad?"

"I didn't say it was bad." He removed his skates, jammed his feet into his boots. "It's just not the way I was brought up. My folks taught me the most important things were honesty and integrity. If you're right and you know it, you don't buckle no matter what the peer pressure, and you don't care what others think about you as long as you know you've done the right thing."

"And arguing with the ref was the right thing to do?"

"Yes. He was wrong. I made that goal."

"And if you'd been mistaken?"

"I'd swallow my pride and admit it."

She looked at him a long moment. A peculiar queasiness assailed him. Had he put her off by being himself? But hell, he didn't know any other way to be. He couldn't pretend to be something he wasn't. He hadn't been schooled in subterfuge the way she obviously had. He wasn't well versed in suppressing his convictions. Nor did he want to be.

"It's my opinion that nothing important was ever gained by sitting back and keeping your mouth shut," he expounded. "If you have something important to say, say it. If you don't let people know what's on your mind, how are they ever going to understand you?"

Kay shrugged. "Is it important for everyone to understand you?"

"Not everyone, no. But the people you care about, the people you deal with on a daily basis."

"I'm not sure I agree with that."

"Fair enough. You're entitled to your opinions, just as I am to mine."

"I think one can say too much and change a good impression into a bad one."

"But if you're just letting people know who you are, where you're coming from, then how can that be a mistake? If they dislike you for what you believe in, then they dislike you. If they admire you simply for the image you portray, then how do people ever get to know the real you?"

Kay said nothing at all. Instead, she studied him silently.

"Like now. You're thinking I'm full of crap, but you're too polite to tell me to go take a flying leap. Right?"

"What gave you that idea?'

"Right?" He cocked his head, gave her his most dazzling grin.

She smiled then, a little sheepishly. "Okay. All right. Yes, I do think you're full of it."

He pushed to his feet, threw an arm around her shoulders, drew her close to his body. "See there, sweetheart? That wasn't so hard, was it?"

"Not too hard," she admitted.

"Come on." He chucked her under the chin. "I'll take you back to Jake's."

She gave him her hand, and he knew then that everything was okay between them. She accepted him for who he was. Her approval lifted his spirits, and his feelings for her took on a new dimension. They could disagree and still respect each other.

He kissed her under the porch light of Jake's establishment. He knew full well that half the town was peering through their curtains watching them, but he didn't care. Let 'em gawk.

A groan escaped his throat and he tugged her flush against the length of him. She kept her eyes wide open during the kiss and so did he. Damn, but it was erotic. They couldn't seem to peer deeply enough into each other. Her pupils dilated and her lips softened.

She tasted ripe, willing, ready. He couldn't wait for tomorrow night. Couldn't wait to see how she responded to the things he had in store for her.

Pulling away, he stroked her jawline with his thumb. "I wish I knew all the thoughts that passed through that magnificent brain of yours. I wish I could know the real Kay Freemont."

"That'd be quite a trick," she said huskily, "since I'm not sure I even know myself."

The weird thing was, Kay already felt as if he *could* read her mind at times, and she couldn't figure out where he'd obtained this amazing ability. Why was this man so different from any other she had ever known? She'd heard that men were supposed to hate talking about things like feelings and emotions and sentiment. Especially masculine men of action like this one.

"Please," he encouraged, his eyes softening, his pupils dilating, "talk to me. Let me in. I'm dying to know everything there is to know about you. What are your hopes, your dreams, your wishes?"

She realized then that he wasn't this inquisitive with all women, that it was she alone who interested him. The thought terrified her. "I'm wishing you would kiss me again."

"I think you're evading my questions, but that's a wish I can't pass by." Quinn smiled so deeply he felt the edges of his eyelids crinkle, and he leaned in to take her lips once more.

She was like velvet heat in his mouth.

He thought of hot-fudge sundaes and chocolate fondue and cinnamon rolls drizzled with melted butter.

Then, irrationally, he thought of all the things he wanted to do with her that he never could. Necking in the balcony of a sexy, romantic movie. Holding hands and ice-skating on a frozen pond. Sharing a banana split and listening to fifties music on a jukebox at Marilyn Hecate's soda fountain in July. With Kay, he wanted to be a kid again, exploring her with the eager enthusiasm of a seventeen-year-old in the backseat of his daddy's car.

What would she think if he told her all this? Would he chase her away with his honesty?

He cupped her firm yet soft fanny with one hand, but the excess padding of her ski suit frustrated him. His fingers ached to glide over her bare skin. His hands cried out to knead her tender flesh. His palm itched to delve into new and exciting places.

Her scent filled his nose. That lovely aroma of jasmine mingled with her own natural windswept smell, and his knees loosened. He wanted to lay her down on the sidewalk and do all kinds of decadent things to her.

"I can't wait until tomorrow," she murmured into his mouth expressing exactly what was on his mind.

"Me, neither." His voice was gruff and his body had

gone rigid from the taste of her. The chase was on. His hunter's instincts were roused. His sporting blood boiled.

"Will we be doing more aurora-gazing?"

"No, I've got something else in mind."

"Oh?" He heard the excitement in her voice and it served to supercharge his erection.

"Yeah." He grinned. "I'll pick you up at five-thirty. But be forewarned. You might want to bring a change of clothes."

HIS CRYPTIC WORDS had sent her into orbit.

What in the heck did he mean? Kay wondered as she rifled through the clothes she had brought with her, excitement racing up her nerve endings until she tingled with heightened anticipation. Had he known what effect his statement would have on her? Driving her crazy with curiosity.

The man was a genius at mind games.

After much deliberation, she dressed simply in black jeans and a sapphire turtleneck sweater, then stashed a pair of woolen slacks and a crimson blouse into her satchel. As she was applying the finishing touches to her makeup, the telephone rang.

"Hello?"

"How's the article coming?"

Kay winced. Judy.

"I was just getting ready for bed and thought I'd give you a call. Is that hunky bachelor keeping you warm on those cold winter nights?"

"Oh, please."

"Go ahead, lie to me if you want to, darling, but don't lie to yourself. Any fool can see there's chemistry between you two. I'm not going to lose my prize reporter to the Alaskan wilderness, am I?"

"Don't be ridiculous, Judy. I'm not about to stay in Alaska. It's dark nearly twenty hours a day."

"I don't know. That Quinn is pretty cute. You're never going to find anyone like him in Manhattan."

"And it's freezing cold. I have to wear three layers of clothing to stay comfortable, even indoors. Hard to get romantic under those conditions."

Then again there was nothing more romantic than body heat.

"So if you're not canoodling with bachelor number one, where were you last night when I tried to call?"

Sampling a taste of heaven.

"Out doing research."

It wasn't a lie. She had been researching Quinn's background for the article, never mind that her research had concluded with some fierce kissing.

Judy didn't need the details. She had nothing to worry about. Once Kay returned to New York a satisfied woman, she would never see Quinn again.

Why that thought made her tummy ache, she couldn't say.

"I hope you got some good info."

Oh, it was good all right. Sinfully good. The best. And just as soon as Judy hung up the phone, she was going back for seconds.

BLUSTERER. BLUFFER. BLOWHARD.

Quinn had shot off his mouth and told Kay he was capable of giving her an orgasm. Now that she was sitting here in his kitchen and the moment was at hand, he was panicking.

Big time.

What if he failed her?

Over the course of his thirty-two years, he'd satisfied many lovers. Several of his former girlfriends had affectionately dubbed him Slow Hand. He loved making love and he loved pleasuring his partner.

But this was different. This was pressure. Kay's whole sexual awakening lay in his hands, and his normal cockiness had deserted him. Especially because that dynamite body of hers drove him to distraction.

Quinn refused to be like the other men of her acquaintance. He refused to let her down, and he intended on devoting himself to the pursuit of her orgasm while putting his own needs on hold. Because that was what she deserved.

Kay was exceptional.

Would ten days with her be enough for him? After Kay, would any woman be enough?

Don't get all romantic, Scofield, he told himself. *This is only sex and you know it. You're getting mixed up because you want to get married. But let's get real for a moment. You could never provide a woman like Kay with the things she needs. She's accustomed to bright lights and the big city.* It was honor enough that she had selected him as her sexual teacher. He took his responsibility seriously. He wouldn't ask for more than she could give.

Kay cleared her throat and he realized several minutes had passed where he'd done little more than stare at her when he was supposed to be making them a cup of hot tea.

"So." She rubbed her palms together, and that was when he realized she was as nervous as he. "So when do we begin?"

Virgins on their wedding night couldn't have been more unstrung.

He took a step toward her, his heart pounding. Damn, but she was breathtaking. She practically glowed, her features arranged in a piquant orchestration of enthusiasm and excitement.

Gone was her normally reserved demeanor. Her mahogany eyes had a fervent gleam. Her mouth was tipped up in a zealous grin. Her brightness, sunny as the twenty-four-hour summer solstice in the Arctic circle, completely bowled him over.

You're the man. The one with the supposed experience in eliciting women's orgasms. Take charge. Do something, dillweed.

But he couldn't do more than stare at her. "You look beautiful," he said.

"Thank you." She ducked her head.

This wouldn't do. Casanova didn't win women with clichéd compliments and an "aw shucks" attitude.

"Well," she asked, sneaking a surreptitious glance at his face, "what's the first lesson?"

"We're going back to the basics," he said, her question unfreezing him at last.

"The basics?"

"Don't ask questions." He reached out a hand to her. "Come here."

And damn, if she didn't giggle just a little bit as she slipped off the bar stool and placed her small, soft hand in his. He would have thought such an elegant woman incapable of giggling. He also never thought a giggle could have such a profound effect him.

"Did you bring a change of clothes?" he asked.

"Yes, and that's been driving me crazy all day. Why did I need a change of clothes?"

"Shh. No questions, remember. I want you to sit here." He patted the tabletop.

"On the table?"

"Was that a question?"

"My mother would have a fit if she caught me sitting on the table."

"All the more reason to sit there."

"You're sure this is necessary?"

"No questions," he growled, feigning sternness.

She clapped her hand over her mouth. "Oops, forgot. Questions, curse of the journalist. I'm sorry."

Without warning, he cupped her under the chin with his fingers and forced her gaze upward so she had no choice but to look him squarely in the face. Her eyes were so deep and brown and inquisitive he immediately felt as if he were drowning in a vat of chocolate.

"Trust me." He could tell this was difficult for her, letting go of control, trusting a man she didn't know very well. But that was exactly why it was so important for her to do it.

"Okay." She nodded in agreement, her expression softening. He was stunned by how much she wanted this. Even enough to go against her instincts.

He put his hands around her slender waist and lifted her onto the table. He could see her pulse racing in the hollow of her throat, and the intoxicating sight caused him to stiffen again.

She watched him as he drew the silk tie from his pocket. Her breathing quickened, grew shallower as he slowly ran his hands over the delicate material until he had one end clutched in each fist.

The tip of her tongue flicked out to moisten her lips. A glimmer of expectation lit her eyes.

She looked from the tie to his face and back again. She swallowed hard.

"I want to ask a question."

"No."

She clenched her jaw. He saw the muscles work beneath her skin.

"You want to know what I'm going to do with this tie. Is that correct?"

She nodded.

"I'm going deprive you of the sense of sight."

Kay gulped and a tremor passed through her at the wolfish expression in Quinn's eyes, at the unmistakable feral intent...but she wasn't scared. Instead, she was very turned on and extremely aware of her body's heated response—the reckless stagger of her pulse, the incandescent spark that shot through her veins and rooted low in her belly, the sudden dryness in her palms and equally sudden moistness in her most feminine place.

He approached like a lion stalking his prey. Leaning forward, his chest bumped into hers as he secured the tie around her eyes. Her nipples hardened in instant response. How she wished they were naked, with his bare, muscled chest pushed against them.

He secured the tie, cutting off her vision.

Blind. Sightless. And questionless, too. She couldn't even ask him why he was doing the things he was doing to her. She was at his mercy.

A spark of fear touched her then. Fear and an accompanying thrill. Trust was not her strong suit. She had resided too long in New York. Lived too many years as a Freemont woman. She wasn't like the Alaskans she'd met, who'd assumed everyone was a friend until proved otherwise.

But she had asked for his help, and he was giving it to her. Too late to back out.

Quinn pressed something into her hand. Her fingers closed around it. She recognized the shape. A metal whistle on a chain.

"Now," he said, "if you start to feel uncomfortable with anything that happens, I want you to blow this whistle. I'll stop immediately. But I ask you to bear with me and give it a chance before you resort to the whistle. Once the whistle blows, the evening is over. Understand?"

She nodded, comforted that he'd given her a way out, but determined not to use the whistle, no matter what.

He took the whistle and slipped the chain around her neck. "We start," he said, "with the sense of taste."

Her tongue responded to his suggestion. It began to tingle and her mouth watered. She realized her entire body was tensed. Waiting.

She felt him move away from the table, heard the oven door open. Her nose twitched at the bewitching scents. The spicy aroma of barbecue, she recognized. And was that fried chicken?

His footsteps sounded on the hardwood floor as he tromped back over to her. His finger touched her chin, and she parted her bottom lip.

"What is this?" he asked.

She bit into the morsel he offered. "Barbecued ribs."

"No, go deeper," he insisted. "What does it taste like?"

She frowned. "I don't understand."

"Dig, Kay."

She felt the pressure of his hand on her knees. Sighing with exasperation, she said, "Pork. It tastes like pork ribs."

"I can see why you have so much trouble with sex. You're too literal in your thinking."

"Frankly," she said, a little annoyed with him, "I don't see what this has to do with sex."

"That's your problem, sweetheart, but don't worry. Quinn's here to help."

She was about to tell him he was acting like a pompous ass when she felt a flutter as his lips brushed her throat. Spicy sparks shot through her system. Okay, maybe she was wrong and he was right about this.

"This is your reward," he said huskily. "Answer my questions and you get more kisses."

"Tangy," she said. "Rich. Full. Smoky. Woodsy. Oaken."

"Yes, ma'am, I'm impressed. See what you can do when you put your mind to it?"

What a heavenly assault! Her senses sung to life and she was aware of everything not visual. Quinn's musky male smell. The scent of spray starch on his shirt. The pressure of his hand on her shoulder. The hardness of the table beneath her bottom. The flavor of barbecue lingering on her tongue. The faint plunk-plunk-plunk of water droplets from a leaky faucet hitting the bottom of the stainless-steel sink.

From head to toe, her body tingled. Tingled and prickled and quivered.

He pressed something else to her lips. An icy coldness that was a brisk contrast to the warmth of his fingers.

"Ice cube," she said as he traced her mouth with it. "Cold. Frosty. Tasteless."

"Stick out your tongue."

She extended her tongue. He dropped the ice cube onto it.

"Now suck."

She wrapped her tongue around the ice cube, sucked gently as it melted.

"What does it taste like?"

"No taste."

"Wrong. Try again. Use your imagination. You're a writer—I know you've got one."

"It tastes like winter."

"More."

"Refreshing. Invigorating. Chilling."

"I'm very proud of you." He rewarded her with a rain of kisses, showering her forehead, the tip of her nose, her cheeks and chin.

She thrilled to his kisses, exalted in having earned them. She had pleased him. This sensory deprivation was driving her mad. She wanted to rip the tie off so she could see his face, gaze deeply into his eyes.

She reached to undo the tie, but he saw her intent and stilled her hand.

"Oh, no, sweetheart. There's much more to do. The night is young and we've only just begun."

He fed her more tidbits and made her describe each one in detail. She got into the spirit of the game, and when he gave her salsa guacamole in corn tortillas she exclaimed, "Lime, tequila, sangria, Acapulco sunsets, hot sand, thong bikinis."

When he handed her a slick, round cob of corn, she bit into it and pronounced, "Crunchy, buttery, hot, salty. Summer. Fireflies. Picnic tables."

He pushed the sleeve of her sweater to just above the elbow and slowly kissed and nibbled a blazing path up her arm.

"Ah," he said. "I think I've made my point. We move on to the next phase."

"You're a wicked man, Quinn Scofield, to torture me so."

He chuckled. The fertile sound resonated in her ears. She could tell so much from his laughter. She heard passion and kindness, humor and an earthy intelligence.

"Come."

His fingers reached for hers and he helped her slide off the table. Her feet touched the floor and she realized she was eye level with his chin. She knew her face was decorated with barbecue sauce and corn nibbles and smears of guacamole. She felt like a messy kid.

She reached out a hand to touch him and he stood perfectly still and allowed her to run her fingers over his features the way a blind person might.

Her fingers trailed over to his nose. A sturdy masculine nose that was neither too large or too small, but bent slightly, knocked crooked from playing one too many games of hockey.

From his nose, her fingertips migrated to his mouth. Oh, this was dangerous territory. Firm and wide. Hearty and willing. His lips parted and he licked lightly at her fingertips, sending a blast of high-voltage electricity coursing through her body.

Startled, she jerked her hand away.

He laughed again, delighted with her, and began to clean her with big, wet kisses. His tongue frolicked over her upper lip.

"Mmm," he said. "You've never lived until you've slurped barbecue off the face of a beautiful woman."

"I think I'll trust you on that one." She laughed. "What's next?"

"Dessert, and in the process, we're going to fully explore the sense of touch."

"Oh." She inhaled sharply.

His hand reached for the button on her sweater. She stiffened beside him.

"Relax," he soothed. "We've got to get you out of these messy clothes. Take a long, slow, deep breath."

She obeyed. What else could she do? She wanted this so much. And yet she felt vulnerable, standing here blindfolded while he got to watch her every move.

Button by button, he undid her sweater, then carefully slid her arms from the sleeves.

He hissed in a breath.

"What?" she asked, then remembered she wasn't supposed to ask questions.

But this time he answered her. "That black lace bra. It's giving me a hard-on that won't quit."

Heat spread from her neck to her face. Blushing, the scourge of the blonde.

"Any woman who wears the kind of lingerie you wear can't be frigid. You've just been waiting for someone to treasure you."

To Kay's horror, she began to cry. Fortunately, she had on the blindfold.

CHAPTER NINE

"WHAT'S WRONG?" Quinn asked. He drew her to him, her naked skin pressed against the crispness of his shirt, the metal whistle imprinted below the hollow of her throat. "Did I say something to offend you?"

She shook her head.

"I shouldn't have made that crack about my hard-on. I just wanted you to know how much you move me."

"It wasn't that remark." She sniffled. "I'm a New Yorker, after all. I hear much worse than that on my walk to work."

"What is it, then?" He sounded genuinely worried, and his tenderness only exacerbated her emotions.

"No one's ever treasured me before." She placed a palm to her mouth and tried to will herself to stop crying.

Her feet left the floor when he clasped her so tightly she could hear the steady lub-dub of his heart. "I know, baby, I know."

And then he just held her for the longest moment.

"Maybe we should call it a night," he said, gently easing her back down to the floor. "I didn't mean to upset you."

"No," she said. "I want to continue."

"Are you sure?"

She nodded, and imagined she looked pretty incon-

gruous standing there in a blindfold, black lace bra and
her black denim jeans.

"I wasn't going to do this yet, but I can't help myself." The next thing she knew he was on his knees in
front of her kissing her belly and easing down the zipper on her jeans.

Kay caught her breath. So this was it. They were
going to make love on the kitchen floor. Couldn't get
much wilder than that. She thought back on some of the
articles she had written for *Metropolitan*. Articles on
spontaneity. Well, for once she was about to practice
what she preached.

Once her pants were undone, Quinn placed a hand
on either side of her and slowly began to nudge the thick
material down over the curve of her hips.

"More sexy underwear." He groaned when he spied
her black thong. "You're going to propel me over the
brink, woman."

His comment filled her with elation. She liked that
she had the power to literally bring him to his knees.
She had never held such control over Lloyd. He had
acted as if her body was nothing special. In fact, he
often prodded her to lose weight, and for heaven's sake,
at five-five she only weighed 115 pounds.

But Quinn seemed to relish her curves, and his appreciation made her feel like a goddess.

"Step out of your pants," he instructed when he'd
pooled the material around her ankles.

Trembling, she did as he asked. She still wore her
boots and her underwear. Would he make love to her
with her boots on? She found the thought incredibly
erotic.

What now? What would come next? Her mind
sprinted ahead of her body, imagining them coiled

in the throes of sex, the hardwood floor pressing into her back.

But then he surprised her yet again by taking her hand and leading her through the house.

"I'm going to push you right to the edge," he growled in her ear, "and then pull you back before you tumble over."

She gasped, heard him open a door and felt a gust of frigid air. He was taking her outside!

He opened another door and a moist, heated blast washed over her. She smelled cedar and dampness. He closed the door behind them.

"My sauna." He directed her to sit on a bench.

Her skin came alive. It seemed separate from the rest of her, as if it were a living, breathing organism all its own. Goose bumps piled up. Everything she touched was greatly magnified. The rough feel of the cedar bench, the damp heat draping over her body, the soft silk of the tie binding her eyes.

"I'll be right back with dessert," he whispered, his lips on her ear. "Don't go anywhere."

She sat in total silence for a moment, soaking in the experience, reassuring herself that this was indeed happening to her, that she wasn't caught in the sleepy midst of one of her explosive fantasies.

The door snapped open again. Quinn pressed something into her hand. "For you."

Her fingers were wrapped around an ice-cream cone. Kay laughed. Ice cream in a sauna?

"Hold mine a minute." He handed her a second cone and stepped away from her.

Her ears, attuned to the slightest nuance in sound, pricked up when she heard the whisper of material and realized he was getting undressed. Not being able to see him catapulted her excitement into overdrive, and she found herself growing hotter and wetter than the sauna itself. When he finally settled himself on the bench beside her, it seemed as if her heart had ceased beating.

Waiting.

Perspiration pearled around her collarbones, trickled down her chest. The silence was deafening.

"Thanks for holding my cone."

He took it from her. By now, her ice cream was melting in a sticky stream down her wrist.

"Oops," he said. "Let me lick that off for you."

He flicked his tongue around her wrist and Kay groaned. Then she felt something cold plop onto her breast.

"Sorry, lost the top of my cone."

Then his tongue was on her skin just above her cleavage, and he was licking with mad abandon.

"Gotta eat it all up before it melts," he gasped.

He went back and forth in rapid motion, first feasting at her breasts, then sucking on her gooey fingers. Kay was mad with the sensation of his hot, wet, sticky tongue seemingly everywhere at the same time. She dropped her cone. It hit the floor with a soft crunch, but she didn't care. She was drowning, falling, dripping into a pool of crazy agitation.

"I want a taste!" she cried.

So he kissed her on the lips, his mouth full of ice cream.

"Mmm, chocolate," she cooed. "No wait—vanilla? Strawberry?"

"Neopolitan."

"Ah. That explains the mix of flavors."

His gooey hands were on her shoulders, then her stomach. Damn this blindfold! She wanted to see him, wanted to watch what he was doing with that awesome tongue.

But then he stopped licking.

"What's wrong?" she whimpered.

"Damn," he said, disappointment winding through the timbre of his voice. "The ice cream is all gone, and we're running out of steam."

Quinn shifted off the bench, and she heard the sound of water being poured over the hot lava rocks. Hiss. Sizzle. Fresh steam rose and rolled over her skin, muggy as summertime in New Orleans. He returned to his seat beside her but said nothing.

Kay waited.

And tried to imagine what he looked like naked.

She wanted to ask what they were waiting for, but he'd warned her not to ask questions, and she was determined to play the game his way.

Finally she couldn't stand the tension any longer. She reached out. Her hand collided with his forearm. Ah, those forearms that stoked an instant flame inside her. She wrapped her fingers around his wrist, crushed his arm hairs now damp with humidity beneath the palm of her hand.

"Quinn, I want you," she whispered.

"Then come here."

He took her by the waist and lifted her onto his naked lap. She straddled him, his incredibly hard erection caught between their naked bellies.

"Oh!" she exclaimed because she could not think of one single thing to say to express her feelings. "Oh."

"See what you do to me, woman?" He leaned close to growl in her ear.

Quinn cupped the sweet curve of her lush bottom left

exposed by those dental-floss-size panties and pulled her even closer.

She made a little noise, soft and low, and the sound drilled a hole straight through his gut. She settled her hands on his shoulders. Her lovely breasts overflowed the lace of her low-cut bra. Like flags of pink velvet, her jaunty nipples peeked out above the delicate fabric gone soggy from the sauna.

Quinn wanted to seize her right then and there. Wanted to lower her onto his throbbing shaft and give her the ride of her life.

Control, he warned himself. This night was about Kay's pleasure, not his own. He was going to drag this out as long as humanly possible. He was helping her explore her erogenous zones so that when she did finally climax, it would be like scaling Mount Everest, thrilling, incomparable, the experience of a lifetime and thoroughly earned.

Damn, but he should have spent some private time in the shower before he picked her up. Mentally steeling himself against the growing pressure inside him, Quinn dipped his head and suckled first one perky nipple and then the other.

Her fingers flew to his hair and knotted there as if she was anchoring herself in place. She wriggled and squirmed and writhed against him.

"Experience this with your skin," he instructed in a voice choked with lust. "Focus on what you're feeling. Tell me about it."

"Hot," she gasped. "Utterly hot."

"And?"

"Wet and slick and slippery."

"More."

"Mucky, sticky, spongy."

"Yes."

"Squishy, sloppy, soggy."

"Don't stop."

"Pervaded, persuaded, invaded."

"Go, go."

"Drenched, saturated, undone." She was breathing heavily, her breasts rising and falling with each ragged pant. The tail end of the tie, soaked with steam and perspiration, trailed down her slender shoulders.

"Burning!" she cried. "Sweating, sweltering, ablaze."

A strand of hair was plastered to her forehead. He would never have believed the cool, sophisticated woman he'd met at the offices of *Metropolitan* magazine could be so completely wanton. And so totally delicious.

Quinn loved it.

Man alive, how he loved it.

He had to grit his teeth and clench his fists to keep from tearing off that scrap of panty and piercing her through with his pulsating sword. The instinct to sheathe himself deep inside her was primitive. If he didn't get her out of here quickly, he'd mangle everything he was building toward.

"Let's go," he said.

"Wh…what?" She bobbed her head at him, raised a hand to her tie.

"Leave it."

"I don't understand."

"Hush." He tugged her off his lap, her booted feet bumping lightly into his shins.

"But Quinn…" she protested.

He didn't give her a chance; he just dragged her from the sauna and plunged them, steam rising from their bodies, into the cold, cold night. The air was brisk, the northern sky filled with dancing light. Quinn realized with a start that Kay wasn't the only one having her senses put through the paces. The moment seemed utterly surreal. Like something from an erotic fantasy poem.

Holding hands, they ran together through the snow. He pulled up short beside the house and leaped with her into a snowbank.

"Omigosh!" Kay exclaimed. "This is absolutely exhilarating. Like a splash of cold water on a muggy August afternoon in Manhattan."

Her skin had pinked, her cheeks flushed red. A huge grin decorated her face, and the sight of her joy tugged at Quinn's heartstrings.

Watch out, Scofield! You're treading on thin ice here. She's not available. She's on the rebound.

"I'm floored," Kay said, apparently invigorated by the experience. "Completely floored."

"Enough," Quinn said. "We don't want to get frostbite."

"How could you get frostbite from something that feels so lovely?"

"Trust me on this." He struggled to his feet, his arousal gone, and reached down to help her from the snowbank.

"You're amazing," she said.

"Me?" He speared her with his eyes, raked his gaze over her body. "I don't think so."

She wagged a finger at him. "Oh, yes, you are."

"Let's get you inside, Miss Eskimo. I'm beginning to think the cold has gone to your head." Feeling inexplicably protective, he placed a hand to her back and swept her up the walk beside him.

She was shivering so hard her teeth were clattering

by the time he got her to the fireplace. He wrapped her snugly in a quilt and seated her on the hearth. "Don't move," he said. "I'll be right back with a hot toddy."

Before going to the kitchen, he hurried to his bedroom and pulled on red nylon jogging shorts and a T-shirt that said, "Mountain Climbers Never Die, They Just Reach Their Peak." He wasn't cold; he did the sauna-snowbank thing on a regular basis, but he didn't want Kay to see him naked. Not yet.

A few minutes later he settled a mug of Irish coffee in her hands and untied the blindfold.

She blinked up at him, the firelight reflecting the golden strands of her disheveled hair. Her mascara had smeared a little, causing her eyes to look wide despite their slightly almond shape.

He liked her like this, Quinn realized. Mussed and rumpled and smiling. Bang, bang, bang, went his heart.

"What?" she asked. "Or am I still not allowed to ask questions?"

"Game over," he said. "And I was just shaking my head in amazement at how beautiful you are."

She raised a hand to her head. "Yuck! My hair's all clumpy with melted ice cream. I must look like a bachelor pad at 4:00 a.m. on New Year's Day."

He sat beside her, stared into her eyes. "You don't need hairspray and makeup and fancy creams to look beautiful, Kay."

"Ha! Tell that to my mother. She'd be appalled if she could see me now. Appalled on so many levels."

"You've spent your life trying to please your parents."

"Well, that's part of why I'm here. To start untying those apron strings."

"I'm your bit of rebellion."

"Kind of," she admitted.

He'd suspected as much, and he shouldn't have been surprised or even disappointed by the knowledge. But he couldn't help but wish that she'd come to Alaska because she liked him, not to piss off her parents or learn how to exceed her sexual speed limit.

Still, she was here and he wanted her, and he certainly wasn't going to send her away. She would be a sweet memory. His time with Kay was teaching him more and more about what it was he wanted from a wife. Maybe that was the whole cosmic reason of their meeting in the first place.

He realized he needed someone more like him. Someone with the same traditional family values, the same kind of experiences, the same love of the land, the same frank ability to speak her mind. He tried to imagine Kay living in Alaska and failed completely. She would survive here about as well as a hothouse orchid.

"So what happens next?" she asked.

"Clean up," he said as they moved to the bathroom. "You're gonna love this."

"Should I take off my underwear?"

She was glad to have the blindfold removed, glad to be able to see him. He was wearing a pair of jogging shorts, but there was no hiding the imposing package that bulged beneath the constricting material.

"Get in the shower." He tested the temperature with his forearm. "Just as you are."

"Aren't you getting in, too?"

"Right behind you, sweetheart."

Giddily she stepped into the warm shower. He climbed in beside her and pulled the glass shower door closed. He took her in his arms and smothered her gig-

gles with kisses. She felt as if she was eighteen again
and experiencing sexual pleasure for the very first time.

Ah, this was what she wanted. This was why she
had come to Alaska. To wipe her sexual slate clean
and start fresh.

He reached around her for the bath gel and squirted a
dollop into the palm of his hand. The almost empty bottle made a wheezing noise that had her giggling again.
He began lathering her up, scrubbing her through her
saturated underclothes.

The sensation of his warm, slippery skin massaging
her through wet lace was intensely erotic. His hand slid
over her smooth mound, and her slick, soapy panties
pulled against the curve of her buttocks and plucked
tightly over her most feminine and sensitive flesh.

Kay closed her eyes and clung to him. With one
hand, he stroked a swollen breast through her bra.

He was a master of exquisite torture.

The steam, the sensuous spray of warm water, the
stimulation of his wet fingers were more than she could
tolerate. He deserved to get a healthy serving of what
he was dishing up.

She smiled devilishly and reached for him.

Quinn gulped. The woman was turning the tables on
him. Didn't she realize how truly dangerous that was?
If she wanted her longed-for orgasm, she'd better stop
rubbing him down there.

Leaning into him, she nuzzled up hard against his
chest. Right then and there he knew he wasn't as in
charge of the situation as he wanted to be. She kissed
him then, sinking her fingers into his shoulders to hold
him still.

The force of her kiss surprised him and stoked his

own internal furnace higher and hotter. She made sweet mewling sounds deep in her throat.

He felt like a fallen mountain climber, dangling precariously from the end of a taut rescue line. Every muscle in his body tensed. His erection was so damned hard he feared he'd turned to granite, and he yearned for her with a desperate urgency that scared the hell out of him.

Ah, he was lost!

"Don't stop," she whimpered. "More, more."

He clutched her hips and ground himself against her far more roughly than he'd intended. The thin material of her thong rubbed provocatively against his nylon jogging shorts, and he about flipped.

"Yes, Quinn, now!" she cried, and pressed her breasts so tightly to his chest that the whistle around her neck made an indention in his skin. The whistle he'd given her to blow if things got too out of hand. "Make love to me right here in the shower. I'm ready."

He was startled to discover she welcomed his aggressiveness. His lack of control hadn't scared her one bit.

But it scared him.

Desperately Quinn reached for the whistle, took it from around her neck, pressed the wet metal tightly against his lips and blew.

CHAPTER TEN

WHEN HE ARRIVED on Friday evening to escort Kay to his parents' dinner party, Quinn didn't say a word about what had happened between them. But he did take her arm possessively. He angled her a glance that made her feel all woman. She was ready to skip the party and head back to his place for another love lesson.

Since Wednesday night, she had been unable to think of anything but Quinn. To hell with the article. To hell with work. She caught herself lying on the bed at the bed-and-breakfast staring at the ceiling and recalling ever nuance of what they'd shared. And she imagined what other wicked treats he had up his sleeve.

The Scofields' large, homey kitchen was crowded with Quinn's laughing family and friends. The decor was an eclectic hodgepodge. Nothing looked as if it fit. Just like at Quinn's place, his parents had rafter ceilings and leather furniture.

A stenciled border featuring moose and bear and salmon ran along the kitchen wall. A carved totem pole in the corner did double duty as a coatrack. Numerous knickknacks graced shelves and corner nooks. Photographs of Quinn and Meggie as children graced the walls. Gingham curtains hung in the kitchen window. Slightly bawdy cartoons were stuck with magnets to the refrigerator. A pot of plastic flowers on the window ledge sang "Let the Sunshine In" and twirled wildly in opposite directions when anyone approached.

Honoria would have blanched at the sight and proclaimed the house "irreparably tacky." Kay found the place both charming and comfortable. It was a real home, not a museum showcase like her parents' penthouse apartment in Manhattan or their summer retreat in the Hamptons.

The smell of sourdough bread and beef stew permeated the room. Everyone was milling around, talking at once, balancing hearty bowls of stew and slabs of buttered bread in their hands. Raucous classic rock music underscored the gathering. Jim Scofield filled his guests' mugs full of frothy ale from a tapped keg. In the next room a lively group of poker players yelled good-natured insults at one another.

Kay had never witnessed anything like this jolly free-for-all at her parents' parties, where guests nibbled exotic tidbits from silver trays and sedate classical music poured through the piped-in system.

At first she had been taken aback by the exuberant rowdiness. But when she thought about how her mother would have turned up her nose at such a party, she began to relax and enjoy the camaraderie. She was here to experience Alaska as it was—sprawling, unruly, wildly independent—not to resort to prejudices against what Honoria would call "common folk."

Even though she had become unhappy with things of late, Kay had never really realized how much she'd lived in an ivory tower or how cruelly snobbish her family was. This new knowledge reinforced her desire to become more open, more accepting, more forgiving of others.

All four bachelors were in attendance at the party. In

fact, the house was crowded with men. Kay and Meggie were the only single women under thirty-five. In fact, they were the *only* women under thirty-five except for six-months-pregnant Candy Kilstrom, wife of KCRK disk jockey, Liam.

Quickly enough Kay learned that Jake was the life of the party, cracking jokes and telling stories. He possessed a keen wit and grinned ninety percent of the time.

Mack, the shortest of the bachelors but by no means small, never seemed to stop moving. He was quick and industrious, the first to volunteer when Quinn's father had asked for help unloading the keg.

Caleb was hard to figure. His calm nature drew her, but he didn't say much and preferred to stay perched in the corner watching the others with a sage smile. She did notice that whenever he glanced at Meggie, his smile disappeared and his dark eyes turned moody and restless. Kay wondered if he disliked the young woman for some reason.

If that was the case, she didn't know why. Kay really liked the straightforward woman, who seemed to have the courage to say all the things Kay thought but wasn't candid enough to express.

But she did wonder where Meggie's husband was. No one had commented on his absence. Meggie seemed in high spirits, however, laughing, joking, cutting up with all the men who looked at her with covetous expressions. At one point Meggie herded Kay and the four bachelors in front of the fireplace for a group photo. And Kay loved it when Quinn leaned over to kiss her cheek just as the flash went off.

Glancing up from where she was sitting next to Linda Scofield at the kitchen table, she caught Quinn watching her with those gray eyes the same brooding color as the snow-heavy clouds that hovered over the town. He winked and Kay felt a now familiar thrill.

Where have you been all my life, wilderness man? The question floated unbidden into her head, lodged there and refused to leave.

She had to be careful. As wonderful as Quinn was, she couldn't allow her feelings for him to become anything more than physical. This infatuation brewing inside her was just that, infatuation. She was intrigued by their differences, turned on by his complete opposition to all the other men she had ever known.

Plus, she liked the way she changed whenever she was around him. Already, in less than a week's time, she'd began to relax, to let her hair down, to explore the part of her psyche she'd kept shut away for so many years and to abolish her old thought processes.

Kay was also impressed with Quinn's family and friends. They were close-knit and yet very welcoming to a stranger from New York City. Yes, she had to be very careful not to mistake this infatuation for something more. The last thing she wanted was to hurt him.

Or herself.

Quinn moved across the room toward her as if called by the glance she'd sent him. He lowered his head and placed a hand on her shoulder. At the pressure of his touch, at the tickling of his warm breath in her ear, Kay's heart revved.

"Are you doing all right?" he asked.

She nodded. His chin lightly grazed her cheek and caused an immediate reaction deep in her center.

"We're a rambunctious bunch," he said. "But don't let them overwhelm you."

She shook her head to let him know she was fine.

"Bet you're not used to this kind of shindig."

"It's different," she admitted, "but a lot of fun."

"Would you like to dance?" he asked.

"To this music?"

"We can fix that."

"Where would we dance?"

"Just watch." He winked again, and Kay was warmed clean through her toes.

Quinn straightened, clapped his hands and raised his voice. "People, we're in need of a dance floor and some dance music."

Kay stared in stunned amazement as soup bowls and beer mugs were deposited on the counter and half a dozen burly men relocated the poker players to the kitchen. They scooted furniture against the wall and rolled the heavy braided living room rug back from the glossy hardwood floors as if they'd done this many times before.

Linda took a seat at the upright piano parked in the corner, and solemn Caleb Greenleaf surprised Kay by retrieving a fiddle from his truck. He perched on a wooden stool pulled up next to the piano and soon the sounds of "Cotton-eyed Joe" filled the house.

"Shall we?" Quinn held out his hand to Kay. Several other couples were already gathering on the makeshift dance floor and forming a circle.

She'd danced at many a cotillion. She'd waltzed with politicians and bankers and stockbrokers. She'd worn five-thousand-dollar dresses and sipped five-hundred-dollar champagne from crystal flutes.

But she'd never danced the two-step in front of a roaring fire on a cold winter night in someone's living room wearing blue jeans and boots and a turtleneck sweater. She'd never drunk beer from a keg or eaten sourdough bread sopped in beef stew.

And she'd never had so much fun.

All these years she'd been unfairly deprived!

From "Cotton-eyed Joe," Linda and Caleb segued into "Achy Breaky Heart" with an ease that told Kay they'd been doing this for a long time. And all the men seemed to be vying for the honor of squiring Meggie around the dance floor.

Kay didn't know the steps, so she had to follow Quinn's every move. For a large man he was amazingly graceful, stepping lightly without any of the awkwardness brawny men often possessed.

"Achy Breaky" melded into "Tennessee Waltz." Quinn took her into his arms, held her close and twirled her about the living room. She was so intent on staring up into his compelling eyes that she didn't even notice for several minutes that they were the only ones dancing.

She vaguely registered that the telephone rang and someone hollered at Meggie that it was for her. Her mind was in a dream where she noticed nothing except Quinn.

Resting her head against his broad chest, Kay inhaled his piney scent, listened to the beating of his strong heart. His hands tightened on hers and he squeezed lightly, letting her know she was safe with him.

Then, for absolutely no reason at all, a lump rose in her throat, forcing her to swallow hard to keep from crying. She was happy. Why this urge to bawl?

From childhood she'd been trained to control her emotions, to repress her feelings, deny her impulses. She'd been taught that appearances were paramount, and you conducted yourself based on what others thought of you.

Growing up rich and privileged was like living on an island with other people exactly like you. The lifestyle imposed on children of the wealthy and powerful entailed certain duties and conditions foreign to the majority of the population. There was no blending into an anonymous background. You were required to watch your step at every moment. No one trod easily on the emotions of others where money and manners mingled. This behavior resulted in an inbreeding of the spirit, too much held in, regret and silent brooding.

And Kay wanted out.

She'd wasted so much time living on her island and pretending to agree with people whose values and beliefs differed so greatly from her own. She'd expended too much effort struggling against her natural tendencies. The truth of the matter was, she'd never felt more at home than she did right now in Quinn's arms.

Tilting her head, she looked into his face. He smiled at her with a lustfulness that made her hot and achy. Then without warning, he dipped his head and kissed her, all the while moving them around the living room.

It wasn't a long kiss. Nor the most passionate he'd ever given her, but it was blindingly tender.

They danced past a clump of men gathered in one corner.

"Will you get a load of that?" old Gus whispered none too softly. "Looks like Quinn's found himself a city girl to play with until the real thing comes along."

The words, when they sunk in, stung. She wasn't considered wife material. No matter how kind, how welcoming these people seemed, she wasn't one of them and never would be.

Oh, Lord, what was she thinking? She didn't belong here. She was a New Yorker, a socialite, a magazine reporter romanticizing her first trip to Alaska.

This was why her mother warned her against public displays of affection. For the first time in her life, she'd dared to let her hair down, and look what happened. She pulled away from Quinn, but he held fast to her hand and refused to let her go. She didn't want to jerk back and make things worse.

"I need some air," she murmured, avoiding his eyes. "It's too warm in here."

"I'll get your coat," he said. "We'll take a walk to the barn."

She shook her head. "I'd rather be alone."

"No, ma'am. I can't let you go by yourself."

"Why not?" she snapped.

"Wolves out there."

"Look, I live among two-legged wolves. I think I can handle myself with the furry variety."

Linda and Caleb had stopped playing. Everyone was eyeing them. Kay clamped her jaws and headed for the kitchen. She retrieved her coat from the totem pole and rushed outside.

She didn't know why she was upset. She only knew she needed distance from Quinn so she could sort out her feelings.

It was cold outside. Very cold. Kay shivered despite the warmth of her heavy coat, woolen gloves and cap. The light from the barn some fifty yards away welcomed her. She hurried toward it and tumbled inside.

To find Meggie Drummond sitting on a bale of hay struggling to light a cigarette with an obviously shaky hand. The minute Meggie saw Kay she flung the unlit cigarette across the barn.

"Oh!" Meggie and Kay cried in unison, and then laughed.

"I'm sorry," Kay mumbled. "I didn't mean to violate your privacy."

"You didn't," Meggie admitted. "You saved me."

Kay arched an eyebrow. "How so?"

"I kicked the ciggy habit years ago, but when I get nervous, that old urge returns. I sneaked out to take a couple of drags off a cigarette Gus gave me. I'm glad you stopped me. I'd hate to harness that old monkey to my back again." Meggie grinned.

"Then I'm glad I interrupted you." Kay smiled back.

"Have a seat." Meggie scooted over and patted the hay bale.

Kay sat beside her. "What drove you to sneak off for a cigarette?" her inquisitive reporter instincts made her ask.

"Mom's ankle. Looks like she's going to have to have surgery. It's not healing the way they hoped." Meggie gave her a convenient excuse, but Kay had a feeling something else was on her new friend's mind. Should she pry?

"I'm sorry to hear that."

"Yeah." Meggie made a face. "Means Mom will need me to stay through the summer, and I hate being away from home that long."

Kay nodded. "Your job?"

"Yeah, the job." Meggie shrugged nonchalantly. But Kay could tell from the expression on her face that there was something else on Meggie's mind.

Suddenly Meggie brightened. "Looks like you and Quinn are really hitting it off."

"We like each other."

"He's a great guy, and I really like you, Kay. But as

one city girl to another, I have to warn you about some-thing if you think you might be getting serious about my brother."

"Oh, don't worry. We're not serious. I know Quinn's looking for a wife, and I'm a New Yorker through and through. Couldn't live anywhere else," Kay denied, and waved a hand.

"That's good." Meggie nodded. "Because you can take an Alaskan man out of Alaska, but you can't take Alaska out of the man."

"Is that how it is with your husband, Jesse?" Kay asked, struggling to tamp down the odd strangeness pressing against her heart. Meggie's words were not a new revelation, but what she'd said underscored what Kay knew. The gulf between Quinn and her was sim-ply too wide to breach.

"Jesse?" Meggie's eyes darkened with an emotion Kay couldn't pinpoint. An emotion akin to pain. Was her marriage in trouble? "Oh, no, Jesse's not a native Alaskan. He moved here as a teenager when his father married Caleb's mother. Jesse is pure big city. Which I suppose is what attracted me to him. I wanted so much to get out of Bear Creek, and Jesse was always talk-ing about the places where he was going to go and the things he was going to do. He really turned my seven-teen-year-old head."

"And everything worked out for you. You got what you wanted."

"Yeah," Meggie said, but it sounded as if she was still trying to convince herself of that fact. She rose to her feet. "I better get back inside. Been nice dishing the dirt with you, girlfriend."

Kay wiggled her fingers, watched Meggie walk away and realized then they had something else in common besides their love of cities. Neither of them liked to trot their feelings out for others to examine, and deep down inside, they were both very lonely.

QUINN GLANCED ABOUT the room and waved a hand. "Everyone go on dancing."

"Can't, the two beautiful single ladies are gone," someone said.

"You're out of your league with that New Yorker, boy," old Gus cackled. "She's too high-class for you. Best to stick with your own kind."

Jake came over and clapped Quinn on the back. "Don't pay attention to Gus. You know how he likes to stir up trouble."

Irritated, Quinn stalked to the kitchen and paced. He wanted to give Kay some space, but he felt antsy. After five minutes of waiting for her to return, he couldn't stand it anymore and went out to find her.

The darkness was thick. The overcast sky obscured any chance of seeing the aurora tonight. A muted light from the barn was the only illumination.

Winding his way past the vehicles parked in an uneven grid across the driveway, he cupped his hands around his mouth and called, "Kay."

Silence.

What was the matter? he fretted. What had he done wrong?

"Kay," he called again.

Still no reply.

He was aware of a strange pounding in his chest, a burgeoning fear he couldn't seem to control. What if something had happened to her? What if she'd stepped into a hole and twisted her ankle, or worse?

His treacherous mind conjured up a hundred different horrific scenarios that had almost a zero percent chance of actually happening. But when it came to winter in Alaska, all bets were off, and Kay was a babe in the woods.

Of course, she probably went into the barn to get out of the wind, he told himself. He increased his stride, reached the barn door in a few paces and flung it open. Startled horses and cows raised their heads from their stalls to gaze at him.

He sprinted across the cement floor, examining each nook and cranny. No Kay.

By the time he burst outside again, his chest heaving, his body drenched in sweat, real fear had latched hold of his gut and wouldn't let go.

"Kay!" he shouted, panic rising.

"I'm right here, Quinn," she replied in a tone as untroubled as a frozen lake.

He skidded to a halt and jerked his head in the direction of her voice.

She was sitting in his truck, and she'd rolled the window down to speak to him. He trotted over.

"There you are." He smiled, goofy with relief.

He rounded the hood of the truck. She rolled up the passenger-side window. He climbed in beside her and started the engine. It responded sluggishly at first, then took hold. He switched on the heater, then turned in his seat to look at her.

"What happened back there?"

She shook her head. "Nothing."

"Liar." He reached out, ensnared one of her gloved hands in his. "We were having a good time, then you changed just like that." He snapped his fingers.

"Really, Quinn, you're making a much bigger deal

of this than it is." Her breath fogged the darkness between them.

"Did I do something to offend you?"

"It wasn't you." She stared out the windshield.

"What, then?"

She shrugged and in that slight gesture, he felt her pain. She was hurting and he didn't know why.

"Talk to me. Please."

"I overheard someone make a valid observation. I guess that's why it hit a little too close to home."

"What did they say?" Quinn asked a second time through clenched teeth.

Kay stared down at their entwined hands. "You heard old Gus. He said I was nothing to you but a playmate until the real thing came along."

Quinn's breath caught. "And you believe that?"

"Yes. You are looking for a wife, and I'm certainly not what you had in mind when you concocted that ad."

"Look at me," he commanded.

She raised her chin, met his eyes with a steadfast gaze. She was so good at cloaking her feelings when she wanted to. She was putting up barriers, keeping him from getting too close.

"Would you like to be more than just my sexual playmate?" Quinn asked, barely daring to hope that she might say yes.

Kay laughed. "Of course not. We're at opposite places in our lives. You're ready for marriage, and I just got out of a lousy relationship. I've got a lot to learn about myself before I can be with any man."

His hopes sank as quickly as they'd buoyed. So much for wishing on a star.

"That man's comment," she continued, "simply

brought home to me how different we really are. How much a fish out of water I am here."

He squeezed her hand. "Sweetheart, don't let what other people think bother you so much."

"That's hard for me. I was raised to believe the opinion of others matters a great deal."

"You're going to have to get over this need to please everyone." He traced a finger along her jawline. "Or you'll never please yourself."

"I know."

"We'll have to address this issue in our next love lesson. Obviously it's deep-seated. In fact, I think we may have stumbled onto the real reason you've never been able to have an orgasm. You are repressed."

"Tell me, Doctor—" she laughed again "—is there any hope for me?"

"As long as you have that sense of humor, there's always hope."

In that moment she looked so forlorn he knew that the laughter was merely a cover. She really feared that she could never have an orgasm.

He shook his head in disbelief, wondering where she'd gotten such an idea. Frigid women didn't wear stockings and garters and sexy black lace bras. They didn't travel more than three thousand miles in search of sexual release. He admired her courage more than he could say, and he was even more determined than ever to help this amazing woman achieve her goal.

Quinn hauled her across the seat toward him, wrapped his arms around her. Her pale hair shone in the darkness, her tantalizing feminine scent filling his nostrils. He was overwhelmed with myriad sensations, and he didn't fully understand a single one of them. Except for a flourishing need that was both distinguishable and unequaled. Lust. Yet wildly stronger than lust.

His body ached to be joined with hers. He wanted to be buried inside her. He longed to hear her soft cries of encouragement, yearned to feel the satisfying clench of her love muscles around his erection as he thrust deeper and deeper until she began to be a part of him.

Kay was as eager as he. Her lips parted in anticipation; her breathing sped up.

"And you want me?" she whispered.

He guided her hand to his rock-solid erection. "You tell me."

She gasped, and in the glow from the dashboard, he saw her eyes widen. "You're so hard."

"That's what you do to me, Kay."

He kissed her then, inhaled her sweet, sweet taste and reveled in the heat of her mouth against his. Every time he kissed her, it felt like the first time. He marveled at everything about her. Her flavor, her scent, the plushness of her pampered skin. He felt as if he was tumbling down a long, dark hole, and he didn't care one whit that it was bottomless.

She made muted noises of pleasure, and he almost came right then and there. He pulled away, panting slightly.

The rasp of their breathing filled the cab of the truck.

"What's wrong?" she asked.

"Nothing's wrong. I want you more than I've ever wanted any woman. I want you so much it literally causes me pain."

She trembled against his chest. "Oh, Quinn, I want you that way, too. I never knew my body's hunger could be so overpowering."

"Neither did I, sweetheart, neither did I."

Then without warning she scooted her tush across the seat until her hot body was flush with his. She pressed those sweet, honeyed lips to the pulse at his throat and lightly bit down. She ran a hand up the nape of his neck, entangled her fingers in his hair and stoked little swirl patterns that sent spikes of hard desire shoving through him.

"What are you doing?" His voice was so husky, so soaked with desire, he could scarcely hear the words.

"Take me home with you," she whispered between nibbles. "Take me home and make love to me right now."

"You have no idea how much I'd like to do exactly that."

"So put the truck in gear and let's get out of here."

He shook his head. "We can't."

"Why not?" Her lips puckered into a pout.

"Because," he said, "you're still not ready."

CHAPTER ELEVEN

WHAT DID HE MEAN she wasn't ready? If he didn't make love to her soon, Kay was going to split in two.

He'd left her on the front porch of the B&B last night with the promise he'd pick her up the following evening to continue her love lessons. But that wasn't enough. She wanted more and she wanted it now.

Kay stared at the screen of her laptop computer, at what she'd written more than four hours earlier and hadn't added a word to since: "During early March in Bear Creek, needle-cold wind rinses every impurity from the air."

But that sharp cold did nothing to dispel her impure thoughts. In fact, the weather seemed to escalate her horniness. Face it, her brain was mush. Courtesy of Quinn Scofield.

The tease.

She was beginning to think he was enjoying torturing her far too much. What was he planning now?

The knock at her bedroom door startled her. She slid off the bed and padded over to throw it open. And was brightened to see Quinn standing there with a large, brown paper bag in his hand.

She glanced at her watch, then back at him. "You're way early."

"I know. Thought I'd catch you off guard."

"I'm not ready." She gestured at her long-sleeved T-shirt layered over powder-blue long johns.

"We're not going anywhere."

"We're not?"

"Nope. I decided to bring the party to you."

"Oh?" Warily she eyed the bag. "What's in there?"

"Curiosity killed the cat."

"Satisfaction brought him back."

"Precisely." He shouldered past her and his big frame seemed to fill the whole room. Kay kicked the door closed behind him.

"Ah." He set the bag down on her dressing table and nodded at her laptop. "You're working on the article. Am I interrupting?"

"Not at all. I was done for the day." She skipped over to the computer and slammed the top down. She didn't want him seeing what pitiful little she'd written and figuring out he was responsible for her writer's block.

"Don't you think you should save your work before you lose it?" he asked.

One sentence. How tough would it be to lose one sentence?

"I already saved." She circled closer to the paper bag, hoping to get a peek inside.

But Quinn was quicker. He clamped a hand around the top. "Ah-ah, no peeking."

"You're driving me right out of my skull. I hope you know that." Then she did something completely out of character for a self-possessed, controlled Freemont. She stuck her tongue out at him.

It felt great. It felt freeing. And it made Quinn laugh. She liked making him laugh.

"Yeah," he said. "You better be careful the way you

use that thing. I can think of several good uses for a sexy tongue."

"You're all talk, big boy," she challenged, squaring off with him toe-to-toe. "You had your chance last night and you blew it."

"That's why I'm here. To make amends."

"Yes?" She perked up at the offer. Was he actually going to make love to her this time?

"The real reason I came over here, instead of taking you to my place, is that Jake's rooms all come complete with those nice, deep, oversize whirlpool-jet bathtubs."

"Meaning?"

Oh, she was enjoying herself.

Quinn reached for the sack and with excruciatingly slow movements removed first a bottle of foaming bath oil and then a package of floating candles.

Kay grinned. Was this guy romantic or what?

"I'll run the bath," he said. "You slip into your robe and pin up your hair."

He went into the adjoining bathroom. Kay heard the water come on and she couldn't get naked fast enough. She stripped off her T-shirt and long johns and wrapped a fluffy white bathrobe around her body. She peeled off her socks, nudged her feet into house slippers, then twisted her hair up off her neck and pinned it in place with a couple of bobby pins.

By the time she edged into the bathroom to join Quinn, the mirrors were already steamed over.

Watching her walk into the room made Quinn's pulse jump. One sleeve of her too-large bathrobe had slipped down on her shoulder, exposing a slender collarbone and an enticing expanse of creamy-white skin. He almost dropped the bath oil and felt himself grow instantly hard with desire for her.

God, she was gorgeous.

She crossed the room toward him. Quinn gulped and backed up as far as he could, until a towel rack poked him in the shoulder blades. Holy cow, what was she doing?

She went up on tiptoe, cocked her head and lightly brushed her lips over his before lowering her heels to the floor again.

Yo, Mama!

She nuzzled his neck, her labored breathing fanning warmly across his flesh. He tried not to think about their perfect fit, his throbbing arousal and how easy it would be to surrender to temptation and take her right here on the bathroom floor. She was extracting her revenge, torturing him the way he'd been torturing her for days. And he was defenseless against her.

He kissed her ear, then ran a tongue along the faint scar traversing her skin from her ear to her jaw. "How'd you get the scar?"

She shivered into his chest. "Who cares?"

"I do," he whispered. "I want to know everything about you."

"Why?" She raised her head so she could study his face.

"You're interesting." He traced a finger along the scar.

She made a dismissive noise.

"You're not going to tell me?"

Dropping her gaze, she shrugged. "Not much to tell. It happened during the one and only time my mother let me play with the maid's children. For weeks I'd begged to be allowed to join in their fun. We were running and diving on a Slip-and-Slide when I slipped off the slide and slammed into a yard ornament." She raised a hand to the scar. "I had to have six stitches."

"Your mother never let you play with those kids again?"

"That was the end of my Slip-and-Slide days. Mummy said the maid's children were ruffians. That they'd maimed me for life."

"I love your scar," he declared fiercely.

"My mother still hounds me about getting plastic surgery. But it's such a small mark, and to tell the truth, I was always a little proud of my battle wound." She smiled.

"I hate to say this sweetheart, but your mother…" He shook his head, let his words trail off. He didn't want to bad-mouth her mother, but the more he found out about Kay's family, the more he understood why she was so emotionally repressed.

"Shh," she said. "No more talking."

Lifting her shoulders, she untied her sash and the next thing he knew, the bathrobe lay in a circle about her feet.

He swallowed. Hard. And waved at the tub.

Kay pushed a tendril of loose hair from her face and met his gaze. There was no mistaking the appreciation in his eyes as he visually caressed her body. That and the slight groan that slipped from his lips let her know how much he wanted her.

Suddenly she felt self-conscious. *Freemont women don't get naked and splash around in the bath with men they barely know.*

That thought overrode her hesitancy. She wanted to do the exact opposite of what a Freemont woman would do. Face it, Freemont women were fuddy-duds who tolerated adulterous husbands and sublimated their sexuality through shopping sprees and plastic surgery. Did she want to end up like her mother and her grandmother and her aunts and female cousins? All superficial women with nothing more to concern themselves with than the latest fall fashions or which bedroom to redecorate next or how many people to invite to their summer soirée. None of them had real marriages or real jobs or expressed authentic feelings.

She raised her head again, determined to see this through, and noticed Quinn was wincing. Her gaze trailed lower, and she spotted the source of his discomfort—the erection pushing against his zipper.

He was watching her, his eyes taking in every curve and dip of her body. His glance traveled from her shoulders to her breasts to her waist and lower. Up and down the length of her legs, then stopped to linger a moment at the blond triangle between her thighs.

Awareness and a dazzling heat prickled her skin. She'd never felt so exposed. She'd thought that night in the sauna had been sexually charged, but then, because of a silk blindfold, she'd been unable to read his reaction to her body. Now she saw every erotic thought that crossed his face. And the power she held over him blew her away.

Her entire body flushed with the heat of his stare. Damn. She'd never blushed so much in her life as she had around him. That unabashed stare of his caused her heart to do the conga against her rib cage. Her hormones were flipping like acrobats in the far recesses of her groin.

He made her feel special, and yet she had no right to feel that way. Quinn was a ladies' man. No doubt about it. From that wolfish grin to the romantic bath complete with bubbles and candles, it was clear he appreciated women. Right now he was appreciating her for all he was worth, and she was helpless against his charms.

It wasn't that men hadn't told her she was beautiful before. She'd had many admirers. The trouble was, because of her own lack of sexual interest in them, she hadn't believed their flattery. She figured that, like Lloyd, they were interested only in her wealth, her family's reputation, her blueblood pedigree.

But Quinn was different. He made her feel a thousand times a woman, and he didn't seem to care one whit that she came from blue-blood stock or that her family oozed money.

Funny that the man she was most attracted to would be the man she couldn't have in the long term.

Ha, ha, good one, Fate. The joke's on me.

Because despite her best intentions not to get emotionally involved with Quinn, he had a sneaky way of flying under her radar, weakening her defenses, slashing right to the root of her intimate longings. It was if he knew what was in her heart and in her mind.

Spooky stuff.

Enough to make her rethink this whole orgasm business.

When had things gotten so complicated?

Just go along for the ride, she told herself. Savor every step of the way with this star-kissed man. Abandon all caution. Bestow yourself on him here and now. Accept what he can offer you; don't pine for more.

This extraordinary man was giving new life to her parched body, waking up her sleeping soul. For that, she would be eternally grateful.

He tipped his head in that rakish way he had, and a lock of whiskey-colored hair fell across his brow. He arched an eyebrow expectantly. "Well? Are you going to get in the bath or not?"

Well, indeed.

Here goes nothing.

Gingerly she stepped into the bubbling water, then sank into the steamy depths. A moan of pleasure escaped her lips as her muscles at first flexed and then relaxed, soothed by the pulsating jets and silky heat of the water. It felt as if she was sliding into a tub of liquefied butter. Hot, thick and sinfully delicious.

"Good girl," he murmured, and knelt beside the tub. "The point here is to get you completely relaxed."

"I'm well on the way."

"Close your eyes."

The corners of her mouth tipped up in a smile, and she let her eyelids drift closed. In a moment she felt Quinn's hand on her fingers, oh-so-leisurely massaging each knuckle.

She didn't know what to expect. Anything and everything he did was a wondrous surprise. From her hand, he advanced to her wrist, then ran his fingers, in a feather-soft stroke, up and down the delicate underside of her forearms.

Kay shivered, alarmed at the intensity of the sensation. "No, don't, it's too much."

"Shh," he soothed, and kept stroking. In a moment the tickling sensation passed and she began to enjoy herself.

He massaged each arm, then turned his attention to her feet.

"Oooh." She sighed as his fingers kneaded her toes, the balls of her feet, her heels.

His tender massage seemed to last forever. When she thought she might fall asleep she was so relaxed, he moved up her legs to her calves and there, he applied hard pressure that made her groan. When his fingers brushed the erogenous area behind her knees, she almost came undone.

She waited for his hand to slide upward to her thighs and beyond, but he disappointed her and stopped. She opened one eye, saw him soaping up a sponge with vanilla-scented bath soap. She smelled the homey, sweet aroma as it clung to drops of steamy air.

He rubbed her shoulders with the sponge, then ran it over her breasts. Kay sucked in a breath. Her nipples beaded and begged for more attention. He washed her belly, then her thighs, but he completely avoided the part of her she most wanted him to touch.

He was doing this on purpose, she thought, working her to a fever-pitch, then dropping her like a skydiver without a parachute.

She shifted position and spread her legs, hoping to tempt him to go farther, explore more. Water sloshed over the edge of the tub, soaking his shirt. She looked up at him and smirked. She could see his nipples had beaded as tight and hard as her own.

"Whoa there," he said, his voice husky. "Slow down, sweetheart, we've got hours and hours yet to go."

She heard a whimpering noise then and realized the sound came from her. "I can't stand much more of this, Quinn."

"Oh, baby, we're just getting started." He pampered her like a mother coddling her small child. He turned off the jets, lit the scented candles and set them in the water to float beside her. The heady aroma of a spring floral bouquet curled through her nose. Jasmine, lavender, honeysuckle.

He got up, turned out the lights, then sat back down

beside her and took her hands. "Now stare at the candles, inhale deeply and concentrate on your body for a few minutes."

She blinked at him.

"Go ahead, do it."

She closed her eyes again, leaned her head back against the tub and inhaled deeply. She'd tried meditation, of course. And creative visualization and yoga classes. She'd heard rave reviews of all these techniques to enhance your sex life, but she'd never been able to relax. Something had always held her back. She felt odd letting herself go in the company of strangers, and she'd never been able to freely express herself like everyone else in the classes.

But here now, for the first time, she felt her body floating as if on a cloud, while at the same time she felt leaden, affixed to the tub. It was an exhilarating experience.

"That's right," he whispered as if he knew she'd achieved an exalted state. "Focus your attention on the center of your belly."

She did as he asked.

"As you breathe in, imagine a warm light settling in your solar plexus and gradually spreading outward."

How had he become so sophisticated about such things? she wanted to ask. Living out here in the wilderness, so far from people and activities.

But she couldn't ask him this, because she was supposed to be concentrating. Yet it was hard to focus when she could smell his masculine scent even over the flowery aroma of the candles.

Warm glow. That was it.

Then like a match to a wick, her belly suddenly did feel hot. Hot and tingly. She rode the sensation, imagining the heat spreading out, coursing through her body, pooling in her groin.

And then she was so hot she couldn't stand it a second more. The power she had over her own body was eerie. She'd never been so in touch with herself.

Her eyes flew open and she found Quinn watching her in the candlelight.

"Pretty awesome, huh?"

All she could do was nod.

"Okay," he said. "Time to get out, your fingers are turning pruney."

He got to his feet, opened a fluffy bath towel and held his hand out to her.

When she touched him, the contact amazed her. Quinn wrapped the towel around her dripping body. He rubbed her dry. The towel was new, mildly scratchy. Her skin was pink from the heat, the water, the brisk toweling.

His affectionate attention reminded her of the nanny she'd had as a little girl. After her bath, Nanny Marie would dust her with talcum powder, help her into her pajamas and then sit by Kay's bed reading one of her favorite books for the millionth time until she fell asleep. Once in a while, on her way to a party, Mommy would pop into her room to say good-night. But she never hugged or nuzzled her cheek the way Nanny did. Honoria wouldn't risk smearing her makeup or mussing her elaborate hairstyle by bending over to kiss her daughter.

Kay blew out her breath, pushed away the melancholy memory. This wasn't the time or place for a stumble down memory lane.

"You okay?" Quinn asked, his gaze on her face.

"Fine." She forced a smile.

Once she was dry, he took her hand and guided her

into the bedroom. "Lie down on the bed on your stomach."

"I feel guilty," she said. "You're doing all these things for me, and I've done nothing for you."

"Hush. My time will come. Tonight is all about you."

She lay then, on her belly, with her face pressed into the pillow. Outside she could hear winter spitting icy rain against the windowpane, but inside they were wrapped tight in a snug cocoon.

Quinn sat on the edge of the bed beside her. The mattress sagged under his weight. His hand, warm and slick with heated peach-scented oil, slid over the planes of her back, lightly caressing.

Had anything in the world ever felt this luxurious?

His hands advanced in ever-widening circles, down her spine to her lower back and then to her buttocks, which he teased with firmer caresses.

She felt sexy deep in the most intimate part of her. Sexy and wet and desperate for this man. She tried to turn over, to face him, to see what he was thinking, but he pushed softly on her shoulder.

"Not yet."

She groaned. "Bastard."

"Now, now. No call for such language." He laughed. "You'll be thanking me soon enough."

"Pretty damn sure of yourself, aren't you?" she said through gritted teeth.

"Don't you know it."

His motions changed but never stopped. Short strokes to long strokes and back again, he swept his hand up and down her back until she felt as if she'd melted into the sheets.

"Turn over," he said.

She barely had the energy, but she managed.

His big hands slid down her neck. Mentally, her mind went where his fingers were. Butterfly pressure on her throat. Tingles in the hollow spot where her collarbones met.

Hot, cold. Soft, hard. She felt so many things.

Her breath caught in her lungs when his right hand made a leisurely foray from her hip to her left breast, kneading with gentle, rhythmic motion that had her squirming even more.

His hand grazed her hardened nipple, and she sank her teeth into her bottom lip to keep from crying out. He leaned in close, ran his tongue over that insatiable nipple, tugging, licking, suckling until her breathing was nothing but shallow, ragged gasps.

His splayed palm felt different than his fist. He used both to fondle her. First one, then the other. Round and square, up and down. Opened, closed. Curved, straight.

After what seemed an eternity, his fingers finally skated to her belly button.

She writhed as his hand lingered there. "Don't," she said breathlessly. "I'm ticklish."

"That means you've got a lot of sexual energy stored there. We need to release it. Let it flow throughout your entire system."

Then he leaned over and pressed his lips to her navel. His hair glinted in the light from the bedside lamp. No one had ever kissed her belly button before, and she found it wildly erotic.

But then the next thing she knew, he'd left there and was headed decidedly south.

What was this?

With one hand he gently spread her knees. "Hold still," he commanded. "Keep your eyes shut."

She closed her eyes, felt his weight shift off the bed.

In a minute he was back. She heard what sounded like jar lids being opened. She cracked one eye to see what in the heck he was doing.

"No peeking."

"What's going on?"

"Lie back and enjoy the ride."

She tried to sink into the pillow, to let her body go limp, but she was so damned curious. "I can't stand this. Tell me what you're doing."

"Pretending I'm Michelangelo. I've always wanted to paint a masterpiece."

"What?" She frowned.

"Shh," he whispered, and she felt a soft feathering of a dry artist's paintbrush sweep against her furrowed brow.

Everywhere the brush touched, she burst into flames. Down he went, traversing her body for a second time.

Eyebrows, eyelids, cheeks, nose, lips. He worked his way around first one ear and then the other, then slipped to the underside of her jaw.

He took the brush away, and when he brought it back, it was warm and wet.

"What's that?" she asked.

"Open your mouth."

She parted her lips. He leaned over and lightly dabbed something on the tip of her tongue.

"Mmm. Chocolate body paint."

"Very good."

With bold strokes, he painted a wide stripe straight down between her breasts to her tummy. Her toes curled at the delicious sensation. He drew a design around her belly button.

"What's that?" he asked.

"A heart." She grinned.

"And this?"

She felt him spell out K-A-Y. "My name."

He switched to a tiny brush and swirled it around her nipples. "Yes," he hissed triumphantly. "I love how they glisten when they stand perkily at attention."

Was she still on planet Earth? Or had she been shot clean into outer space?

He returned to her knees, edged them apart again. "There we go. I'm switching to my smallest tool."

"Wh…?" she started to ask but got no further.

His sizzling-hot hands rested at the apex of her thighs. And he was manipulating that brush like Michelangelo himself. The tip was wet and hot and sticky and oh-so-fine. And he definitely knew how to use it. He gently eased back the flesh protecting her womanhood and caressed the hard, thrusting nub with the warm, damp sable of the brush.

The sensation was nothing short of electric.

She inhaled all the way to her feet. She felt every velvety strand of the brush's thick fur as it fluttered back and forth over her flowering cleft. She swung her hips, gyrating against the brush, reveling in his sounds of approval.

"Yes, baby, yes," he purred.

He flicked the brush. Back and forth, back and forth until she was covered in steamy chocolate.

"Now," he said, "I'm going to lick you clean."

He dipped his head. His hair rasped against her belly. He was licking at the high recesses of the inside of her thigh. So near the area where she was dying for him to be. She was tired of this torment. She wanted to feel his hard, throbbing member thrusting deep inside her.

She smelled his maleness, and his scent spurred her arousal. Her body, which minutes before had been soft and pliant from the bath and the sensual rub, was now stiff and ready. She was wet, so incredibly wet. She wanted it. This spectacular release everyone spoke of. This colorful, vibrant fantastic orgasm. It was possible. Within her reach at last. She could feel it building, feel herself getting more strung out and desperate.

She tossed her head like a restless mare. She arched against his mouth, wanting, no, needing more, more. Her nerves were raw, ragged.

His tongue, oh, sweet heaven, his tongue! She unfurled to him like a rosebud opening to the sun, exalting in the heat, blooming, growing, expanding.

He was too slow. He was taking too long. This was maddening. This was incredible. This was hell. This was heaven.

Was it possible to feel so much driving need and not collapse if that need was not met?

"Take me, Quinn," she begged, unable to stand this one second longer. "Make love with me. Get inside me. I want you."

But he diligently ignored her pleas, still slowly, gently licking her with his tongue.

He inched closer and closer to the prize, his mouth now between her thighs and her outer lips. He drew circles with his tongue and each lick felt like a stinging-hot brand. Whimpering, she pushed her hips upward, her lower back clearing the bed.

And then he was flicking his tongue across her aching cleft while at the same time stroking the sensitive area just below with his fingers. She cried out at the dual sensation. She was falling, stumbling, careening into a caldron of heat.

Boiling, baking, blistering heat.

Hijacked, bushwhacked, shanghaied.

He'd kidnapped her, mind, body and soul.

She tried to say something, but her tongue wouldn't work. Her ears rang.

I need, I need, I need.

So this was what it was all about. This was why everyone extolled sex as if it was some great curative. She felt as if she was hanging on the edge of a precipice by her fingernails.

She was aflame, ablaze, incandescent. She was the aurora borealis, and Quinn's dangerous, exquisite mouth created sunspots, shooting highly charged energy through her until she was aglow with electricity.

She gyrated and rotated. She writhed and bucked.

Make it happen, she begged silently, hungering to tumble over into that magical abyss.

His tongue loved her, caressed her, lifted her to the pinnacle.

She waited for the drop, entwined her fingers in his hair and waited with bated breath, knew that orgasm was only seconds away. At last. After twenty-seven years. At last.

And then, just before she came, he stopped.

CHAPTER TWELVE

"No," SHE WHIMPERED. "No. You can't stop now."

Quinn looked down into her face, scrunched tight with both pain and pleasure, and his gut torqued. How he wanted her! If only she knew how difficult this was for him, holding back when more than anything in the world he ached to bury himself deep inside her and stay there forever.

She raised herself on her elbows, flicked out her tongue and licked his throat. "Please," she whispered, her eyes still effulgent with the sheen of lust. "Please."

He almost lost his minuscule shard of control and took her, but his overwhelming desire to confer upon her the precious gift of her first orgasm kept him tethered to his goal.

"One more night, sweetheart." He pressed his mouth to her ear. "Just one more night. Trust me on this."

Kay groaned and sank against him. "Quinn, this is cruel and unusual punishment."

"I know, baby, I know." He gently caressed her head. "But it's for your own good. Tomorrow night, my place. I promise."

But could he keep that promise? She'd been close to orgasm just now, but if he'd continued stroking her, would she have plunged over the edge or remained on the precipice, unable to make the plunge? Was that the real reason he'd pulled the plug on tonight's proceedings? Because he was afraid that, when push came to shove, he couldn't deliver on his promise?

The thought of letting her down, of not being able to fulfill her sexually, caused a clutch of anxiety in the bottom of his heart. God, how he wanted to be the one to make her happy.

That was why he wouldn't give in to those pleading eyes and his raging hormones. That was why they had to wait one more night. Everything had to be perfect. Tomorrow night he was pulling out all the stops, unpacking his arsenal, opening his bag of tricks. He was going to make sure she had the sexual experience of a lifetime and returned home to New York with treasured memories of Alaska that would never fade.

For some odd reason he felt empty at the thought of her leaving. He'd known from the beginning that this could not be a long-term relationship, that for many reasons they weren't well suited as a couple, but he'd hardly had any time to get to know her the way he wanted to know her.

"Quinn?" She reached up and traced his lips with a finger. "Is something wrong?"

Wrong? Oh, only that he was holding an exquisite angel in his arms and soon he would have to let her go. He feared that consummating their passion, joining their bodies and taking their relationship to the highest physical level would make things that much harder.

And yet, he could not, would not, let her down, even if it meant getting hurt himself. She was worth the sacrifice. He would award her all he had to give.

"Nothing." He smiled. No point tormenting himself over something that could not be changed. "Just planning tomorrow night."

She curled against his body. "I can't wait," she whispered, "to see what you've prepared for me."

Oh, boy. The pressure was on, and somehow, he would rise to the challenge. But how could he provide Kay with what she needed while at the same time keeping himself from falling head over heels in love?

"Kiss me again," she whispered. "Just kissing and nothing else."

How could he refuse that?

Kay sighed into his mouth. This man was so powerful and yet so tender. He was controlled and yet willing to do whatever she asked of him. She'd never met anyone like him.

They lay on the bed together, side by side, his tongue softly exploring her mouth.

In her mind, a vision appeared. She saw him in her mind's eye as clearly as if it was happening. He was cuddling a sweet newborn baby in the crook of his arm, gazing tenderly into the baby's face. His hands were bigger than the baby's tiny head. The explicit contrast was startling.

He would make a wonderful father.

Kay opened her eyes, stared at Quinn, who was looking right at her. Why was she picturing him as a father? Why was she thinking about babies? When she'd been with Lloyd, she'd barely given babies a second thought. Oh, she supposed she wanted a child someday. But she'd been too consumed with her career, too unimpressed with Lloyd to spend much time fantasizing about babies. Now, in a sudden rush, all those maternal feelings she'd suppressed came to the forefront of her mind, confusing the hell out of her.

She couldn't have him. She could never be the kind of wife he needed, so why daydream about having his baby? She pulled away from him, disturbed by her feelings.

"What's wrong?" His husky words clobbered her thoughts, demanded entry into the part of her she kept most private—her heart.

She struggled for her famous Freemont control, tried to force her features into expressionless lines.

And failed miserably.

She couldn't keep dragging that tired facade over her face, couldn't keep hiding her true feelings.

Quinn reached out and gently massaged her shoulder. "Tell me, sweetheart, have I done something wrong?"

In that moment Kay lost it completely, and to her horror, she began to cry.

"What is it?" Alarmed, Quinn sat up. His heart thundered. What had he done wrong? He gathered her to his chest. "Talk to me."

"Nothing." She shook her head. "It's just that no one man has ever treated me so gently, so kindly."

He squeezed her tight. "Well, darling, your luck has just changed."

Concern for her, and another emotion he wasn't quite ready to name, filled his chest. He searched for the right words to say, to tell her how special she was, when the beeper he wore for fire-call emergencies went off.

THEY CAREENED DOWN the street, headed for the fire. Kay's blood was pumping through her veins like Freon. Quinn had agreed to take her along as a journalist as long as she promised to stay clear of the fire. He gripped the steering wheel in his hands, his gaze focused intently on the icy road in front of them. Through the two-way radio mounted on the dash, he was in touch with the other firefighters and had learned that Millie Peterson's house was on fire.

Millie, Quinn told her, was an eighty-five-year-old widow who lived just outside Bear Creek. She'd grown absentminded of late, and he worried that maybe she'd forgotten to turn the stove off before she went to bed. He gave the truck more gas and took the curve far too fast. Kay, thankful for her seat belt, gripped the armrest and prayed that Millie was all right.

Quinn braked to a stop outside a small, two-story frame house at the same instant that Mack, Jake, Caleb and a couple of other men arrived in the fire truck. Orange flames licked their way across the roof. The acrid smell of smoke consumed the air. Quinn sprinted over to the truck.

Kay got out and watched him quickly and methodically go about the business of putting out a fire. She wanted to help. Needed to keep busy so she wouldn't worry so much about Quinn and the other firefighters. Glancing around, Kay saw an elderly woman standing on the lawn. She hurried over.

"Millie?" she asked.

The elderly lady, dressed in long johns and a bathrobe, was shivering, her glasses askew on her wrinkled face. Kay whipped off her coat and draped it around Millie's shoulders.

"Doodles," Millie cried. "My little doggy, Doodles, is inside."

"I'll tell the firemen," Kay said, and raced over to Quinn, who was breaking out an ax from the back of the truck. "Quinn," she called to him. He raised his head. "Millie's dog is inside."

Quinn glanced toward the house. In the short time they'd been here, the flames had grown taller, arched higher into the night sky. Mack grabbed Quinn's arm. "Don't do it, man. The house is about to go."

"Doodles!" Millie wailed, and wrung her hands.

"I've got to try," Quinn said. "Millie would give up and die if anything happened to that dog."

"Quinn," Kay whimpered, "be careful."

"Don't worry, honey. I'll be back." He leaned down and placed a quick kiss on her lips. "I promise."

While Mack and Jake turned the fire hose on the house, Quinn charged through the front door.

Kay's heart crammed into her throat and stayed there.

"I'm scared," Millie said.

Kay surprised herself by confessing, "Me too." Since coming to Bear Creek, she'd found it easier and easier to express her feelings. She didn't know if that was good or bad. She only knew that in New York she would never have felt comfortable enough to throw her arm around a frightened little old lady she didn't know and hug her close.

For what seemed an eternity, Kay and Millie huddled together, waiting. More cars arrived. A crowd gathered. At one point Kay looked around and realized the whole town was here, people running to and fro, doing what they could to help. Someone threw a blanket over her and Millie.

Kay turned to see Meggie standing behind her, a worried expression on her face. Kay nodded.

Meggie reached over, took Kay's hand and squeezed.

A huge lump of emotion formed in Kay's throat.

I'm among friends, she realized. Honest-to-gosh friends. Not just people who pretended to like her because she was rich.

Suddenly she felt a part of Alaska, a part of the community, a part of Quinn's family. But almost as suddenly, her fear quickly pushed aside her quiet feeling of acceptance. Quinn should have been out by now. Where was he?

Just as Jake said, "I'm going in after Quinn," a form appeared in the doorway of the burning house and Quinn staggered out, something clutched tightly in his arms.

Doodles.

Millie sprang forward to snatch her dog from him, and Kay sprang forward to scoop her smoky, cinder-smeared man into her arms, unmindful of the hubbub surrounding them.

Quinn picked her up. She wrapped her legs around his waist and her arms around his neck.

"You're safe," she whispered.

"I told you I'd be back," he said gruffly. "And I always keep my promises."

"I was so worried, so scared I'd never see you again."

"Were you really?"

"Of course, you big goof."

"Hey, what's this?" he asked.

Tears were streaming down her cheek and she didn't even realize it until he kissed them gently away.

TONIGHT'S THE NIGHT.

It was six o'clock on Sunday evening as Kay parked the Wagoneer that Quinn's parents had lent her, then made her way up the frozen walkway. The smell of wood smoke hung in the air. The snow crunched delightfully underfoot.

At last, at last, at last, she mentally chanted.

Underneath her coat she wore a red silk dress, sheer red-tinted stockings, a racy red garter belt and three-inch red stilettos. But in the short distance from the heated car to Quinn's front door, the icy bite of wind had turned her legs into Popsicles. Alaska in late winter was no place to wear seductive clothing.

But the sexy outfit made her feel ultrafeminine, her gift to Quinn. She hadn't considered wearing anything else.

Tonight was the night.

He opened the door and let her in.

She tilted her head at him, and the sight of his rugged profile caused a hitch in her breath. He was so handsome, so masculine, so unabashedly male. She couldn't wait to see him naked. Couldn't wait to have him inside her.

He caught her watching him and grinned. She looked away but not without holding his gaze for a long moment first. He led her inside to the rug by the fire.

"Sit," he instructed, then took her coat and went to hang it up. When he returned, he sat beside her.

An awkward silence hung between them for the briefest minute, then they both chuckled at once.

"Your feet look pale." He said. "Give 'em to me."

Languidly, as if moving through a pool of pudding, Kay raised her legs and plopped her feet in Quinn's lap. He slipped off her high heels and tossed them into the corner. The sensation of his warm fingers on her cold toes caused her to hiss in her breath.

He rubbed her feet between his palms. First the left and then the right. "I'd lecture you on dressing warmly," he said, "but you look so damned sexy in that outfit I'm not saying a word."

She laughed, pleased at his compliment. He made her feel like a seductive vamp, and she loved the feeling.

"Mmm," she moaned softly against his tender ministrations, lying back against the stone hearth and closing her eyes. "That feels wonderful."

"Are you hungry?" he asked. "Dinner's keeping warm in a Crock-Pot, so we could eat now or whenever you're ready."

"Just keep rubbing," she said, her body going eagerly limp. She amazed herself at how easily she relaxed with Quinn.

His fingers rubbed and kneaded, caressed and massaged. He moved from her feet to her ankles, then up her calf.

"How does this feel?"

"Heavenly."

"How about this?"

"Ooh, you wicked devil."

"At your service, angel."

She thrilled at his words, at the sex in his voice. Her body erupted in a shower of mind-numbing tingles.

"You have gorgeous legs," he said.

"And you administer a mean foot rub. Your hands are like a touch of silk."

"Your legs were the first thing I noticed about you. You know, on the plane to JFK."

"Really?" She opened her eyes and peered at him in the flickering glow from the firelight.

"Uh-huh. What was the first thing you noticed about me?"

"The way you kept staring at my legs."

"No kidding."

"It wasn't hard to miss. Your eyes were practically bugging out of your head."

"I didn't know you were paying any attention to me at all."

"You're a hard one to miss, Quinn Scofield."

His hands were on her knees now and climbing higher. She felt herself swept away as if drugged by a magical potion and carried off into an X-rated fantasy land.

She and Quinn are Russian nobles traveling at high speed across the snowy landscape in their troika. Their thick fur wraps protect them from the harsh Siberian winter.

Suddenly highwaymen seize them, haul them from their sled.

"Strip," the brigands demand, and in the bitter cold they peel off their garments. Now, they're going to freeze to death, together, in the bitter cold.

But highwaymen are not completely merciless, even though they are laughing at their nakedness. Before they leave, the bandits toss down a fur rug.

They wrap the skin around them and stagger toward a wooden hut at the edge of the forest. He builds a fire, and she falls asleep in his arms.

She awakes to find him rubbing the fur between her legs. Suddenly he seizes her around the waist, flips her onto her belly and he takes her from behind, while his hand stimulates her from the front. As she sinks down into the throes of climax, she hears a snowstorm howling outside the hut and knows they will not be rescued for days.

"Let me in on your fantasy," Quinn whispered. "Tell me what you're thinking."

Kay's eyes flew open and she blinked up at him. She realized his hand was on her upper thigh and so very close to the most dangerous part of her. "I don't know what you mean."

"Don't lie to me, Kay, you're no good at it." He

reached out a finger and lightly stroked her cheek. "You're having an awesome sexual fantasy."

"How do you know?" Her lip quivered. She was amazed at his powers of deduction. He seemed to know her most intimate thoughts.

"You've been holding your sexuality at bay for so long you're bound to be brimming with fantasies. Tell me and we'll reenact them."

She hesitated. She'd never revealed her wildest sexual fantasies to anyone.

Was she brave enough to do this?

"Trust me," he murmured. "Share. Let me go there with you."

"Snowbound," she murmured after a long moment. She was giving him the highest degree of trust she was capable of bestowing. "In the frozen Russian tundra. We're rich nobles who've been stripped of all our wealthy trappings by bandits and left to die in a storm. But we have a fur coat, and we find a shack on the edge of the forest."

"Hang on a minute." He jumped up and disappeared down the hall. Shortly he returned carrying a plush sable coat, an open bottle of red wine and two glasses. "This coat belonged to my grandmother back before fur was politically incorrect." He filled the glasses with wine, rested the bottle on the hearth, then spread the coat over the rug. "Lie down."

Kay sank into the fur and gasped at the luxurious sensation. "Oh, my."

"You know," he said, "I've been going about this whole seduction the wrong way."

"How so?" she purred and rubbed her body into the coat like a kitten curling up to its mother.

"I've been doing to you what I thought would make you responsive."

"And you've been doing a damn fine job of it, too."

He shook his head. "I was off base. You need to learn what turns you on, to learn to control your own body before you turn it over to me." He sat down cross-legged beside her. "Let's get that dress off."

With incredible slowness that pushed her to the limits of endurance, he unbuttoned her dress and slipped it over her head. Her underwear was next. He unhooked her bra and tossed it into the corner. A second later her red satin thong followed. The fireplace gave off enough heat to warm her bare skin.

"Give me your hand," he said.

She did as he asked.

He took it, guided her hand to her belly. "Touch yourself."

"What?"

"Just do it."

"While you watch?"

His gray eyes had turned stormy slate. "Yes."

"I feel silly."

"Stop that thought right now. You're anything but silly. Have a sip of wine." He held the glass to her lips. Obediently she raised her head and swallowed the tepid liquid. "Good girl. Now close your eyes and let your fingers do the walking. Pretend you're alone. I'm not here."

Hesitantly Kay traced her fingers over her breasts, amazed at how good it felt.

She was really embarrassed at first, but the more she let herself go, the more Quinn made appreciative noises. She loved hearing that she turned him on. She snuggled into the fur coat and tugged at her nipples. When she twisted gently, they came to life. A warm, wonderful tingling spread from her belly to her thighs. She followed the sensation with her hands.

She could hear Quinn's breathing, and his raspy intake of air spurred her on. She caressed herself and slowly slid one finger into her folded flesh. This felt great, but lonely. She wanted to see Quinn. Opening her eyes, she was shocked and yet thrilled to find him naked and hard.

Quinn had never watched a woman pleasure herself, and it was driving him beyond insane. He'd done well to hold on this long.

"Help me," she whispered. "I don't want to do this by myself."

Yes! He surged toward her, came to rest beside her on the fur coat. He began by kissing her and took his time working his way down to her other pair of lips. When he ventured too close to her delicate cleft, she hissed in her breath.

Easy, he told himself, easy. That pretty pink cleft was a shy little devil. Gently he wet her with his mouth and when he pulled away, she moaned.

He retrieved the lubricants he'd bought for her, moistened his fingers with a smooth gel and rubbed them across her blood-engorged flesh. With the first two fingers of his right hand he carefully edged them apart.

Starting directly to the left of her pulsating cleft and inching clockwise, he brushed against her with fast, short, circular stokes, looking for the perfect combination that would rocket her to the moon.

So as not to abrade her tender membranes, he made sure her cleft stayed wet and slick by dipping his fingers into her warm recesses and drawing out a trail of love juices to rub over her burgeoning womanhood.

The small cleft changed as her arousal reached new

heights. It swelled, grew harder and finally climbed eagerly from its hooded cave.

"I don't want to hurt you," he whispered, "or ruin your arousal. Show me what feels good to you. Talk to me. Tell me."

She brought her hand to his. He followed her lead, memorized her every move. It was the most intimate thing he'd ever indulged in with anyone.

"Oh, Quinn," she breathed, and writhed beneath him. "Yes. Right there. Like that."

His own arousal was beyond anything he'd ever felt before. Together they massaged and stroked and caressed her, both working in tandem to achieve the same goal. But after forty minutes, Kay still wasn't anywhere near the summit. Maybe it was because she was too nervous about having him watch her.

Then he had an idea. It was something he'd heard once, supposedly a favorite sexual trick of Marilyn Monroe's. It would solve the problem of Kay's embarrassment and yet allow her to have full control over her own orgasm. It was worth a try. If it didn't work, well...

Since their relationship had no foundation other than a physical one, Quinn didn't even want to think about that. He would present her with what she so desperately craved. He would, he would, he would.

Kay whimpered in frustration. "I'm so close," she moaned. "Why can't I get there?"

"You will, baby," he soothed. "You will. I promise. Keep stroking, I'll be right back."

Kay almost burst into tears the minute Quinn left the room. She had a feeling he was at his wit's end. She bit down hard on her bottom lip. Everything he'd done for her felt so good. He'd treated her like a princess—she couldn't let him down. If she had to, she'd fake the orgasm for his sake.

"Get off the coat," he commanded.

She rolled over and looked up at him. He had a plastic tarp under one arm and a bottle of baby oil in his hand. His erection was still as big as the state of Alaska. He took the coat from the rug and tossed it on the couch. Then he spread the tarp across the rug.

"What's going on?"

"Shh." He began coating the front of her body in baby oil. "Now," he said, when he'd finished, "you oil up my back."

He lay facedown on the tarp. Puzzled, Kay took the bottle of heated oil and squirted some onto his back. He groaned deeply as she ran her hand along his naked torso, down his buttocks and legs until he was as wet with oil as she was. She loved the feel of his firm skin beneath her fingers.

"Now what?" she asked when she'd finished the task.

"Lie on top of me."

This was a weird request. Feeling awkward, she lay down atop him, her breasts smashed flat against his shoulder blades.

"Your breasts feel like velvet," he murmured.

"Your back is so muscular. Hard as a rock." She breathed into his ear.

"I'm going to stay completely still. This is all you, babe. You're at the helm. You're in control."

"But what do I do?"

"Slide your hands down my arms."

She wasn't sure what was going on, but she enjoyed feeling the wide expanse of his back beneath her, and she trusted him. She raised herself enough to lean forward, clasp her hands around his wrists and slip her arms down the length of his.

It felt like the time she went shooting over that Slip-and-Slide with the maid's kids.

"That's right. Keep touching, keep moving," he coached. "Make love to my back. You're looking for a certain spot. Go down a little."

Spurred by the easy glide from the baby oil, she got into the rhythm, rode on the motion. She rocked her hips in slow, small circles pressing her pubic bone directly against his tailbone.

And then she found it. The spot on his body that was a perfect fit for her cleft to snuggle into. A nice, welcoming groove.

She let loose with a shout of glee and wriggled happily.

Nothing had ever felt so good. She kept rocking, stoking her own fire. Her aching cleft set the pace, as she rubbed it up and down, up and down his oil-soaked skin. Up and down and around and around. She surfed his body like a wahine cruising a curl off Oahu's north shore.

"Quinn!" she cried, desperate to share her experience with the big, motionless man beneath her. "This feels phenomenal."

"Go, baby, go. Get it anyway you can."

"I'm getting so close. I can taste it rising up in my throat."

She clasped her arms around his waist, squeezed him tight. His heart was pounding so loudly she could feel it vibrating throughout his whole body and up into hers.

"Glory!" he cried, startled at the extreme intimacy this unorthodox maneuver wrought. "I can feel every twitch you make, Kay."

"Quinn, it's happening. I'm coming."

And then it hit her with the force of an oncoming freight train. Her entire body was engulfed in a hot, flushed, quaking release that started in her sensitive cleft but unfurled in a jerking starburst all the way to her toes.

She shuddered as wave after wave crashed into her. It was a force more powerful than an erupting volcano, more awe-inspiring than an ageless glacier. It was as if every dam in the country had broken at once, spewing torrents of wild water over the land. Seven days of sweet torture, years of hungry fantasies, a lifetime of repression burst forth from her.

At last! At long last!

Panting, she slid off Quinn's back. He rolled over, tucked her into the curve of his arm and smiled down at her. "My only regret," he whispered, "was not being able to see your face."

She was dishrag limp and unable to speak for a good five minutes. When she finally caught her breath, all she could say was, "That was…incredible."

In that fortuitous moment Quinn's telephone rang.

He leaned in to kiss her. She raised her head.

The phone rang again.

"Are you going to answer that?" she murmured sleepily, his lips so close the air vibrated off his mouth back to hers as she spoke.

"Let the machine pick up." He lightly ran his tongue over her upper lip.

By the time the machine intercepted the call, her arms were entwined around his neck, her legs around his waist, and their lips were fused.

"Quinn, this is your mother. Are you home? If you're home, please pick up."

"You better answer that," Kay said into his mouth.

"Do I have to?"

"It might be important."

Sighing, Quinn untangled Kay's limbs and got to his feet. "I'm here, Ma," he said, picking up the receiver and running a hand through his hair. His gaze slid over to his sexy Kay and he winked at her. "What's up?"

"Liam is rushing Candy to the hospital in Juneau. It looks like she might be in preterm labor. Your father's been at the station all day, and I need him at home. My ankle is giving me fits. Is there any way you can sub for Liam tonight?"

"Right now?"

"Yes, dear. Meggie's at the station for now, but Liam and Candy want her to fly with them."

Quinn took a deep breath. He loved his family and he was distressed to learn that Liam and Candy were having a crisis, but tonight of all nights? When he'd promised Kay he would make love to her?

He glanced at Kay again. She'd gotten to her feet and was looking at him with a quizzical expression on her face.

Helplessly he met Kay's gaze. "I gotta go," he muttered, holding a palm over the phone so his mother couldn't hear. "Minor emergency."

Kay nodded.

"Okay, I'll be right there," he told his mother.

"You're a good son."

He told her goodbye, hung up and gave his attention to Kay.

"I hope everything's all right," she said.

Briefly he explained what was happening. "I'm so sorry," he apologized. "I intended for us to spend the whole night together."

"Hey, it's not your fault." She shrugged. "There'll be other nights."

"But you're leaving on Saturday."

"And this is only Sunday. Go. Help out your family."

"You're sure?"

"Don't be silly, of course I'm sure."

Her forgiveness and easy understanding filled him with an odd sensation. When he first met her, he'd been attracted to her physically, but he'd thought that was as far as the attraction went. In all honesty, he'd seen her as a spoiled, rich socialite. But here she was acting anything but spoiled. And in that moment Quinn knew his attraction had jumped to a whole new level.

CHAPTER THIRTEEN

How could she get upset with Quinn, even though her body was aching for his attention? Devotion to his family was one of his most attractive traits. She loved that his family meant so much to him, that they were so close. She wished his family was hers. She wished she could be a part of such a loving community.

In six days, she would be gone. His family was here for a lifetime. How could she begrudge him his choice?

She didn't, but as she watched him shrug into his coat, she couldn't seem to tamp down the torrent of loneliness washing through her.

Alone again.

Alone and super horny. She wanted more sex. More orgasms. More of him.

"Stay here," Quinn instructed, coming over to brush her lips lightly with his. "I'll be back after midnight. Eat some supper, watch a movie, finish off that glass of wine, take a nap, but don't you dare go anywhere. Got that? We're not through yet."

She nodded, even though a nagging voice in the back of her head was urging her to go to the bed-and-breakfast, pack her things and head back to New York right now. They'd yet to take that irrevocable step toward becoming full-fledged lovers. This was her chance to back out before she made a fool of herself. Before she got seriously hurt.

Because she was already starting to care for Quinn far more than was prudent.

"Say it." He leaned over to nibble on her earlobe. "Say you'll be waiting here for me when I get home."

What was it about this man? He seemed to know every errant thought that passed her mind. How? She had spent so much of her life learning to cloak her feelings, keep her countenance unreadable, her head clear, her mind undisturbed, and yet she could never fool Quinn. What gave her away? she wondered. How had he known she was panicking?

His gentle nipping of her earlobe was more than she could bear. "I'll be here," she promised huskily. "Now go."

"I could get used to this," he said. "Having you to come home to."

Kay inhaled sharply. "It's not me you want, Quinn. It's a wife."

He stepped back a moment, studied her in the foyer light. Too bad she couldn't read his mind the way he seemed to read hers.

"Yeah," he said. "You're right. Long term, I do want a wife, but for tonight..." His gaze raked over her body. "I can't forget what sizzling, sexy blonde will be waiting for me."

He turned and walked out the door, leaving Kay feeling more confused than ever. She wandered about the house, snooping a little and finally ending up in the large room upstairs where he'd taken her the night he'd shown her the northern lights.

She didn't open any closets or drawers, but she did touch the things that were lying out. His ice skates, the blades cleaned and freshly sharpened. His gloves. His heavy snow boots—good grief, he wore a size fourteen. She fingered his hockey jersey, which she held to her nose to breathe in the scent of him. The smell aroused her with a perplexing kick to the belly. Immediately she dropped the jersey back on the chair where she had found it.

She drifted over to the stereo system, flicked on the radio, then settled herself on the couch with her wine to watch the show outside the window. The northern lights were in full swing, flickering and dancing hypnotically.

"Hello, listeners." The soothing sound of Quinn's voice came through the speakers and wrapped around her like a thermal blanket. "You're listening to KCRK, number 840 on your AM dial. Sorry folks, but you're stuck with the native son tonight. Mack's flying Liam and Candy into Anchorage as we speak. Seems little Liam Junior is trying to put in his appearance two and a half months too early. I know they'll appreciate any prayers you can send the family's way."

A knot formed in Kay's throat. Bear Creek was such a caring community. Small, intimate, cozy, a place where neighbors looked out for one another and nobody worried about stupid, inconsequential things like what kind of wine went with what kind of meal, or which pair of earrings to wear to an art-gallery opening.

Kay realized she'd invested too much of her life worrying about things that didn't really matter.

"On a lighter note," Quinn was saying, "Millie Peterson and Doodles are doing just fine. Millie's staying with her sister over in Haines for a while in case anyone wants to run by and say hi. And thanks to everyone who donated money and clothes. Also, I'd like to thank everyone for helping out our visitor from New York City, Kay Freemont, with her article on Bear Creek. The magazine will be hitting the newsstands in mid-

May, so be sure and drop by Leonard Long Bear's to get your copy."

Kay grinned at the radio, brought her wineglass to her lips and took a sip.

"And speaking of Kay, I'd like to dedicate this next song to her."

Rod Stewart's "Hot Legs" soon issued forth.

Kay hooted her approval and started tapping a foot in time to the lively music. After it was over, Quinn came back on. "It's an open request line tonight, folks. So call in—577-5555 for those of you with bad memories—and let me know what you'd like to hear tonight."

Getting to her feet, Kay padded back downstairs, took her cell phone from her purse and punched in the numbers to the radio station.

"I'd like to request a song," she said.

"Yes, ma'am, what can I play for you?" He gave no hint that he knew it was her, but how could he not know?

"'Natural Woman' by Aretha Franklin. Do you have that one?"

"Why, yes, ma'am, I believe we do."

She grinned again, sat down in front of the fire and kept the cell phone in her lap. She hummed along with the song that expressed her sentiments exactly. Quinn did make her feel like a natural woman. Sexy, feminine, loving.

"We gotta another dedication, folks," he said, when "Natural Woman" was over. Then he played a very provocative Barry White number, and Kay knew he was playing that one for her as well.

It was naughty, suggestive, and Barry's deep-throated voice sent spikes of hot desire down her spine. Damn! At this rate she wasn't going to last until midnight, which was when the radio station went off the air and Quinn returned home.

Kay felt herself go soft and moist and warm inside. She picked up her cell phone and dialed the station again. "How about 'You Sexy Thing'?"

"Coming right up," Quinn replied. He played her request followed by "You Can Leave Your Hat On."

That gave her an image to giggle about. She programmed the radio station to speed dial and whispered seductively when he answered, "'Let's Get It On.'"

"Your wish is my command."

Kay giggled again and pressed the back of her hand to her mouth.

He topped "Let's Get it On" with "Feel like Making Love."

"Keep those requests coming," Quinn said, when the song had played. "Oh, wait, I've got a call right now. Go ahead, caller."

"Hey!" Kay recognized the voice as that of old Gus. "Why don't you two have sex, already?"

Quinn sputtered into the microphone. "Er...I don't know what you're talking about. I've only been taking requests."

"Stop yanking my chain, Scofield. Obviously the lady's hot for you, and the rest of us would like to listen to something a little less arousing. Play something decent, like big-band tunes." Gus huffed loudly, then disconnected.

Kay burst out laughing.

Quinn put on "In the Mood," which only made her laugh harder. Why was she sitting here? Kay wondered. Why not toddle on over to the radio station and surprise him?

She grabbed the bottle of wine from the hearth where

Quinn had left it, hurried into the kitchen, dug a wheel of cheddar cheese from the fridge and scooped a loaf of crusty sourdough bread off the counter.

Then, just before she put on his grandmother's fur coat, she took off her dress. Wearing nothing but stockings, garter belt, stilettos and the heavy sable coat, she got into the Wagoneer and drove to the radio station.

At nine-thirty, the main street of Bear Creek was deserted. Fat snowflakes spiraled from the pitch-black sky. The only vehicles she passed were the few trucks and cars gathered outside the Happy Puffin bar. Her heart hammered as she parked in front of the KCRK station. She could see Quinn through the window, seated in the booth, headphones over his ears.

The sight of him made her stomach go all jiggly.

Her breath came in frosty puffs. She knocked on the door, balancing precariously on her too-high heels, the bottle of wine in one arm, the cheese wheel and loaf of bread in the other.

A second later Quinn pulled open the door with such force he knocked her off balance, and she tumbled into his arms.

"Whoa." He grabbed her shoulders to steady her. "What are you doing out in this weather?"

"Coming to see you." She grinned up into his face. "I realized old Gus was right. It is high time we had sex, already. Real sex. Not just playing around."

"You called what we did earlier 'just playing around'?"

"Uh-huh. Now I'm ready for the hard stuff."

"Get in here." He tugged her inside and shut the door against the swirling cold. "Silly woman." He pressed her to his chest, breathed into her hair.

"I brought sustenance." She held out the wine and bread.

His eyes glimmered. "You're one hell of a woman, Kay Freemont, you know that?"

He parked her on a tweed couch in the studio. "Have a seat. I gotta go give the call letters and put on some more music. Got a request?"

"You pick." She smiled and settled back against the seat.

He did so in record time, the strains of Nat King Cole's "Unforgettable" seeping into the room. In his hands he held two paper cups. He appropriated the wine from where she'd set it on the floor, filled the cups and passed one to her.

"To the sexiest woman on the planet." He raised his glass.

"I can't drink to that. I'm not the sexiest woman on the planet."

"You are to me," he growled softly.

She drank then to the sexuality she'd repressed for so long. The sexuality that Quinn had so lovingly cultivated and coaxed from her over the course of the past eight days.

"I'm ready, Quinn," she said, finishing the wine and blinking in surprise at her sudden boldness. "No more games. I want you. Right here. Right now. Right this very minute."

GOD, BUT SHE WAS gorgeous, swaddled in his grandmother's fur coat with nothing showing but her legs from the calf down encased in crimson silk stockings. Her sweet feet were in sexy stiletto heels.

Her hair, normally perfectly controlled, was mussed,

and her lipstick had come off on the edge of her paper cup.

He liked her this way. Relaxed. Natural. Asking for what she needed from him.

She was so beautiful and yet so out of place here on the worn tweed couch in his parents' radio station in Bear Creek, Alaska. She deserved to have her first orgasms at the Plaza Hotel in New York City while dining on chocolate-covered strawberries and expensive champagne, not supping on stale sourdough bread and third-rate wine. She deserved so many things he couldn't provide.

She reached out a finger, ran it along the crease cleaving his forehead. "Stop worrying," she murmured. "Everything's going to be all right."

But was it?

Quinn studied her, knowing she didn't belong here, knowing he had no right to want her as badly as he did. She was on the rebound, after all, looking for sex as a way to rebuild her self-esteem. He was a vehicle to her goal, and although he couldn't blame her for that, he couldn't seem to stop himself from wanting more.

Take what you can get. When the ad comes out in the magazine, you'll be knee-deep in women and Kay will be nothing but a pleasant memory. Make the most of it.

"Let me just make sure we're not interrupted." He went to the door and slipped the lock into place with a resounding click. He flicked off the overhead fluorescent bulb, leaving them bathed in the glow of red and green lights from the control panel.

Her almond eyes widened, and she ran the tip of her tongue along her lips, making him hotter than the volcanic Ring of Fire bubbling beneath Alaska's crust.

She was like Alaska itself. A cool, perfect beautiful exterior with a hot, smoldering center just waiting to erupt. He'd sensed this about her from the moment he'd seen her on the plane.

And her exciting combination of fire and ice stirred something inside him, just as his homeland did.

He admired so many things about her. The way she carried herself, regal and self-confident. The little noises she made when he caressed her. The taste of her mouth. Her unexpected laughter, her inquisitive mind, the special smile she gave him when he'd pleased her.

How he loved making her smile. He was ready to please her any way he could. All night long.

Kay shifted on the couch. She lounged against the armrest, swung her legs across the cushions until she was sprawled out provocatively. Her teeth sank into her bottom lip as he sauntered nearer.

He grinned wickedly, and his fingers went to the buttons of his flannel shirt. Kay sat up straighter, her eyes riveted to his fingers, watching as, one by one, he undid the buttons and stripped off the shirt.

Next came his sweater, then his T-shirt and at last his thermal top. When his chest was completely exposed, Kay's mouth dropped open and she rubbed the back of a hand across her forehead.

He winked, stepped closer. He was almost to the couch, his clothes strewn in a haphazard path behind him. Looking at her made him hungry all over again. And this time not for bread and wine, but for a taste of that sumptuous skin. He licked his own lips.

Yum.

Kay's gaze traveled from his chest to his mouth and remained transfixed on his lips. Enjoying himself immensely, Quinn rounded the couch and slowly lowered himself beside her, his blue-jeaned thigh brushing against her stiletto heel. He watched the pulse at the base of her throat jump, felt a corresponding surge of blood through his body.

Tonight his goddess was going to come during intercourse. Tonight she'd be screaming his name in reverence.

He leaned across her legs, her knees hitting him midchest, the crush of fur against his nipples. He idly toyed with a strand of her hair, then oh-so-gradually traced his finger down her right ear.

She shivered.

Violently.

And closed her eyes. He watched the column of her throat work as she swallowed.

"What," he whispered, "are you wearing beneath that coat?"

"Why don't you see for yourself?" she invited.

His finger tracked a path from her ear to her cheek to her chin, then slid down that hot, hot throat to her collarbone, where he parted the fur coat, splayed his hand beneath it and found nothing but bare skin.

And he'd thought he had a raging hard-on before. That erection felt puny compared to this shaft of steel rising from him now. If he didn't watch himself, this whole endeavor would be over in a matter of seconds.

He pushed his hand farther down, relishing in the feel of her silken flesh. He peeled back the coat, watched his man-size fingers glide over her smooth breasts. He inhaled as deeply as she when his thumb rasped over her nipple and he cupped the full globe, bent his head to kiss it, then looked up to meet her gaze.

Her eyes were glazed, her breathing thready.

"You look more delicious than red-velvet cake,

sweetheart. I could eat you right up with my hands tied behind my back."

"Oh, Quinn, you say the nicest things to me."

"I mean what I say, Kay. I'm not a man who tap-dances around the truth."

"And I love that about you."

"Honesty can make a guy unpopular at times."

"Not with me. I find it refreshing."

"I find you refreshing." His eyes gobbled her up. Strangely his heart felt too big for his chest.

"Nobody's ever appreciated me the way you do."

"By nobody, I'm assuming you mean that sorry son-of-a-dog you used to date."

Kay nodded.

"Forget about him," Quinn growled. "He was a jerk and he didn't have any idea what a treasure he threw away. I appreciate you, darling. And don't you ever forget it."

"Don't," she said, her voice oddly choked, "be so nice to me."

"Why not?"

"Because if you're nice, I'll want to stay, and we both know I don't belong here."

He said nothing to that because he wanted to beg her to stay. But Bear Creek had nothing to offer a blue-blood magazine reporter from the most cosmopolitan city in the world. He could offer her no more than this. If Alaska hadn't been enough for Meggie, who'd been born and raised here, how could it be enough for Kay? Most women, his sister included, considered Alaska a lonely place. He had no right even to ask her to stay. None at all. He was going to take what he could have and give her a night to cherish always.

"Let's not talk anymore," she said huskily. "Let's just

make love. Send me into orbit, big guy. I want to know what it feels like to frolic with the aurora borealis."

Quinn wrapped his arms around her narrow waist, then leaned back against the opposite end of the couch and pulled her on top of him, until they were touching head to toe, her bare breasts flattened against his bare chest, the warm apex of her womanhood flush against the zipper of his jeans.

She let out a low, feral sound that inflamed him beyond measure. She nuzzled her face in his neck and whispered his name.

His hands skimmed down her luscious body, then back up again beneath the plush material of the fur coat. He kissed her throat, then licked and lightly sucked because he couldn't get enough of the taste of her.

He rubbed her calves through the silky material of her stockings, and it was almost his undoing. He fondled the backs of her knees, then toyed with the garter at her thigh. His hands roamed higher, kneading the tight muscles of her compact tush until he was hot as a blowtorch and hard as the arctic tundra.

How was he going to last long enough to give her the pleasure she needed? The top of his head was going to blow off if he didn't get some relief soon.

Kay writhed above him. "Quinn, you make me so wild. I never knew I could lose control the way I do with you."

"Wild women wanted," he murmured, repeating the tag line of his ad copy. He slid his fingers down between her thighs, found her wet and hot. "Are you wild for me, Kay?"

"Wild, savage, frantic."

"That's good. 'Cause I'm going to have to make love to you now, darling, or go insane."

HE WAS BEYOND handsome to her. Beyond strength and size and manliness. He was clean and raw and unspoiled. He was pure man and pure animal. He and his instincts, his ancestry, blended together against all the edicts of the polite society from whence she came, and Kay loved him for that.

His mouth claimed hers. Roughly, sweetly. He tasted of heat and wine and soul. He smelled of Sitka spruce, wood smoke and lemony soap.

The life she'd always lived to satisfy the needs of her civilized culture was erased, as he framed her face with both hands and stared deeply into her eyes.

The pressure in her very center that had been building night after night was coiled tight, waiting to burst forth again in sweet release.

"Straddle me," he whispered, gently pulling his lips from hers. "I want you to be in control. You need it this way."

She arranged her thighs on either side of him. She felt the hard bulge of his erection throb against his pants, against her bottom. Her hands fumbled frantically with his belt, unbuckling it and jerking it through the loops with a slithering swish. She grabbed for the metal button, but was trembling so hard she couldn't free it from the buttonhole.

"Let me."

She shifted, rising on her knees and leaning her right side into the back of the couch. He raised his hips, undid the button, tugged down the zipper and shucked both his pants and underwear at the same time, shimmying them past his hips.

Kay took it from there. Grabbing the denim and his long johns, she pulled the garments off his legs and tossed them aside. Panting, she returned her attention to him, and her eyes widened as she surveyed the long, hard length of him, getting her first really good look at his impressive package.

When she'd dubbed him Paul Bunyon that first day on the plane, she hadn't been far off the mark.

She stared, openmouthed. "You're incredible."

"You're not so bad yourself, sweetheart."

"I've got to have some of that." She swung her legs over his torso again, her body clenching in anticipation of riding his erection into oblivion.

"Wait," he said in a strangled voice, and struggled to sit up.

"What?" She stared. Dazed, glazed, starving beyond measure.

"I don't have a condom," he croaked. "They're back at my place."

Her face broke into a smile as she slipped her hand into her pocket and produced a small foil packet. "Let me deal with this one, fireman."

Then with the inexpert fumbling of a woman who'd researched and written about such tricks but never tried them herself, Kay scooted down until she was sitting on his knees. She placed the condom in her mouth, leaned forward and, after a few failed attempts, successfully rolled it over his shaft.

Quinn groaned and shuddered so hard she thought he was going to come right then and there. "Give me a minute, sweetheart."

She sat up, watched his face as he fought for control.

"Okay." He held out his hands to her. "Come back up here."

With the fur coat slapping seductively against her naked behind, she straddled him once more, facing forward. Remembering all those sexy tomes she'd read,

Kay curled her hand around his shaft and slid him into the length of her.

She spread her hot wetness across the head of him, then lowered herself, impaled herself just half an inch, no more, then pulled up again. She rubbed her yearning cleft all over his swollen end, then let him slide a little deeper. She pulled away again.

And repeated the steps several times until, desperately, he grabbed her around the waist and yanked her down hard until her tight, wet, warmth engulfed his flaming erection.

Simultaneously they hissed in their breaths as they were fully joined for the first time.

Quinn was rigid as a slab of marble beneath her, his hands spanning her waist, his face twisted in a grimace of pure pleasure. He penetrated her, filled her up, filled the emptiness that had been inside her for so many years. Filled her beyond her knowledge of herself. She had never been so physically possessed.

Peals of pleasure unfolded and sang through her blood. She moved with him as if she'd been doing it all her life. Moved as graceful as horse and rider. Up and down. Agonizingly slowly at first, getting her bearings, adjusting to the thickness of him. She stretched out on top of him, her legs over his, her face cradled against his neck. She rocked her hips, pushing lower and lower until her cleft pressed directly against the base of his shaft.

"That's it, sweetheart, that's it," he encouraged. "Take charge. It's your turn to be in the driver's seat."

She reveled in her ability to do this for him, and she gave a cry of joy at the mystery of her woman's magic, which allowed her to accommodate his maleness. She sat up, squatted over him, feet planted precariously in the yielding couch cushions just outside his thighs, hands on his chest for balance.

In an instant she was flying. Riding up to the tingling tip of him, then pounding back down. Every smack of her bottom against his hips produced in him the most erotic groans she'd ever heard.

He was close to jettisoning off the edge of reason. She heard it in his voice. Not yet. Not yet.

She stopped, then turned carefully, keeping him embedded inside her as she moved. She leaned her back against his chest, begged him to reach around and caress her breasts. She pulled her legs together on top of him and squeezed, the muscles of her thighs and buttocks effectively became a velvet vise around his manhood.

"Kay," came his muffled, garbled cry, and she felt an awesome sense of power. "I'm about to come."

"Hold on. There's more."

She knelt over his hips and leaned forward. She knew for him this was an incredibly erotic position. He had a spectacular view of her bouncing bottom. He could actually watch himself slip in and out of her.

Instinct urged her to quicken the pace, and soon she was thumping him so hard the couch vibrated. Soon, it seemed, the whole room was vibrating, singing with heat and energy and the dark pulsating power that emanated from the frenzied meeting of their bodies. Kay worried crazily that the small room couldn't hold the blizzard force of their grappling union.

"Unforgettable," Nat King Cole sang for the umpteenth time.

Kay felt both exalted and afraid. Her body was a glorious temple and he, Quinn, exalted her.

And that's when she flew apart.

A tingly, heated buzz that started inside the deepest, wettest part of her and rushed forth to encompass every nerve ending, every cell.

She came. Hard.

It was explosive. The twisted emotions of a lifetime came pouring out of her. The frustration, the shame, the avoidance of intimacy all evaporated.

She was laughing, she was crying. Tears streaked her face, giggles shook her body. She'd done it! She'd had an orgasm during intercourse! She felt like the queen of the world. And Quinn was her king.

I'm not frigid, Lloyd. I'm not. You were wrong. So damned wrong about me.

She gasped, slid off him, turned around and collapsed against his chest. She'd always hoped it could be like this. Hoped and wished and prayed.

He wrapped his arms tightly around her, tenderly kissed her forehead, then brushed his fingers through her sweaty hair. "There, there, sweetheart. You did good."

"Thank you," she whispered, tears still choking her voice. "Thank you, thank you, thank you."

CHAPTER FOURTEEN

QUINN FELT PROUDER than he had the day he had scored a hat trick to beat the Ketchikan Freeze in intramural hockey play-offs. He had done it. He had helped Kay achieve the orgasms she so deeply deserved, and he had still managed to hang on to his control. He hadn't come, and he wasn't through with her yet.

But for the moment, he lay basking in his accomplishment, her head resting against his chest, his fingers entwined in her hair, her scent all around him, her sweet taste in his mouth. He lay listening to "Unforgettable" play on and on, past the time when the station should have signed off the air. But he wasn't about to get up and break this wondrous spell.

She'd taught him so much in a short period of time. How to be patient and tender and understanding. Unwittingly she'd shown him how to be a good husband, skills he would need when he found his life's mate. By teaching Kay about her own body, he'd learned serious self-control. He'd also learned to put her needs ahead of his own. He felt grateful for these lessons and forever indebted to her.

She was an extraordinary woman.

As he lay watching her breathe, he began to kiss her. She roused and met his gaze with a lusty gleam of her own.

"More?" she asked.

"Don't you know it?"

She purred deep in her throat. "Come here my burly bear of a man."

He treated her to more foreplay, then when she was once again fully aroused, he moved her around and entered her from behind, his belly against her back, one hand kneading her breasts and the other steadying her pelvis.

Kay flung back her hair and cried encouragement. Her frenzy excited him. Harder, faster he moved, driving deeper into her willing body.

When she said, "I can't bear any more, Quinn. I'm going to shatter into a million pieces," he knew the time had come. A second climax was upon her. He slipped his hand from her breasts to her protruding nub and rubbed with a gentle, ceaseless caress until he felt the beginning of her contractions.

"I'm coming, Quinn!" she cried.

He groaned.

Nothing had ever sounded so beautiful. Nothing had ever galvanized him as much as those words. Her cries pushed him over the edge, and he let his body's streaming heat launch him into oblivion.

Afterward they lay spent and content, suffused with well-being. They slept briefly. When they awoke, they talked of the sensations of their bodies, their physical desire for each other. Both avoided speaking of something deeper, of the emotions they were experiencing but afraid to express.

They reinvented kisses, warmed by the rhythmic blending of their breaths. No one had ever kissed like her. Kay's mouth traversed erotic areas he never knew he possessed—the nape of his neck, a sweet section of skin on the tender side of his upper arm, the back of his ear. He returned the favor, licking and nibbling in unusual spots.

They murmured to each other, lips muffled against breasts, throats, bellies. Neither of them spoke of the future or the past. Nothing existed but now.

They held each other, cuddled and spooned. They pulled the fur coat over their naked bodies and reveled in their new discoveries. Both were happier than they had ever been. Or so it seemed to Quinn.

SOMETIME AROUND FOUR in the morning, a steady pounding on the back door roused Kay from deep slumber.

"Hey," she whispered, poking Quinn gently in the ribs. "Someone's outside."

"Quinn," a woman called. "Are you in there? Is everything okay?"

Quinn grunted and sat up, blinking and yawning. His disheveled hair stood in spikes all over his head. "I feel like I've been trampled by Kong."

"There's some woman outside, knocking on the door," Kay said.

"Tell her to go away." He grinned. "I've got more woman than I can handle right here."

She pinched him lightly on the arm. "Don't get cute."

"Hey!" He rubbed the spot where she'd pinched, pretending it hurt. "You're vicious."

"Quinn!" the woman at the back door demanded. "Open up this minute or I'm gonna get J.C. to knock down this door."

"J.C.?" Kay clutched the fur coat to her bare breasts.

"Sheriff's deputy from over in Haines. But don't worry. Even though it's only five minutes by plane from here to Haines, it's eight hours by road. She's just making idle threats.

"Hang on, Meggie," Quinn called, searching the floor for his clothes. "I'll be right there."

He dressed, then pulled open the door, Meggie tumbled inside.

"My gosh, Quinn, what happened? Did you fall asleep or something?" Meggie shivered and stomped snow off her boots. "I just got back from taking Liam and Candy to the hospital. I drove by the station and saw your truck was still here and the Wagoneer, too. Then Mack called me and said that on his way home he had the radio tuned to KCRK and you were playing 'Unforgettable' over and over again. So I came here to see what gives."

"How's the baby?" Kay asked from her place on the couch.

"Oh," Meggie said, apparently noticing her for the first time. "You've got company." She wiggled her fingers in greeting. "Hi, Kay. Listen, I'm so sorry, I didn't mean to interrupt anything."

Grinning, Meggie started backing up.

"You didn't." Kay returned her smile. If her mother had taught her nothing else, it was how to make the best of awkward situations. "The baby?"

"Oh, they stopped Candy's contractions. Looks like Liam Junior's going to stay put until May, the way he's supposed to."

"That's great news," Kay said. "I'm glad to hear it."

"I'll just be going now." Raising a hand to her face to hide her expanding grin, Meggie turned and rushed out the door.

"Guess we surprised her," Quinn said. While she and Meggie had been talking, he had given Nat King Cole a rest and signed off the radio station.

"Guess so."

He held out a hand to her. "Come on, sweetheart, let's go home."

LATER, IN QUINN'S four-poster, king-size bed, Kay lay looking up at the ceiling and listening to the reliable sound of his steady breathing.

He was sleeping on his stomach, one arm thrown around her waist, one leg pressed against hers. She loved that he wanted to touch her. Loved it and feared it.

Because as his body heated hers, his kindness, his tenderness, his unselfishness melted her heart. How had she grown accustomed to him so quickly? How had she come to anticipate his touch, to listen for the sound of his voice, to long for the flavor of his unique taste?

And how would she adapt when this was all gone? How could she ever be satisfied with her lonely New York apartment now?

He'd worked hard to give her a most precious gift. He'd held his own orgasm at bay, pushed his own needs aside for her. She'd never known a man like that. In fact, she had secretly doubted such men existed outside the pages of a romance novel.

But here he was. The man who'd taught her so much about herself.

Oh, the things he'd taught her.

Kay smiled into the darkness. His lips had branded her in the most private of places, marking her as his own. And she'd not only let him, but begged him for more. He knew her body inside and out.

All she wanted to do was bask in the afterglow, revel in the glory of their lovemaking. But she was afraid of her escalating feelings for him. Worried that she might be falling in love.

You can't fall in love with him. It simply isn't prudent. He's from a different world. And besides, it's not really love. You're just infatuated. Grateful to him because he gave you the one thing that had eluded you for so long.

Sexual fulfillment.

No! her heart cried. It's not infatuation, it's something deeper, something more meaningful.

But her troubled mind, which for too long had been indoctrinated in staid thinking, wouldn't let her indulge such nonsense.

Okay, challenged her brain. *What if you are in love with him? There's no guarantee he loves you back.*

And even if he did love her back, she wasn't the kind of woman he needed. A man like Quinn needed a practical wilderness woman. A woman who could start her own fires and bake sourdough bread. A tough sort of woman who didn't turn blue in the cold and wasn't scared of a tame moose. He needed much more than a lover. He needed a companion and a friend. But most of all, he needed a woman who wasn't afraid of her feelings. A woman who could express her emotions and give herself to him wholly.

She could never be the kind of woman he needed. Never in a million years. If she'd learned anything from this adventure, she'd learned you have to be yourself. You can't pretend to be something you're not in order to please those around you.

She simply didn't have what it took to make it in Alaska. And the sooner she accepted that, the quicker she could start getting over him. Because deep in her heart, she knew that if she let herself, she could fall madly in love with him.

THEY AWOKE AROUND NOON on Thursday. They'd spent the past few days in bed, barely coming up for air, packing a lifetime of sexual memories in four short days. Good thing she'd already completed the research for her article. Quinn made blueberry pancakes, and then they bundled up and took a frosty walk through the forest, both of them revved into overdrive with excess energy from the long nights before.

In silence they tramped through woods muted with snow. Overhead a pair of bald eagles soared. They stopped for a few minutes and watched the regal creatures wing their way across the sky.

Quinn took her hand in his, helping her to step over fallen logs and frozen creekbeds. He marveled at how small and delicate her hand felt in his.

When they reached a clearing, she pulled away from him, took a deep breath and looked up at the gray, cloud-strewn sky, awash in only a modicum of pale yellow light. Her elegance and private nature never failed to stir him on an elemental level. She was so damned self-contained.

Somewhere along the way—maybe it was living in a big city with so much stimuli to block out, or maybe it came from putting on a game face for the high-society crowd she came from—she'd learned the art of withdrawing quietly into herself. Just another facet of her personality that drew him to her.

He admired the graceful way she moved and the way her mouth tipped up at the corners when she was pleased with him. He adored the way she blushed so easily at things he said or did, and the way she'd tilt her head in his direction when she was listening to him.

Face it, he told himself, making love to this woman had been a gigantic ego boost. He would never have believed a wilderness man from Bear Creek, Alaska, could attract the likes of Kay Freemont.

Somehow he'd managed to have done just that.

But soon she'd be leaving.

Leaving him alone with this empty space in his chest. Quinn didn't like that sensation. It made him feel helpless and vulnerable. And he hated feeling unprotected.

His emotions ran deep. So deep he was afraid to explore them. What if he actually spoke the word *love*?

You'd get hurt, stupid. That's what would happen.

Kay was rich, well-bred, classy. She would never move to Alaska, and the notion of him moving to New York was unfathomable. It was best not to speak of his feelings, to deny them even to himself. Despite the fact he'd spent the better part of the past two weeks trying to get her to express her feelings, he was not going to follow his own advice. His best bet was to simply live in the moment and stop thinking about the future. He'd always been good at that.

Sometime soon he'd find a wife, and he'd forget all about Kay Freemont.

Liar!

He would never forget her. Not if he lived to be a 108. She was unforgettable.

The tune played in his head and, damn, if an odd lump didn't rise in his throat.

"You look cold," he said to her. "Maybe we should go back."

"Okay," she said simply.

Then for no reason other than he wanted to nurture her, Quinn scooped her up in his arms and carried her back to the cabin. He took her upstairs to the bed and undressed her. They made love again, slow and leisurely.

Later, when he looked down into her face, he saw tears glistening in her eyes.

"What's wrong?" Sudden panic gripped him. "Did I hurt you?"

She gave him a watery smile. "Nothing," she whispered. "I'm just so happy."

He kissed the tears away, understanding immediately what she was feeling. Her tears tasted of her salty happiness. The happiness tinged with sorrow that this thing between them could never be more than it was right this moment.

He was the rebound guy. The tonic that gave her the strength to go forth and face the world again after being cheated on by her boyfriend. He'd served his purpose. He'd helped to heal her. That was enough.

Besides, tourist season was fast approaching, and he had a lot to do to get ready. They were adding new rafting trips to the itinerary for the cruise-ship excursions, and he had signed up to serve on the mountain-rescue squad once a week. And besides, he had a wife to find.

"I better go," she said. "I've got to finish my article. I checked my voice mail, and Judy's already left six panicked messages."

"Will I see you again before you leave Bear Creek?"

"I've got an early flight on Saturday morning, so Mack's flying me into Anchorage tomorrow night. I've booked a room in a motel near the airport."

"This is your last day, then." Amazing how they'd spent the past few days together without discussing the details of her departure. But they'd both been avoiding the inevitable, choosing not to speak of it until they absolutely had to.

"Yes."

"I'll come with you to Anchorage. We can share the room." He quirked a smile. "One last orgasm for the road."

THE LAST TIME they made love was bittersweet. Kay memorized everything. The way Quinn moved above her, the feel of his hands on her skin, the taste of him on her tongue. She imprinted the decor of the room, what they wore, the room-service meal they ate.

I'm making memories, she told herself. To sustain her through the hard days ahead. She had a lot to think about, a lot of soul-searching to do.

What did she want in her future? She knew one thing—she had to face Lloyd again, to confront him about how shabbily he'd treated her. Before she could move on, she needed that closure.

No one was going to believe the change in her.

But it was high time. And thanks to Quinn, she now had the courage to proceed with her life.

He sat holding hands with her in the terminal while the ramp workers de-iced the plane. Her heart lay heavy in her chest. A wave of feeling welled up in her, and she had to fight to keep from expressing it. He'd trained her too well. And there was so much she wanted to say, but the old Kay reminded her that silence sometimes was golden. She figured it was better to stay quiet and not tell him what she feared. Because what would he do with that information?

"I can't thank you enough," she said when boarding for her plane was announced. She stood up, and he rose to his feet beside her.

"Sweetheart, I didn't do anything but take the lid off the box." He smiled tenderly, ran a finger down her cheek. "You had it in you all along."

"Thank you for believing in me. No one else did."

"They didn't see in you what I saw."

"And what was that?" she asked breathlessly.

"Passion." His eyes met hers. "Fire beneath the ice. Heat simmering under that unruffled surface."

"I'm glad you're so perceptive."

"And I'm glad you picked me to help liberate you."

"If you're ever in Manhattan, please call me."

"And if you talk your boss into doing a follow-up story on the bachelors of Bear Creek, I'll pick you up at the airport."

"I'll put a bee in Judy's ear."

He took her hand. He started to say something, then hesitated.

Over the intercom, the gate agent announced last call for her flight.

"I gotta go," she whispered.

He pressed his forehead to hers, looked deeply into her eyes. "You take care, Kay, you hear?"

"Same to you, big man."

"Maybe I'll call you sometime."

"I'd like that."

She slung her carry-on bag over her shoulder and started for the jetway.

"Hey, Kay," he shouted as she reached the mouth of the jetway.

She turned, her heart hammering.

"Remember when I told you there's supposed to be a lot of sunspot activity this summer?"

"Yes."

"Mean's the aurora will be highly visible. Maybe as far away as New York. Plus, the aurora does strange things to radio signals. If you're lonesome some night, turn to KCRK. Maybe you'll hear a song that reminds you of our time together."

"I'll do that." Damn. She had to go before she burst into tears.

Luckily the flight attendant rescued her. "Please, ma'am, if you don't move along, we're going to have to shut the plane door without you."

"Bye." She waved gaily over her shoulder at Quinn, putting on her game face and pretending that her heart wasn't splitting in two.

THE ADVANCE COPY of the June issue of *Metropolitan* magazine arrived in his mailbox in mid-April with a short note from Kay stuck to the front cover.

"Hope you like how the ad and article turned out," she'd written in her elegant script. "My publisher was very pleased. See page 110."

That was it? His spirits plummeted. He flipped to page 110.

There was the advertisement and on the opposite page was Kay's article. "The Bachelors of Bear Creek Beckon; But Are You Gutsy Enough to Become a Wilderness Wife?"

He read slowly, cherishing every word, knowing Kay had written them. In glowing terms she exalted all the bachelors and their little town. Quinn's chest filled with emotion when she lauded his skills as both a hockey player and a volunteer fireman.

She wrote of the stark beauty of the land, the soul-stealing majesty of the mountains, the water, the wildlife. She described the northern lights. She wrote about the fierce independence of the Alaskans, their old-fashioned values, their love of the land.

Pride filled Quinn's heart. For his home, for Kay,

for his life in Alaska. Obviously she'd fallen in love with the place.

But then came the negatives. Cold and darkness. Moose freely roaming downtown streets. Wolves and bears lurking in the woods. Danger aplenty. No convenience stores. No movie theaters. No shopping centers. No restaurants. She wrote of Liam and Candy's baby scare, how the hospital was a long plane ride away. She wrote of the isolation. She wrote about the lonely sound of the wind whipping through the Sitka spruce on frozen winter nights.

And any hope Quinn had been holding out that she'd come back disappeared. Much as she might love Alaska, it was too different from anything she'd ever known. Asking her to move here would be like asking a salmon to sprout wings and fly, or asking an eagle to unhinge his feathers and dive into the depths of the ocean.

Their differences were what had attracted them to each other, but it was those differences that kept them apart. And the main reason he hadn't called her.

Many times over the course of the past six weeks, he would start to pick up the telephone. But on each occasion, his doubts held him back. He feared he wasn't good enough for her. He told himself she needed her space, needed time to get her life in order. Needed to see if what she felt for him was real or merely the result of him being the one to open her up to her own sexuality.

Hell, truth be told, he had no idea what she felt for him.

Besides, if he kept picking at the wound, his heart would never heal.

He closed the magazine. Closed his eyes. He could see her as plainly as if she was standing in front of him, cloaked in his grandmother's fur coat and nothing else.

She was the sexiest, smartest, most savvy woman he'd ever known, and he'd been lucky to have her in his life even for a short while.

But he couldn't stop thinking about her. Since her visit, he'd lost ten pounds, because without her, food had no taste. He couldn't sleep—the bed seemed too empty, so he threw himself into getting ready for the tourist season. He'd added a whole new wilderness adventure to his regular offerings. The business kept him occupied from six in the morning to very late at night. That was the point. To stay so busy he had no time to think of her.

Except it wasn't working.

Quinn couldn't comb her from the snarl of his thoughts. No one smelled as good as Kay. No one he knew spoke with her smooth, polished voice. No one had her sleek hairstyle, her dynamic way of walking.

She was special and he was never going to find anyone else like her, so he might as well stop trying and start concentrating on what he could have. Like the cute new guide he'd hired last week. Or any of the women who would undoubtedly show up when *Metropolitan* hit the newsstands in May.

Except he couldn't seem to work up the energy even to think about dating.

Good grief, he thought suddenly. Was this more than mere infatuation? Could he actually be in love with Kay Freemont?

CHAPTER FIFTEEN

QUINN.

How she missed him, Kay thought as she sat in her office staring at page 110 of the June issue, which had come out in May and had been on the stands for three weeks now. Her gaze riveted on one of the four bare-chested bachelors stretched out like movie idols.

With a heavy sigh she traced a finger over his one-dimensional image and recalled what it felt like to touch him in the flesh. All sinew and muscle. All hard edges and solid tissue.

She thought about his winsome smile, his self-confident stance, the tender way he gazed at her when he didn't think she was looking. She thought of his loving family, his good-hearted, down-to-earth friends.

Since coming home to her own family, she'd been doubly struck by how shallow and image-conscious they were. Lloyd had begged her to come back. Her father had demanded she reconsider his proposal. Her mother had clucked her tongue and told her she was no longer behaving in a manner becoming of a Freemont. And when she finally spoke her mind—letting loose with a stream of opinions she'd kept cloaked for twenty-seven years, opinions that differed vastly from Charles and Honoria's rigid rules of conduct—they'd told her they didn't want to see her again until she had come to her senses.

Kay had told them not to hold their breaths.

That's when Kay realized exactly how much she had changed.

She no longer cared that her father was angry or that her mother was upset. She didn't care if Lloyd got his nose out of joint or if her mother's friends were furiously whispering gossip behind their hands. She was ready to make her own way, lead her own life, unfettered by the expectations of others.

Those two weeks in Alaska had transformed her.

Two weeks in Quinn's arms enjoying orgasm after orgasm and learning how to take control of her life.

"Knock, knock," Judy called from the doorway before strolling into Kay's office, a manila envelope tucked under her arm. An ear-to-ear grin split her face.

"Hi." Kay managed a smile.

"Guess what?"

"I'm not in the mood for guessing games, Judy."

"Still pining over the Mighty Quinn?"

"No." But even to her own ears, the denial rang false.

"Liar. But cheer up, I've got fabulous news." Her boss perched on the edge of her desk.

"I'm listening."

"Between the Bear Creek bachelors, your article and the contest, sales of our June edition are already up sixteen percent."

"You're kidding!" Kay gaped.

"Nope. And as a result, Hal's not only giving you a tidy bonus, but he's prepared to offer you the position of head writer when Carol leaves next month." Judy clapped her hands.

"That's nice."

"Nice? Is that all you're going to say? Kay, this is an opportunity of a lifetime."

What Judy said was true. Kay had dreamed of being head writer ever since she graduated from Vassar and hired on at *Metropolitan*. But somehow it no longer seemed like such a big deal.

"You're going to take the position, aren't you?"

Kay shrugged. "I don't know."

Judy stared at her. "You've been acting downright weird ever since you got back from Alaska."

"I've changed the way I look at things."

"Yeah, you've taken several steps backward. You used to be so focused, so centered, so ambitious. What happened?"

What had happened indeed?

She'd learned a new way of being. She'd learned to listen for the cries of bald eagles soaring overhead. She'd learned to enjoy the sight of moose trotting down the main street. She'd learned to love a place where the northern night sky lit up in a dancing swath of colored lights.

Unmindful of Judy's presence, Kay reached out to caress the photograph she'd framed on her desk. The picture Meggie had taken of her with the four bachelors at the Scofields' party and mailed to her when she'd gotten them developed. They'd even exchanged a few emails since then, but Meggie only mentioned Quinn in passing, and Kay had been reluctant to come right out and ask direct questions about him.

In the photo Quinn was standing to her left, Jake to her right. Quinn's arm was draped over her shoulder, and he was gazing at her with a tender expression on his face.

"Oh, my God!" Judy exclaimed suddenly. "It's all so clear. Why didn't I see it before? You've been moping around here for weeks like a sick puppy. You're in love with the lumberjack."

Kay's head jerked up. "I'm not," she denied.

"Oh, yes, you are."

"Don't be ridiculous. Quinn and I were just…" What? Friends? No sir. Considering the sexual adventures they'd shared, they were so much more than that. Lovers? Well, not really. The word implied a long-term relationship. Two ships that passed in the night?

"Yes?" Judy arched an eyebrow, waited expectantly for her to continue.

"We had a good time together, but that's all it was."

"You sure about that? Your article was great. Full of emotion. You've never written anything so passionate," Judy enthused. "And you showed both sides of the coin. The sexy bachelors, that homey little town, the beauty of Alaska versus the serious negatives. Any woman that snags one of those guys can't say she wasn't forewarned."

Kay nodded.

"I was thinking, in case any of those bachelors does get married as a result of the article, maybe we could do a follow-up story. Would you like to go back?"

"I…I don't know." She would love to go back, but what if one of those bachelors was Quinn? Could she stand to see him with his new bride, his face shining with a happiness that had eluded them?

"Just think about it," Judy said. "In the meantime I brought these for you to look at. Thought you might enjoy picking the winning contest entry." She handed Kay the fat manila envelope.

"Thanks." Kay put the envelope in her top desk drawer. "Anything else?"

"No, that's all." Judy turned to go, but stopped when

she reached the door. "Kay, if you really are in love with this man, don't let him go without a fight."

SEVERAL HOURS LATER Kay carried the manila envelope in her briefcase as she walked swiftly down a side street in the misting rain. She'd been late leaving work after a powwow with Hal about the possibility of taking over Carol's job as head writer. She'd tried for a taxi, but getting a cab in rainy weather was like getting good Chinese takeout in Bear Creek.

She'd gone through the bulk of contest entries Judy had given her, and while several were well written, none had jumped out at her. She had a few more to read, so she was bringing the rest home with her. But she couldn't really concentrate on the contest. Her thoughts were on Quinn, and she allowed her usual mindfulness to slip. She didn't even notice that she was the only person on the block, and when she passed a Dumpster, she didn't even look behind it.

Big mistake.

A man grabbed her from the shadows and held a knife to her neck.

Kay was so startled she couldn't even scream. Her brain went numb.

"Give me your purse, lady," the man demanded. "And the briefcase."

This simply could not be happening to her again. Mugged for the third time in as many years!

Resigned, she handed him her purse. But the clasp on her briefcase hung on her purse strap. He snatched at her things while at the same time throwing her to the ground. The briefcase burst open, and the manila folder fell to the ground beside her. The man ran off into the night, leaving Kay alone in the wet darkness bleeding from scrapes on her palms and knees.

It was almost midnight by the time she arrived home from the police station.

She plunked the manila envelope wearily on her bed. Her hometown. The place of her birth suddenly seemed like an alien and hostile place. Outside the window she heard the wail of an ambulance.

If only she had someone she could talk to. Someone who understood. She thought of Quinn.

Call him.

But what would she say? How would she begin? She wandered over to the radio, turned it to 840 AM as she'd been doing almost every night since she'd returned from Alaska. Even with her high-power radio, she'd picked up KCRK only a couple of times, and neither time had Quinn been manning the control booth.

She got nothing but a few staticky crackles. Glumly she sat on the bed. The manila envelope had torn during the encounter with the mugger, and one of the remaining contest entries was poking out. Idly Kay reached for it.

I want to go Alaska because I'm very timid, and more than anything in the world I long to be brave. If Alaska can't save me, nothing can.

The heartfelt words reached out to Kay. The writer had touched something inside her. She, too, had gone to Alaska seeking salvation. And she'd found it. But in the end, she'd been too scared to act on her instincts. She hadn't trusted herself. Or her true feelings.

She glanced at the name on the entry form. Cammie Jo Lockhart from Austin, Texas.

"Well, Cammie Jo," Kay whispered. "Let's see if you can do better than I did. This is your chance to test your courage. You win the contest."

She closed her eyes and leaned back. Behind the static she heard a faint trickle of music. She cocked her head and strained to listen.

Paul Anka's "Having My Baby." She sat up, reached over and fiddled with the dial. The reception improved.

Kay's heart clutched at the sound of that voice she knew so well.

"I'll be standing in for Liam for the next couple of nights since Liam Junior got here. Hope you folks will bear with me. Since I'm at the controls and there's one hell of an aurora tonight, I'm going to be talking to a friend of mine, hoping she can hear me. Kay, baby, if you're out there, if you're listening, these next two are for you."

He played "New York, New York" and followed that with "Unforgettable."

She promptly burst into tears.

What on earth was she so scared of in Alaska? If she could live in Manhattan with the muggers and the pollution, why couldn't she make it in Alaska with a little darkness, a little cold weather, a few wild animals?

She missed that beautiful land. She missed Bear Creek. She missed the kind and welcoming townspeople.

And most of all, she missed Quinn.

What the hell was she doing in New York when everything she cared about was in Alaska?

THREE DAYS LATER Kay waited in line to board a plane bound for Anchorage. She was ready to begin her new life. She'd not only gone out on a limb, but sawn off the branch behind her. She'd sold off most of her belongings. And she'd quit her job at the magazine. Hal had been appalled at losing his best writer, but Judy had given her a thumbs-up and a ride out to JFK.

"Go get him, honey. He's a keeper," Judy had whispered in her ear as she gave her one last hug in the terminal before Kay passed through security.

The scary thing was, she hadn't spoken to Quinn. She was taking a huge chance, and she knew it. But if she'd learned anything from her first visit to Alaska, it was how to take a risk.

Thanks to Quinn.

Showing up unannounced had seemed like a terribly free-spirited, romantic, un-Kay-like thing to do. But now that everything was in motion, she started to panic.

Shifting the shoulder strap of her carry-on bag, she shuffled forward as the line moved. To distract herself from her anxiety, she studied the jetway neighboring her gate. A plane from Anchorage had just arrived and a gate agent moved to open the door. A steady stream of people began to disembark. From her peripheral vision, she caught sight of a tall, broad-shouldered man.

And did a double take.

Her heart thundered like a calving glacier.

Could it be him?

Nah.

Her line moved forward as her plane began to board. The big man in flannel and jeans was almost rounding the ticket counter. *Was* it him?

"Quinn!" she shouted, not caring that people stared. "Quinn!"

The man turned his head.

Gray eyes met hers. Recognition dawned. Then he stared in stunned disbelief.

"Kay?" A huge grin split his face.

He dropped his bag. She dropped hers.

She ducked under the roped-off area separating the departing passengers from their visitors.

He dodged a mother pushing a stroller.

In four, long-legged strides, he had her, catching her under the arms and swinging her high in the air as if she weighed no more than a toddler. Strong emotions surged through her—joy, excitement, wonderment.

And something else.

Love.

Quinn held her tightly to his chest. She could hear his heart pounding as heavily as her own.

Then he captured her mouth and kissed her.

Ah, the taste of him. How she'd missed his flavor!

"Isn't that sweet," someone in the crowd murmured.

"Makes me remember our courting days, Melinda," said someone else.

But it was all background noise to Kay, who only had eyes and ears for Quinn.

She kissed him hard and long. Kissed him in the airport terminal in front of dozens of openmouthed onlookers. She didn't care what anyone thought. She didn't care who she shocked or outraged. There was nothing wrong with expressing your love. And she refused to be ashamed of her physical urges any longer. He kissed her back until they were both gasping for air, and then he pulled away ever so slightly.

"What are you doing here?" she asked, at the same moment he said, "Where are you going?"

"I'm moving to Manhattan," he answered at the same moment she announced, "I'm moving to Bear Creek."

"What?" they cried in unison.

"Last boarding call for flight 1121 to Anchorage," intoned a voice over the loudspeaker.

Kay looked over her shoulder at the gate.

"You're not going now!" he exclaimed.

"No." She shook her head ruefully. "But everything I own is on its way to Alaska."

"And Meggie's staying in my cabin. Jesse's left her for an eighteen-year-old, and she's devastated. She's taken a leave of absence from her job, and she needed a place of her own to think things through."

"Oh," Kay said, genuinely sorry to hear about Meggie's trouble. "I feel so bad for her." As soon as she could, she'd give Meggie a call.

"It's been a long time coming." Quinn shook his head. "Jesse and Meggie were always too much alike to make a good couple."

"That's such a shame. Hadn't they been married a long time?"

"Six years. But let's not talk about Meggie's problems right now." He put his hand to Kay's back and ushered her toward a row of chairs. "What happened to make you decide to move to Alaska?"

They sat down. His hand curled over hers. He couldn't seem to let go of her. It was as if he feared that without his hands on her body, she'd disappear.

She told him then about everything that had happened. Her realization that her family were snobs and would never change. How she'd confronted them about their attitudes and behaviors toward those less fortunate. How her parents had withdrawn from her after she'd expressed herself. She told him about being offered the head-writer position and not wanting it. About getting mugged. About reading Cammie Jo Lockhart's winning contest entry. And about hearing him dedicate those songs to her on the radio.

"I got the distinct impression the universe was trying to tell me something."

"Sweetheart." He kissed her forehead.

"It was the mugging that made the biggest impression. I kept thinking that if something like that happened to me in Bear Creek—and what are the chances of that? A million to one?—the whole town would come to my rescue. Meggie would doctor my scrapes. You and Jake and Mack and Caleb would track him down. Even cantankerous old Gus would be there to lecture the guy when you captured him."

"You're right about that."

"I gave up my apartment. I quit my job. I wanted to go to Alaska. To come home. Quinn, Alaska has been in my blood and in my brain every since I left. I couldn't stop thinking about Bear Creek, and I couldn't stop thinking about you."

"Are you sure, Kay? You'd be giving up a lot. Success, social position, access to world-class shopping and cultural events. I can't offer you the kind of things your father can. But I can offer you respect and a sense of community, and most of all my love."

"Oh, Quinn." She looked into his eyes. "Yes, I'll be giving up a lot of *things*. But they're only things, after all. I'll be gaining my freedom and friendship, and most of all your love."

"You really feel that way?"

Tears glistening in her eyes, she nodded. "Can't you tell? But what about you? Look at the sacrifices you were willing to make for me. I can't believe you're moving to Manhattan. How were you planning to make a living?"

"Testing sporting equipment for Adventure Gear. I've already got a job."

"What about your mountain-guide business?"

"I hired someone to manage it for me."

"You'd be miserable in New York. This place would suffocate a wilderness man."

He cupped her chin in his hand. "No, it wouldn't. Not as long as I had you, sweetheart. It doesn't matter where we are as long as we're together. I decided I wasn't going to let my stubbornness get the best of me anymore. I have a problem with compromise. It's what came between me and my best friend Kyle. It's what came between me and Heather. After a lot of soul-searching, I realized I wasn't willing to give you up. This time I wasn't going to let pride and stubbornness keep me from the woman I love."

"You want to tell me more about that?"

"I gave you a hard time about not expressing your feelings, but when push came to shove, I couldn't tell you what was in my heart. I was worried I wasn't good enough for a classy lady like you and too damned proud to admit it. Then I remember that because of my stubborn pride, I lost my friendship with Kyle."

"Oh?"

"I got angry with Kyle when he let Lisa wrap him around her little finger. It hurt when he chose her over me and Bear Creek. Lisa was the best thing that ever happened to Kyle, and he was smart enough to see it. I called Kyle recently and we talked for a long time. He made me see that I was throwing away a lifetime of happiness with you by being too set in my ways to change. I love Bear Creek, Kay, but I love you even more."

"You mean it?" Emotion clogged her throat. She laced her fingers through his.

"I love the soft, little snoring sound you make when you sleep. I love that scar below your ear. I love the way your brain works, the way you figure through problems intelligently and methodically. I love that you understand my need for independence. I love the way your body feels curled against mine. I love the way you look at me. As if I'm something."

"You are something." She was trembling. Trembling with a deep yearning for this man. "I want you so badly I ache, but I'm still scared."

"Fair enough," he murmured, and pulled her onto his lap. "You know the drill by now. Talk to me, babe. Tell me what's on your mind and in your heart. Don't hide your feelings from me. Lay them on the table."

"I'm afraid of bears," she whispered.

He threw back his head and laughed. "Whew! You had me going. I thought you were afraid of loving me."

"No! Not that. Loving you is the best thing that's ever happened to me."

"Well, don't you worry about those bears. We'll bear-proof our garbage cans, and I'll stock the house with bear repellent. You can wear bear bells wherever you go. I promise, honey, you're far more likely to get mugged in New York City than mauled in Bear Creek. Besides, you've got me to protect you."

It felt good to know that was true. She didn't need him for protection, but she wanted him. She was brave enough to make it on her own, but why should she have to when she had a man like Quinn?

"I'm so hot for you I can taste it," she whispered, running a finger along his lips. "Now let's find a hotel. When you made love to me, big man, you started something big."

TWENTY MINUTES LATER they were ensconced in a hotel room near the airport. Quinn tipped the bellboy, closed the door and turned to Kay with his best George-Clooney-on-the-make imitation.

"Come here, you." He crooked a finger at her.

Kay ran to him.

He whisked off her clothes, and to his utter delight discovered she was wearing a garter belt and those black seamed stockings underneath her blue jeans.

"You kill me, woman, you honestly do," he said, pinning her to the bed.

"How so?"

He raked his gaze over her body. "Those stockings," he croaked. "Have you no idea the effect they have on a man?"

Kay could feel his body heat radiating through her bare skin. Teasingly she turned her head and nipped at his wrist.

"So take your clothes off," she said, "and let's make up for lost time."

"Hang on. There's something I've got to do first."

"What?" She sighed, too hungry for him to wait any longer.

He rolled off her and perched on the edge of the bed. Kay sat up and tucked her legs beneath her. He reached into the pocket of his mackinaw and withdrew a small, black, velvet box.

"Oh, my God!" Kay put her trembling hand to her mouth as Quinn cracked open the box with his thumb. A beautiful heart-shaped diamond ring in a platinum setting winked up at her.

"I'd intended on waiting. After I got to New York. Found a place. Romanced you some more. But I can't wait anymore. I put out an ad for a wild woman to become my wilderness wife. And from the moment I met you, even though I tried to deny it, I knew you were the one for me. Kay, you're beyond my wildest dreams. I never believed I was good enough for you, but you've never made me feel that way. You've made me feel like twice the man I was before."

"Oh, my God," she repeated, staring into the depths of his eyes.

"Will you marry me, Kay?"

"I can't…I mean, I will…" Her hand was shaking so badly she couldn't hold it still. Her stomach fluttered as if someone had let a million mad butterflies loose in it. "Oh, just let me show you."

She wrapped her arms around his neck and kissed him with all the passion she'd stored for just the right man to shower it upon. By taking a chance, by opening up and sharing her feelings, she found that intimacy she'd craved for so long.

"Is that a yes?" Quinn gasped a few minutes later.

"Yes."

He had to capture her hand at the wrist to hold it steady while he slipped the ring onto her finger. "Marry me in New York. Marry me today. Marry me now."

She shook her head. "No. Not today. I want to get married in Bear Creek. With all your family and friends. I'll marry you when we get home."

Home.

The band of emotion that had been getting tighter and tighter the closer he got to New York and Kay loosened, and his eyes stung with tears of hope and happiness.

"I love you, Kay, I always will. Now and forever. Here or in Bear Creek."

"And I love you." She touched his heart. "I can't wait to start steaming up those northern nights with you."

"I'm not waiting until we get back to Bear Creek for that."

In a flash Quinn shucked his clothes, lay down on the bed and pulled Kay on top of him.

"You know," she said as he planted kisses over her bare belly, "there are going to be a lot of disappointed women when they show up in Bear Creek and find there're only three eligible bachelors instead of four."

"But think of the article possibilities," he said, and made a frame with his hands. "I can see your title now—One Down, Three to Go. How I Landed the Wilderness Guide."

"Well, it definitely needs some tweaking, but you just might have something there, big guy."

"I'll show you what needs tweaking," he murmured, his tongue heading for a very sensitive place.

And the next thing Kay knew she was shooting into space with Quinn piloting the rocket, proving once and for all that she was indeed a very wild woman.

* * * * *

A THRILL
TO REMEMBER

CHAPTER ONE

W<small>HO WAS THAT</small> masked woman?

Spellbound, Caleb Greenleaf watched the auburn-haired lady in red strut through the front door of the Bear Creek, Alaska, community center and into the rowdy, masked costumed ball hosted by New York City's trendiest women's magazine, *Metropolitan.*

"Red, hot and rockin'" he muttered under his breath, narrowing his eyes and studying her more closely in the muted, atmospheric lighting.

Tall. Curvy in all the right places. Good legs.

Correction. Very, very good legs.

In fact, showcased so fetchingly in those four-inch, heartbreaker-red stilettos, they might even be the most stupendous pair of gams he'd ever clamped eyes upon.

The tight, scarlet bustier she wore snugged her luscious body like a second skin. The satiny material flared out provocatively over those generous curves before nipping in again at her narrow waist.

Below the bustier she had on crimson tap pants that barely covered her bodacious bottom. Then came vermilion fishnet stockings topped with a black lace garter that set his pulse charging like a stampeding bison. She was as vibrant as a Vegas showgirl and three times as sexy.

The term *brick house* permeated his brain.

He recognized the lingerie. Had seen similar attire at

Dolly's House, a brothel museum in Ketchikan, gracing the voluptuous wax figure of Alaska's most notorious gold-rush madam, Klondike Kate.

What a costume.

What a body.

What a woman!

Who was she?

Brazenly, Caleb ogled, not the least bit ashamed of himself, which wasn't like him at all. No hound dog, he. In fact, he was leaning against the wall in the insouciant slouch he'd carefully perfected for unwanted social occasions such as this.

An introvert by nature, he found his job as a naturalist for the state of Alaska suited his personality. Caleb spent a great deal of his time alone, in the outdoors, and he treasured his freedom. He avoided big parties, but since he was one of the guests of honor, he couldn't steer clear of this shindig. Even though townspeople, husband-hungry wannabe brides, curious tourists and an assortment of media types packed the community center, he was suddenly very glad he had come.

Just inside the foyer, she hesitated. He observed her make the conscious decision to proceed in spite of her fear. She squared her shoulders, pasted a smile on her luscious lips and sallied forth. That split second of vulnerability, followed by her resolute marshaling of courage, touched him in an oddly tender way, and he almost applauded.

In she stalked. *Boom-shaka-boom-shaka-boom.* Her breasts bounced jauntily.

Wowza!

Watching her bottom sway caused Caleb's body to tighten, his temperature to spike and his breathing to quicken. A seething longing gripped his gut. In conjunction, the wistful flavor of yearning burned on his tongue. He wanted her. Badly.

She aroused him with the stunning impact of blunt force trauma. No woman had aroused him quite like this since the object of his very horny teenage fantasies—Meggie Scofield.

He grinned crookedly at that memory. At one time he'd been so infatuated with his best friend's sister Caleb had thought he would never get her out of his head. And unfortunately, Meggie, who was two years older, had never seen him as anything more than a surrogate kid brother. It had taken both a stint in college and his stepbrother Jesse marrying Meggie for him to let go of his youthful obsession.

As the last of the four Bear Creek Bachelors who had advertised for wives in *Metropolitan* magazine, Caleb had just about surrendered all hope of finding someone who inflamed him in the same way Meggie once had. But then, out of the clear azure sky, in marched sexy Klondike Kate, piquing his interest and stirring long dormant passions.

Was she a tourist? He knew everyone in town. She certainly wasn't a local. Maybe she was with the magazine.

He couldn't stop staring at her. She sashayed over to the bar, ordered a glass of wine and started chatting up the bartender. Lucky bastard.

Look at me, Caleb willed her. *Forget that joker and look at me.*

As if compelled by his silent entreaty, she raised her head and glanced across the room.

Their gazes clashed like lightning striking. Hot. Intense. Compelling.

Heavy-duty.

Her eyes widened behind the showy red-feathered mask that hid the upper portion of her face. She moistened her lips with the tip of her pink tongue and Caleb just about came undone. In an instant, his overactive imagination transported him to a world of his own making.

She's splayed spread-eagle across his big, king-size bed in that daring damned underwear.

"Come here," she invites.

He's out of his clothes and beside her quicker than you can melt butter in a microwave.

She kisses him with a vital pressure, thrusting her honeyed tongue against his. Heat rushes to his groin, whetting his voracious appetite.

He unhooks her bustier, allows it to fall open and expose her full, creamy breasts. When he growls low in his throat, she closes her eyes and softly coos, "Help yourself."

Bending his head, he takes one budded pink nipple into his warm mouth. She hisses drawing in a breath. Desire shoots through him. She encourages him to continue by holding his head in place.

"Harder," she whimpers. "Don't be gentle."

Reaching down, she runs her hand over the length of his shaft, greedily signaling to him exactly what she needs. Her fingers tangle with the leather strings on his pants and she gives a series of short firm jerks that send a shower of sparks scorching through his groin.

He is beside himself with cravings for this marvelous creature. He could take her right here, right now, with no thoughts except to quench his undying thirst for her. But he doesn't. He wants her to be as desperate for him as he is for her.

Hungrily, he cups her breasts together, filling his

*palms, so he can easily drift from one to the other with
a quick flick of his tongue.*

*Her moans almost send him over the edge of rea-
son, plunging him headfirst into a world of sensation
of which he has only dreamed.*

Pure heaven.

*He feels himself grow stiffer, not even realizing such
hardness was possible. His brain is addled by the sweet
scent of her womanhood, the luxurious touch of her
hair, the heavenly taste of her skin, the hypnotic sound
of her voice.*

More. He had to have more.

"Hey, guy." A lithesome brunette dressed as Elvira,
Mistress of the Dark, sidled up to him and shattered
his reverie.

"Yes," he replied rather curtly. *Gee thanks, lady, for
interrupting the grandest fantasy I've had in years.*

"Ooh, the dark, brooding type. My favorite." She
circled her index finger around the rim of her champagne glass and batted her eyelashes at him.

Aggressive women had approached him many times
before. Especially after he'd made it rich and even more
especially after the June issue of *Metropolitan* had hit
the stands. All too well he recognized that flint-edged
expression in her eyes, and he could almost hear the
cha-ching sound of a cash register echoing in her head.

Gold digger, he diagnosed, right off the bat.

"So, who are you suppose to be?" Elvira purred.

"What?"

Her gaze roved over him. "Let me guess. Zorro?"

"No."

She snapped her fingers. "I know. You look like
Johnny Depp in that movie *Don Juan Demarco.* You're
supposed to be Don Juan, the infamous Latin lover."

"Uh-huh." Caleb nodded, barely glancing at the woman. He wished she'd go away and let him resume his fantasy.

"So say something sexy to me." She winked.

He frowned.

"Brooding and silent. Okay, then I'll say something sexy to you. I really love the way your leather pants fit, if you catch my drift."

Great. He was lusting after Klondike Kate but he'd gotten stuck with Miss Hot-for-Your-Wallet.

Undaunted by his lack of response, Elvira continued. "Somebody told me you're that millionaire bachelor. Is that true?"

"Sorry." He shook his head. "Don't have a penny to my name."

"Oh." Her eyes rounded in alarm as if she'd just stepped in a big pile of something unsavory with her expensive designer shoes.

And his friends claimed he was too cynical. Well, he had his reasons.

From the beginning of this whole advertising-for-wives venture, Caleb had been reluctant to join his friends. Not that he was afraid of commitment—he did yearn for the same intimacy and happiness the ad had generated for his three buddies, Quinn, Jake and Mack. But given his family's history of numerous weddings and divorces, stepfamilies merging and then dissolving, he was a bit leery of marrying for any reason other than true love.

You're paranoid, Greenleaf. Terrified of getting involved with a woman like your mother who ditches rich husbands for even richer ones. Or of winding up like your dad, down and out after two failed marriages.

Okay, all right. Perhaps he *was* sensitive on the subject. And maybe he did have trust issues when it came to women.

At age twenty-seven, he had amassed a small fortune by translating his love of the wilderness into a lucrative dot-com company that supplied indigenous flora and fauna to universities and laboratories. When he'd sold the company in the midst of the bull market and parlayed his hobby into a cool million, he'd discovered that other than impressing his hard-to-please, social-climbing mother, the money had been a hindrance rather than a boon.

He realized too late he shouldn't have worn the attention-grabbing Don Juan costume. He couldn't say why he'd chosen the guise of the infamous lothario. Perhaps because he was nothing like the gregarious Spanish lover and it was easier pretending to be something he wasn't. More than likely it was because the outfit had been fairly simple to put together.

But if he was honest with himself he would admit the Don Juan masquerade *did* elicit a certain confidence in him. Something about these leather pants, shiny black boots, dashing cape, dapper fake mustache and billowy white pirate's shirt stoked his confidence in a way he couldn't explain. The costume served as a conduit for the darker side of his personality and dared him to act upon impulses he normally would have suppressed.

Like the urge to glide across the room and introduce himself to Klondike Kate.

He had never been one for casual sex, although in college he'd indulged in a few short-term flings in an attempt to douse his desire for Meggie. But the woman in red made him so darned hot that he was ready and willing and open for just about anything.

Short-term, long-term. He didn't care. He just wanted to get to know her.

And, after much speculation, he was ready to call off the wife search and plunge headlong into a reckless affair in order to ease his sexual frustration.

Tonight he was suave Don Juan.

Anything was possible.

Go on. Do it.

He searched for his crimson goddess, but she had walked away. He was bereft for a moment, but then he caught a flash of red as she disappeared into the costumed throng gyrating on the dance floor in time to a jivey disco version of "Wild, Wild West."

He exhaled.

"Wild, Wild West" morphed into "Super Freak." Blood strummed in his temples and his heart pounded like a headhunter's drum. Panic scratched through him at the thought she might leave the party before he could speak to her.

Where had she gone?

"Will you excuse me?" he asked Elvira, and before she could reply, he pushed off from the wall and went to prowl through the crowd.

After several minutes of searching, he spied Klondike Kate sitting alone in a cloth-backed chair positioned in a dimly lit alcove just off the main hall.

He smiled to himself.

Gotcha.

One high-heeled shoe dangled from her hand and she was slowly massaging her foot. At the sight of those delicate toes, painted not stark scarlet as he might have suspected, but a beguilingly innocent cotton-candy pink, Caleb's heart lodged in his throat. She inclined her head, exposing the gentle sloping curve of her neck, and he had to bite down hard on the inside of his cheek to keep from moaning out loud. His gut constricted, his muscles loosened, his body warmed—an extreme reaction he recognized but could not seem to control. His unexplained nervousness scared him, smacking of a weakness he did not want to accept.

Don't let her get to you.

It had simply been too long since he'd had sex. That was why he was so susceptible to her allure. No other reason.

Yeah, right. If mere horniness was what motivated him, then why not take advantage of the dozens of women who'd thrown themselves at him all summer?

Nope, this was different, even if he couldn't say why.

Klondike Kate started to lean forward to slip her shoe back on, but stopped short. His gaze tracked her movements. He noticed one of the hooks on her bustier had snagged the chair's tweed cloth.

Squirming, she tried unsuccessfully to dislodge herself.

This is your chance to meet her, Greenleaf. Don Juan to the rescue.

Heart thudding, he hurried over, boldly leaned down, pressed his mouth to her ear and heard himself whisper in a debonair Spanish accent that sounded nothing like his natural voice, "Please, allow me. It would be my greatest honor to assist you."

DON JUAN'S MANLY HANDS rested on her bare back, his fingers finessing the hook of her bustier.

Meggie Scofield caught her breath, stunned that the drop-dead gorgeous man in the black leather mask who had been staring so blatantly at her ever since she strolled into the community center was touching her in a most intimate fashion and causing a frisson of heat to spread fanlike over her tender flesh.

No. No. This was much too soon. The guy was more than she had bargained for. She wasn't ready for this much masculine attention.

It had taken every ounce of courage she possessed—plus generous encouragement from her friends and a hefty quaff of chardonnay—to stroll into the party wearing this skimpy outfit. If she hadn't been so darned determined to shed her goody-goody image she wouldn't have made it this far.

But now she was paralyzed, intoxicated by the smoldering nearness of this stranger. He stood so close his spicy cologne filled her nostrils with the bracing combination of orange zest, piquant cinnamon and rich licorice. He smelled like a holiday feast.

Anticipation, charged and fiery, crackled between them. Adrenaline shot through her veins, prickled her sensitive skin, seeped beneath the auburn wig she wore over her coal-black tresses.

Who was he? And why did he seem so fascinated with plain ordinary Meggie Scofield, when a man like him could have any available woman in the room?

It's the costume, ninny.

Disquieting heat waves shimmered through her body as his fingers tripped down her spine. She shivered and shifted away from him.

"Hold still," he murmured in a low Spanish accent so erotically seductive it caused the fine hairs at the nape of her neck to lift. "I fear sudden movement will render your beautiful garment worthless."

"Sorry."

"No reason to apologize."

Her heart hammered restlessly. His leather-clad hip

was level with her shoulder. She dropped her gaze to his knee-length, shiny leather riding boots, and had to force herself not to shiver again.

For some reason she could not fathom, Meggie envisioned rubbing her fingers over the soft, fluid folds of his silky white shirt. The unexpected image sent goose bumps skittering up her arm, and the budded tips of her breasts stiffened against the lace of her bustier.

She gulped.

This whole moment felt weirdly surreal, as if she were moving in slow motion through a favorite recurring dream. When she was younger her secret fantasies had been chockful of ferociously naughty characters like Don Juan. Rock stars and motorcycle men. Pirates and Vikings and irascible black sheep. But those days were gone. She'd had her fill of rogues, and she was finished with living vicariously through risk-taking men.

She wanted her own adventures.

Except her body wasn't listening to her mind's vehement denial.

"There," he pronounced. "You are free."

Meggie leaped from the chair, almost careening into him in an urge to remove herself from his disconcerting proximity.

"Thank you," she murmured.

Unable to resist peeking, she shot him a sidelong glance. The intense blue eyes lurking behind his black leather mask rocked her, upsetting her equilibrium.

"You're most welcome."

He kept his voice low, and she wondered if the Spanish accent was real or if it was simply perfected for his Don Juan persona. She remembered then that she was supposed to be in character, too, and she should be speaking with the bawdy, teasing drawl of Klondike Kate. But bowled over by her body's unexpected response to this stranger, she couldn't force herself to speak above a whisper.

Whoever this guy might be in real life, in costume he was a dead ringer for the infamous Spaniard. Had he chosen his costume because he was indeed a masterful lover?

He caught her watching him, and Meggie's stomach fluttered. Deliberately, he raised a hand and slowly traced an index finger over his pencil-thin mustache in a surprisingly intimate gesture.

Her gaze darted from his eyes to his mouth and back again and her chest squeezed.

Look away! Look away!

But she could not.

His audacious gaze collided head-on with hers. Smoldering, fervent, deeply blue. He possessed the sort of eyes to make any woman tremble with sexual anticipation. Eyes that promised a thousand taboo pleasures.

He didn't smile; his expression remained one of inexplicable containment. His lips were full; his jawline solidly masculine.

Who was he?

There was something incredibly powerful about the secrecy of his masquerade. Was the man beneath the mask just as potentially explosive as he appeared?

His masculine aura of supreme self-confidence seduced her, while at the same time made her extremely skittish. Her heart galloped and she did, indeed, tremble. Meggie hated the torturous, achy sensation and the helpless vulnerability that such potent physical attraction implied.

"You are cold."

Say something flip and flirty. Something Klondike Kate would say, the voice in the back of her head urged.

But overwhelmed by this man and her body's response to him, she couldn't find her tongue.

He whipped off the black cape from around his neck and settled it over her shoulders. At the simple pressure of his hands, Meggie's heart popped.

"There." He stepped back. "Warmer?"

"Much," she croaked. The cloak smelled of him, all delicious spice, rugged leather and masculine male.

He was staring at her again, and everywhere his gaze roamed, her body burned.

Helplessly, she found herself imagining his fingers traversing the same ground his eyes had just traveled. Her breasts engorged with heated desire. She was very aware of him as a virile, potent man.

Disconcerted, she stared down at her feet and realized to her chagrin she was wearing only one shoe.

Good grief, why had she just now noticed that? What was the matter with her?

Why didn't he say something?

Why didn't she?

Meggie glanced around the room, desperate to distract herself from the intensity of his scrutiny. The community center was crowded with tourists and townspeople alike, everyone decked out for the lavish, end-of-summer masked costume ball. Excitement and mystery tinged the atmosphere as everyone tried to guess who was who.

The costume theme was "notorious characters from history," and guests wore a wide variety of attire, from Attila the Hun to Bonnie and Clyde.

Animated conversations buzzed around her. A cavalcade of delicious scents wafted from the buffet—onions, garlic, rosemary, freshly baked bread, a banquet for the senses. Liam Kilstrom, the disc jockey from KCRK—the local radio station her parents owned— spun a kicky, raucous song by Pink that had everyone on their feet. But Meggie couldn't seem to focus on anything except the perplexing pull of the exotic masked stranger and his unwavering stare.

She wished he would cut it out.

Now she could say she knew exactly how a goldfish felt.

Exposed.

He leaned over, picked up her orphaned shoe and indicated her bare foot with a nod. "May I?"

Numbly, Meggie plunked back down in the chair and extended her leg.

Don Juan sank to one knee, cupped her heel in his palm and, like Prince Charming with Cinderella, gently slipped the scarlet shoe onto her foot.

The warmth from his hand was too much. She felt as if she'd slipped into a vat of melted chocolate.

He stood. Unbidden, her gaze tracked a path down the length of him. His body was hard and lean and muscular. A honed body that spoke of time spent outdoors, not lingering behind some desk.

Impressive.

He was a provocative specimen, from his thick unruly black hair, which contrasted starkly with the pristine white of his collar, to his broad-shouldered torso that tapered down to the narrow waistband of those exquisite leather pants.

This was way too much excitement for one night. This evening was supposed to be her coming-out party. The first time she had attended a public function since her divorce six months earlier. The first time she'd done anything remotely social since taking a leave of absence from her job as a pediatric nurse in Seattle.

She'd returned to Bear Creek under the auspices of helping her mother while she recovered from ankle surgery. But in truth, Meggie had come back to the safety of her hometown in order to regroup and lick her wounds.

She refused to get trapped in a rebound situation. She wasn't about to repeat her past mistakes by falling headlong for some totally inappropriate guy.

You could just have a wild affair.

Impossible.

She felt her face heat at the very suggestion. Meggie Scofield was not a wild affair kinda gal. She was too sensible, too responsible and too darned cautious to leap without looking.

One thing was clear. Because she couldn't seem to trust her own emotions, she had to get away from this guy. Fast.

Grabbing her clutch purse, which had slipped into the crack behind the chair cushion, she jerked a thumb in the direction of the ladies' room.

In a tight whisper she stammered, "I'm gonna…I just gotta…go."

A smile curled his lips, as if her nervousness amused him. He looked as if he might say something else, but Meggie didn't wait to hear it. She darted from the chair and made a beeline for the bathroom, her heart pounding as it never had before.

CHAPTER TWO

SEVERAL MINUTES LATER her three best friends found her hiding out in the ladies' lounge, head tucked between her knees as she tried not to hyperventilate.

"Meggie! Are you okay?" Kay Freemont Scofield, Meggie's new sister-in-law, settled herself on the sofa next to her and draped an arm around her shoulder.

Woefully, Meggie raised her head. "Fine if you consider a five-alarm hot flash fine."

"Does it have anything to do with that hottie in the Don Juan costume we saw you talking to?" Classy, native New Yorker Kay looked stunning in her Mata Hari costume. Then again Kay, a Charlize Theron look-alike, would be stunning in a tow sack.

"Certainly not. I just got overheated in that crowded room."

"Don Juan looks like he could definitely steam up the sheets. Need an ice pack?" Sassy Sadie Stanhope, dressed as Marie Antoinette, wriggled her eyebrows and parked her fanny in front of the vanity mirror to freshen up her makeup.

"No," Meggie declared, reluctant to admit her helpless attraction. But then she ruined her nonchalant pose by asking, "Do you know who he is?"

"Nope." Kay shook her head. "But he is ador-able."

Adorable? That wasn't a label Meggie would have

chosen for that studly slab of manhood. Her heel still burned from his touch.

Reaching over, Cammie Jo Lockhart rubbed Don Juan's silk cloak between her fingers. "Cool cape. Did you two play superhero and damsel in distress?"

"Don't be silly, I did not play anything with that man. I was cold. He lent me his cape. End of story."

"Wait a minute. I thought you said you were over-heated."

"That was before."

"Before what?" Cammie Jo grinned.

"Before Mr. Hot-Bod draped his cape over her shoulders." Sadie measured off an inch with her thumb and forefinger. "Come on, Megs, are you sure you're not just the teeniest bit interested in him?"

Meggie shook her head. "Okay. So the man is sexy. Big deal. I'll tell you what the real problem is—this costume. I told you guys it was a big mistake. I look like some third-rate hooker. He probably thought I *was* a hooker."

She got up to lean over Sadie's head and peer at her reflection in the vanity mirror. Kay had helped her get ready for the party, and she'd spread enough makeup on Meggie's face to frost a cake.

But at the same time she was protesting, a quiet thrill of pleasure rippled through Meggie. She had managed to attract the attention of a very handsome man. Still, in this racy disguise she felt like an inexperienced driver behind the wheel of a souped-up muscle car.

So much flash. So much power.

So darned much potential for disaster, whispered her voice of reason.

The same confounded voice that had kept her tied to outmoded values for far too many years. The same stick-in-the-mud voice she had desperately tried to quell when she had allowed her friends to talk her into this outrageous costume.

"Don't be silly," Kay said matter-of-factly. "Klondike Kate is the perfect alter ego, and you look fabulous in that bustier."

Meggie twirled, the cape whirling about her waist as she peeked over her shoulder at the mirror. She sighed. "It makes my butt look big."

"Stop cutting yourself down," Kay said. "You've got a great figure."

"Not according to Jesse," she muttered blackly, narrowing her eyes at the reflection of her well-rounded bottom.

"Oh, screw Jesse."

"Not anymore, thank you very much. I'll leave that to the eighteen-year-old groupies," Meggie said in a tart tone that caused Sadie and Cammie Jo to lapse into gales of laughter.

"As well you should." Kay nodded.

Jesse's leaving hadn't hurt nearly as much as his cruel parting shot. He had told her point-blank she was a lousy lay and that's why he had been forced to stray from their marriage bed.

"Face it, Meggie. You're a dud in the sack," he had said, lashing out at her. "Sock puppets are more fun than you."

Meggie winced at the memory. His words hurt because they were true. She wasn't very adventuresome when it came to sex, and she'd always preferred snuggling to the actual act. Not that her ex had been much of a cuddler.

Kay, Sadie and Cammie Jo had rallied around, just as they were now, helping her through the rough spots with too much chocolate and lots of laughter. Most surprisingly, and most comforting of all, however, was the support she'd gotten from Jesse's stepbrother, Caleb.

Caleb was such a sweet guy, concerned that she might be humiliated or worried that the rest of the family thought ill of her. He had come to see her at her parents' house right after he'd found out about the divorce, just to assure her that everyone understood and sympathized with her.

"You've got to stop judging yourself on what other people think," Sadie advised, "and find your authentic self."

"Thank you, Dr. Phil."

"Sadie's right. You are much too good for Jesse's sorry ass." Kay picked up on Meggie's sadness.

In a moment of weakness, she had confessed to Kay the whole sordid details of their breakup, which included finding black thong panties that definitely weren't hers dangling from the kitchen ceiling fan.

"You shouldn't let him squash your self-esteem. If I can come out of my shell, so can you," Cammie Jo said. After meeting her husband-to-be, bush pilot Mack McCaulley, she had recently been through a startling transformation of her own.

"Cammie Jo makes an excellent point." Sadie nodded. "You need to reclaim your womanhood. Declare your independence. Redefine your sexuality. It's way past time you started to live a little."

Live a little.

Just the mention of those three short words caused Meggie's heart to flutter with anticipation. She thought of Don Juan and her stomach did cartwheels. Did she have the guts to go back out there and start a conversation with him?

A conversation that might lead to...where?

An edginess nibbled at Meggie, challenging her to do something forbidden. She felt concurrently hot and cold and bizarrely excited.

"If you've got it, flaunt it," Kay said.

"I'm not much of a flaunter."

"It's time you started. You've spent too much of your life taking care of other people. Your mother's ankle has healed. You're going back home to Seattle tomorrow to begin your new life as a single woman. What better time to start taking care of numero uno than right this minute?"

Kay spoke words of wisdom, but Meggie felt uncomfortable admitting her vulnerability. She was a nurse. She was supposed to be the strong, reliable one. She blew off her shortcomings with a laugh, pretending a sharp sticker of emotional pain did not skitter low in her belly.

It wasn't so much sadness over Jesse's betrayal. Truth be told, she was relieved to be out of the unhappy union. Their marriage had died long before the divorce; she just hadn't had the gumption to bring it to its natural conclusion.

Rather, the tight coil of anxiety resulted from realizing she'd wasted so much time trying to be what Jesse had wanted her to be in order to hang on to something that wasn't right in the first place.

A nurturer by nature, she'd never put her own needs first. Meggie had spent her entire life looking after others in one way or another. As a kid, she had taken in every stray animal she had stumbled across, and she'd helped her mother care for her invalid grandmother. As an adult, her natural ease in providing moral, emotional and physical support had led to a career in nursing, which was a source of constant pride.

Unfortunately, her need to be needed had also led her into an unsatisfactory marriage. She'd fallen for Jesse because he was everything she was not. Lively, animated, adventuresome, freewheeling. He played in a hip-hop band, drove fast cars and was always surrounded by people.

She had mistakenly believed he could give her the courage she lacked, while at the same time convincing herself she could offer him stability and security. She'd been drawn to the fact that he'd needed her, but not long after their wedding, the problems surfaced.

All too clearly now, she could see her mistakes.

What she'd once perceived as Jesse's ability to take life nice and easy was in actuality irresponsibility. He was always on the road, leaving her at home to take care of everything—the bills, the house, the cars. She'd been as good as single for the past five years, but without the freedom to choose for herself what kind of life she really wanted.

"Remember," Kay said, uncannily reading her mind. "The best revenge is a life well lived. Come on, Meggie. Let your hair down. Don't be ashamed to explore."

"You're absolutely right." Sounded good, anyway.

"This is your chance. You've been stagnating and you need something to snap you out of the doldrums. Don't be nervous about spreading your wings. Now is the time to fly." Sadie threw in her two cents' worth.

Why not? Under the protection of her Klondike Kate guise, Meggie could flirt with Don Juan to her heart's content. No one in Bear Creek, other than her three friends, would ever know whose face lurked behind the red-feathered mask. She was anonymous.

Why that thought should thrill her so, she had no idea, but it did.

She would flirt with Don Juan and dance with him.

And?

Who knew? She might do something totally out of character for her, like make out with the guy in a darkened alcove.

Live a little.

Take a chance.

Carpe diem.

Just the idea of taking a walk on the wild side caused her throat to constrict and her palms to perspire.

"Go back out there and flirt with Don Juan," Kay insisted. "You've got nothing to lose."

"Yeah," Sadie agreed. "What's the worst that can happen? He has no idea who you really are. Play the game. Have fun. You deserve it."

"And just in case…" Kay opened her Gucci handbag and produced a roll of condoms.

"Kay!" Scandalized, Meggie slapped a hand over her mouth. She had never in her life had a one-night stand. Did she dare start now?

"Always be prepared." Kay grinned and slipped the condoms into Meggie's purse.

"I don't need those. I'm not going to be doing anything like that."

"You never know what might pop up." Kay winked. "Better safe than sorry."

Meggie nibbled her bottom lip. She was very open to suggestion right now—susceptible, vulnerable, fragile—and she knew it.

But that knowledge couldn't quell her long-ignored need to shake up her complacent world. She would take

Jesse's betrayal and use it as a stepping-stone to a whole new Meggie. Why not?

And here were her dear friends, supporting her, encouraging her, egging her on with their spunky you-go-girl attitude. They recognized that she needed a little masculine admiration to repair her tattered ego. It seemed they knew her better than she knew herself.

She wanted this, Meggie realized with a start. She was twenty-nine years old, newly divorced and fighting off a deep-seated dread that life was sprinting by her at a dead run. This might be her last chance to really explore her limits and relish her youth.

Question was, did she have the courage to go for the gusto? Was she brave enough to reach for what she wanted? To explore the secret sexual fantasies she'd never shared with anyone? A weird sense of panic scampered through her. Did she possess enough chutzpah to initiate something wickedly wonderful with Don Juan?

Or was she going to end up a lonely old spinster with a houseful of Siamese cats, pining sadly for what might have been?

Take a risk. Who knows what you'll discover about yourself? whispered an audacious voice in the back of her mind—the voice she'd spent a lifetime denying because it scared her so.

Go for it. You may never have a chance like this again.

"METROPOLITAN WOULD LIKE to thank the Bachelors of Bear Creek for taking out that wonderful advertisement. You guys single-handedly boosted the magazine's circulation by twenty percent." Kay Scofield stood on the stage at the back of the community center, microphone in hand, her husband, Quinn, by her side.

She smiled at Quinn with a shining love that made Caleb's gut hitch with jealousy. All the bachelors had found someone to love except him.

"And on a more personal note…" Kay stared deeply into her husband's eyes "…I want to thank you for making me the happiest woman in the world, Quinn. I'm honored to be your wife."

"Aww!" The crowd sighed in unison when Kay stood on tiptoes to kiss her husband, who was dressed, appropriately enough for his size, as Paul Bunyon.

"This party is also to celebrate the impending marriage of Sadie Stanhope and Jake Gerard." Kay scanned the audience. "Sadie and Jake, please take a bow."

Liam, the disc jockey, shone the spotlight on Jake and Sadie, who were swaying together in the middle of the dance floor. Jake waved his hand and Sadie blew kisses to the crowd.

Caleb shook his head and grinned to himself. Those two were a pair. He'd never thought fun-loving Jake would settle down, but Jake had met his match in Sadie.

"Wedding is December 16 at our B and B," Jake said. "Remember, you're all invited."

"And Cammie Jo Lockhart and Mack McCaulley," Kay continued, "are you out there?" She raised a hand to her forehead to scan the crowd.

Liam flashed the spotlight to the corner of the room, interrupting the two lovebirds in the throes of a deep kiss.

Someone whooped with delight. Cammie Jo blushed and ducked her head. Mack grinned like a kid caught with his hand in the cookie jar. The audience applauded.

In a very short time Bear Creek had changed considerably, and mostly for the better. Not only had Caleb's three best friends gotten hitched or engaged, but the population had grown from fifteen hundred to almost two thousand.

Some of the ladies that had arrived in response to the ad had fallen in love with Alaska and decided to stay, even though they hadn't found a husband. Some of the fellows from surrounding communities had moved in, hoping to catch the eye of one of those ladies. Bear Creek was growing and changing from a summer tourist resort into a real town. Part of Caleb liked the changes. Another part of him feared his hometown might one day lose its rustic appeal as an increase in population tamed the wilderness.

"The ad's success rate stands at seventy-five percent," Kay continued, once everyone had settled down. "That's pretty darned impressive, but the magazine would love a hundred percent success rate. There's only one bachelor left. Caleb, where are you?"

He took a step back, not interested in being thrust into the spotlight.

"Caleb?" Kay called out. "Come on up here."

That's when he realized no one knew he was dressed as Don Juan. Relief washed through him. All he had to do was keep quiet. He didn't want Klondike Kate to know he was the millionaire bachelor, which would seriously alter her perception of him. At least for tonight he wished to remain incognito.

"Caleb, where are you?" Kay coaxed.

Meggie cocked her head to one side and peered through the crowd, hoping to spy her ex-stepbrother-in-law. She hadn't seen much of Caleb this summer—he'd been too busy fending off love-starved ladies, while she'd been sequestered at home taking care of her mother.

But since she was catching the first plane out of

Anchorage tomorrow morning, this would be the last chance she'd have to say goodbye. She was very happy that her divorce from Jesse hadn't caused any hard feelings between them; Caleb was a good, stable, honest man. The kind of guy she should have married.

"Caleb?" Kay repeated for the third time, but he did not appear. "Anyone seen Caleb?"

Meggie wasn't surprised, although she felt disappointed. Caleb wasn't much of one for parties or crowds.

"Well, I guess all you single ladies are out of luck. Seems our most eligible bachelor has flown the coop," Kay said. "But on a positive note, the buffet is now open for business. Enjoy, everyone."

Meggie kept searching the crowd, but when her gaze landed on Don Juan, she forgot all about Caleb.

Don Juan was talking to a razor-thin woman in a black cat suit. Meggie immediately felt fat and dumpy in contrast. She shook off that feeling. She wasn't going to think negatively. So what if she was a size twelve and not a size two? Just because her ex had preferred rail-thin women, that didn't mean everyone did.

Don Juan turned slightly, and she could see his stunning profile made all the more intriguing by the camouflage of his mask. She stared at his full, ripe mouth.

What would he taste like?

She knew the answer deep within the most hidden parts of her. He would taste like sin. She pursed her lips and slowly released a pent-up sigh.

He angled his head, caught sight of her from his peripheral vision and smiled very, very slightly, as if he harbored a hundred sexy secrets. No one else in the building would have noticed the glance, the smile, so subtle was his execution.

But Meggie did.

Go on over and put on a show. Pretend to be Klon-dike Kate.

She wanted to, but she was afraid of so many things. Like making a mistake, or getting in too deep.

How deep could you sink, Meggie? You're leaving town tomorrow morning, never to see Don Juan again.

Not knowing exactly how to deal with her unexpected sexual desires, she sought sublimation. The buffet beckoned. She hurried over to the table, picked up a plate and started down the serving line.

With a cocktail fork, she leaned over to spear a moist, pink shrimp, but before she could retrieve her succulent prize, someone on the other side of the table got to it first.

"Hey," she protested, then raised her head and caught Don Juan's stare head-on.

He stood before her, the fat, slick shrimp impaled on his fork. Leaning forward, he dangled the seafood mere inches from her lips. Damn if he didn't possess a small, wicked smile tilting up one corner of his mouth.

Meggie's stomach did the hula and her knees loosened. She had the sudden urge to sit right down on the floor so she wouldn't topple over from his body heat.

"I will share with you, belladonna," he murmured with his captivating Spanish accent, rolling the word *belladonna* around in his mouth, savoring it as if it was the finest Belgian chocolate money could buy.

Slowly, Don Juan lowered the shrimp until it lightly brushed her bottom lip. Meggie flicked out her tongue to whisk away a drop of juice. Audibly, he sucked in his breath, his eyes never leaving her face.

Her heart careened into her rib cage, and she felt oddly enchanted. Determined not to let him know exactly how much he had affected her, Meggie shrugged and stepped back.

"On second thought I think I'll skip the shrimp," she said, affecting Klondike Kate's uncultured inflection.

"Why is that?" he whispered. "Are you afraid?"

"Afraid?" She avoided looking into his eyes again. "What's there to be afraid of?"

"Some say shrimp is an aphrodisiac."

"Old wives' tale," she pronounced, really getting into the gold-rush madam's brogue.

"So why not take a bite and see?"

He was flirting with her, no doubt about it. Meggie didn't know what to do. It had been a very long time since someone had flirted so openly with her. She wanted the attention and yet she didn't.

"No, thanks."

"Ahh," he said knowingly. "I understand."

In spite of her best intentions not to meet his eyes again, Meggie had to slip a quick glance his way to see what he was ahhing about. She was immediately sorry she had. Sympathy for her shone on his face.

Damn. She didn't need his pity. She didn't want anyone's pity, and she'd spent the past six months trying to convince everyone in Bear Creek of that fact. Now here was this masked stranger, reading her every emotion as if he truly knew her.

"You've been hurt by love."

She rolled her eyes. "Oh please. Anyone over the age of eighteen has been hurt by love."

"But you've been hurt recently and you're afraid to try again."

"Hush up," she insisted, but her pulse sprinted through her bloodstream.

How could he know this about her? Who was he?

Was he from her hometown? If so, then who was he? No local man had ever set her libido to whirling the way this guy did. Bear Creek was too small, everyone too much like family.

"He has made you doubt your desirability as a woman," Don Juan said. "He is a terrible bastard. Do not concern yourself with him."

Her chest suddenly felt tight and she had the strangest urge to laugh and cry all at the same time.

"Look at me," he insisted. "Look me in the eyes and tell me you're not in pain."

For pity's sake. With a sigh of exasperation, Meggie stared him squarely in the face.

And lost herself.

With that warm smile and lusty expression in his eyes, Don Juan made her feel womanly, wanted and appreciated. Cherished. It was a feeling she hadn't experienced in a very, very long time.

Entranced, she felt ensnared in a provocative reverie. A dreamy vagueness settled over her, wrapping her in a warm envelope of altered perception. She didn't know if it was the masks or the wine or Don Juan's solicitous smile, but she experienced a drowsy sense of peace.

Something about him seemed comfortingly familiar, as if she'd met him in another life. Except Meggie didn't believe in that stuff. Even though she couldn't exactly explain why, she felt safe in his presence.

Don Juan was the tonic she needed. The physical vehicle for her emotional healing. This magnetic man could be the cure for the psychic malaise that had dogged her for years.

In that instant, Meggie knew she was going to sleep with him.

MAGIC.

His costume was magic. It had to be. Caleb could think of no other explanation for his miraculous ease with the beautiful mystery woman. Wearing the mask and fake mustache was a liberating experience. He could be anyone. He could say and do anything.

Hell's bells, he felt as if he were channeling Don Juan himself.

He was breathing hard, and roughly, the shrimp still dangling from his outstretched fork as he waited for Klondike Kate's sweet, crimson lips to part and sheathe the tender morsel.

Their gazes locked. Who was she really?

She was breathing as hard as he, the gentle swell of her chest rising and falling in a mesmerizing rhythm. Holding him enthralled.

She reminded him vaguely of someone. But who? His mind probed the question but arrived at no answer.

Kate's green eyes were lively and intelligent, the top half of her face hidden by the red-feathered mask. She wielded her tongue like an instrument of torture, touching it lightly against her upper lip as if purposely trying to make him lose control.

The visual impact slugged him. Hard.

His blood flowed hot and viscous through his veins. The way she gazed at him, like a curious innocent intent on exploring a brave new world, clutched something deep inside him and refused to turn it loose.

In that brief endless moment, as they faced off across the buffet table, the wet, pink shrimp as the prize, Caleb memorized everything about her not swaddled by the mask. The way she smelled of fresh summer rain, making him ache to bury his face in the curve of her neck. The fine brown freckles that lightly decorated her upper

chest, exposed so engagingly by that red bustier. The ir-
regular pounding of her pulse at her jawline. The sweet
ruby bow of her lips.

And the completely gut-scorching realization that
beneath the satin and lace of her flimsy undergarment,
her nipples were standing at erect attention.

He almost groaned aloud.

"Excuse me," Genghis Kahn interrupted, leaning
across the table between them, tortilla chip in hand.
"Could I get at that crab dip?"

Flustered, Caleb moved aside at the same time Klondike Kate blushed prettily, smiled and turned away.

Damn. The moment was lost.

Or was it?

Caleb ate the shrimp himself, hurried around to her
side of the buffet table and boldly took her elbow. Instantly, his fingers tingled at the warmth of her soft
skin. He pressed his mouth next to her delicate ear and
murmured in a muffled growl, "What is your name?"

She lowered lashes so dark and long they brushed
against her mask with a whispery rasp. "Now, now,
that's not part of the game."

"And what is the game?" he asked, his voice thick
with feeling.

"Secrecy. Anonymity. Mystery. That's the fun."

"You're not going to tell me your name?"

"My name is Klondike Kate. Don Juan, I presume?"

He took the hand she offered him and pressed the
back of it to his lips, as if he'd performed the courtly
gesture a million times. He clicked his heels and bowed.

"At your service."

"I am flattered. The famous lothario gracing the
halls of my brothel. Perhaps, Señor Juan, we can teach
each other a few tricks."

Ah, but she was extraordinary. One minute blushing shyly, the next sassily playing at being a brothel madam in that whispery tone that obviously wasn't her real voice. Just like him, she was playing a part. Her words hung between them like a physical entity, their meaning sinking into his brain one vivid movie-reel image at a time.

She wanted to teach him a few tricks.

Holy macaroni!

He was going to combust right there on the spot. What a game. Suddenly, he knew he had to get her alone.

"Wrap up your plate," he said, barely remembering to keep up his Spanish accent. "Take it to go. We'll have a picnic in the forest."

"The forest?" Her eyes widened and for a moment he thought he'd panicked her and she was going to back out of their little masquerade.

"Twenty yards right outside this door, and you're in the Tongass National Forest."

"You don't say."

He waited. "Well?"

"I don't think I'm really in the mood for food," she murmured.

"No?"

"My appetite is of a different nature."

Caleb thought he was going to break out in a sweat right then and there. "Mine as well."

"You go on ahead." She cast a surreptitious glance around the room and settled her plate on an empty table. "And I will follow. One can never be too careful. There might be spies."

"Spies?" He knew this was just part of her charade,

but damn if he wasn't turned on by the thought of being observed. "Who is watching us?"

"Why, any number of your women, or my men." She winked. "We must keep our clandestine affair secret. No sense making our other lovers jealous."

Caleb gulped.

Potential scenarios tumbled through his head, each more stimulating than the next. He was cast iron hard, and the leather pants did nothing to arrest his arousal. All she had to do was glance down and she would know his every illicit thought.

"Go," she urged in an imperative whisper that charged his libido. "Hurry, before we are spotted. I will meet you in the forest. Wait for me."

She pressed her hand to his forearm, setting off monster ripples of sensation straight up his shoulder and into his chest, to his belly and beyond—a tautness, an electrical impulse, a dynamic combustion that made it difficult to string two words together.

"Don't stand me up," he growled.

"I won't. Now just go." She pushed him toward the front door.

Then, before he could respond, she turned and disappeared out the side exit adjacent to the stage.

Caleb had never done anything like this before— scheduled an amorous rendezvous with a woman he did not know and might never meet again. He was by nature a quiet, solitary man guided more by his brains than his body or his heart. But ever since putting on that Don Juan costume, he'd been transformed.

Tonight he was different.

And so was she.

Caleb sensed this was as much an erotic adventure

for the mysterious Klondike Kate as it was for him, and he was bound and determined to make it a night neither of them would ever forget.

CHAPTER THREE

WHAT IN THE HELL had she just done?

Had she gone completely mental? Could the stress of the past six months have caused her to take leave of her senses and chase after the first man who showed her some attention? So what if Don Juan was sexy and handsome as Hades, and apparently more than willing to indulge in flirtatious games? None of this explained her uncharacteristic behavior.

Her brain squawked, telling her how foolish she was to take such a chance, but a tiny voice in the back of her head whispered, "Seize the moment. For once in your life, Megan Marie Scofield, live a little."

Then again, maybe her real motivation was more of a compulsion than any sincere desire to take charge of her life. From the moment she'd spied him lounging so lawlessly against the wall, she'd felt...well, something special.

As she picked her way through the forest in the twilight, her condom-filled clutch purse tucked beneath her arm, Don Juan's cape flapping about her shoulders, her heart rate thudded faster and faster, headed straight for the danger zone. Still, she couldn't seem to make herself turn around and go back to the party.

She was like a songbird unaware it had been caged until one day the door was left open and the opportunity to fly presented itself. Should she take wing and explore the brave new world extending before her? Or stay safely hunched on her perch, watching life pass her by?

The answer wasn't difficult, even to her conflicted brain. Don Juan was simply too exciting, and too good-looking, the prospect of making love with him far too sweet to be denied.

Besides, when was the last time she had been so sexually aroused? Never? Ever? Could he actually teach her to let go of her hang-ups in bed? She owed it to herself to find out.

Her shoes bogged in the mossy carpet of undergrowth beneath the towering hemlocks and swaying Sitka spruces. She was glad she'd taken the time to change into the sensible footwear she kept stashed in the trunk of her car.

A blueberry bush, devoid now of its berry harvest, grazed her leg, startling her. The air was heavy with moisture and she heard nothing beyond the gurgling creek and the faint hmm of voices and music from the party she'd left behind.

Oh dear. Where was Don Juan? She had expected him to stay close to the perimeters of the forest, where she could find him easily.

"Come."

She heard the whisper, low and seductive. She wasn't certain from which direction it originated.

He was concealing himself from her, ratcheting the game up a notch.

Meggie bit down on her bottom lip, tasted the opulent flavor of her own lust. She was nervous, confused, curious and extremely turned on.

What was going to happen next?

"Don Juan?" She heard a faint rustling in the trees, then nothing more.

In the phantom of rapidly dwindling daylight, she walked through the forest, pushing back vegetation, stepping gingerly over tree roots, eager not to fall and sprain her ankle. A sprained ankle would definitely blow the moment.

And the last thing she wanted was a dose of reality. She wanted to escape, as she had of late in the pages of fantasy romance novels. What she longed for was to disappear in this dreamy netherworld. She could easily envisage unicorns and fairies, woodland sprites playing flutes and dancing around magic toadstools. She ached for a pretend world of virginal maidens, stalwart knights and deep, undying passion.

Her friends had regaled her with their own tales of acute throbbing desire. Of lust at first sight. Of being drawn helplessly into earthly pleasures beyond emotional control. She'd never really believed those stories, even though she had desperately wanted to. Hadn't known such intensity of physical feeling was possible.

Until now.

She stopped walking.

He'd been here. On this path. Right where she was standing. She could smell him. As individual as a fingerprint, his scent hung in her nostrils like a primal memory.

A faint fear, tinged with escalating anticipation, pinched her solar plexus in a dazzling heat that hastened her footsteps and sent her heart staggering headlong into a restless, thrashing rhythm.

Another step deeper into the gloaming. Another and then another.

Twigs crunched beneath her feet. A fingered fern

crept across her ankle. A bubble of fear caused her to jump, and then laugh at her own spooked state.

Nothing to be afraid of. She was in control of the situation. She wasn't little Red Riding Hood evading the Big, Bad Wolf. She could turn if she wished and go back to the party. Nothing was keeping her here except her own inquisitiveness and her escalating imagination.

Walking up a slight embankment, she glanced left and then right, saw only the tall, thin thrust of tree trunks and the full orange moon rising over the horizon.

Was it possible to breathe any faster and not faint from hyperventilation? Could her stomach possibly squeeze any tighter? Could her knees grow any weaker and not dissolve into noodle soup?

He was enticing her, this man. And she wanted him to capture her, no matter how sinfully foolish her subterranean desires.

Goose bumps pricked a warning, raising the hairs on her forearms and the nape of her neck.

He was near. She could feel him.

CALEB WAS IN his element. The forest. The wilderness. Home.

He inhaled her on the cool evening breeze. Sweet, ripe, glowing. Soap, perfume, saltiness. The luscious aroma stirred a pulsating pressure of impulsive hunger deep within his masculinity.

Like predator to prey her scent drew him. His mouth watered and every fiber of his being grew taut, every male sense alerted to the wondrous female encroaching on his territory.

Relentlessly, her womanly bouquet lured him. Silently her body entreated, *Come to me*. Pheromones. Nature's mating call. As surely as any hapless male moth enticed to a flame, she ensnared him with her spinning scent song.

He could not resist.

Through the copse of trees he caught a flash of crimson, a glimmer of her auburn hair, the sound of her teasing laugh.

"I see you," he crooned in his heavy Spanish accent.

"Come and get me," she dared, and darted from his sight.

He heard the sounds of her feet crashing through the woods. Grinning, he followed.

The hunt was on.

Every cell in his body strummed to life in a way he'd never experienced. Feverish heat punched through his system like a fist through a paper bag, tattering any shred of civilized behavior. A savage hunger dogged him, his feral passions mounting in shocking disregard for decorum.

He wanted her—in a way he'd never wanted another. Not even Meggie in his teenage years.

He moved with long, easy loping strides, knowing he could effortlessly outlast her.

This was his every naughty fantasy come true.

SHE'D CAUGHT A GLIMPSE of him back there. Silhouetted at the top of the embankment, with the fat full moon at his back, he'd been watching her with hooded eyes.

Consumed by both thrill and trepidation, she slipped away the minute she realized he had spotted her, too. She had issued a challenge that reverberated in the silent air.

Come and get me.

She pushed through the undergrowth and then realized with a start that she was lost. It had been a long time since she'd visited the Tongass, and she had no idea which direction Bear Creek lay.

Licking her lips, she furtively scanned the forest, every muscle in her body tense with anticipation. In the moonlight, she spotted a clearing just ahead of her.

She moved toward the opening, not knowing if she should go there, risk exposing herself to him and foiling the fun, or stay secluded and draw out their play. But she needed to get her bearings and discover her location.

Cautiously, she emerged and peeped through the trees to see a pond shimmering in the moon glow. Beside the pond squatted a small skaters' cabin, meticulously maintained by the forest rangers. As kids she and Quinn, Caleb, Jake and Mack had shared many happy memories there. Ice skating on the frozen pond, laughing, joking, teasing each other, and then slipping inside the cabin to warm up with hot chocolate and marshmallows toasted over a fire in the black potbellied stove.

Her heart gave a strange tug of nostalgia at the memory. As a young woman, she couldn't wait to leave Bear Creek for big-city lights. She'd thought she would never miss anything about living in the isolated wilds of Alaska. But seeing that little cabin again reminded her that Bear Creek could provide her with something special that Seattle never could—cherished childhood memories.

She heard the rustle of leaves and slipped back into the sheltering trees.

Don Juan was behind her. Coming quickly but quietly, as if he knew every step of the path.

Hide! a giddy, childish impulse urged her.

Trying her best not to giggle and give away the game too soon, Meggie looked for a good hiding place. Trees trunks loomed on either side of her, tall and imposing but narrow and thin.

She crawled behind a spruce, hoping that if she stood sideways and stayed as still as possible he wouldn't immediately spot her in the gloom. Pulling herself tall, she pressed flat against the trunk, closed her eyes tight, strained to hear, and waited.

Nothing. Except for the wind whispering faintly through the trees and her own blood roaring in her ears, there was only silence.

She held her breath.

Her heart lub-dubbed

Had he gone? Given up already?

Oh, no. Please don't let that be so.

She wanted to look, to move, to breathe, but hated to end the suspense. Not just yet.

Sweat popped out on her brow despite the chill.

An uneasy minute passed.

Still nothing.

Finally, unable to hold her breath any longer, she let out a soft whoosh of air and inhaled deeply.

She waited, breathing hard.

That's when his viselike arms clamped around her waist.

Meggie let out a shriek, the sound reverberating throughout the forest, and dropped her clutch purse. But he did not let her go. In fact, those ropy, muscled arms wrapped more tightly around her.

"You are mine now, slippery minx." His lyrical Spanish accent stroked her ears, transporting her deeper into the magical dream.

He was standing behind her, securely holding her bottom pressed flush against his groin. She could feel the heat and hardness of his throbbing erection through the inconsequential restriction of his leather pants. His hand came perilously close to her womanhood, cloaked so thinly by the satiny tap pants. Her flesh felt seared, achy, desperate.

She wanted to see his face. To read the expression of the eyes beneath that mask. As if intercepting her thoughts, he spun her around, clasping her wrists in his hands, and held her restrained.

"You make my blood race," he said.

God, she loved the way he'd been masterfully setting the tone from the moment he'd approached her at the buffet table. He seemed to know exactly what she needed to hear.

Two could play this game. Meggie swallowed hard, valiantly tilted her chin and met his gaze. "*You* make my body ache."

"And you bring me to my knees."

She saw sexual hunger in his eyes, yes, but tenderness as well. He caressed her with his gaze, as if he knew precisely where to touch and how to torment her with sweet, exquisite pleasure.

"You're feeding into my most taboo fantasies," she told him.

"I know."

"I want to feed yours as well. What are your most wicked desires, Don Juan?" Meggie thrilled to her own bravery. "How can I captivate you?"

He pulled her flush against his strong, solid chest and she inhaled the arousing scent of a man in his prime. They generated so much body heat, pressed together, that Meggie could almost feel the steam rising from their contact.

"Can't you guess? I like to play games."

Anonymity had all sorts of benefits, she decided,

nuzzling his neck. She was catching the early morning flight to Seattle. The whole population of Bear Creek was inside the community center. No one would ever know she had slipped into the forest with Don Juan. It was just their little secret.

"But we must make sure neither of us does anything to truly scare the other," he said. "Agreed? Nothing too freaky."

"So you're kinky, but not freaky."

"Exactly."

"No S and M."

"No."

"Bondage?"

"Not unless you want it."

Meggie licked her lips. "Maybe just a little."

He chuckled. "We need a word. Or a sign. In case things go too far."

"You're right."

"How about something simple, like 'enough'?"

"All right. Things get out of hand and if either one of us cries 'enough,' the other backs off."

"Agreed."

"Okay, the ground rules are set. What next?"

What next indeed?

His lips were so near, his warm wafting across her mouth.

She wanted to ask him what he was going to do next, but the words would not come. If her very life had been threatened she could not have spoken. She could do nothing but wait in suspended animation for the abracadabra magic that would break his spell.

And then he kissed her.

His lips were warm, soft and perfect. Damn, but the man could kiss. She moaned wantonly into his mouth.

Not in a thousand years could Meggie have predicted the earth-cracking impact of Don Juan's kiss or her body's out-of-control response to him.

The excitement of pretending to be an accomplished seductress, the scintillating ego boost from Don Juan's admiration, the titillating secrecy of their masks, the sexy hide and seek, the frank discussion of their sexual limits had dissolved into something much more primal than mere play-acting the very moment his lips brushed hers.

The friction of his kiss unraveled every firm lecture she'd given herself about protecting her heart and staying far away from bad boys. Because none of that mattered at this wondrous moment, when the baddest of bad boys was sweetly, tenderly cajoling her with the silky slide of his mouth across hers, taking time and care to draw her deeper, ever deeper into dangerous territory. Meggie had no defenses against his special brand of languid seduction and beguiling charm. And when he carefully eased her back against the trunk of the tall Sitka spruce and slanted her lips more firmly beneath his, she came utterly undone.

No way out. Absolutely none.

For support, she gripped his corded forearms, which were covered only by his thin shirtsleeves, and held on for dear life. Even though their masks rubbed together as they kissed, Meggie had no desire to remove the barricade and reveal herself.

She liked this experience—anonymous, provocative, daring.

This secrecy was what she craved. As Klondike Kate she was a bold, brash, seductive woman who knew lots of sexy tricks. As Meggie, she was an ordinary twenty-nine-year-old nurse who'd been dumped for a younger woman. She wanted to live this fantasy if only for a short while. Wanted to feel feminine and desirable again.

His eager tongue dipped inside to taste her, tormenting her with silken assaults that liquefied her knees and set her nerve endings tingling. Brazenly, she hunted for a more in-depth sampling of him. At the delicious flavor of man and shrimp and red wine, she shivered.

Ah, sweet lover, thy name is Don Juan.

She shouldn't have been so surprised to find he was a man who took his time and did a thorough job. He kissed her with a scrumptious sleepiness, as if he possessed all the time in the universe captured in the flat of his hand. He seemed intent on exploring every indulgence her mouth had to offer, as if he was memorizing every nuance of taste and texture.

And perhaps he was, for Meggie was doing the same, committing every flavor, every smell, every touch to memory. In the days ahead, whenever she felt lonely or dowdy or depressed, she would take out this moment like a treasured photograph and mentally review it over and over and over again.

He pressed his hips closer, making her all too aware of his burgeoning erection, pinning her hard against the tree trunk. The smell of tree and man combined into an earthy, sprucy scent that sent voluptuous flourishes of sensation coursing throughout her eager body.

With his thumb, he traced her jaw, and her skin caught fire. His wide chest was pressed firmly against hers. Beneath the bustier, her breasts swelled and her nipples tightened and ached. His masculine thigh insinuated itself between her trembling legs and she felt his penis, covered by that tight stretch of black leather, grow even harder against the curve of her hip. Heated desire uncoiled deep within her parts most feminine.

She had never kissed a man with a mustache, and the hair on his upper lip was soft and smooth. She'd expected it to be bristly and uncomfortable. Their masks chafed together in a maddening way and she found herself wanting to rip away their disguises, but she was too afraid of what she might find. Too afraid he would no longer want her once the secrecy had been dispelled.

When he took the kiss even deeper, Meggie responded with an enthusiasm that terrified her. Never had she experienced a passion this all-encompassing, spontaneous and fierce. She had never with such careless abandon wanted a man. Not even in her most untamed daydreams.

What was happening to her, the woman who until tonight had never really cared that much about sex? Nothing had ever prepared her for this kind of concentrated, consuming hunger and desperate, painful need. She was flummoxed, stunned by the intensity of what was happening. Without even realizing it, she'd been searching for something to make her feel alive again, and now, here it was. With one explosive kiss Don Juan tapped into her secret yearnings and made her crave more. So very much more.

What had he done?

While her love-famished body wanted to find out where this irresistible delight might lead, her rational brain reminded her that she wasn't the kind of woman who indulged in one-night stands. Neither a madam costume nor a single kiss, no matter how thrilling and mind-bendingly awesome, could change her into someone she wasn't.

Sensing the shift in her mood, Don Juan slowly

dragged his lips from hers. He was breathing heavily, his forceful blue eyes locked on her gaze, his mouth glistening wet from her moisture.

"You've stolen my control," he murmured hoarsely into her ear. "And, I fear, my heart as well."

This was part of the game, she reminded herself. He didn't really mean that she'd stolen his heart. Nor did she want him to mean those words. This was about animal attraction, pure and simple. She wasn't prepared for anything else.

To prove her point, she took his hand and lifted his index finger to her lips. In deliberate, measured increments, she slowly took his thick, round digit into the recesses of her mouth.

He groaned. Loudly.

The searing wet velvet of her tongue had him writhing. Oh, she was wickedly good. His cock bulged against his pants and he feared the seam was going to split right open. He couldn't stand this torture a minute longer.

She looked up at him. Caleb watched her irises grow dark as velvet emeralds and her pupils widen with stark, desperate desire. She wanted him. Savagely.

And best of all, she didn't know that he was the wealthy, unattached Bear Creek bachelor. She didn't want him for his money or what he could buy her.

A surge of fire sped through his veins. Her bare thigh brushed his leather-covered one and he heard her hitch in her throat.

Unable to let the moment pass without indulging himself in one of his milder fantasies, he raised his hand and gently glided his rough fingers along the outline of her chin, relishing the soft smoothness of her feminine jaw, wondering what her cheekbones looked like beneath that sexy red-feathered mask.

They were face-to-face and chest-to-chest. A shadowy expression of pent-up passion clouded her gray-green eyes.

He reached up to touch her hair, his fingers almost trembling from the tension that was building layer upon layer, but she blocked his hand with hers.

"No. Don't," she said.

"Why not?"

"It's a wig."

"What color is your real hair?" he asked, aching to dispose of the wig and plunge his fingers through her sleek locks.

"Let's not ruin the fantasy."

"All right."

He cradled her in his arms, all the while plumbing her ripe, rich mouth. She responded in kind, sending the flames of his libido higher and higher with each flick of her fiendish tongue. Her fingers traced enticing circles over his face and along the edge of his mask. He could feel the steady drubbing of her heart. He stared down into her eyes and felt himself falling, falling, falling.

Playfully, Klondike Kate bit his bottom lip and growled low in her throat, sending his control shattering into a million pieces.

"I need...." she whispered, and that was all she said. It was all she needed to say because he understood her perfectly.

"I know."

His arousal matched hers. Their intrepid game had generated a craving in him he feared might never be sated, and he knew without words that she felt the same way.

Her lips parted and her eyes remained transfixed on his as if she were mesmerized. Slowly, she lifted her hands and softly traced her fingertips along his mouth. Her feathered touch triggered a reaction in him so potent he was ready to explode. As the real Don Juan most assuredly would have, Caleb took advantage of the situation and surrendered to his basic male instincts.

He kissed her again.

Soft, slow and sweet. Gently, tenderly. He knew if he didn't approach this with care, his control would be shot.

Easy. Take it easy.

But what an almost impossible task it was not to slake their desire with rough, spontaneous pleasure.

"The skaters' cabin," she whispered.

"What?"

She nodded toward the clearing. "I saw a skaters' cabin near the pond. This time of year it's sure to be empty, and far more comfortable than the forest floor."

He stared at her, incredulous. "Are you saying what I think you're saying?"

Bending down, she retrieved her fallen purse, tucked it under her arm, then raised her head to meet his gaze.

"Take me," she said.

CHAPTER FOUR

HE SCOOPED HER into his arms, carried her through the forest and into the clearing.

It felt like a dream, a fantasy, a fairy-tale romance.

Without the happily ever after ending, of course. But that was okay. She didn't believe in happily ever after anymore. What she believed in now was living in the moment.

She wanted wild, mind-blowing sex and lots of it. She wanted to prove once and for all that she was not a lousy lay. She wanted to explore, experiment and enjoy. She wanted to reach for and achieve her maximum potential as a woman.

His boots clattered on the wooden steps to the cabin. Giggling, she reached out to open the door and he carried her over the threshold like a virgin bride—cherished, treasured, prized.

The cabin, which would have no electricity until the pond froze over for the winter and Caleb or one of the other naturalists brought over a generator from the ranger's station, was awash in darkness.

Don Juan set her on her feet and put out a hand to steady her. Even with moonlight slanting across the wooden floor, she could barely make out the shape of a sofa pushed against the wall. Then he closed the door behind them, smothering all light and plunging them into blackness so thick Meggie caught her breath. The utter darkness disoriented her. It was too dense, too absolute.

His heady masculine scent enveloped her, drowning out the musty, stale cabin smell. Leather, oranges, cinnamon, licorice and a bracing woodsy aroma. His large hand tightened around hers and he slowly waltzed her toward the sofa. They knew they'd arrived at their destination when their shins brushed against the vinyl material. He eased her down on the seat, then let go of her hand and stepped away.

"Don Juan?" Fear and excitement in an invigorating combination charged through her.

Nothing.

She inhaled shakily. The vinyl was cool and slick against her barely clothed bottom. Meggie strained to hear sounds of him moving. A whispered breath, a creaky floorboard.

"Are you still there?"

Nothing.

Then from out of the ether, a heavy hand settled on her right knee.

She jerked.

Because she could neither see nor hear anything, the hand seemed disconnected, detached, the touch of a phantom lover straight from some erotic hallucination. Warm fingers crept up her knee to her inner thigh.

She tensed, with anticipation or apprehension; she couldn't really say which. The feelings surging through her were electrified, distorted by the sensation of both time and place suspended. Nothing felt real, and yet at the same moment her body hummed with heightened intensity that channeled all her focus to this minute stroking of her skin.

The hand continued, moving upward to skim over

her bustier to her waist, and finally stopping to lightly caress her tormented breasts through the stiff lacy material.

No more!

She couldn't tolerate idly waiting. She had to participate in this exquisite teasing. Palms extended, she reached out for him and found his chest. She hissed in air when her fingertips grazed bare, muscled skin and she realized he'd discarded his shirt. Her fingers sank into the soft tuft of chest hair, and the strangeness of his body heightened the dark fantasies revolving through her head.

The texture of his skin, the sculpted configuration of his musculature felt alien but oddly right. She and her unfamiliar lover were alone—in the dark, deep forest, in a deserted cabin. Her normally taciturn body had become wickedly willful, silently begging for more mystery, more suspense. She knew neither this man nor her new self that his caresses had unearthed. And she liked the indefiniteness of it all.

Her hands roamed, learning this different man by the sense of touch. His flesh was damp and hot beneath her palms. The heaviness of his breathing filled her ears, and as she kneaded first his chest and then his shoulders, she felt his fingers work the numerous tiny hooks at the back of her bustier.

Meggie explored him thoroughly, touching here, there, everywhere.

She sensed the raw energy pulsing through his pores. He untied the cape from around her neck. She felt the bustier fall apart in the back, experienced the blaze of his hot, wet mouth as he planted it on her sensitive shoulder blade.

"Are you sure this is what you want?" he asked. "To lie with me?"

He was giving her a way out. She was eternally grateful for his consideration, his kindness in fact heightening her desire for him.

"I'm sure."

"I would hate for you to have regrets."

"No regrets. I promise."

"What would you like?" he whispered. "I want to please you."

"Being with you and playing this game pleases me."

"I need more information. I need specifics."

"Like what? I'm not sure what you mean."

"Where should I touch you? And how? Soft? Hard? Slow? Quick?"

"Anything." She moaned softly and arched into the curve of his body. She wished to sample it all. "Everything."

"You are an adventuresome woman."

"Thanks to you, I am now."

She shivered at the wonder of what was happening. An electric power gushed between them, a vital power strong enough to light the whole of Alaska. They needed neither lamp nor torch. Their passion gave them the vision to see each other as they really were.

Open, vulnerable, ready.

"Where shall we begin?" he whispered.

"Kisses. Lots of kisses."

"Hmm." He pulled her onto his lap so that she was facing forward, her bare back flush against his naked chest, her legs astride his leather-clad thighs. "A very good start."

And then, for what seemed like an eternity of bliss, he kissed her. Brief, velvety kisses on the back of her neck, over her shoulders, down her spine. She tossed her restless head back and he kissed her jaw, her ear, her throat.

He shifted her position, turning her around until they faced each other in the darkness. The sizable bulge in his pants grew harder against her silk-covered womanhood as he planted long, moist kisses on her lips, her chin and the hot pulse throbbing at her collarbone.

Lower and lower he roved, moving her for comfort as he went. First kissing, then licking and at last gently nipping a trail from her neck to her nipples and down her rib cage to her smooth, flat belly. She ended up with her back on the vinyl couch cushion and his taut male body positioned over her, one leg planted on either side of her thighs.

Meggie groaned. "No fair," she whispered. "My turn to tease you. What do you like?"

"Talk dirty to me," he whispered. "Tell me exactly what you'd like for me to do to you."

"Oh, my." Meggie felt the color drain from her face. She wasn't sure she could be *that* boldly uninhibited.

Dull in bed.

The mean-spirited words rang in her head.

Do it. Tell him what you want.

Meggie panted, short and hard, at the thought.

"Tell me," he insisted in a commanding tone that curled her toes.

"I...I can't."

"Why not?"

"I don't know how."

"Open your mouth and say the words."

She hesitated.

"What are you afraid of?"

"That I won't do it right," she confessed.

"Why would you think that?"

She shrugged.

"Let me guess. Some jerk you've been with has misled you about your desirability."

"He said I was dull in bed."

"Dull! You?" Don Juan's vehement reaction warmed her heart. "You are anything but dull. Now talk to me."

"I don't have the guts."

"Yes, you do. Let me hear you say it."

Pretend you're Klondike Kate. She's not dull. Forget the past. Lose yourself. This isn't really real. It's just a dream. Play-acting.

"What do you want?" His low, husky Spanish accent dragged her into the fantasy. She could do this. She would prove that she was brave and exciting and wildly sexual.

Meggie swallowed. "Take off my panties."

"That's good. Very good."

In an instant he slid the silk of her tap pants down her hips, past her knees to her ankles and then over her shoes. A blast of air cooled her heated flesh and she shivered.

"Now what?" he asked.

"Finger me."

"Where?"

"Down there."

"Down where?" She heard the teasing tone of amusement in his voice.

"You know."

"Down here?" He lightly entangled his fingers in the curly hairs at the juncture between her legs.

"Lower." She was panting so hard she could scarcely speak.

His three middle fingers slid over the slick mound

of her womanhood and edged toward her aching center. One finger went left, one right, the other straight down the middle.

"Here?"

She nodded, breathless.

"Shall I go on?"

"Uh-huh," she whimpered.

"Say it."

"I…I…"

His face was pressed against her ear, his leather mask rubbing her cheek. She could see absolutely nothing; the darkness was as pure as her desire. Gulping, she squeezed her eyes tightly closed. The hypersensitive sensations spurring through her groin were incredible.

"You've got to tell me or it won't happen."

Say it, Meggie!

Oh, the risks she was taking, the things she was learning about herself.

Dull no more.

"I want to feel your fingers inside me," she said, surprising herself with a strong voice of authority.

He obeyed, sinking his middle digit deep within her warm recess. Meggie gasped out loud and clutched his hair in both her fists.

"You're so wet," he whispered. "So hot."

She tightened her muscles around his finger and his responding groan made her smile into the darkness.

He raised up to kiss her again, his body wedged between her and the back of the sofa, his mouth searching for hers as his inquisitive finger continued gently to investigate her delicate nook. When she arched her pelvis against his hand, he chuckled with satisfaction.

Stroking, rubbing, massaging.

The pressure built inside her like a balloon being

blown up…and up…and up…to the point where one more expanse of air would cause it to explode.

Then he stopped and removed his hand.

Meggie cried out in despair. "Don't torture me."

"Do you want me to make you come?" he asked.

She pushed her hips higher and whimpered, low and impulsive.

"Tell me."

"I want you to make me come. Please, please, please. Make me come now."

Caleb's ego soared. He tenderly sucked on her bottom lip while slowly moving his finger in and out, in and out of her magnificent softness. Her moans spiraled steadily, filling the empty blackness with her throaty, feminine noise until his ears rang with the splendid sound.

Her tongue thrashed against his. Her breasts quivered. Her hips undulated madly. And when he slid a second finger inside to join the first one, she momentarily stopped breathing.

Her entire body stiffened. He felt her hover on the edge, her muscles taut, straining. When he touched his thumb to her clitoris she let loose a high, keening sound of pleasure.

"Don't…stop," she begged, her voice muffled with the expectation of climax. "Oh, oh, oh…"

And then, in one shattering moment, she came.

Her muscles spasmed around his fingers, her buttocks arching off the sofa cushions. He'd never witnessed anything so lovely.

An indescribable emotion tightened his chest. He felt as much satisfaction as if he himself had climaxed. This was his purpose—to pleasure this beautiful woman and help her heal whatever demons it was that pursued her.

For he knew without knowing how he'd come by the knowledge that she had followed him into the forest as a tonic for what ailed her. He was so happy that he had been able to give her this small respite.

She sagged against him and he held her close. He murmured sweet nothings in made-up Spanish, listened as her heart slowed from a racing gallop to a sedate pace.

He felt oddly sated, to the point that when she reached up in the darkness, cupped his chin and said, "Now it's your turn." He shook his head.

"No," he said softly.

She pushed against his chest, struggling to sit up. "Why not?" she asked.

Caleb frowned. It had been bugging him for a while now, ever since she'd forgotten to speak in her Klondike Kate vernacular. Her voice sounded naggingly familiar. Did he know her?

"I would rather wait."

He realized it was true. He had to see her again, and he feared if they fully consummated their passion he never would. But if he left her aching for more... who knew how long this game might last? Maybe, just maybe, she'd want to return for seconds.

"Wait?" Panic settled in her voice, obscuring the familiarity. "Wait for what? I don't want to wait."

He had her exactly where he wanted her. Caleb reached for her hand and held it tightly in his, even though she tried to pull back.

Eventually the throbbing in his groin would abate. Eventually.

"I want to see you again," he told her.

"No," she said adamantly, reverting back to her

Klondike Kate drawl. "This is supposed to be a one-night stand. Now take your pants off."

"Relax. There's nothing to be afraid of."

"You don't understand. I don't want anything more from you than sex."

"I'm not saying I do, either," he cajoled, but his stomach pitched. Truth be told, he would like to see where this attraction might lead. See if the powerful sexual pull might take them to something deeper, more meaningful. "But I think dragging out the seduction will make it so much more memorable when we finally do go all the way."

Her nails bit into his palms. "It's not such a good idea."

"Why not?"

"Tonight we were overcome—by hormones, the full moon, by our costumes. It was magical, special. Why ruin it? Just make love to me now so things aren't lopsided, and then I'll slip away into the darkness. Let's leave this a wonderful flight of fancy."

"I can't accept that."

What was the matter with him? What she was proposing was every guy's wildest fantasy. Anonymous sex with a beautiful stranger. No strings attached. No consequences. No regrets. Except more than anything in the world, he wanted to see her again. He was taking a risk, pressuring her like this, and he knew it, but he felt it was a risk worth taking.

"I must see you again," he insisted, unable to quell the urgency building inside him. "I must know more about you."

"Impossible."

"But why?" Then he froze as an ugly suspicion dawned. "Are you married?"

"No."

Caleb exhaled in relief. Thank heavens. He wasn't a home wrecker. "Then why deny us this pleasure?"

"Simple logistics, my dear Don Juan. I'm leaving town tomorrow morning."

"You're not from Bear Creek then?"

"No."

"I'm sorry, but I cannot let you get away." Stubbornly, he clung to her hand.

"Please, Don Juan, this was nothing more than an extravagant game. We both got turned on, but it's no more than that. Please, let it go."

"It's more than a game and you know it."

"It's not," she insisted.

"All right then," he said, scrambling for something he could say that would change her mind. "Let me help you get dressed and I'll walk you back to the party."

Several minutes later, they were clothed again and walking through the forest hand in hand. His body was still stiff from wanting her. His mind raced with ways to convince her to see him a second time. Things couldn't end on this disappointing note.

Caleb led her into a moonlit field not far from the community center where the party still continued. Laughter, music, the sound of car doors slamming echoed in the still of the night.

He stopped, drew her closer to him and stared into that unfathomable face hidden so dramatically behind the red-feathered mask.

"What if I happened to come to where you lived? I travel a lot on business," he lied, still speaking in his Don Juan accent, reluctant to release the disguise and break the enchantment. "Could I see you then?"

She paused for a long moment. "Perhaps. I don't know."

His heart leaped with hope. "You realize this was special. How often have you felt this way?"

She inhaled deeply. "I'm not sure this is such a good idea."

"Think of all the fun we could have."

"Do you swear that it would only be fun? Nothing else? I don't want anything else."

"Nothing else," he promised. At this point he would promise her anything to get her phone number.

"I'm doing this against my better judgment, but you're right," she said. "I've never felt anything like what happened between us tonight. You've made me feel like a desirable woman."

He made a deep sound of approval. "You *are* a desirable woman."

"Okay." She swallowed audibly. "Here's the deal. I'll whisper my phone number to you and if you can remember it, then you can call me."

Caleb's pulse pounded in his ears. He was beset by the riddle of her. He wanted her so badly it hurt. Wanted to be inside her, buried deep.

"Sweetheart, I could never forget," he crooned, meaning every word.

She whispered the number.

"What?" Startled, he shook his head, certain he had heard incorrectly. "Please say that one more time."

She repeated herself.

With the rapidity of lightning striking, his blood froze. His world skidded to a screeching halt. His ears echoed with the sound of her voice mouthing those digits. Realization dawned. He knew that number. Had called it many times over the years.

"Good night," she whispered. "And if I never see you again, goodbye. I'll always remember the precious gift you gave me in the skaters' cabin, Don Juan. Thank you."

Then, without another word, she turned and started toward the community center, her graceful body illuminated in moon glow.

He literally could not speak. His senses reeled. He splayed a palm over his heart. He knew now who she was. No wonder she had sounded familiar. No wonder he had been so inexplicably attracted to her.

She was the woman who had dominated his teenage fantasies. The very same woman who had once been married to his stepbrother Jesse.

Klondike Kate, the lady upon whom he'd just performed sexual maneuvers, was none other than his unrequited childhood crush.

Meggie Scofield.

CHAPTER FIVE

"HOT DAMN, WOMAN. I love the hair!" Wendy Roseneau, Meggie's next-door neighbor and good friend for the past five years, declared.

It was three days after her return home to Seattle. Wendy, a brown-eyed, bottle blonde with Kewpie doll cheeks and a Cindy Crawford beauty mark over her upper lip, settled her hands on her hips and nodded approvingly as Vincent, a tattooed, nose-pierced, fuchsia-haired stylist at En Avant!, the trendiest salon in Seattle, put the finishing touches on Meggie's dashing new coif.

"Your friend's right, darling. You look absolutely plucky," Vincent enthused.

Plucky? Her?

Sure. Why not? Yes, by gosh. Her. Plucky.

"You were in desperate need of a change," Vincent continued, waving his hand with a theatrical flourish. "That bland Buster Brown blunt cut you were sporting was just too, too retro. I'm sooo glad you chose me to be the artist of your transformation. You are my masterpiece, my muse, my Mona Lisa."

Okay, so Vincent was a bit of a drama queen but he did have a point. The conversion was startling.

Meggie stared into the mirror. The difference in her appearance astounded her. The spiky cut flipped out from her head in short, sassy wisps. The style not only slimmed her face and accentuated her green eyes but also lent her a hip, dynamic edge.

She looked like the kind of woman who took life full throttle. It was exactly what she'd been seeking when she'd plunked herself in Vincent's chair and asked him to create a wild, new, independent persona for her.

"Wow," she murmured and reached up to lightly finger her hair. "Wow."

"Wow indeed," Wendy concurred. "You should have gotten divorced years ago. Freedom definitely agrees with you."

"It's not just the divorce," Meggie whispered to Wendy as she slipped Vincent a tip so big he actually purred.

Normally, she wasn't the kind of woman to kiss and tell, but she was filled to the bursting with thoughts of her erotic night with Don Juan.

"Oh no?" Wendy rubbed her hands gleefully. "I smell a juicy story. What's up?"

"Come on. I'll tell you later. In the meantime I'm buying a whole new wardrobe at La Chic Freak."

Wendy plastered a hand over her heart. "You? In La Chic Freak?"

"Yep. I'm going for leather and lace and chains. And who knows? Maybe I'll even get a henna tattoo."

"Omigosh, I thought I'd never live to see the day you decided to recognize your full potential and rebel against that good-girl image that's kept you trapped in that tight little black-and-white box. I'm so proud of you, Megs." Wendy wrapped her in a honeysuckle-scented hug.

"Me, too," Vincent chimed in. "You go, girlfriend."

Geez. She knew she'd been something of fuddy-duddy but she had no idea everyone had been holding their breath just waiting for her to cut loose. This had certainly been a week of prolonged self-discovery.

And it's all because you stepped outside your comfort zone and took a gamble.

The evening she'd spent in the skaters' cabin with Don Juan had been the most liberating experience of her life. Ever since that fateful night she felt changed in ways she couldn't explain. Ways that made her long for all the things she'd missed. Why had she hidden her light under a bushel all these years?

Well, no more. From now on, everything was going to be different.

She and Wendy left the salon and headed for La Chic Freak. An hour later she emerged wearing a red mesh blouse and a matching red leather miniskirt so short it would have caused even Klondike Kate to blush. In her hands swung a shopping bag filled with equally intrepid clothing.

"Okay," Wendy said as they wandered down the street. "We're out of earshot of anyone. Spill it. What in the world happened to you in Alaska?"

She tried not to smirk, but couldn't help herself. "I met the most awesome guy."

"Get out!"

"It's true."

Wendy stopped walking and smacked her forehead with a palm. "No, no, no. Please say it ain't so."

"What?" Meggie felt perplexed. "I thought you would be happy that I met someone."

"Yes, in a year or so. Maybe. Not yet. It's too soon after your divorce, sweetie."

"I've been divorced for six months."

"No good can come of this relationship. He's nothing but the transition guy. A temporary fix. You need to live a little before you get involved with anyone else."

"Give me some credit, will you? I totally realize that. Why do you think I got this new haircut and bought new outfits? Believe me, this thing with Don Juan was nothing but a fling."

"Don Juan? Oh, please tell me you're kidding."

"Settle down. Don Juan's not his real name and, besides, I'm never going to see him again."

"You? A one-night stand?" Wendy shook her head, incredulous. "Not that there's anything wrong with a good, lusty romp in the hay once in a while, but I just never thought you of all people..."

"Not only that," Meggie whispered. "I don't even know his real name."

"What?"

Leaving out the most intimate details, Meggie told Wendy about Don Juan, the costume party and the cabin in the woods.

"From what you describe it sounds like there was a whole lot of sexual chemistry going on," Wendy said when Meggie had finished. "That kind of passion can be hard to ignore, particularly with a guy who has obviously made you feel special. I have been there and I've been burned. Be careful, sweetie. I'd hate to see you get hurt."

"Don't worry. He doesn't know my name, either. We were two ships passing in the night."

"Well," Wendy said, linking her arm through Meggie's and continuing down the street to where they'd parked the car, "maybe you're right. Maybe this was exactly what you needed. I certainly approve of the changes in you."

"Honestly, I swear, it's just what the doctor ordered.

I've never felt so free. It's like I've unearthed this confidence in myself I didn't even know I had."

"And you promise you're never going to see this guy again?"

"I promise." Meggie held up two fingers. "Girl Scouts' honor."

"That's good. As long as you're not tempted to jump into a relationship with a man you don't know just because the sex is stupendous."

"Absolutely not."

"Then congratulations on stretching the limits of your imagination."

"Thank you," Meggie said, but a nagging little voice reminded her that she wasn't being completely honest with her friend. She *had* given Don Juan her telephone number.

But what were the chances of him even remembering her number? And if he did remember it, what were the odds of him calling her or ever coming to Seattle to see her?

Very slim to none. She was safe with her lusty memories. She didn't have to worry about falling hard for some stranger in a black leather mask. All Meggie cared about was exploring her newfound sense of adventure in whatever form it might take. New hairstyle, new clothes, new experiences.

And speaking of new experiences...

She stopped in front of the dance studio sandwiched between La Chic Freak and En Avant! Through the window she spied a group of costumed belly dancers executing a series of mesmerizing gyrations.

For the longest time she had hankered to take belly dancing lessons, but because Jesse had called her an awkward klutz the time she had tried to do a striptease for him, Meggie had felt too self-conscious about her body to give belly dancing a go.

Well, phooey on her ex and his stupid opinions. Thanks to Don Juan she was more than eager to rip the envelope of adventure wide open.

Purposefully, she pushed through the door of the dance studio.

"Hey," Wendy said. "Where you are going?"

Meggie glanced over her shoulder at her friend and grinned. "To stretch the limits of my imagination."

"MAY I SPEAK to you in my office?" Meggie's boss, Jenny Arbenoit, asked three weeks after her shopping spree with Wendy.

"Sure," Meggie said, wondering what was up.

She didn't think she'd made any mistakes lately, but perhaps she had gone overboard with her newfound confidence. Recently, she had stopped kowtowing to the doctors' every whim, and she'd also started making more decisions based on her own assessments without asking for corroboration from her colleagues as she once had. A sinking sensation settled in her stomach.

It was a slow afternoon in the emergency department. The nurses had been enjoying a welcome respite from earlier in the week, when they'd been deluged with nearly an epidemic of children suffering from high fevers related to a recent outbreak of a Lyme disease type illness. Meggie had been catching up on paperwork when Jenny singled her out.

Mouth dry, and prepared to offer an apology, she followed Jenny into her office.

"Have a seat." Her boss indicated a chair and closed the door behind them.

Meggie sat and nervously eyed the older woman.

"Meggie, ever since you returned from your leave of absence, I've noticed a change in you."

"Mrs. Arbenoit, if I've done anything—"

Jenny held up her hand. "Please, let me finish. Several of your co-workers have also commented on your new attitude. You've always been a good nurse—kind, caring, considerate of others—but until these last few weeks you have lacked the kind of self-confidence that would make you management material."

"Excuse me?"

"Your exemplary performance during this latest public health crisis has not gone unnoticed by the doctors. You've assumed more responsibility and presented yourself as a thorough professional."

Meggie's head spun. She wasn't being taken to task. She was being praised.

"We were hoping you would accept a position on the community health education board. Do you think this is something that might interest you?"

"Absolutely." Ideas sprouted in her head. She loved teaching patients, and this was a marvelous opportunity to boost her career.

"Excellent, excellent." Jenny Arbenoit got to her feet and extended her hand. "I'm looking forward to working on the board with you."

"Thanks." Meggie shook her hand, a sense of pride filling her chest. A new job offer because of her increased self-confidence. Just one more debt of gratitude she owed to Don Juan.

CALEB STARED OUT the window of the ranger station at the vast white expanse of new-fallen snow. It had been six weeks since that fateful night he'd discovered his new lover was none other than his teenage fantasy woman.

Six weeks since his world had been turned completely upside down. For the first time in his life, the wilderness he loved so deeply felt desolate and lonely.

With Meggie gone, everything in his world seemed quiet, dull, empty. He got through his daily routine, but nothing brought him joy. Listlessly, he dug in the pocket of his crisp, hunter-green uniform shirt and pulled out a photograph he'd gleaned from an old album—a picture Jesse had taken of him and Meggie together on the rare occasion he'd visited them in Seattle.

It had been Christmas Eve. He and Meggie were sitting on the couch together. He had on a Santa hat, and she wore a blue package bow stuck in her hair. They'd had too much holiday eggnog, and Meggie, with one arm thrown over his shoulder, was mugging cutely for the camera. He'd been staring at her with a look of such deep admiration it was a wonder neither Jesse nor Meggie had ever noticed. Hell, even Caleb had never realized before how much like a lovesick puppy he looked.

And he'd told himself he'd gotten over his childhood crush. Ha! One glance at the photo and he knew he'd been lying to himself for years.

The photograph was frayed now, the edges curled from wear. As he did every day since discovering Klondike Kate was actually Meggie, he traced a finger over the picture and murmured her name.

He recalled how she'd looked the last time he'd seen her, dressed in that scarlet bustier and auburn wig. He thought of her sweet scent, and his imagination supplied the aroma he was searching for—jasmine soap, strawberry shampoo and a hint of Obsession cologne.

His brain didn't stop with scent memories. He thought about those cinnamon freckles that decorated her collarbone and those intelligent green eyes the color of verdant summer grass. He envisioned her soft, womanly curves, the creamy taste of her full, rich lips and the way she'd felt wrapped in his arms. The way her body had responded to his touch.

In a twinkling, he was transported back to that astounding night.

Slowly, tenderly, he removes her red-feathered mask and the long auburn wig in order to reveal her own coal-black hair. She does not resist. She is not ashamed to let him see her face. And when he removes his mask, she is not alarmed or upset. He sucks in his breath, overwhelmed. His heart thumps at her easy acceptance of his role as her lover.

She wants him. In fact, she lifts her arms to him and a tempting smile teases her lips as she slowly undoes the top hook of her bustier.

Another tiny hook undone. Another and then another, until the stiff lacy material lays open just beneath the swell of her breasts. The cool evening breeze causes her nipples to tighten into pink pouting buds.

Her eyelids drift closed. Loose tendrils of dark hair curl invitingly over her forehead. Her lips part. She tips her chin up.

"Kiss me," she commands.

His blood is at the boiling point, and he's clutched so hard with need he doesn't know if he'll be able to control himself.

But he must. For her sake. No matter how much his body aches for a frenzied coupling, he will not surrender to the instincts raging within. Not yet.

Apparently, however, she is feeling just as desperate as he, for she opens her eyes, takes hold of his shirt in her fists and rips the garment from his body. She splays her palms against his chest and then savagely sinks her nails into his flesh. Her breath hisses out through clenched teeth in a sultry sizzle.

His bulge is straining hard against his leather pants. Roughly, he grasps her wrists and pins her hands above her head.

"Is this how you want it? Fast and hard?"

In answer, she just growls and raises her head to nip at his throat.

He claims her mouth with a merciless kiss that leaves them both gasping for air. He glides his fingertips down her raised arms to her exposed breasts. She shivers at his featherlight touch, obviously confused, but also delighted by his change in tactics.

Using great care, he unhooks her bustier completely and pushes it open until her flat, ivory-white stomach is bare. He makes quick work of the tap pants, shoving them past her hips. The delicate wisp of red satin tangles around her ankles. She helps, kicking the panties off into the darkness.

Restlessly, she undulates her hips, calling him back down to her. When he lowers his head and takes one of her pert nipples into his mouth, a low guttural moan slips from her lips.

He caresses his hands along the smooth, firm planes of her body, exploring every inch of her. She is any man's dream lover. The fantasy woman to end all fantasies, and at long last, she is his.

He wants her so badly he can barely think, but at the same time, he wants to draw this night out and make it last forever.

Cupping her hips in his palms, he lifts her up and she gyrates against his erection.

"Take off the pants," she commands. "Now. I want to see you. Touch you. Taste you."

At the notion of her tasting his shaft, he almost comes right then and there.

Control. Hold on to your control.

But how impossible this wonderful woman was making that task. She was actively licking his chest while he fumbled with the drawstrings of his pants.

Then he was naked, his pants flung out into the empty cabin, and her fingers—oh, her wicked fingers— were wrapping around his hard cock.

"I've spent my life waiting for you," she whispers. "Take me, Caleb. Make me your own."

"Mail call!" Quinn Scofield's booming voice, and the loud thumping of his feet on the staircase, yanked Caleb from his X-rated reverie.

Cricket on a crutch! He'd been fantasizing about his best friend's baby sister, and now here was Quinn, coming through his front door.

Caleb tossed the Christmas photograph aside, grabbed the high-powered field binoculars from the table and pulled them into his lap to disguise the vestige of his arousal.

"Hey, Greenleaf." Quinn came grinning into the cabin, stomping snow off his boots and bringing the cold, late-October air with him. "What's happening?"

If only you knew, you'd probably punch my lights out.

"Morning, Scofield. You didn't have to make a trip up here. I was headed into Bear Creek tomorrow to pick up supplies."

Quinn dumped the mail onto the table. "Truth is, buddy, we were all a little worried about you. I know you're the strong, silent type, but we've hardly seen you in town since the *Metropolitan* party."

"No need to worry about me. I'm just tired of the

matchmaking and having women throw themselves at me. It's getting harder and harder to tell the sincere ones from the gold diggers."

"Old Gus commented that you might have a harder time finding an honest woman because of your money."

"Don't you people have anything better to do than gossip about me?"

"As the last remaining bachelor, Greenleaf, you're a cause for much speculation."

"Lucky me. Let me guess—old Gus has got a pool going about my future marital status."

Quinn's grin was answer enough.

Caleb shook his head. "So what's your bet?"

"I'm predicting you'll be swept off your feet by the pretty interim park ranger who takes your place while you're in Seattle. You'll get married here in the ranger station next summer—I forecast a June wedding—have sixteen kids and live happily ever after."

"What are you talking about? I'm not going to Seattle."

But even as he denied this statement, Caleb's heart rate accelerated. There was no way Quinn could know he'd spent the past six weeks debating whether or not to go to Seattle after Meggie.

Quinn reached in the mail sack, withdrew a letter and passed it over to Caleb.

"Have you been reading my mail?" He frowned.

"Didn't have to. Talked to Meggie this morning."

"Meggie?"

"You know, my sister. Your ex-stepsister-in-law."

"I know who she is. What does her calling you have to do with me going to Seattle?" His gut twisted with a mix of excitement and hope.

"Read the letter."

Caleb stared down at the return address of King County Health Department, Seattle, Washington, then flipped the envelope over and opened the flap.

The letter was from the director of public health services. There had been a massive outbreak of a tick-borne illness in Seattle and the surrounding counties. The ailment mimicked Lyme disease. The local medical community was woefully lacking in knowledge about the type of ticks that caused the condition. They needed an expert to come to Seattle, all expenses paid, and give a series of lectures at area hospitals for the next four weeks. Caleb's name had been recommended by one of the board members, Meggie Scofield. The director had worked out a deal with the park services of Alaska. In exchange for Caleb coming to Seattle, one of Washington's naturalists would take his place in the Tongass during his absence.

It was the perfect excuse to go to Seattle. At the thought of seeing Meggie again, Caleb's chest squeezed.

He had to remind himself this meant nothing. Meggie didn't know he was Don Juan. She had suggested his name to her superiors simply because he knew more about insects than anyone in the Pacific Northwest, not because she secretly wanted to see him again.

Unless something on a subconscious level was at work here. He looked over at Quinn. "Meggie recommended me?"

"Sure. Why not? You are the best bug guy around. She's on the board. In fact, she's on the committee that's throwing a Halloween charity ball to raise money for public awareness of Lyme disease and other tick-borne illnesses. If you take the job, maybe you'll be in time to attend."

Caleb pushed the envelope away. Apprehension took

hold of him. What if he did go to Seattle, tell Meggie he was Don Juan, and she rejected him?

"I don't know. A month is a long time to be away."

"Come on, Greenleaf. You need to get out of the forest every once in a while, and you said yourself you're tired of all these women throwing themselves at you. No one in Seattle except Meggie will know you're a millionaire bachelor. Take off—have a good time."

"I suppose it would be a vacation of sorts."

"Darn right. Go for it, man. Get Meggie to show you around town and introduce you to some of her cute single girlfriends."

"I thought I was suppose to fall in love with the interim ranger and have sixteen kids."

"Come on, everyone needs a plan B. What if the interim ranger is a guy?"

"Good point."

Caleb thought of the Don Juan costume stuffed in the top of his closet. A Halloween party charity event put on by Meggie's hospital. He could show up a few days early, take the costume with him to Seattle, wear it to the party, and then he could take off the mask and show her face-to-face that he was the man who'd enflamed her that night in the forest.

Take a gamble. Roll the dice. Go to Seattle.

He had nothing to lose.

Nothing, that is, except his heart.

CHAPTER SIX

"SO TELL ME more about this cute, rich friend of yours giving the symposiums."

"Caleb?" Meggie glanced over at Wendy.

"You got more than one cute, rich, lecture-giving friend?"

"No." Meggie chuckled. "Just Caleb."

They were taking their daily jog around the park adjacent to their downtown apartment complex. A foggy mist had settled on trees resplendent with a vivid splash of autumn color, dampening the ground and lending a slight chill to the air.

"Caleb." Wendy rolled his name on her tongue. "I like it. Sounds rugged and woodsy and he-mannish."

"He is."

"Ooh." She gave a little shiver of delight that for some unknown reason irritated Meggie. "Tell me more. What's he like?"

"He's really not your type."

"What's that suppose to mean?" Wendy slowed, but Meggie kept going.

"You're a party girl," she called over her shoulder.

"And?"

"You'll spend a month's salary on a pair of Manolo Blahniks."

"So?"

"Caleb lives in a park ranger station in the middle

of the Tongass National Forest, Wendy. He uses a two-way radio for a telephone. Not too many occasions turn up for putting on the Ritz."

"Hey, wait up! I'm falling behind," Wendy hollered, but Meggie never slowed her pace.

Why should she care who Caleb went out with? Besides, the guy needed a little fun in his life. He was much too serious, and if anyone could lighten him up, effervescent Wendy could do the trick.

You feel protective toward him. He's practically like a brother. You don't want to see him get hurt, that's all, Meggie reassured herself. Her feelings for Caleb were strictly platonic.

Then why are you feeling jealous? a tiny voice in the back of her head whispered. But she ignored the obnoxious nudge. Meggie had enough trouble dealing with this obsession she'd developed for Don Juan without throwing Caleb Greenleaf into the mix.

What was wrong with her, anyway? Why couldn't she forget about Don Juan? She knew he wasn't good for her, and yet night after night she had hauntingly erotic dreams about the masked man coming to her bed and making fierce, passionate love to her.

Probably because he had curtailed their sexual adventure that night in the cabin. Meggie felt certain if they had consummated their romantic assignation she would not be fixated on him. It was a clear case of wanting what she couldn't have.

Wendy, panting and red-faced, finally caught up with her. "Witch. Why didn't you slow down?"

"Interval training. You burn more calories this way," Meggie said, slowing at last and feeling a bit ashamed of herself for sprinting ahead. She reduced her speed to a fast walk, and Wendy shot her a grateful smile.

"So about Caleb…"

Obviously, her friend wasn't going to let go of the subject. Meggie sighed. "Yes?"

"What's he like?"

"Tall, dark hair, deep-blue eyes, handsome as a Greek statue."

"Yum, tell me more."

"He's quiet, somber, deeply into nature and very intelligent. That's why I recommended him as a lecturer. Actually, I'm pretty surprised he accepted. He generally hates to leave Alaska."

"The strong, silent type." Wendy licked her lips. "I'm intrigued."

"He's a great guy." Meggie gazed across the street at a schoolyard where a group of kids played soccer. Why watching those kids at play should make her feel wistful, she had no idea. Maybe because she was beginning to wonder if she'd ever have any kids of her own. "A good listener. But you would probably think he was boring."

"Hmm." Wendy stopped walking.

Meggie halted. "Hmm, what?"

"Why don't you want me to go out with him?"

"I never said that."

"Come on, you tell me how great he is on the one hand but warn me off on the other. Saving him for yourself, are you? That's a little selfish, considering your almost religiouslike conversion after your naughty costumed tryst with the suave Don Juan."

"Don't be silly. I'm not interested in Caleb."

"Why not? He sounds perfect."

"For one thing, he's younger than I am."

"Oh, big deal." Wendy waved a hand.

"And he's Jesse's stepbrother."

Wendy made a face. "I can see where that could cause problems, but still…"

"He loves Alaska, and I love Seattle."

"True love conquers all."

"I just don't have *those* kinds of feelings for him."

"Okay then. Since we got that cleared up, you gotta introduce him to me."

Meggie swallowed. She wasn't sure Caleb would appreciate being fixed up, but Wendy was a lot of fun to be around. Even if she and Caleb didn't click, maybe they could at least have a good time together.

"All right. I'll introduce you."

"Hot dog!" Wendy did a little jig, and then gave Meggie a hug. "A decent date prospect for the first time in weeks. Megs, you're a doll."

Yeah. But how was Caleb going to take the news?

THE MINUTE HIS PLANE touched down at SeaTac Airport, Caleb remembered why he didn't like big cities.

Crowds. Noise. Traffic congestion. Pollution.

He'd been to Seattle only once before and he'd had the same reaction. The frantic pace gave him a headache. Hurry, hurry. Where was everyone dashing off to in such an all-fired rush?

It took him a good forty-five minutes to find the baggage claim terminal and retrieve his luggage. Then another ten minutes wading through the jostling throng to find the taxi stand.

Feeling like a stranger in a strange land, he suspected the cabbie was driving him around in circles, but he had no proof. When the guy pulled up in front of his hotel and told him the fare was thirty-six dollars, his suspicions were confirmed.

He tried arguing, but the driver suddenly pretended

he didn't speak English. Grudgingly, Caleb paid the fare, but as he turned to deliver his bags to the bellhop, a scruffy-looking teen on a bicycle darted up the hotel's circular drive, leaned down and scooped up his briefcase. The kid disappeared before Caleb realized what had happened.

Dammit!

All the notes for his lecture were in that briefcase. Stupid kid was going to be disappointed when he pried open the case and discovered it contained nothing more than a treatise on ticks and half a power bar.

An hour later, after a powwow with hotel security and a Seattle police officer who was not optimistic about Caleb's ever seeing his briefcase again, he was finally ensconced in his room.

If it wasn't for Meggie, he would have been sorely tempted to turn around and head straight back to Bear Creek. But she had staked her reputation on him, recommending him as a guest lecturer. He wasn't going to let her down. Even if he would have to wing his speech.

Besides, how could he leave Seattle without seeing her again? At the very notion of meeting up with her his heart went *thumpa-thumpa-thumpa*.

Call her. Let her know you got a lower fare by coming in on Friday night instead of Sunday, a little voice whispered.

Caleb circled the phone. "Go ahead, Greenleaf. Call her."

Determined, he perched on the edge of the bed, reached for the telephone and punched in her number.

It rang three times and he almost hung up.

"Hello."

Meggie's voice was so breathy, so overwhelmingly

sexy, he sat stunned for a good ten seconds, his fingers wrapped tightly around the receiver.

"Hello?" she repeated.

Heat, sultry and sudden, swamped his body. How he wanted her!

Caleb opened his mouth to say, "Hi Megs, it's me. I just got into town," but instead it seemed as if alien forces captured his throat and took possession of his larynx. He'd never in a million years intended on saying what he said next.

"*Buenos dias,* belladonna," he crooned in Don Juan's husky accent. "Are you surprised to hear from me?"

MEGGIE ALMOST DROPPED the receiver as her stomach slid into her sensible bedroom slippers.

Oh dear, oh dear, oh dear.

She plastered a palm against her bare chest above where her towel covered her breasts. She had just stepped out of the shower, following her jog with Wendy, when the telephone rang.

Water from her wet hair trickled down her back. She heard the distant whizzing of cars on the freeway. Tasted the tangy flavor of her own desire on the tip of her tongue.

For the past six-and-a-half weeks she had scarcely thought of anything besides that magical night with Don Juan when she'd dared to let go of her inhibitions and had discovered a whole new side of herself.

Meggie Scofield could be as wild and wanton as the next girl.

Her pulse was pounding a rhythmic tyranny. She hadn't really expected him to come to Seattle, or even call her, for that matter.

Meggie's knees loosened. She groped for one of the

straight-back chairs gathered around the kitchen table, and sat down hard.

"Don Juan?" she whispered.

"Do you have any other Spanish lovers?"

Ripples of desire undulated up her spine. What was it about the man that caused such sensations to engulf her?

"I have been unable to forget you."

She heard the sly smile in his voice, felt a corresponding hitch in her belly. She laughed as much to dispel the strange achiness inside her than anything else.

"You're a little hard to forget yourself."

"So it was not my imagination. You felt for me the same as I felt for you." His rich masculine sound wrapped around her like a blanket.

"It wasn't your imagination," she murmured, having no idea why she said that. What in the heck did she want from him? What did she think she was doing?

"I dream about you day and night. Night and day."

"Oh?" She forced herself to sound cool, casual.

"Yes. I think of the way you move, so graceful, like a swan skimming over a peaceful lake."

It was corny and hokey and blatantly a line but, heaven help her, she was falling for it. With shaky fingers, she shoved a spike of soppy hair behind her ear.

"Your walk is so sensuous. Perhaps because you have such beautiful legs. The shape of them, so slender and feminine, excites me beyond measure."

"Really?"

She was a weak, weak woman. The man was no good for her and she knew it. She should hang up the phone on him right now and forget he'd ever called.

But she did not.

"Your legs and your butt excite me."

"My butt?" His use of frank language both startled her and turned her on.

"Yes, you possess a fine bottom. Nothing inflames a man more than a woman with a narrow waist and generous hips."

He thought her big rear end was sexy? Pensively, Meggie reached around and patted her fanny.

"If I were there with you right now, I would pinch your butt. Not too hard, just enough to let you know how much I admire it."

Hang up! Hang up!

Meggie cleared her throat. "Then what?"

His chuckle was smooth and seductive. "Ah."

"What's that supposed to mean?"

"You know what it means."

"I don't."

"But you do."

What was he insinuating? That he wanted to have phone sex with her? She'd never talked dirty over the telephone and she wasn't about to start now.

Prude.

I'm not, Meggie silently insisted.

Prove it. Step outside the box.

"What are you wearing?" he asked.

She glanced down at the beach towel wrapped around her midsection and winced. Think dowdy. Stop this before it gets started.

"A sweatsuit," she lied.

"I do not believe you."

"Okay, what do you think I'm wearing?"

Dammit, Meggie, why did you say that?

"I think perhaps you are wearing baby doll pajamas. Or maybe a silky, sheer black negligee."

Meggie laughed.

"Or maybe…" his voice, already deep, dropped another octave "…you're wearing nothing at all."

Whew, that was too close for comfort.

"But I hope you are wearing something," he continued. "Because I'd like to imagine undressing you. I'd like to slowly slide those skinny black negligee straps off your shoulders."

"Umm."

"I wish I could kiss you," he said. "Would you like that?"

Unbidden, she imagined Don Juan there with her, nibbling her lips, his tongue gliding over her mouth. She realized then she was panting in short, fevered gasps.

"Yes," she murmured helplessly, "yes."

"And then I would like to run my hot tongue over your gorgeous bare breasts."

She sucked in her breath and unknotted the towel.

"Stroke yourself. Pretend I am there. That it is my fingers touching you. Remember what it felt like?"

She did as he commanded, rubbing her nipples and delighting in the erotic sensation.

"Does that feel good?"

"Yes," she gasped.

"I wish I could lick you. Kiss you. Hold you. I'm getting hard just thinking about you."

"I'm getting excited, too," she panted, thrashing about in the chair as she ran her hands down her belly to the triangle of hair between her legs.

"I wish I could slip my hands into your panties and stroke your warm, wet…" He spoke a word that made her blush and ache to come all at the same time.

Perspiration beaded on her forehead as her brain spiraled off into another seductively vivid scenario. She imagined him sliding her naked body down the length of his until she was on her knees, her lips even with the hard length of his erection. She envisioned wrapping her warm, moist mouth around his manhood until he groaned with ecstasy and begged for mercy.

She saw herself pinned under his hard, masculine body, his manly fingers tangling in her hair, holding her prisoner while he ravished her with his mouth, feasting on her nipples, dragging his tongue along her belly, then lower to her heated depths.

A sharp shudder thrust its way through Meggie's system and she shifted in her seat, crossing one leg over the other in a desperate attempt to stay the sensations flooding her groin.

"I count the moments until I see you again," he whispered. "Until I can kiss you and gaze into your beautiful green eyes."

Absently, she ran a hand along her throat, fingered the erratic pulse beating there and was surprised to find her skin so warm to the touch. Desire heated her from the inside out and made her crave this man's presence.

"I must see you again." His voice through the phone line was a low, masculine rumble of urgent sound that grabbed hold of her and aroused the most secret places of her body.

"I'd like to see you, too."

"To finish what we started."

She felt her face flush hot, but, yes, this was what she wanted, what she had dreamed of for the past seven weeks.

"Yes," she murmured softly.

"I will be arriving in Seattle in the morning. I have business to attend to during the day, but my evening is reserved for you."

"I can't tomorrow night. I'm attending a Halloween charity event."

"I'm only in town for one night. I must see you tomorrow or not at all."

He was pressuring her, but damn if she didn't want to see him again. "You may come to the Halloween party if you like. If you've got a pen, I can give you the name and address of the hotel where it's being held."

"Should I come as Don Juan?"

"But of course."

A thrill ran through her at the mental picture of his tight leather pants and shiny black boots. She certainly did not want him to come without a costume. If she was going to have a red-hot, mindless affair with this man, she must not know his real name or see the face behind the mask.

She bit down on her bottom lip. Molten passion seeped through her being with a heat that obscured all rational thought.

"Are you there?" he asked, his devastating accent fueling the fire between her legs. "Are you all right?"

Meggie blinked and realized several seconds had gone by while she had indulged her fantasies. She cleared her throat.

"Fine. I'm fine."

"Until tomorrow night," he whispered.

"Until tomorrow night," Meggie echoed, not knowing how she was going to make it through the next twenty-four hours.

CALEB HAD STUNNED HIMSELF. He couldn't believe he had said those provocative things to her over the telephone. And after he'd hung up, alone in his hotel room with nothing but erotic visions of Meggie pleasuring herself, he had been forced to take matters into his own hands. There was only so much control a guy could command before the dam burst.

Now here he was, dressed as Don Juan, in a taxi on the way to the Halloween party. His blood surged feverishly with thoughts of the night ahead. How and when was he going to reveal himself to Meggie?

While he was enjoying this masquerade, he couldn't keep it up forever. And dammit, call it ego, but he was ready for her to know that he, the guy she considered no more than a friend, was the one pushing her sexual buttons.

But he also knew that Meggie was loving this game they'd built, and wearing a disguise was what gave her confidence to move into uncharted territory, just as the Don Juan costume supplied him with the courage to take a chance on fulfilling his fantasies.

He smiled to himself. Meggie Scofield. What a woman! Brave and smart and sexy as hell.

The taxi parked in front of the Claremont Hotel. Caleb paid the fare and got out. As he walked through the elegant, upscale European-style lobby, numerous feminine heads turned to stare in his direction.

He barely noticed. All his thoughts were concentrated on one woman and one woman only. In a brash move, he stopped at the front desk and made a room reservation for the night.

Are you sure this is such a smart thing to do? his practical side argued. *Aren't you assuming a lot? And what if you do make love to Meggie? What if it turns out to be terrible and you end up ruining your friendship?*

He thrust out his jaw and shoved aside the voice that kept him trodding the straight and narrow. Keeping quiet, holding back, had never gotten him what he wanted. The only time he'd achieved success was when he'd pursued something with passion.

When he crossed over into the packed ballroom, he realized he had no idea what costume Meggie would be wearing tonight. Feeling at a loss, he found a vantage point by the front entrance from which to peruse the crowd.

Suddenly, two hands slipped around his mask and covered his eyes, her dainty pinkies tickling his fake mustache. "Guess who."

Caleb started at the sound of her voice, so familiar and melodious. He began to turn toward her, but a hand on his shoulder stilled him.

"Wait."

She was so close he could feel her soft breath fanning the nape of his neck, and despite the crowds in the ballroom, he felt as if they were totally and completely alone.

"Guess who," she repeated.

"I need a clue."

"Think extravagant."

"Well, that narrows it down."

"Someone sinfully rich."

"Don't tell me. Wait. I've got it. Bill Gates is flirting with me?"

Meggie's laugh sent an arrow of pure sexual energy shooting straight to his groin. "Not that rich and further back in history."

"Marie Antoinette."

"Closer, but not so headless."

The lush, velvety material of her sleeve scratched gently against his cheek. She rested her elbows on his shoulders and he could feel her breasts brushing seductively against his cape.

Alarmed, Caleb became cognizant of the very stunning effect this new game was having on the other parts of his body. He felt a swift stirring of arousal. If she didn't step away from him soon he was bound to embarrass them both.

"Guess who," she whispered into his ear again, her hands still locked in front of his face.

He'd never noticed before what cute palms she had, and her fingers were long and delicate. Refined. Certainly not the hands of an Alaskan woman. She belonged here, he realized with a twinge. In this city.

And he did not.

Before he could follow that depressing train of thought too far, Meggie did something that completely knocked him for a loop. She stood on tiptoe, leaned in close and ran her hot little tongue along this ear.

It was the most incredibly erotic thing anyone had ever done to him. He felt his control unraveling fast. What was she playing at?

"Come find me if you can," she whispered, then turned and disappeared into the crowd.

CHAPTER SEVEN

DRESSED AS Catherine the Great, Meggie slipped across the room and found a place to hunker down behind Dracula, the Wolf Man, Michael Jordan and John Wayne, who were discussing the pros and cons of extended antibiotic therapy in the long-term treatment of tick-borne illnesses.

Her pulse was pumping with enough endorphins to kick-start a Harley. She was high on adventure and the thrill of the chase. Crazed with a bright excitement as memorable as childhood Christmas mornings.

She certainly hadn't planned this little escapade. She'd simply spied Don Juan standing in the crowd and had gone to greet him, but by the time she'd made her way over, he had his back to her. Impulse had driven her to stand on tiptoe, rest her elbows on his shoulders and cover his eyes with her hands. Impulse and animal instinct.

His sharp intake of breath at her presence, his rich masculine scent, the way his broad shoulders had tensed beneath that silky white pirate shirt had compelled her to take things a step further. To dare him to figure out what disguise she was wearing and try to find her in the midst of the costumed congregation.

She should have known better. Hadn't that night in the forest taught her that hunting and capturing a mate was a compulsion written in a man's genetic code? By extending him this challenge, she'd effectively pitted herself against thousands of years of evolutionary conditioning.

And now Don Juan was on a quest, stalking through the gathered horde with a confident, ground-eating stride and an expression of serious intent riding his tightened jaw: he was searching for her.

What a buzz! What a lark! What a fantasy!

Meggie's mouth was dry, and she shivered from her head to her feet. She felt warm and jittery, as if she'd downed a half-dozen espressos in one sitting.

Was she losing control of the situation?

This masquerade was in danger of becoming an obsession. Don Juan made her feel things she had never felt before. Wonderful, delicious things she wanted to explore more fully.

Did she truly dare finish what they had started in the Tongass?

Dracula shifted to one side, leaving Meggie exposed to the crowd. She glanced around the room, looking for a new place to hide, but when she tilted her head to the right, there was Don Juan, standing just a few feet away, an inscrutable smile on his enigmatic lips.

The minute their eyes met Meggie knew she was in trouble. He started toward her. Meggie gulped. What was he going to do?

Wicked intent glistened in those commanding blue eyes, made even more powerful by the erotic frame of his black leather mask.

Her stomach fluttered. A jolt of pure, raw sexual energy rushed through her and her world narrowed, shifted into agonizing slow motion.

Stomp, stomp, stomp. The noise of his boots striking the marble floor was sharpened and elongated, echoing loudly in her ears with each resounding step. His black hair was wildly tousled. The material of his silky shirt rippled when he walked, fluid as water. His gaze was locked on hers and she was helpless to look away, even to move. In what seemed both an eternity and a mere whisper of a second, he was at her side.

My God, he was handsome.

He reached out and wrapped a hand around her right elbow. The pressure of his fingers caused her to disintegrate into a quivering mass of organic matter. His body heat muddled her brain.

When the two of them came in contact it could only be described as chemistry, electrical conductivity, spontaneous combustion. Oh, how seriously pathetic to be reduced to bottom-level biological rubble by a man.

He slipped a key card into her palm, then pressed his lips to her ear and whispered in his robust Spanish accent, "Come to room 716 as soon as you can get away. I will be waiting."

THIRTY MINUTES LATER, a short, firm rap sounded at the door of room 716.

Forcing himself to remain calm and in control, he let her knock again before pulling open the door to find Catherine the Great leaning against the doorjamb looking like a billion bucks.

He was about to speak, to say something comforting to soothe their nervousness, when she took him totally and utterly by surprise. Meggie splayed a palm across his chest and pushed him back as she stepped over the threshold. With one delicately slippered foot, she slammed the door closed behind them at the same time as she wadded his shirt in her fist and pulled him forcefully toward her. Her green eyes lit up like a lynx's and she pounced on him, growling softly. His knees went weak with lust and he felt a curious tingling sensation in the back of his throat. She planted a kiss on him with such ravenous aggression that he found himself propelled backward onto the bed. She followed, melding her mouth to his, straddling his prone body and tugging his shirt from his waistband, all in one smooth move.

Her brazenness bowled him over. Holy buried treasure. What had he wrought?

He was both pleased and disconcerted by her overt onslaught. This wasn't the sensible, restrained Meggie Scofield he'd known his whole life. This was the lusty, uninhibited wench from his fantasies.

Wait a minute. Maybe he was dreaming all this. Maybe he should pinch himself.

But no, she was nibbling on his bottom lip with her straight white teeth, and it felt very real indeed. Apparently their role-playing had unleashed a long-dormant tempest within her.

She wrapped her arms around his neck, pressed her body against the length of him and eagerly ran her tongue over his lips.

No. Wait. Stop the presses. This wouldn't do. At the rate she was moving, he wouldn't last five minutes.

Reaching up, he untangled her hands from his hair at the same time he disengaged his mouth from hers. He lifted her off him, placed her to one side and sat up.

"Sweetheart," Caleb crooned. "Slow down. This isn't a race."

She pulled back, her chest rising and falling rapidly. She blinked and then a red flush ran up her neck to color her cheeks.

"I'm sorry. I don't know what came over me. I've never acted like that."

He pulled her to him. "Shh...don't be embarrassed. I liked it. We just need to slow down."

"You're right." She nodded. "I guess I was just wanting to get to it before I lost my courage."

Aw hell.

Was she trying to rush through sex with him just to get it over with? Was she trying to prove something to herself, using him as a means to her end?

He took her hand. "I don't want you to do anything you don't want to do."

"I'm not," she insisted, and rested her head against his shoulder.

"Good." He exhaled, troubled by the unsettling sensation tromping around in his gut.

"But I do have two requests."

He would do absolutely anything for her, Caleb realized. If she asked him do handstands atop the Space Needle, he would have asked her how many and done one extra for good measure—even in the face of his fear of man-made heights. He would grant her every whim, from the simplest appeal to the most sublime demand. He wanted her that much.

"We must leave on our masks."

She didn't want to see his face. What did that mean? Caleb bit down on the inside of his cheek. He'd intended on revealing himself to her tonight, but he had promised to comply with her desires, and he was a man of his word.

"All right."

"And turn out the lights. All of them."

"Whatever you wish."

He did as she asked, drawing the curtains and turning off each lamp until the room was pitch-black, the way it had been that night in the cabin.

With no lights anywhere, he had to feel his way in the darkness. His other four senses pricked in awareness. He could not see her, but he felt her presence, heard her breathing, smelled the wonderful womanly scent of her, tasted her unique flavor on the tip of his tongue.

And he had to admit, not being able to see was highly erotic. The anticipation had been building for seven weeks and his nerves were as taut as newly tuned guitar strings just waiting to be strummed.

He moved toward where she had been standing, but felt her slip past him.

She giggled. "Find me if you can."

Caleb smiled in the darkness. Obviously, she liked playing tag.

He lunged for her, came into contact with some soft part of her body, but she squirmed away before he could clamp a tight hold on her.

She pattered across the room, and he heard rustling noises.

Caleb went after her, his blood chugging through his veins, thick as syrup. He moved slowly, listening for sounds of her. He kept his arms outstretched, feeling for obstacles.

Table, chair, lamp.

"Where are you?"

Curtains. An armoire. The television set.

And then his hand brushed bare breasts, and the impact of connecting with her ripped through him like a detonated time bomb. He realized with a shock that Meggie had shed her clothing.

Like a blind man reading braille, he skimmed his palms over her smooth naked skin. He felt goose bumps raise on her flesh, and experienced a corresponding tactile reaction of his own.

She reached up to stroke her fingertips over his face and his body caught fire, singeing him internally from head to toe.

He cupped her pert full breasts in his hands and wished like the devil he could see the pink tips of her nipples poking out at him. He had to satisfy himself with tenderly pinching those straining buds until she murmured a soft, "Oh my."

He lowered his head, ran his tongue across first one nipple and then the other.

"You're wicked," she gasped.

"Isn't that why I intrigue you?"

"Yes, yes."

"You never know what I might do next."

She inhaled sharply.

"That's why you don't want me to remove my mask. You like an outlaw."

"Uh-huh."

He grasped her hands, raised them over her head and pinned her to the wall.

"You don't know what you're getting yourself into, *señorita*." He had to force himself to stay in character as Don Juan although this game was driving him right over the edge of reason.

She was his prisoner now, trembling with excitement and need. "Please," she whimpered, "don't…"

"Don't what? Ravish you?" He'd sensed that she was taking their game to a new level, and he would play along.

He felt her nod, and a rush of blood drained straight to his groin.

"I could take you right here, right now. Up against the wall. Hard and fast. It's dark. You can't see my face. You couldn't even describe me to the authorities. It's best if you don't give me an excuse to punish you."

"But I've been a very bad girl. I've told the police where they can find you."

The playful tone in her voice let him know he hadn't gone too far. He amazed himself at the boundaries he was able to cross with her.

Helpless to resist her plea for more sex play, and wanting to give her as much pleasure as he possibly could before taking his own release, Caleb lowered her arms to her sides and then sank to his knees.

"Uh-oh. That means I'm going to have to give you a thorough tongue-lashing."

He spanned the curve of her waist with his hands and then slowly began to run his tongue from her rib cage to her navel. She entangled her fingers in his hair and clasped him tightly against her belly. His mask must have scratched her tender flesh for she made a moaning, mewling sound of heightened awareness that nourished his own arousal. He ran a hand down the voluptuous curve of her hip to cup her buttocks, and discovered she still wore thong panties and thigh-high stockings.

Man alive. She was volcano hot and seducing him without even moving.

He hooked his thumbs under the ribbon of silk hugging those spectacularly feminine hips and started the exhilarating procedure of inching the flimsy morsel of fabric down her warm, firm thighs. She gasped, an erotic sound that reverberated like a prayer in his head.

When he feathered his fingertips along her skin in languid exploration, her grip on his hair tightened. He touched the inside of her thigh, the top of her legs, drew circles on her tight fanny. He stroked every inch of the area between her navel and knees, except where he knew she most wanted him to touch.

"You're vicious," she moaned. "I thought you promised me a tongue-lashing."

"Punishment, sweetheart, takes many forms."

"Bastard!" She uttered the word with clenched teeth. He laughed.

She leaned back against the wall and arched her pelvis up toward him, planting her womanhood right near his face. Begging.

"Brazen wench," he declared.

"If you can't take the heat, then get out of the kitchen."

"I'll ignore that, because I know you don't really mean it."

Her sigh in response was like a caress in the darkness, inching down his spine, spilling through his bloodstream, setting him on fire with escalating desire for her. Swelling need seized him and his pulse knocked wildly in his temple. To wrest back a modicum of restrait, he compelled himself to disregard the provocative smell of her, the seductive rhythm of her undulating hips, by resolutely turning his attention back to the thong caught around her knees.

He skimmed the scrap of satin down to her ankles, his hands brushing against the enticing silkiness of her nylons.

"Step out of your panties," he demanded.

She obeyed.

"You really are as mercurial as the wind," he said. "One minute aggressive, the next coy, the next acquiescent. Who are you, really?"

"My identity is secret, just as you are a complete mystery to me."

She liked not knowing him. Controlled, sensible, honest-to-a-fault Meggie liked adventure and rowdiness and subterfuge in the bedroom. As long as he remained behind the mask, as long as he was the sensual, roguish Don Juan, he could provide her with all the things she needed. But what could he do for her as plain, ordinary Caleb Greenleaf? The unsettling thought disturbed him and quashed his libido.

But not for long.

"I'm naked, and now you must get naked, too," she declared.

The mental imagine of her standing completely unclothed before him dispelled his self-doubts and goaded illicit visions of untying his leather pants, freeing his ferocious erection and plummeting deep inside her feminine recess.

But not yet. She deserved much more than a blazing quickie.

She began unbuttoning his shirt, her cool fingers tracking lightly over the heated flesh she slowly unveiled. She plunged her fingers into the curls of hair on his chest.

Caleb groaned, clasped her to him and delivered a series of searingly desperate kisses to her smooth, flat belly. She moaned and slid her body down his until she was on her knees in front of him, her breath flowing hot and fast against his skin.

She explored him with her honeyed tongue, tasting the skin she uncovered while completing the task of removing his shirt. She stripped it off his shoulders and over his biceps before flinging the garment across the room. Splaying her palms against his chest, Meggie muttered a pleased sound of discovery and traced her fingers down his torso to the hard planes of his stom-

ach. His body tensed and flexed in response to her inquisitive, reverential exploration.

"I wish I could see you," he croaked.

"No," she said sharply. "No lights."

He wanted to ask why, but dammit if she didn't start
licking his ear in the provocative way she'd done in the
ballroom. The very same maneuver that had caused him
to press the room card key in her hand and invite her
up for a midnight romp. It seemed they both operated
better in disguise.

Was secrecy what fed the flame between them? What
would happen once the mystery was gone?

Caleb didn't want to think about that eventuality. He
didn't want to think about anything. He just wanted to
be in the moment.

As a man accustomed to spending much time alone
in the wilderness, appreciating and living in the moment
was his specialty. He could give both Meggie and himself the gift of total concentration. He would. Just for
tonight, no more doubts, no more fears of what might
happen once she discovered a familiar face behind the
Don Juan mask.

"Nibble on my neck," Meggie requested in a jag-
ged whisper.

His blood pulsed, fiery and brutal. As if hypnotized,
he followed her instruction. Nestling his mouth to the
hollow of her slender throat, he bared his teeth against
her fevered skin. She cried out and squirmed against
him when he took her flesh into his mouth and nipped
lightly. He shivered in awe that he'd produced this reaction in her.

The taste of her succulent saltiness wasn't nearly
enough. He was famished for her. Had been for years.
He nibbled on her like a banquet feast, sucking and

licking, swirling his tongue over the sweetness of her. Caleb plunged his fingers through her hair and cradled her naked body in his arms.

She was all soft swells and generous curves. Her nipples thrust hard against his chest, begging for attention. He left her neck and went straight for the eager buds, curling his tongue around one puckered peak and gently tugging. She hissed like a hot griddle doused with ice-cold water.

"You inflame me."

"Shh. Don't talk, just lick."

He laved her with his mouth. A tremble shuddered through her and a slow, deep groan unfurled from her throat.

"That's it, don't stop."

He savored her, claimed her and ached to possess her on a baser level. He gorged on the sugary taste of her, indulging his whims.

Caleb caressed her with his hands, kneaded her skin, massaged her, quickly learning which spots produced the most explosive reactions. He discovered where she liked it firm and where she preferred a whisper-light touch. Which stroke made her quiver and which made her sigh with restless longing.

Steadily, relentlessly, he pushed her toward the edge of reason. He experienced it, too—the heady anticipation, the measured buildup, the escalating wildness.

She strained her hips against the hard ridge of his erection. He knew what she wanted because he wanted the same thing. Wanted it more than he had ever wanted anything in his life. Passion throbbed between them, blistering them both. They hovered on the verge of stepping completely out of bounds of all rational behavior.

Whimpering, she sought his mouth and kissed him with a yearning, soulful need.

Scuttling his hands up her naked back, he crushed her to him, hugging her breasts—still damp from his tongue—tightly against his chest. Their hearts raced in unison, ratcheting upward in a building crescendo. Frenziedly, he dragged his mouth from hers, gasping for air and attempting to stay his frantic lust.

God, how he wanted to see her face, to examine her eyes and learn exactly what she was feeling. Did she want him as much as he wanted her?

Stupid question.

Even as he sought a small respite from this ever-increasing whirlwind of want, Meggie clearly had another plan in mind. To garner his notice, she bit down lightly on his earlobe and tugged the susceptible flesh with her teeth.

"Show me what you like, Don Juan. Take my hand. Guide me where you want me to go."

"Ah, *señorita,* it is my place to please you, not the other way around," he managed to gasp. If she were to suddenly start plying those lips of hers in his most sensitive areas, he wouldn't last two seconds.

"This can't be one-sided like that night in the cabin. I have to know I can please you as much as you please me."

He shook his head.

"You must. It's very important to me."

"All right," he said with an exasperated groan. "If it really means that much to you."

Spellbound, he plunged his fingers through the silky strands of her hair and began with a long, heartfelt kiss simply because he could not get enough of the flavor and texture of her mouth. He leaned backward, taking her with him until he was splayed flat on his back and she was straddling him.

After a few heated minutes, he tenderly broke off the connection and gently steered her moist, parted lips down his chin, over his throat and, in measured increments, along his chest.

Her tongue fluttered across his ridged nipples, and she did to him what he'd earlier done to her. She was making every single one of his most forbidden fantasies come true, and he loved her for it.

She tracked a path from his nipples to his belly, scooting her bare fanny down his leather-clad thighs as she moved lower, ever lower.

Although he wished he could see her, there was something unspeakably erotic about total darkness—not being able to spot her next move, unable to predict what else she had up her sleeve, because he wasn't privy to the naughty gleam in her eyes.

Everywhere her mouth touched, his skin sizzled. He moaned as her lips traveled to where his belly hair disappeared into his waistband. When she stretched her mouth over his hardness through the pliant leather of his pants, he almost came right then and there.

He raised his hips and hissed with sharp, greedy need. "That's it."

She drew back and her fingers went to work on the drawstrings at his fly. Without faltering, she tugged his pants past his hips and chortled out loud when she realized he wasn't wearing underwear.

"You're going commando." She giggled, obviously delighted by the fact.

"No boxers or briefs for Don Juan."

"Guess with those drawstrings you don't have to

worry about anything…er…important getting caught in a zipper."

Her lighthearted, teasing tone touched his heart. She was happy. He'd made her happy.

She wrapped a hand around his rock-hard penis and his smile vanished as he fought his natural instinct to explode at her searing touch.

"And my, Don Juan, may I say, what an impressive package you have."

"The better to—" He almost said "make love to you with, Little Red Riding Hood," but he figured "make love" was the last thing she wanted to hear. Instead he used a crude street term that seemed to rev her engines, for she made short work of his pants, peeling them right off his body.

"That's right, talk dirty to me."

She returned her attention to his throbbing organ, and he was unable to speak at all, much less talk dirty. She stroked him with her fingers, squeezing and rubbing, revelling in the raw and ready hotness of his sex, exploring the paradoxical velvet and granite texture.

Tentatively, she sheathed her mouth around him, tasting his masculine essence with the tip of her tongue. She ran her lips up and down his shaft in a maneuver that caused his entire body to quake helplessly.

Oh mercy. Mercy.

She took her time, trying out a variety of experiments. She blew hot little puffs of air against his skin. She swirled her tongue around the head of his penis. She sucked and licked, teasing him, drawing him ever closer to the brink of climax.

He shuddered when she discovered the sensitive ridge lurking below the proud, jutting tip. In that moment, he almost called out her name. In fact, the first syllable was past his lips when he remembered the game and her rules. He bit down on his tongue.

"Mmm."

"You like?"

"If you keep doing what you're doing, then we're both in trouble."

"Good."

Before Caleb knew what was happening, she took his engorged shaft as deeply into her mouth as she could possibly manage in a blinding, white-hot kiss that turned his world inside out. He whimpered as she engulfed him in a way that made him absolutely mad-dog crazy for release. For her.

His hands searched for her in the darkness, clutched her hair in desperation and tried to get her to break contact. If she didn't quit he simply would not be able to stop the force of nature that had kidnapped his body.

But she would not be denied.

He gasped, he writhed.

She moved faster, sucked harder.

He could not think. Could not reason. Could only let himself be swept up in her vortex.

Up, up, up, she took him. Climbing higher and higher. When she gently cupped his balls in the palm of one hand, he knew it was the end for him. Every muscle in his body tensed. He stopped breathing and for one brief second in time felt as if he hung suspended on the edge of the world.

The searing orgasm red-hot and mind-blowingly powerful, shot up through his shaft in a blinding rush. Intense, blistering pleasure shuddered throughout his system in a kaleidoscope of sensation.

He tried to pull her away but she ignored his attempts. The moist, warm recesses of her mouth stole

his restraint, and he could do absolutely nothing but ride
the roller coaster down, down, down as he plummeted
earthward into heavenly release.

Meggie! Meggie!

What a gift. What a surprise. What a woman.

Emotion pressed into the corners of his eyes, and for
the first time since turning out the lights, he was grateful she couldn't see him.

Panting, she raised her head and whispered in his ear.
"Make love to me with your mouth, Don Juan. Make
love to me right now."

CHAPTER EIGHT

TAKE A RISK, she had told herself when she'd accepted Don Juan's key card. *Take a chance. No telling what you might discover about yourself.*

Boy, had that been an understatement.

She knelt beside Don Juan, trembling in the darkness, stunned and amazed at what she had just done. She'd never done anything so intimate with a man before.

How would he react? What would he do?

In answer to her question, he gave a groan and she felt him get to his feet. He fumbled for her in the darkness and latched his arms around her waist with a possessiveness that both frightened Meggie and delighted her. Without speaking, he scooped her into his arms and gingerly made his way to the bed.

What was it about him that drew her? What made her yearn to throw caution aside and proceed with the reckless abandon of a horny teenager? He fascinated her like no one else on earth, and she didn't even know his real name.

This is just for tonight, Meggie. Don't for a moment forget that. You can lose your head if you wish, but don't give this guy your heart.

But of course not. She had learned her lesson the hard way. Don Juan was a dalliance to help her repair her shattered self-esteem. As long as she understood that, she wouldn't get hurt.

By providing her with a safe outlet for sexual exploration, Don Juan was giving Meggie her femininity back. Because of his precious gift, when she did find the right man and fall in love, she would come to her new lover with a free heart. Whatever happened tonight, the knowledge that she would be better prepared for a loving relationship in the future because of Don Juan buoyed her hopes.

She could find love again. She would. And next time, it would be with the right guy.

Tonight, however, was about cutting loose, experimenting and finding out just how far her limits stretched.

Don Juan deposited her gently in the middle of the mattress. He stepped back and she reached for him.

Sudden fear struck her. What if he wasn't taking this affair as casually as she? She didn't want to hurt him any more than she wanted to be hurt.

"Don Juan?"

"Yes?" His sexy, disembodied voice floated from the blackness, causing her to shiver with expectation.

God, how she loved the way he spoke. Never mind that the accent was fake. She knew he wasn't really Spanish, but she ignored that knowledge for the sake of fantasy, and reminded herself she would not ruin everything by delving into reality.

"This is just a game for you, isn't it? I'm just one in a long string of your lovers. Right?"

He said nothing. Silence roared in her ears. Oh, no. What if he wanted more than she could give? She wasn't about to get involved with another rogue, no matter how sexy or how good at foreplay he might be.

"Right?"

"Remember," he whispered at last. "I'm here for one thing and one thing only. Your pleasure. Do you understand?"

Relief washed through her. Yes. The last thing she wanted was to hurt him. Thank heavens they were on the same wavelength, because it would have been next to impossible to walk away from him at this point.

She felt the mattress sag from his weight as he settled himself on the bed. From nowhere, it seemed, his fingers made contact with her arm and roved up her shoulder to her collarbone and then down to her aching, engorged breasts.

"I want to reward you. To thank you for the perfect present you just gave me. I wish to reciprocate."

Meggie hitched in a deep breath as his fingers trailed lower, inch by exquisite inch.

"You are so beautiful."

"I'm not beautiful." She laughed. "You've only seen me in a mask, with a costume on. For all you know I look like Quasimodo."

"And I could say the same. Isn't that part of the attraction? Not knowing what is behind the mask and getting excited anyway?"

"Yes," she admitted, and moistened her lips with her tongue.

His fingers were getting closer, ever closer, to the place where she wanted him to be.

"I could be anyone. No?"

"Yes."

"That excites you, doesn't it?"

"Uh-huh."

He stroked her lower abdomen, stoking the flames that were building inside her. After several minutes of this, her entire body was rigid and she wanted to grab him by the hair and tell him to get on with it.

When she didn't think she could stand the teasing one second longer, he let his hand drift to the hair at the juncture between her legs. Gently he stroked a finger over her right upper thigh.

"Open for me. Nothing is more erotic then the moment a woman parts her legs for her lover."

He didn't have to ask twice. Meggie shifted, moved her legs apart, welcomed him in, opened herself to the greatest vulnerability a woman could experience.

"The holiest of holy spots. The gate to heaven."

He made her feel attractive and powerful and womanly. His reverential sigh brought a tightness to her chest. No wonder women fell at Don Juan's feet. He was irresistible.

And then his hot, wet mouth was on her. He kissed her belly, while his cheek caressed her soft, bushy thatch of hair.

She realized then he wasn't wearing his mask, and panic gripped her. What if she saw his face?

Calm down, calm down.

The room was dark. She would insist he put his mask back on before turning on the lights. Besides, she couldn't freak out right now because the things he was doing to her down there were way beyond her realm of experience.

"Sweetheart," Don Juan murmured. "I want to drink you up."

"Yes. Yes, please."

He was between her parted thighs, his head lowered. She tensed, waiting.

And then he slipped his tongue inside her dewy folded flesh and licked her. One small quick flick, as if getting a drop of ice cream before it melted off the cone and ran down his hand.

She gasped.

"Mmm, you taste delicious."

A sigh escaped her.

"You are so hot, so wet."

"You make me that way."

She felt his lips, which were pressed against her, curl up in a grin. Oh, he was arrogant about his prowess, but with good reason.

He unwrapped her like savoring the opening of a birthday present, using his tongue to explore layer after layer. The ridges and folds of her womanhood blossomed beneath his seductive ministrations. She felt the delicate tissue swell in sultry response to his devilish sucking as his saliva mixed with her natural juices.

He changed tempo. Whereas before he'd been delivering light, rapid flicks over her protruding cleft, he dawdled and pressed more firmly.

Slow, long, deep strokes. Down, then up, in a mesmerizing configuration.

"Aaah."

"So you like things nice and slow."

She nodded her head and twisted her fingers through his hair. "Stop talking."

He laughed and returned to his task. He varied his patterns. One minute circles, the next a grid, after that a haphazard zigzag. Meggie felt a gigantic pressure building beneath the hood of her cleft, building and growing and throbbing.

Ever so slightly he nibbled on her inner lips, and she just about leaped off the bed, the sensation was so excruciatingly incredible.

"More. More." She trembled and clutched the bed-spread in her fists.

Sucking very gently, he drew her cleft into his mouth. In and out. In and out. Tugging. Releasing. Tugging. Releasing.

Entranced by the erotic decadence of the act, Meggie could do nothing but enjoy. How was it she didn't feel tense and anxious about this? What was different about Don Juan?

Because he's a stranger.

Odd that she could let down her guard with a man she didn't know, and allow him do the most private things to her when she'd had trouble relaxing and letting go in the midst of a long-term relationship.

You weren't in the right relationship.

She'd been with Jesse for all the wrong reasons, and she knew it. Jesse had been her ticket out of Alaska, and she'd lived vicariously through his wild ways. But now, no matter how irrational her actions might seem to her practical self, she was having her own adventure, embracing life on her own terms.

It felt damn good. No more taking care of other people's needs first. This time, she was doing what was right for Meggie.

Don Juan glided his silken tongue around the tiny base of her, and then skated up to the tender, surging tip. The hood of her cleft slid back and the sensitive nubbin strained for his attention.

There was danger here. One slip of his teeth and the fun would be all over.

But he understood. He was a careful lover. Oh, so very careful. Everything he did elicited unbelievable tides of carnal bliss.

She shivered and quivered and groaned.

He blew a steady stream of cool air against her, before returning to the hot licking. He alternated: chilly air; scalding, wet tongue. Frosty, fiery, icy, boiling, until Meggie thought she wouldn't be able to bear this sweet torment one second longer.

But he wasn't finished.

On and on he went until she lay limp, wrung out, and when he gently inserted one finger inside her, she lost all self-respect.

"Make me come," she cried out. "Please. Make me come. Now!"

The ache that had been coiling tighter and tighter inside her unfurled then in one blinding, clear starburst that radiated outward in an exploding rush.

No one had ever brought her to orgasm this way. Tears sprang to her eyes, and as she shuddered and trembled, Don Juan positioned himself beside her on the bed and drew her into his arms.

He kissed her tenderly, hauntingly. He tasted of her feminine flavor. Full and rich, robust and healthy. Nothing had ever tasted so sexy. Meggie snuggled into his body, rested her head against his chest and, in her warm, sated state, happily fell asleep.

NEVER IN HIS LIFE had Caleb known such total rapture. And to think he had been so very afraid that making love with Meggie could never live up to his teenage fantasies. Instead, their glorious encounter had exceeded all his previous expectations.

The woman was better than his most provocative daydream. One more night with her was not going to be nearly enough. That much was clear.

He lay in the darkness listening to her breathing. She was spooned into him, her fanny curled against him, his arm thrown over her waist. He squeezed her tighter and his gut clenched.

He wanted more of this.

Of her.

But first, he had to come clean and tell her the truth—that he, Caleb Greenleaf, was her secret Don Juan lover. What was the best way to do that? Let her wake up, look over and see his face?

Nah. He immediately discarded the idea. Too jarring. He didn't want her to regret their night together, and if he didn't handle this just right he ran the risk of having her never speak to him again. He had to find another way, a better time and place to reveal himself to her.

But where and how?

He would have to think about it. In the meantime, he was going to have to slip from the room while she slept.

Inwardly, he groaned. The last thing he wanted to do was leave this bed and her warm, soft body. He wanted to languish here, savor this moment. He wanted to wake her with kisses and make love to her all over again, not just with his mouth this time. He wanted to be inside her, consume her, claim her as his own.

But he wouldn't. He couldn't. She wasn't ready to learn the truth. If she had been, she wouldn't have insisted he douse the lights.

Caleb wondered if deep down inside somewhere she knew that he was Don Juan and she simply couldn't face the reality. That thought caused a twinge of anxiety to pierce his heart. His fingers gently stroked her sleeping form, and sorrow paralleled desire in the immense complexity of these new emotions.

He wasn't going to pursue that line of thought. For

now, he would do what he had to do, even though the
thought of leaving her was killing him.

Much as it hurt, he had to go.

MEGGIE AWOKE WITH a start, confused and disoriented.
The hotel room was still dark, but sunlight shadows
were seeping beneath the drawn curtains, casting
enough illumination to let her see that the space on the
bed beside her was empty.

Breathing in a deep sigh, she pushed her tangled hair
from her face and sat up.

"Don Juan?" she called, thinking he might be in the
bathroom. If he was in there and not wearing his mask,
she didn't want to see him.

The thought of coming face-to-face with her lover
caused her pulse to accelerate. She threw back the covers and hopped out of bed. But she needn't have worried. He didn't answer, and no sounds came from behind
the closed bathroom door.

She knocked. No response.

Whew. That was a relief!

Okay, so if she was so happy that he'd abandoned
her, why the heavy sadness settling low in her belly?
Was this the morning-after-a-one-night-stand blues?
She stepped into the bathroom and flicked on the light.

"Eeek!"

Who was that woman in the mirror? Her lips were
slightly swollen, her hair a rat's nest, her mascara-
smeared eyes like a raccoon.

She studied herself for a long moment. The thought
of Don Juan hung like a mist between herself and her
reflection. As if in a dream, she saw him before her.
She gazed at that shadowy image, memorizing it to forever carry him with her, knowing she would treasure

it for fear if it might break up and scatter like paper-weight snowflakes.

"Stop being so fanciful," she told her reflection. "It's not like you."

She had no reason to feel blue or abandoned. She had nothing to complain about. She'd gotten what she wanted—a thrilling night of no-strings-attached sex. Raw, animal intimacy to help her overcome her fears and regain her femininity.

"Don't feel sad, Meggie. You just reclaimed your sexuality," she declared to her bedraggled reflection in the mirror. "Be happy. Be proud. Go forth from this moment knowing that you are not dull and predictable either in bed or out."

She made herself grin.

Feeling a little better, she showered and dressed, then realized she was going to have to sneak out of the hotel room just after dawn, wearing her Catherine the Great costume and no makeup. Hopefully she wouldn't run into anybody she knew.

"Better get a move on, Scofield," she muttered under her breath.

Groaning, she slipped her feet into her high-heeled shoes and headed for the door. That's when she saw it dangling from the doorknob.

Don Juan's mask.

That was all? No note requesting to see her again? No phone number where she could reach him?

But that was a good thing. Right?

Except she did want to see him again. No matter how irrational the thought.

If you want to know who he is, it's easy to find out. All you have to do is call the front desk and ask who reserved this room.

Quickly, she slammed the door on that idea. She did not wish to pursue a long-term relationship with the man. It was over.

For the longest moment she stared at the mask, trying to find a double meaning that wasn't there. This was it then. With a sigh—of disappointment or relief, she couldn't say which—Meggie balled the mask in her fist and flung it into the wastepaper basket.

CHAPTER NINE

"WHERE HAVE YOU BEEN?" Wendy demanded, sizing up Meggie's bedraggled costume. She was sitting on Meggie's front stoop, the Sunday morning newspaper tucked under one arm, a box of doughnuts resting on her bent knees. "I've been ringing your doorbell for a good ten minutes."

"You got Krispy Kremes? I love you."

Meggie reached for the doughnuts in an attempt to sidetrack her friend, but Wendy was having none of it. She hunched forward, shielding the box with her body.

"No way, sister. You don't get one until you tell me where you were."

"You're not my mother," Meggie said defensively. She didn't want to talk about her night with Don Juan. It was too special.

Besides, she was afraid that if she spoke of their lovemaking, and of how he had left her without a single word, she would start crying. For no good reason at all. She had *wanted* a no-strings-attached fling. What was there to bawl about?

"No talkie, no Krispy Kreme."

"Fine. Keep your doughnuts." She stepped around Wendy to insert her key in her door lock.

Looking startled, Wendy jumped to her feet and followed Meggie into her apartment. "You're seriously turning down doughnuts?"

"Seriously." She tossed her keys on the table and kicked off her shoes.

"Ooh, this must be really juicy." Wendy opened up the doughnut box and fanned the lid. "Mmm, smell. Got your favorite. Plain glazed."

"Forget it. I'm not talking."

"If it was the other way around, I would tell you." Wendy pursed her lips in a pout.

"That's beside the point. You love to blab." Meggie pulled a carton of orange juice from the refrigerator. "Want some?"

"With doughnuts? Yeck. You've gotta be kiddin'."

"Suit yourself." She shrugged and poured a glass for herself.

Wendy set the doughnuts on the counter. "I'm getting kinda worried about you, Megs."

"Don't be."

"How can I not? You're my best friend. And at first, when you came back from Alaska all charged up after your romantic encounter with this Don Juan dude, I thought it was really cool the way you were taking charge of your life. Cutting your hair, getting new clothes and speaking up for yourself at work."

"But now?"

"Well." Wendy eyed Meggie's rumpled dress. "You're not acting like the Meggie I know and love. I mean, obviously you were with some man last night."

Meggie said nothing.

"Why won't you tell me?"

"It's personal."

Wendy slapped her palm over her mouth. "Omigosh. It's that hometown guy. You spent the night with your old buddy."

"Caleb? Don't be silly. His plane isn't even due in

until this afternoon. Of course I wasn't with Caleb. Why would you think I was with Caleb? I told you I don't have romantic feelings for Caleb."

Meggie realized she was talking too fast, denying Wendy's accusations too vehemently and using Caleb's name too often. Why?

And why the sudden tightness in her breasts at the thought of making love with Caleb? Good grief! What a mental picture. Maybe she was losing all control when it came to men. Maybe Don Juan had turned her into a sex-crazed nympho.

"I don't know. Whenever you talk about Caleb, your eyes light up and you get this glow about you."

"You're nuts."

"Then who *were* you with?"

"I don't want to discuss it."

"Oh no." Wendy groaned. "It's that Don Juan dude, isn't it?"

Meggie looked away, refusing to meet her gaze.

Wendy bit her bottom lip. "I care about you and I'm afraid you're getting in over your head. You know after going through a divorce some women go wild and do things they would normally never do. Things they regret afterward. Don't get swept away by lust, Meggie."

"I appreciate your concern, I really do. But I really am okay."

"Promise?"

Meggie nodded.

"All right then, but if you need anything, anything at all, I'm here."

"Thank you for that. Now, if you don't mind, I think I'd like to take a nap."

Wendy nodded. "I'll leave you a couple of Krispy

Kremes, even if you won't tell me about your sordid night of pleasure."

"It wasn't sordid."

"What fun is that?" Wendy grinned impishly.

"Go on, get out of here."

"See you later." Wendy put three doughnuts on a saucer, covered them with a paper towel and then retreated with the box.

After Meggie closed the door behind her friend, she wandered into the living room, intent on checking her answering machine. The green light blinked. One message.

A bubble of hope expanded inside her. Maybe Don Juan had called to tell her what a wonderful time he'd had. Or maybe he'd even called to make another date for the next time he was in town.

Don't be ridiculous. You made it clear you didn't want to see him again. He didn't call.

She depressed the play button, crossed her fingers and strained to hear the voice spilling into the room.

"Hi."

For one moment she thought it *was* Don Juan.

"Meggie, this is Caleb."

She exhaled and sank onto the sofa. Why was she so disappointed?

"I just called to let you know I got into Seattle a little early, so you don't have to pick me up at the airport. I'm staying at the Crowne Plaza. I've got some things to do today, so I guess I'll catch you at the lecture tomorrow. Can't wait to see you. Bye."

Well, at least somebody wanted to see her. So what if she never heard from Don Juan again? No sense feeling sorry for herself. It was all for the best. Besides, Caleb was in town. If anyone could cheer her up, that man, with his understanding smile and soulful blue eyes, most certainly could.

DESPITE THE LOSS of his notes and reference material, the lecture was going really well. Caleb knew his entomology as intimately as he now knew Meggie's luscious body.

He fielded questions and comments from the audience, which consisted of various medical personnel interested in knowing what they could do to educate the public about Lyme disease and related illnesses. He hadn't made a single mistake.

That is, until Meggie slipped in through a side door and took a seat on the aisle just a few feet from the podium.

He had been in the middle of a sentence, but the moment he spotted her, every bit of knowledge he possessed flew from his head. She looked exquisitely gorgeous, no matter that she wore shapeless pink hospital scrubs and not a speck of makeup. A catwalk supermodel would not have looked any better to him.

"The...er, I...um," he said, desperately wishing he had papers to shuffle, a pencil to tap, anything to help him focus.

Meggie caught his eye, broke into a beaming smile that lit her face from corner to corner and winked at him.

"Sorry I'm late," she mouthed silently.

His heart pinched. A half-dozen conflicting emotions converged upon him, clogging his throat and tightening his chest. Guilt, excitement, longing, fear, desire and inexplicable tenderness.

Thoughts of Saturday night flooded his mind. He recalled those lips, soft as rose petals and tasty as taffy.

How he wished he could have kissed her awake Sunday morning, massaged her taxed muscles and then served her breakfast in bed.

Instead, because of this deception he had been forced to perpetuate, he had slipped from her bed, sheepish and embarrassed. He wondered what she'd thought when she found the mask dangling from the doorknob, and if he'd hurt her feelings by leaving her without so much as a goodbye kiss.

Had she awakened in the cold dark and reached for him, only to find him missing? Had she looked for comfort and found only sharp emptiness?

Perhaps he was being fanciful. Perhaps she was relieved he'd crept away like a sneaky thief, glad she did not have to face him in the sobering light of day and discover his true identity.

He looked at her and his heart tore.

She was still smiling. She wriggled her fingers. She seemed fine. In fact, there was a distinct sparkle in her eyes he hadn't seen there in a very long time.

Apparently orgasms with unknown masked men agreed with her.

Jealousy clenched his jaw.

Dumb-ass, you were that masked man. What? Are you envious of yourself?

Yeah, okay. Maybe he was the guy who'd put the rosy color in her cheeks, but it just as easily could have been someone else.

Caleb realized he was staring at her and silence had settled over the room, while everyone waited for him to speak. But he couldn't continue. He had no idea what to say next.

"Why don't we take a break for lunch?" He glanced at his watch. "The lecture will resume in one hour."

He had to talk to her and find out how she was doing. He had to make sure he hadn't irreparably harmed her.

She rose to her feet. He stepped off the podium and hurried toward her.

Calm down. Chill out. Take it easy.

"Meggie," he said, feeling rather awkward and unsure of himself.

What now?

"Caleb." Her smile crinkled the corners of her green eyes in a way that rendered him useless. She held out her arms and motioned him closer. "Come here and give me a hug. It's so darn good to see you."

And so he embraced her, pressing her tightly against him and patting her back. She smelled fragrantly sweet, like springtime in the Tongass. They were friends, after all. The hug meant nothing more to her than *good to see you, old buddy* and he knew it.

But that didn't stop him from wishing and praying for more. Her body heat infiltrated his consciousness on a primordial level and sent a bolt of desire shooting through his groin.

This wouldn't do. He had to get away from her before he got hard and she discovered that her good old buddy wanted to be *way* more than just friends.

He stepped from the circle of her embrace and looked into her eyes. She gazed at him, a quizzical expression on her face. She blinked and the look was gone. Had she begun to suspect he was Don Juan?

In that moment, he almost confessed everything, but something about the way she was looking at him now, as if she were honestly happy and excited about him being in Seattle, rendered him mute.

This clearly wasn't the time or place for true confessions.

"I'm taking you to lunch," she declared. "There's a lovely little French bistro on the corner."

He nodded, tongue-tied.

She squeezed his hand. "You'll never know how pleased I am that you decided to teach the symposiums. For one thing, we were in desperate need of a knowledgeable instructor, but the truth is I've really missed you since I left Alaska."

"You're kidding. You missed me?"

"Of course I'm not kidding, doofus." She slung her arm over his shoulder, leaned into him and reached up a hand to tousle his hair. "You're my surrogate kid brother."

His hopes sputtered and died.

Surrogate kid brother. Not exactly the sentiment he was hoping for. When he finally got around to telling her that he was Don Juan, he would remind her exactly why he'd been forced into this pretense. She refused to see him for the grown man he was and not the gangly teen he'd once been. The Don Juan outfit had been the only way to burrow under her prejudices and expand her mind.

Problem was, would she appreciate the underhanded education?

MEGGIE PEERED AT CALEB over the rim of her teacup. It was a little after one o'clock and they were sitting across from each at other at La Maison sharing a thick turkey croissant and bowls of hearty French onion soup.

Damn, but she'd never really noticed how very handsome he was. There was no way she was going to get out of introducing him to Wendy. If she refused, her friend might never speak to her again. Good-looking, caring men like Caleb didn't come along every day. He would be good for Wendy, who had a tendency to get tangled up with freeloaders.

But would Wendy be good for Caleb?

Why do you care so much? Introduce them and they can sort it out for themselves.

She had enough problems of her own without fretting over other people's love lives. Absently, she fingered her lips, her thoughts traveling back to Don Juan and the erotic night she'd spent in his arms.

Truthfully, she was still a little shaky over what had transpired, both shocked and pleased by her uncharacteristic behavior.

Does it stick out all over me? Have I changed? Am I different? Can people tell by looking at me? Can Caleb?

She shot another glance his way and found him studying her with such a peculiar expression on his face that for one halting moment she believed he must be privy to her every thought and know exactly what she'd been up to.

But that was fanciful nonsense. How on earth could Caleb possibly know that she'd been with Don Juan?

And if he did know, why would he even care?

Embarrassment frosted over her like an icy film, followed by an unexpected blast of heat. She felt her face flush pink.

This had to stop. Her obsessing over Don Juan was beginning to bleed over into other aspects of her life, causing her to imagine all kinds of crazy things.

Not good. Not good at all.

Meggie peeped up at Caleb again. He was still staring at her as if she were some ageless riddle he couldn't quite decipher.

"Umm, delicious soup," she said, although the soup

could have been swamp water for all the flavor her taste buds registered.

"Excellent choice of restaurants."

His comment sounded forced, or was she imagining things? Surely Caleb was no different than usual. He'd always been quiet, observant, contemplative. His steady, unwavering calmness was what she liked most about him.

Maybe guilt was causing her to read more into his expression than was there. She cringed, imagining what he would say if he knew she'd just had a two-night-stand with Don Juan. He would probably be as protective as her brother Quinn and want to beat the guy up.

Ack!

This was one of the reasons she no longer lived in Bear Creek. Too many people knew her too well and tried to run interference for her when life didn't go her way.

But what was she saying? Life simply couldn't be better. Thanks to Don Juan, she'd found herself again. She had nothing to be ashamed of and everything to be grateful for.

"Penny for your thoughts," Caleb said.

"What?" She blinked.

The corner of his full mouth tipped up in a rueful grin. "You've been a thousand miles away. Is it the company?"

"Oh, no. I'm sorry."

"Trouble at work?"

She shook her head.

"Come on, you can talk to me. This is your buddy Caleb."

"It's nothing. Honest. I was just woolgathering."

"Okay. But if you ever need to talk…" He patted his shoulders. "These are pretty broad."

"Thanks." She smiled.

He was just the nicest guy. She was most definitely going to have to introduce him to Wendy. They both deserved someone special.

And right now Caleb deserved her undivided attention. Resolutely, she relegated all thoughts of Don Juan to a closet in her mind, stuffing him in there as her first skeleton.

She folded her hands one on top of the other. "So, tell me, how's the wife search going?"

He shrugged. "I've given up on that."

"Really? How come? That ad in *Metropolitan* worked wonders for Quinn and Mack and Jake."

"Yeah, but you know me, Meggie. I need my space, and here were all these strange women crowding me. I couldn't help but wonder if they wanted to be with me or with my money."

"Oh. I keep forgetting you're rich."

"Well, you're the only one."

"Not all women are gold diggers."

"Like my mother, you mean?"

"I didn't say that."

"No. You're too nice to criticize. But I haven't given up on the idea of getting married. I've just decided to let nature take its course. I'm not answering any more correspondence from the ad, and to tell you the truth, that's why I accepted the lecturer position. I needed to get out of town."

"Bear Creek can be kind of claustrophobic," Meggie admitted with a laugh, "despite the wide expanse of geography."

"Tell me about it."

Caleb tilted his head and looked at her in the light through the stained-glass window. Her silky hair glistened darkly; her green eyes sparkled, verdant and alive. She was so pretty and seemed to have no idea how appealing she looked bare-faced and smiling. No artifice, no disguises.

Son of a bear, if he didn't ache to claim her right then and there, consequences be damned. He wanted to drive his fists into his thighs and bellow her name with such passion that every diner in the place would turn to stare at him. He wanted to wrap his hand around the nape of her neck and pull her across the table in a kiss so fierce it left no doubt what he needed from her. He wanted to jump to his feet, scoop her into his arms and carry her all the way back to Bear Creek like a caveman, a Viking, a marauding pirate.

Instead, he did the polite, civilized thing and lied through his teeth.

"You've got a little something there on the side of your mouth." He pointed with his index finger.

"Oh?" She raised a hand to the right side of her mouth and brushed at the nonexistent particle.

"The other side."

She dabbed a finger at the left side of her mouth. "Did I get it?"

"Allow me." Caleb leaned across the table and gently swept his thumb along her lower lip.

The contact was electric.

Meggie's eyes widened.

His heart thumped.

"Did you get it?" she whispered.

"Uh-huh."

"That's good." She sank back against the vinyl booth safely out of his reach.

Damn. That was all he was going to get? One slight touch of her lips?

Not enough. Not nearly enough.

He had to take some kind of action to ensure he would see her often during his month-long stay in Seattle. He wanted Meggie to give him a chance. He wanted to see if he could spark the same feelings without benefit of that confounded disguise.

A simple plan came to him.

He told her about his trouble with the taxi driver who had taken him the long route to the hotel, how his briefcase had been stolen. He embellished the story, playing on her sympathies.

"I feel like such a small-town hick. I want to go sightseeing while I'm in Seattle, but I'm worried about making more mistakes and getting taken advantage of. I feel like a fish out of water."

"You're not as helpless as all that." She laughed and the sound burst through him like a song.

"I am. I'm pathetic in the city."

"No, you're not."

"I swear it. I get lost just crossing the street. Call me a backcountry boy, but I've spent my life with moose and bear and salmon and trees. I don't know much about navigating traffic or getting the best deal at the fish market or how to spot a con artist. Come on, Megs. You gotta take pity on me. I'm begging you. I need someone savvy to show me the city or I'll be stuck in my hotel room for a month."

Her smile broadened. "Why, Caleb, that's an excellent idea."

"It is?" His heart soared and his grin matched hers.

"And have I got just the woman to escort you around town."

He felt confused. Was she talking about herself? "You do?"

"Uh-huh. My best friend, Wendy. She's in between jobs right now and she'd love to show you Seattle. Here, let me give you her phone number."

CHAPTER TEN

MEGGIE RUMMAGED in her purse for a pen and paper to jot down Wendy's phone number, then looked up and ran smack into Caleb's deep blue eyes.

He placed one of his large hands over hers. The warmth, and the corresponding jolt of awareness, surprised her as much as the odd expression on his face. She felt flustered, knocked off balance by his unexpected touch.

"I'm sure your friend Wendy is a terrific woman, but I was hoping that *you* could show me around."

"Oh."

She blinked, not certain what to say next, not really sure what she was feeling. She wished Caleb would take his hand back. The weight of it against her fingers was disconcerting.

"That is, if you don't have other plans. I don't want to intrude."

"No, I have no plans." She stared, owl eyed, uncertain of this strangeness stretching between them.

Caleb couldn't be asking her out. Could he?

Come on, why would she even suppose that? He was her friend, her buddy, the guy she used to baby-sit when he was still stuffing tadpoles in his pocket. He just wanted someone to hang out with, and here she was blowing it all out of proportion.

She shook her head to dispel her crazy thoughts.

What was the matter with her? Had rediscovering her sexual prowess gone to her head?

Imagine. A handsome, rich, younger man like Caleb interested in her? Simply ridiculous.

It had been a very strange forty-eight hours. She was still hungover from her night of sinful luxury with Don Juan, and she was misreading things. That had to be the answer to her confusion.

"Nothing against your friend, Megs. It's just that over the past few months I've grown tired of the dating scene and I just wanted someone I could kick back and relax with. Do you realize that in the past four months I've been on sixty-seven first dates?"

"You're kidding."

"I wish I were. Frankly, it's exhausting, having to make idle chitchat with someone you don't have anything in common with. Especially for a guy who spends most of his time communing with flora and fauna. And, believe me, most of the women I've met are not the type to sit and watch glaciers melt."

Why would they be watching glaciers melt when they could eyeball the likes of Caleb's handsome physique?

"No second dates?"

He shook his head. "Not a one."

"But why not?"

"It never felt right."

"Oh."

"So you don't mind spending a few hours a week dragging a greenhorn tourist around Seattle?" he asked.

"With you, Caleb, I could spend twenty-four hours a day." Now why had she said that?

Jeez, what was happening to her? She had no idea receiving oral sex from a sexy masked man could so disorient a woman. She had to stop thinking about Don

Juan and cease reading sexual innuendo into something as innocent as an old friend's touch.

"What I mean is," she said, backpedaling, "I'd love to show you my city."

CALEB AND MEGGIE strolled through the bustling Saturday afternoon crowd at Pike Place Market. The cool autumn breeze rolled in off Puget Sound, carrying with it the earthy aroma of fish and salty sea air. The day was unexpectedly sunny, and behind them, Mount Rainier was visible over the top of the city's skyline.

Meggie was dressed warmly in woolen leggings, a vivid red tunic sweater that complemented her dark hair and ivory complexion, stylish thick-heeled black boots and a black leather jacket. A crimson tam was cocked jauntily on her head, the color reminding him of the bustier she'd worn at the *Metropolitan* party.

He had on black jeans, a black turtleneck and a green-plaid mackinaw. Meggie teased him about the mackinaw, joking that you could take the man out of Alaska but you couldn't take Alaska out of the man. But Caleb saw plenty of other guys dressed as ruggedly as he.

Although a thriving metropolis, Seattle had managed to hang on to its wilderness roots. Things were a bit more casual here than in classy New York or hip L.A. If he were forced to live in a big city in the lower forty-eight, Seattle would be the one he'd choose.

The city, he decided, was a lot like Meggie herself, an interesting mix of sophisticate and earth mother.

A wide array of vendors had their wares spread out in a smorgasbord of selections, from fish to fresh fruits and vegetables to spices and cheese. Tantalizing aromas assaulted their noses.

Also interspersed between the buildings and food stalls were artisans with handmade crafts on display. Leather belts and wallets. Beaded rugs and pottery. Portraits and seascapes. Sculpture and jewelry.

"I come here almost every Saturday morning." Meggie inhaled deeply. "I love the fresh food."

"How about we pick up something for dinner and I cook for you?" Caleb offered. "To thank you for showing me a good time."

"You don't have to do that. We can just grab a pizza and rent a video or something."

His heart skipped a beat. So she had planned for their outing to extend into the evening. This was a good thing. A very, very good thing.

"How about linguine with clam sauce?" he suggested enticingly. "Garlic bread and a tossed salad."

"Okay." She laughed. "You're on."

They wandered through the buildings, picking out the ingredients for their meal. When she casually linked her arm through his, Caleb almost stopped breathing.

He sneaked surreptitious glances her way, trying to decipher what the gesture meant, but she seemed so tranquil he could only conclude she felt relaxed enough in his presence that she hadn't giving a second thought to slipping her arm through his.

Was that a bad sign or a good one?

Meggie chatted gaily about the market, about Seattle, about her job and his lecture series. He hung on her every word, but he was so dazzled by the feel of her arm against his side and the heavenly smell of her that he forgot what she said the minute the words left her ripe, sweet mouth.

She purchased a sack of tangerines from a fruit vendor and, as they strolled, peeled one with her long, slender fingers. Dropping the scalped peel into her sack, she then broke off a segment of the citrus fruit and slipped a wedge into her mouth.

"Mmm."

Her soft sound jolted him straight back to that night at the Claremont Hotel. A shiver sliced through Caleb at the vivid memory.

"Oh, this is *so* good."

Helplessly, he dropped his gaze to her mouth and spotted a glistening bead of wet nectar clinging to her lush bottom lip.

That tiny droplet mesmerized him more surely than a pocket watch entranced a hypnosis enthusiast. And his agony didn't end there. When her tongue darted out and whisked the luscious liquid away, the sight reminded him even more of the erotic adventures they'd shared.

"Here, you've gotta taste this." Meggie stopped walking, reached up and lifted a section of tangerine to his mouth.

With an indrawn breath, Caleb allowed his lips to part. Meggie slipped the tangy, sweet, pulpy fruit between his teeth. Her fingertip, soft and inviting, lightly caressed his lower lip, and Caleb's mouth exploded in a riot of sensation. Between the sugary burst of tangerine on his taste buds and the lingering imprint of Meggie's warm finger on his lips, he seriously considered that he might have just died and gone to heaven. The sound of appreciation he made had nothing to do with the fruit and everything to do with Meggie's closeness.

She beamed at him. "It's a perfect tangerine, isn't it?"

"Perfect," he agreed.

"Want another?"

Baby, you can feed me tangerines all day long, was

what he wanted to say, but instead he said, "Nah, I don't want to fill up before dinner."

"Okay, but you're missing out." She polished off the tangerine with a satisfied smirk, and then daintily licked her fingers in a casual move so frigging hot it left Caleb aching to kiss her to taste the heady flavor of Meggie mixed with the perfect tangerine.

They continued walking. A couple of times she paused and tilted her head, looking at him as if he was a familiar pair of slippers or a comfy bathrobe.

That thought disturbed him. He didn't want to be comfortable and familiar. He wanted to be a dangerous, exciting risk taker like Don Juan.

But he shouldn't be complaining. For now, he had her all to himself. His real self. Not the consummate lover he pretended to be when he was behind that mask.

Ah. The sticking point. Would Meggie rather be with him or some long-dead lothario that Caleb had resurrected in order to romance the woman of his dreams?

Things were getting way too complicated.

He should come clean and tell her the truth about Don Juan, but he didn't know how to start. Besides, he wasn't sure she was ready to hear the truth, and he couldn't bear the thought of losing her friendship.

Meggie leaned her head against his shoulder in a guileless gesture that captured his heart. She pointed to a vendor selling porcelain figurines.

"Ooh, dolls. Let's go see."

Okay. All right. He wouldn't tell her about Don Juan. Not yet, even though he was bursting with the need to scoop her into his arms and kiss her.

He would wait. He would slowly romance her, as Caleb. By the time she realized her true feelings for

him, he hoped she would be ready to discover the identity of her mystery lover.

Caleb swallowed hard. He didn't feel particularly
good about his plan, but saw no way around it. The
outcome hinged on what he did in the next few weeks.
Could he get her to see him as boyfriend potential?
Could he convince her that she would rather have him
than Don Juan?

He had less than four weeks to win her heart. The
clock was ticking.

CALEB SEEMED DIFFERENT and Meggie couldn't quite put
her finger on why. Usually whenever she was around
him she felt as relaxed as she did around her own family, but ever since his arrival in Seattle, there was an
odd uneasiness between them.

When she'd leaned in close to feed him that slice of
tangerine, she'd felt his whole body tense, and when
her fingers grazed his lip she could have sworn she
saw his skin pale.

Was he angry with her for some reason? Meggie had
no idea why. She glanced over at him. The afternoon
sun had slipped from behind the ever-present clouds,
catching them for a moment in a swathe of orange light.

His hair glinted darkly. A five-o'clock shadow had
begun to sprout on his rugged jaw. His brow was pulled
down in a brooding expression. His eyes, as blue as the
ocean beyond the pier, shimmered with an intensity that
grabbed hold of her belly and squeezed. In that moment,
he was a complete stranger to her.

Meggie gulped and the oddest sensation came over
her. She couldn't begin to name her emotion. Anxiety
maybe, but a nicer feeling than that. Apprehension? No,
not really. She wasn't afraid of Caleb.

Excitement? Weirdly enough there was an element of that. Fondness? She'd always been fond of Caleb, but the sensation was deeper, more complex, than fondness.

Knocked off balance by the abnormal emotion—whatever it was—Meggie shook her head and hung back.

Caleb stopped and turned to look at her. The crowd flowed around them, but it was as if they were the only two people in the marketplace. The sun was retreating into the clouds, but left behind enough light to silhouette him in a surreal, ethereal glow.

He looked like...who?

Meggie stopped breathing as a dark, unthinkable thought skittered across her consciousness, but she quickly shoved it aside before it had time to take root in her head and bloom.

She needed something to distract her. Now.

The dolls. That was the answer. They'd been on their way to look at the doll vendor's stand. With her blood darting rapidly through her veins, she hurried over to the vendor without glancing in Caleb's direction again.

Inexplicably, her hand trembled slightly as she picked up a doll and pretended to examine it. But, in truth, she couldn't seem to focus on the porcelain figurine in her hand.

Calm down, Meggie. What's wrong with you?

She felt Caleb come up behind her and stand so close he almost touched her. Meggie's body flooded with a sharp rush of adrenaline. She had the wildest urge to either flee or spin on her heels and snap at him to back away.

The fight or flight response.

But why on earth was she experiencing that cornered-animal gut reaction to a man she had known her entire life? It made absolutely no sense.

Was she *attracted* to Caleb Greenleaf?

At once, she knew it was true. When the switch had been flipped, she couldn't say, but she wasn't about to let Caleb know of her feelings. He was her ex-step-brother, for crying out loud. He was two-and-a-half years her junior, and Meggie had no doubt that he considered her nothing more than a friend.

Whoa! Slow down. What is going on with you, Meggie? So what if you're attracted to Caleb? It means nothing. Probably just some temporary transitional thing you're going through. Like when patients fall in love with their therapists. Displacement. That was it.

Okay. She was calming down. *See? Deep breath in, deep breath out. Calm. Controlled.*

She was attracted to Caleb because he was familiar. He had been kind to her. And this probably had something to do with Don Juan stirring up a lot of sensual feelings she'd kept buried for a long time. Her unexpected desire for Caleb was simply a result of her rebounding femininity. This would pass.

"See anything you like?" Caleb murmured, his warm breath fanning the hairs on the nape of her neck.

Meggie forced herself not to shiver. She started to shake her head, but then her gaze landed on a black porcelain mask. A glass miniature of the same type of mask Don Juan had worn. She reached out to touch the mask in the bizarre hope of grounding herself.

"Ah, you're attracted to the unknown," the doll vendor said. She was a gray-haired woman with an unlined face and mystic aura about her. She wore a dreamy, blue gauze dress and too much jewelry.

"What?" Meggie blinked.

"The mask. It represents what we keep hidden deep within us. The veil that separates the civilized part of our psyche from the uncivilized. The mask symbolizes our secret desires, our forbidden passions, our clandestine affairs."

A coldness passed through Meggie. It was as if the woman possessed a strange telepathy that allowed her to look straight into her heart.

"We'll take it," Caleb told the woman.

"No, please. I can't let you buy this for me." Meggie shook her head.

"You like it and I want to get you something to repay you for squiring me around town."

"Showing you Seattle is my pleasure."

"We'll take it," he repeated insistently, and pulled a wad of cash from his pocket.

"Caleb." Meggie leaned back against his body to whisper a warning. "Don't be such a tourist. This isn't Bear Creek. Don't go flashing your money."

His face colored and he looked chagrined. He peeled off two twenties and handed them to the doll vendor to cover the cost of the mask, then stuffed his money clip back into his front pocket.

Meggie realized she'd embarrassed him and immediately felt bad. "I'm sorry to make a fuss," she mumbled.

"Don't be," he said. "You were absolutely right."

The doll vendor wrapped up his purchase, made change and handed him the sack. He turned the package over to Meggie. "To mark the event of my visit to Seattle."

She clutched the sack to her chest, felt the solid weight of the mask inside the package correspond with the solid lump of emotion lodged in her chest.

"Thank you. It's a lovely gift and awfully sweet of you to buy it for me."

Their eyes met. Something meaningful passed between them. Something more than mere friendship. Something she was too afraid to name.

"You're welcome."

He smiled, and for one starstruck moment she thought he was going to touch her face, but instead he clapped his palms together. "Now how about we get those ingredients for that clam sauce?"

Two HOURS LATER they were ensconced in Meggie's apartment, with a crackling fire in her gas fireplace and a feast laid out across the dining room table.

They had prepared dinner together, chopping and mixing, slicing and dicing, stirring and sautéing. They'd sipped wine as they worked, and Caleb had fiddled with the dial on her radio, jumping from station to station until he caught an edgy salsa beat and left it tuned there.

They had bopped around the kitchen to the lively tunes while the exotic Spanish sound brought unbidden thoughts of Don Juan. Would she ever see her mysterious lover again? Did she even want to?

But she pushed those questions aside to listen to Caleb talk about the lectures, his impression of Seattle and what tourist attraction he wanted to see next.

A fissure of pleasure broke through her earlier anxiety because things seemed to have gone back to normal between her and Caleb.

They were friends again and nothing more.

Thank heavens.

Meggie discounted the weird flush of emotions she'd felt at the Pike Place Market, chalking everything up to her fascination with Don Juan. She was so intrigued by the man she was imagining the most ridiculous things. She really had to do something about her obsession with Don Juan before it started causing her serious problems.

"This clam sauce is the best I've ever tasted," Meggie told Caleb, determined not to think of Don Juan for the rest of the evening.

He grinned at her. "Thanks."

"You're going to make some lucky lady a very good husband someday."

"You think?"

"Oh, absolutely."

She waved a hand. She was feeling a little tipsy from the wine. A soft, warm glow settled over her. She was happy to be sitting here with her friend, and she was glad he hadn't let her fix him up with Wendy. While she had boiled the linguini, he'd set the table and lit the candles that had been sitting on her dining room table for years. When she looked at him across the table, she saw twin candle flames reflected in his eyes.

"For the life of me, Caleb, I don't know why some woman hasn't already snapped you up."

He shrugged. "Guess I just haven't met the right one yet."

Why *wasn't* he married yet? The man was beyond gorgeous. And kind and trustworthy and wealthy and very, very sexy.

As far as she knew he'd never even had a serious relationship. Quinn had mentioned once that Caleb had sown a few wild oats in college, but no one in Bear Creek could ever recall him having a steady girlfriend.

Why not? He didn't seem like a one-night stand kind of guy.

Yeah, and seven weeks ago you weren't a one-night stand kind of girl.

She thought of Don Juan again, felt a flush of heat rise to her face.

Dammit! She was not going to think about him anymore. The affair was over and that's the way she wanted it.

"Let me speculate," she said, looking for any excuse to distract herself. "You're a wee bit commitment phobic because of your family history."

"On the money." Caleb gave her a wry smile. "When your mother has been married three times and your father twice, and you have a total of eleven stepsiblings or half siblings, it sorta shakes your faith in happily ever after."

"Tell me about it." Meggie shook her head.

"You're thinking of Jesse."

"Well, we were together six years."

"How come you married him, Megs? If you don't mind me asking."

"I messed up. What can I say?"

"Was it an opposites-attract kind of thing between you two? Or did you have that silly romantic notion women sometimes get, thinking they can change the bad boy? Because I never understood what you saw in him and I always thought you deserved better."

"My, my. What a big speech for a guy who doesn't talk much," Meggie teased, but the hitch in her stomach made it hard to breathe.

"I won't get offended if you tell me it's none of my damned business. Because it's not. But I'm curious."

Meggie stared into her wineglass and took a swig of the tepid liquid. "To tell you the truth, I've been struggling to answer that question myself."

"Come up with any stunning insight?"

He cocked his head to one side. In that moment he

looked so endearingly boyish, Meggie felt something warm and slippery melt inside her.

"Other than I was young and dumb?"

"Yeah, other than that." He grinned.

Caleb made her feel safe. Like she could tell him anything and it would be all right. She recalled then pleasant snippets from their childhood. Because of his jumbled family life, Caleb had often stayed with the Scofields, especially during the summer when school was out and his stepsiblings had shuttled off in a half-dozen different directions on vacations with their respective parents. Homebody Caleb had always preferred staying in Bear Creek, and Meggie's loving parents had readily opened their home to him.

They'd had the kind of routine that had stayed with her as a model of how summer mornings were suppose to be. As kids, they rose early, listening to the birds trilling. They'd make themselves breakfast if her parents were still asleep. Cold cereal or frozen waffles if Meggie convinced the boys to eat properly. Cookie dough or leftover pizza or even ice cream if they had their way.

Then her parents would get up. Usually her father first, shuffling into the kitchen in his bathrobe to make coffee while her mother showered. Then her mom would make them a picnic lunch if they were going exploring. Cheese and bread, fruit and juice that she put in brown paper sacks. She'd wave them off with instructions not to get lost or fall into the fjord.

"Remember when we were kids and you used to spend the summer with Quinn?"

"I remember."

"You guys were nice to let me tag along with you, even though I was such a cautious scaredy-cat."

"I think your mother made us."

"Yeah, well, there was that." She smiled at him. "But somewhere along the way, I picked up this craving for adventure. Funny, though. At the very same time I was always afraid of letting go, of being out of control."

"You're a complicated lass, Meggie Scofield."

She laughed. "That's one way of looking at it."

"So what did Jesse have to do with any of this?"

Meggie moistened her lips. "Okay, here it is. My theory on why I was with your stepbrother."

Caleb pushed his plate aside, propped his elbows on the table and dropped his chin into his open palms. "I'm all ears. Go on."

"The way I figure it, with my limited knowledge of pop psychology, Jesse provided me with a safe outlet, a way to get my vicarious thrills. I could watch him skydive or bungee jump and I never had to take a risk or put myself out there. I inhaled the fumes from his high and that got me by. Secondhand adventure, so to speak. Does that make any sense?"

Caleb nodded. "I can see where you might find my stepbrother exciting."

"Also makes sense that he would eventually leave me for being too dull."

"You're not dull," he declared vehemently. "Not in the least."

"Oh, believe me, I was. I spent all my time working. My job is everything to me. I never wanted to try anything new, do anything different. I had my routine and I liked things that way. I've got to thank Jesse for that at least. He shook me up and made me realize how I'd been sleepwalking through life."

"If you say so."

"But that's all changed now. I've starting taking a

few risks of my own and I'm amazed at what I've discovered about myself."

"How? What happened?"

Meggie ducked her head, suddenly embarrassed. Should she tell him about Don Juan?

"Megs?"

She raised her chin and met his gaze. She saw nothing but calm acceptance reflected in those big blue eyes. Maybe if she told him about Don Juan she could start getting over her obsession with the fantasy.

Caleb was a great listener and an even better friend. He wouldn't go back to Bear Creek and gossip. If she told him about Don Juan, no one else would ever find out.

"I've got big ears and tight lips."

"Your ears aren't big." She swatted playfully at his shoulder, almost fell out of her chair and realized belatedly she was a tad tipsy.

"Whoa there." He put out a hand to steady her and his touch did very strange things to her skin. It sizzled, fizzled and tingled.

It's just the wine, ninny.

"Thank you, kind sir."

Caleb's eyebrows dipped in a frown. "Are you okay?"

Gosh, he seemed so serious. Meggie hiccuped, lifted a palm to her mouth and giggled. "Oops, sorry."

"Don't feel embarrassed around me. How long have we known each other?"

"Years and years and years."

Man, he really was cute, especially when you focused on his perfect mouth.

Meggie narrowed her eyes and stared unabashedly at his lips. Gee. His mouth looked a lot like Don Juan's. She must have a thing for really great mouths.

"Exactly. So you should feel free to say anything to me. Anything in the world."

"Anything?"

She would bet her last quarter that wasn't really true. What would he do if she told him she thought she might be developing a serious crush on his mouth? And that she was fighting the strongest urge to kick off her sneakers, run her toes up his shin and play a down-and-dirty game of footsie?

Ha! He'd probably make a human-size hole in the wall as he ran away from her.

"Anything," he reiterated.

"Okay, then. I think I've had too much wine."

"All right." He took her glass away. "Is there anything else you want to tell me?"

Damn, he seemed to know something was gnawing at her, and he obviously wasn't going to let it lie. Served her right for knowing him more than half her life.

"Meggie, it's me, Caleb. You know you can trust me with your darkest secrets."

He reached out and squeezed her hand, giving her the courage to spill out her heart and ask his advice on how to stop fixating on yet another bad boy.

That did it. The giddiness of the wine, the warmth of this hand and her desperate desire to overcome her sexual obsession all culminated into one unstoppable urge to come clean about what she had been up to with that dastardly Don Juan.

"Caleb," she whispered, "I've got something to confess."

CHAPTER ELEVEN

ONE SECOND. Two. Three. Was she going to tell him about Don Juan?

"Why don't we go sit in front of the fire?" she invited with a coy little smile that jerked his heartstrings. "Get comfortable."

"Okay." He held out his palm. She hesitated only the briefest second before sinking her hand into his and allowing him to lead her into the living room area.

He wanted to kiss her so badly he couldn't think, but he had to be careful, had to move slowly. When he'd bought her the mask this afternoon and she'd acted so oddly he thought maybe he'd already ruined everything. But tonight, preparing the meal together, and just now, when she'd agreed to tell him her darkest secret, Caleb felt the old sense of camaraderie return.

He also felt a nasty stab of guilt. Because she was tipsy, she was about to entrust him with her vulnerability, and he was the one lying to her. Should he stop her before she got started?

God forgive him, but he couldn't. He had to hear what she was going to say.

They sat crossed-legged on the rug in front of the fire. Meggie pushed her hair back from her face. Lord, she was lovely. She leaned her head against his shoulder and sighed contentedly. The weight of her against him caused a sweet ache in his soul.

Her lashes drifted half-shut as she stared at the mesmerizing flames. Caleb's anxiety mounted with each passing moment that she didn't speak, but he was not going to rush her.

Finally she said, "I met this guy."

Struggling to maintain a cool facade, he simply nodded.

She gave him a sideways glance, as if gauging his reaction, and seemed reassured. She told him then about how she'd met Don Juan at the *Metropolitan* party, how she didn't even know his name but she'd recklessly given him her phone number. How he'd turned up in Seattle for one glorious night.

"He's so wrong for me, but I'm afraid I'm hooked."

Caleb pursed his lips but said nothing.

"Don't get me wrong. I'm not thinking of this guy as happily ever after material. Not by a long shot."

"No?"

"Honestly, I'm not. I didn't want anything more from him than great sex."

"Megs, this falls under the category of a little too much information."

"I've embarrassed you. I was afraid of that. You still see me as an older sister figure, and here I am talking about sex."

"I'm not embarrassed," he growled. *And the last thing I see you as is my sister.* "Keep talking."

"You sure?"

"Positive. I told you I'm here for you, no matter what."

"Okay. Like I was saying, the last thing I want is any kind of a relationship with this guy."

Caleb didn't know what to think about this latest development. Or how to feel. He wanted her to want him, not Don Juan. But if she just wanted Don Juan for sex, what did that mean for him?

Damn. This whole deception was turning into a real mess. What had started out as a daring game had veered into dangerous territory.

"This guy is just a bit of the hair of the dog, if you know what I mean. I suppose I'm using him to get this wildness out of my system, to boost my ego. Doesn't that sound terrible? Using a guy for sex."

"Not if it's what you need."

"And it seems to be working."

"Does it?"

"Well, except for one thing."

"Yes?"

God, what a struggle to keep his tone noncommittal and not say anything that might do irreparable damage to their friendship.

"I'm completely obsessed with him," she whispered.

He looked into her eyes, two glorious green vortexes shimmering with the seductive double whammy of shame and thrill. Her upper teeth sank into her full lower lip, and Meggie dipped her head a bit to hide her expression from his perusal.

Her confession caught him by surprise, while at the same time filled his heart with an inexplicable joy. Meggie was obsessed with him!

Not you, dimwit. She's obsessed with a fantasy. When she finds out the truth, she's gonna be mightily pissed off.

"I can't stop thinking about him. I know it's foolish, but there it is." She knotted her fingers and dropped her hands into her lap.

"It's just an infatuation."

"I know. And even if it wasn't, I realize this guy's

not right for me. I know nothing about him, and besides, how could a relationship built solely on sex ever stand a chance?"

"Do you want a real relationship with him?" Caleb dared to ask.

"No." She shook her head vehemently. "I just wish I could stop thinking about him."

"It's the mystery that's intrigued you. That's all."

"You're absolutely right and that's what I keep telling myself. I'm betting if I were to meet this guy without his mask and costume I wouldn't be attracted to him in the slightest."

Ouch. That wasn't pleasant to hear. The whole Don Juan thing was backfiring on him. In the beginning, Caleb's rationale for hiding behind the disguise was to convince Meggie to see him as a virile, potent man who desired her.

What had started as an impetuous impulse upon meeting Klondike Kate had turned into a driving desire to indulge his long-held fantasies, once he'd discovered who she was.

He recalled the first time he had became aware of Meggie as a woman. It was the summer he was fourteen and she was sixteen. She'd shown up to go sailing with him and Jesse and Quinn, wearing white short-shorts and a blue polka-dot halter top. He could still remember how the soft material had clung to her breasts. How he'd been completely fascinated by the sight.

He swallowed hard. He was slipping, sliding, tumbling headlong to a place he wasn't sure he wanted to go because it was simply too overwhelming. And the realization that he wanted more from her, that two nights of anonymous sex were never going to be enough for him, scared the living hell out of Caleb.

What did it all mean?

"It's getting late and the rain is drumming pretty hard on the roof," he said, unnerved by the thoughts and memories rushing through his head. "I should go."

"You don't have to leave."

"No?" He looked at her, and she was giving him a smile that was quintessential Meggie. His heart tripped. What was she implying?

"The couch makes into a bed," she said, dashing his foolish hopes that she'd meant something else. "I keep an extra toothbrush in the cupboard in case of company."

The idea of staying the night was incredibly tempting. Too damned tempting. He thought of lying on the couch while she slept in the next room, and he knew he'd never be able to do it.

"I think I better go. I have some paperwork to catch up on."

"Oh, okay."

She walked him to the door. They stood there a minute looking at each other.

"What I told you tonight was strictly confidential," she said.

"Of course."

"Thanks, Caleb. It helped, talking to you about my little, er…problem."

"Anytime."

She rose up on her toes, leaned in and planted a kiss on his cheek. "You're the greatest."

"See you tomorrow?" he asked.

She shook her head. "I've got to work and then I've got a committee meeting."

"Monday?"

"I've got belly dancing class."

"Oh."

"But maybe after? We could go to a movie or a comedy club or check out a local band."

"Sounds good." He didn't care where he went or what he did as long as Meggie was there.

"Why don't you pick me up at the dance studio? My class is over at seven."

The thought of watching Meggie belly dance drove a spike of hot, achy need right through his spine. And the imprint of her lips still burned his cheek, feeding his libido. It was all he could do not to kiss her back, and this time not on the cheek.

She gave him the address of the studio, then ruffled his hair. "Good night, little brother. See ya on Monday."

Caleb left her apartment gritting his teeth and clutching the pink paisley umbrella she had given him, knowing one thing for certain. He would have to take some very determined steps to show Meggie exactly how unbrotherly he could be.

But where and how to start?

He had no idea how to go about seducing her without that damnable mask.

MEGGIE SHUT THE DOOR behind Caleb and sagged against it, thankful he'd decided not to stay the night. But she was not really sure why she was so relieved. Probably because she felt pretty darned vulnerable after spilling her guts to him about Don Juan. Why had she told Caleb all that stuff?

Or maybe you're glad he left because of the way he's starting to make you feel, an irritating voice in the back of her mind whispered.

Frowning, Meggie began putting their dinner dishes

in the dishwasher. That was ridiculous. She wasn't feeling any differently toward Caleb than she ever had.

Oh no? Then why were you noticing how nicely his long legs looked stretched out across your carpet? Why were you admiring the way his dark hair curls around his collar? And I saw you staring at his chiseled-from-granite biceps.

"I wasn't," she retorted, jamming forks, spoons and knives into the silverware holder.

Liar.

What about the way he'd listened to her confession about Don Juan, without a hint of judgment or condemnation on his face?

"So he's a good friend. I already knew that."

You kissed him.

"On the friggin' cheek."

First comes the cheek. The lips are bound to follow.

"Oh, shut up."

She scrubbed her large cooking pot, attacking the starchy linguini residue with a vengeance.

And then you went and invited him to come watch you belly dance. Now tell the truth, what in the hell was that all about?

What indeed?

"This is preposterous," she muttered. "I'm not attracted to Caleb Greenleaf, for heaven's sake."

Why not? This time it was Wendy's voice echoing in her head. *He's handsome and smart and rich. Reliable and trustworthy and kind.*

Why not, indeed?

Meggie rinsed off a dinner plate. Well, for one thing, he had shown absolutely no indication of being interested in her.

He bought you the porcelain mask.

"Big deal. He's a generous guy."

He cooked dinner.

"He was just thanking me for showing him around town."

Why are you showing him around town?

"He's an old friend!"

Yeah, right.

"He is," Meggie stubbornly insisted to herself.

Okay, so why haven't you introduced him to Wendy yet?

"Because he's all wrong for her."

Really? Maybe it's because you think he's all right for you.

"Come on, he's *not* interested in me!"

And even if he was interested in her, which she seriously doubted, Meggie wasn't about to embarrass herself by coming on to a younger man. No way, no how.

I'd rather be an old man's darling than a young man's fool. One of Wendy's favorite reasons for dating older men flitted through her head.

And Meggie was a little gun-shy about taking a risk and laying her emotions on the line, which no doubt explained her interest in her no-strings-attached relationship with Don Juan. With him she didn't have to worry about getting hurt. Caleb, however, was another story completely. Just thinking about Caleb in this strange new way caused her to hyperventilate.

No. Absolutely not.

Meggie cringed, imagining what her mother would say, how the gossip would fly from one corner of Bear Creek to the other.

"We're just friends!" she shouted to the wall. "Nothing's changed."

But in her heart, she wasn't so sure she believed that.

THE DANCE STUDIO was chockful of attractive women, but Caleb had eyes for only one. He was standing outside the door of Meggie's belly dancing class, peering through the glass partition and trying hard to work up the courage to step inside.

So strong was his desire for her, Caleb didn't trust himself not to have an overt physical reaction, and he didn't want to embarrass them both in public with a gigantic erection.

When had he lost control over his own body? What was it about Meggie that caused him to act like a horny teenager in the throes of a hormonal storm?

He watched greedily as she undulated in the middle of the room with the other dancers. She wore a gauzy little *I Dream of Jeannie* outfit that showed far too much of her smooth flat belly.

She was the most conspicuous woman in the room, moving with the grace of a true performer. Her arms were raised over her head as she clicked tiny cymbals attached to her fingers. She turned with the group, but she was much more graceful than the others. She was facing away from him now, rolling those curvaceous hips as if she were personally beckoning him to her.

Come.

God, she was hot!

Shake it, baby. The crude, yet thoroughly masculine thought bounced through his brain. He felt like a voyeur, like some kind of a Peeping Tom pervert, but he simply could not stop himself from watching...and wishing she was performing this erotic dance just for him. He hated the thought that anyone else might see her and lust after her.

He realized he was jealous and there was no one to be jealous of. The room contained only the other dancers and the female instructor. No one else was peeking through the glass partition with him.

Cricket on a crutch! He was in deep, and like a quicksand victim, the harder he struggled the deeper he sank. He was falling for her. Fast.

And the misguided jealousy streaking through his heart told him he couldn't fool himself any longer. The desire he felt for her went far beyond the physical. He'd been kidding himself when he decided making love to Meggie would once and forever quell his sexual fantasies about her.

What an idiot he'd been, thinking he could take this lightly and then just walk away.

Meggie executed a series of complicated shifts and steps that had Caleb almost swallowing his tongue. He found his own body swaying in time to the seductive Middle Eastern music seeping under the door and oozing out into the corridor. A mesmerizing sound that had him aching to dance with her. To press her body against his as they moved in tandem.

Stupid urge. He had no idea how to dance.

And yet here he was, his hands burning to touch that wavering waist, to grind his pelvis against those incredible, womanly hips.

The costume she wore was almost as provocative as the scintillating dance she performed. The silky material clung to her well-developed curves and rippled with a stimulating flow that incited his hormones to riot. And a filmy purple veil cloaked her mouth, hiding those full lips he loved so much and adding a tantalizing layer of mystery to her dance.

God, she was gorgeous. The memory of her scent came to him, clinging to his nostrils as surely as if she were standing next to him—the sweet, erotic elixir of lavender, strawberries and Obsession. He recalled the taste of her as well—hot, rich, creamy.

If he wasn't careful he was going to start salivating right there on the spot.

He realized his palms were pressed against the glass, his eyes trained on her. He was a kid outside a toy store with no money in his pockets.

Why had she invited him here?

The thought struck him from the blue and the answer came to him.

This was another one of her fantasies, entitled Just Watch Me, or Let Me Drive You Wild. She was playing a game. Teasing and tantalizing him. But he didn't think she'd been consciously aware of what she was doing when she had encouraged him to come by and pick her up. In fact, he knew that if he were to point out this astounding fact to her, not only would she deny it but she would probably get defensive.

This sudden insight into her psyche jerked like a string attached to his heart. There was only one reason why her subconscious would prod her to ask him to come to the dance studio so he would see her performing such a rousing routine in that electrifying costume. On some uncharted subterranean level she wanted *him*.

A surge of hope, more uplifting than he thought possible, rose inside him. A powerful updraft of expectancy that said yes, maybe he stood a chance of winning her over on his own—without that damned mask.

The music ended. Caleb shook his head, breaking from his reverie as he realized the dance class was over. The door opened and women began streaming out.

Meggie was the last one through the door, and the minute she spotted him, her face lit up with a smile that twinkled like the myriad of holiday decorations the

Scofields had put up around their house every winter when he and Meggie were kids. His own parents had been too busy marrying and divorcing to bother much with Christmas ornamentation.

Her excited expression underscored his hope. Caleb was jubilant. He wanted to dance a jig right there in the hallway with her classmates streaming around them. He wasn't wrong on this matter and he knew it, even if Meggie wasn't yet ready to admit to herself what game she was playing.

Did she suspect, at least on a subconscious level, that he was indeed Don Juan?

"Caleb!" She thrust herself into his arms for a quick hug.

The gossamer material of her outfit grazed his hand and spent a spark of awareness leaping up his nerve endings. She smelled of sweet perspiration and earthy woman, a scent that drove him to the very brink of distraction.

She stepped back. "Have you been here long?"

"A few minutes."

She lowered her lashes, dabbed at her neck with a small, white gym towel. "Did you see me dance?"

Ah, coyness. This *was* a mating game, whether she would admit it or not.

What a rush.

"I saw you." His tone was sexier than he intended, but dammit, he couldn't help himself.

She lifted her head. Her green eyes were startled, her pupils wide.

She honestly doesn't realize what she's doing to me. This is all subconscious.

"You're very good," he said.

"Thank you. I really love to dance."

"You could be a professional."

"Nah. I'm a nurse at heart, but dancing is my passion."

"I remember."

"You do?"

Caleb stuffed his hands in his front pockets, mainly to keep himself from touching her. His fingers itched to trace the fabric of that sparkly costume and feel her body heat beneath.

"One year for your birthday—I think you were probably eight or nine—your mom got you that pink ballerina outfit and you spent the whole summer twirling up and down the streets of Bear Creek. I recall thinking you looked just like a stick of cotton candy."

And, boy, how he loved cotton candy. He'd been stone-cold addicted to the stuff.

"You remember that? But you were only, what? Six, maybe seven?"

"I remember a lot of things, Meggie."

She seemed flustered. Her cheeks darkened and she glanced away again, jerking a thumb in the direction of a door marked Ladies' Locker Room.

"Listen, I'm going to go hit the showers and change. I'll be ready to leave in about twenty minutes. Is that okay?"

He motioned to a nearby bench positioned beneath a bulletin board. "I don't mind waiting. I'll just have a seat. Take your time."

"You're a doll."

She reached over to ruffle his hair in her irritatingly familiar fashion, but halfway to his head, she seemed to realize what she was doing, stopped and dropped her arm. Without another word, she turned and scurried into the locker room.

Grinning, he settled himself on the bench. *Mark this day on the calendar, folks.* Meggie Scofield had stopped ruffling his hair. One small step in the direction he wanted her to go, but it wasn't enough. He wanted to move faster. He needed a major weapon in his campaign to persuade Meggie to stop seeing him as just an old childhood friend and start picturing him as a potential lover.

What would it take to convince her?

He leaned his head back and collided with the bulletin board behind him. A pushpin fell from the cork, bounced off his head and skittered across the floor. An orange flyer swooped through the air and slid under the bench.

Caleb got up, retrieved the pushpin and fished under the bench for the flyer. He moved to tack it back to the bulletin board, but as he read the page, he stopped and an idea took shape.

SALSA CLASSES START FRIDAY.
Looking for an exciting new way to romance your ladylove? Try salsa dancing. She'll be putty in your hands, guaranteed. Even if you've never danced a day in your life, our instructors, the renowned flamenco dancers Raul Roman and his lovely wife Luisa will have you doing the tango, the merengue, the cumbia and many more in a matter of ten easy lessons. Sign up in the office today!

Caleb stared at the flyer. It was as if the thing had been conjured up by divine intervention. He was looking for an exciting new way to romance his lady. And Meggie loved to dance.

Salsa dancing. It was the perfect solution to his dilemma.

Resolutely he pinned the flyer back to the bulletin board and went in search of the office.

CHAPTER TWELVE

WHY WAS HER PULSE hammering so hard? Meggie wondered as she stripped out of her belly dancing outfit and stepped into the shower.

Er...maybe because you spent the last fifty minutes belly dancing?

Ha! She wished.

Unfortunately, she had a sneaking suspicion her accelerated heart rate had nothing to do with exercise and everything to do with the way Caleb had been staring at her.

Don't be silly. Don't be ridiculous. Caleb wasn't looking at you any differently than he's ever looked at you.

And if by some chance he *was* looking at her differently, it was only because of her sexy costume. He was a normal red-blooded male. She was a skimpily dressed woman with a bare midriff. What did she expect?

She shouldn't have asked him to pick her up at the dance studio, especially on a night they were performing a dress rehearsal for an upcoming competition. What had she been thinking?

Well, on the practical side, the studio was much closer to the Space Needle—where she'd intended on taking him for dinner—than her apartment. But if she were being honest with herself might she not admit that maybe, just maybe, she'd wanted Caleb to see her dancing in costume?

Why?

That was the sixty-four-thousand-dollar question.

She shook her head to dispel the notion and concentrated on soaping down her body. As she scrubbed, she found her thoughts wandering back to Caleb.

He was such a great guy. Too bad he hadn't been able to find the right woman, particularly after all his friends in Bear Creek had paired up with the ladies of their dreams. He had to be feeling left out.

She slid her hands down her body, lathering her belly and beyond. Her skin tingled where she touched. She was glad Caleb had come to Seattle. He had badly needed the vacation, time away from home. And she was happy she'd been able to show him the town. It'd been fun reconnecting with her old friend again.

And then without warning, an image popped into her mind that was anything but platonic. Meggie pictured Caleb right there in the shower with her. His hands were washing the triangle of hair between her legs. He was taking his long masculine fingers and slowly rubbing her in private places, stimulating her to a fevered pitch as she pressed herself into his hard, naked, wet body.

Yikes!

What in the hell was she thinking? Caleb was the guy next door, the kid she'd spent her summers playing hide and seek with. She should not be having these thoughts about him. Caleb simply was not fantasy material.

Oh yeah? I've seen you giving him the once-over. You can't deny he's gorgeous. Admit it, Meggie. Caleb grew up real nice.

"WHERE ARE WE GOING?" Caleb asked as they left the dance studio. He'd just signed up for ten salsa lessons, and he could barely keep from grinning. Was Meggie ever going to be surprised when he took her salsa dancing.

"Seattle's number one tourist attraction."

"Which is?"

"The Space Needle, of course."

"What?"

Balking, he stopped walking. He wasn't sure Meggie knew of his fear of man-made heights, such as tall buildings, and he hated to admit a weakness, but the thought of going up to the Space Needle made his gut torque.

"I made reservations at SkyCity, the revolving restaurant at the Needle. They make a killer Dungeness crab cocktail, and their famous dessert, the Lunar Orbiter, is to die for. Afterward, I thought we could go up on the observation deck and gaze out at the city lights. I haven't been up there in such a long time, I'm really looking forward to tonight."

Caleb looked at her standing in the glow of the light from the dance studio and his heart slipped in his chest. She held her workout bag in one hand and her car keys in the other.

She wore a flowing rust-colored skirt, the hem just skimming the tops of her calf-high, brown leather boots, and a black long-sleeved Lycra top. She had a cream-colored sweater draped over her shoulders. Her short black hair, still damp from her shower, curled enticingly around her face. She had applied fresh lipstick, and a light dusting of mascara to her lashes, enhancing her natural prettiness without overdoing the cosmetics.

She wasn't a raving beauty in the way of models and movie stars, but in his eyes, Meggie was the most gorgeous creature on the face of the earth. Just looking at her changed him in ways he could not verbally express.

She made him want to spend less time alone in the wilderness and more time in the world with people. It was a strange sensation for an introvert, and he didn't completely understand his new emotions.

Her smile encompassed her face and her green eyes came alive with excitement. If she wanted to go to the Space Needle, then, by damn, that's where he would go. Phobia or not.

His bravado held until he was faced with climbing into the toothpaste-dispenser-size elevator at the Space Needle. At the entrance, they were greeted by a pleasant attendant who was extolling the virtues of the glass lift to a handful of other visitors.

"Time to face the fear, Greenleaf," he growled.

"What?" Meggie blinked at him.

"All aboard," the attendant announced, unclipping the velvet rope blocking the entrance to the elevator.

Caleb hung back.

"Come on." Meggie smiled and took his hand.

You can do this. There's nothing to be afraid of. It's just an elevator.

He took solace in the feel of Meggie's warm palm pressed against his, and reluctantly stepped into the small glass cage. The attendant asked them to move farther back in order to make room for more people. Gritting his teeth, Caleb shifted toward the outer glass wall with a vertigo-inducing view of the ground below.

Up, up, up. The elevator moved with a series of jerky clicks. Was the damned thing supposed to be so noisy? It wasn't natural for the scenery to blur so fast.

Take the risk. You can handle it. Not just for Meggie's sake but also to prove to yourself that you're not set in your ways. You can do different things. You can face your fears. You can adjust to life in the city.

Much to his relief they made it to the restaurant without incident. The hostess escorted them onto the rotating dais and they were seated at an intimate table for two with a spectacular view of Seattle.

He felt a little quivery, but took in a deep breath and managed to quell the jitters by gazing into Meggie's face cast so beautifully in candlelight. He wasn't going to let a bad childhood memory control his life.

"Isn't this fabulous?" Meggie enthused, turning her head to look out the window and revealing the smooth expanse of her long, graceful neck.

"Yes," he said.

But much more fabulous than the panorama below was the stunning view right across from him. Meggie beamed at him and he felt as if he'd been given the most precious of gifts.

He did as she suggested and ordered the crab. She chattered gaily and, it seemed, a little nervously, as if frightened to leave the opportunity for silence. Caleb wondered why. He and Meggie had sat in companionable silence many times before. It was one of the things he loved most about her. In the past, she'd waited patiently in the forest with him in the hopes of spotting a mama bear with her cubs or a bald eagle building a nest. Why this sudden need to fill the air with talk?

"What do you think of Seattle?" Meggie asked.

"It's a very romantic place, as far as cities go. Of course, nothing can beat Bear Creek for sheer beauty."

"Romantic?" There was laughter in her voice. "Can't say I've ever thought of Seattle as romantic. Too much darn rain."

"Rain can be sexy."

"Oh?"

"Sure. Like the other night at your apartment. A roaring fire, good company, rain drumming seductively on the roof."

"You thought *that* was romantic? Dear Caleb, you've got to get out more."

"That's why I'm here."

"Is it?"

His gaze met hers. "Yep. I came to Seattle to explore the perimeters of romance."

"Ah, now you're pulling my leg."

"A little," he admitted, enjoying the teasing banter between. "But I confess—I am searching for something."

He waited to see what she would say. He felt sexual chemistry shimmering between them, but he had to wonder if it was all in his imagination.

"Have you found what you're looking for yet?"

"Maybe. I can't say for sure."

"Oh."

He glanced at her. She was slowly scooting her food around on her plate.

"Is something wrong?" he asked.

"No." She shook her head.

"Not still pining over this Don Juan guy?" he dared to inquire.

"Nah," she muttered, but dropped her gaze.

"You've beaten your obsession?"

"Yes. Talking about it with you the other night helped immensely. Thanks."

He wasn't sure that he believed her. Something was different between them and he didn't know what. Or why.

The waiter cleared their dinner plates, brought coffee, two spoons and one serving of the spectacular Lunar Orbiter dessert, which turned out to be a massive ice cream concoction delivered with fanfare amid swirls of dry ice to simulate Seattle fog.

She scooped up a spoonful of ice cream. Caleb's gaze tracked her movements, fixating on her lips as she daintily slid the cold ice cream into her warm, wet mouth.

"Mmm," she moaned, soft and low.

When she flicked out her tongue to whisk away a drop of melted ice cream from her bottom lip, he shivered so hard he felt it straight down through his bones.

"Caleb, are you okay?"

Easy, Greenleaf. You're going to give this gig away before you have a chance to put Operation Salsa Dancing in action.

"Yeah...I—" His voice cracked. "Uh..."

Oh, that was about as smooth as gravel.

She reached out and placed her hand over his. "Is something wrong?"

Other than the fact that her touch was causing him to get a high-voltage hard-on?

"Fine," he lied. "Absolutely fine."

They lingered for a while, talking softly, enjoying the city lights, savoring the dessert. Meggie tried to pay for the meal, and when Caleb refused to let her, she lobbied for dutch treat.

"No," he said adamantly. "This one's on me."

"Okay, I give up. You win. Pay away." She waved a hand.

"Thank you."

"You know, most guys would jump at a chance to let their date pay."

"I'm not most guys."

She studied him with a pensive expression. "No, no, you're not."

"And we're not on a date."

"We aren't, are we?"

"Nope."

Caleb rose to his feet, took her sweater from the back of her chair and held it out for her to slip her arms into. She seemed flustered by the gesture and missed the armhole twice before getting it right.

"Ready to go out on the observation deck?" she asked just a bit too brightly.

"Uh-huh." He didn't want to go, but he wanted to be with Meggie. Anything to prolong this evening. Even if it entailed peering down from a great man-made height.

He gulped.

Meggie guided him from the restaurant and up a short flight of stairs to the observation deck. The minute she took his hand, her heart started the same crazy stuttering it had back in the shower at the dance studio. What on earth was the matter with her? Wrong time of the month maybe?

But of course not. PMS triggered crankiness and cramps, not this strange, inexplicable euphoria that set her heart to skipping beats.

This was Caleb, for crying out loud, not Don Juan. Had her hormones gone haywire?

Disconcerted, she dropped his hand and moved out onto the observation deck. Clutching her sweater more tightly around her in the wind, she meandered to the edge of the railing and stared out into the night.

When Caleb didn't move to join her, she turned to find him still hovering in the archway between the restaurant and the deck.

The sight of him standing there, his hair whipping sexily in the breeze, his coat collar flipped up around his strong, muscular neck, made her feel very mixed up indeed. She had an inexplicable hunger to feel his arms wrapped around her waist. She wanted to lean against his chest, rest her head on his shoulders.

"Come on." She motioned him over.

"I'm fine right here," he called.

"The view is terrific." She pointed. "Come look at the harbor."

"You go ahead."

"What's the matter, Greenleaf? You chicken?"

"Actually, yes."

"You?" She laughed. "I don't believe it."

"Guilty as charged. I'm afraid of heights."

"But you climbed Mount McKinley with Quinn and you serve on the mountain rescue squad."

"I'm not afraid of heights per se. Just man-made heights. Towers, tall buildings that sway, elevators that go farther than ten or twelve floors. It's sort of a claustrophobia-acrophobia combo."

"That's right. I remember Jesse saying something about that. You got lost in an elevator at the Eiffel Tower when you were a kid."

"Lost, my ass. Jesse abandoned me."

"No kidding?"

"No kidding."

"He was supposed to be watching me but instead he got distracted by some girl and let me get into the elevator by myself. Just so happens the elevator hangs up and I'm stuck in there alone for two hours."

"He was an irresponsible butthead even back then."

"Yes, he was."

They smiled at each other.

His admission of vulnerability surprised her. Strong, capable Caleb afraid of something? She would never have imagined it. She thought of Don Juan and what he had shown her about herself. He'd taught her how to take risks, and she would be forever grateful for that lesson.

Meggie extended her hand to Caleb. "I've recently learned a powerful lesson about facing your fears."

"Oh yeah?"

"Yeah."

"And what is that?"

"If you want to find out what you're really made of, you've got to take a few risks. Come on. Join me on the ledge of life." She swept a hand at their surroundings. "I have faith in you."

"Meggie, you have no idea what a challenge this is for me."

"But that's wonderful. The bigger the risk, the bigger the payoff."

"You think so?"

"I know so."

"Lady, when you throw down a gauntlet, you throw down a gauntlet," he grumbled, but even as he shook his head he was slowly edging one foot toward her.

"You'll thank me in the morning."

"Humph."

"Come to me," she beckoned, wriggling her fingers at him.

He started toward her. The floor beneath them swayed ever so slightly in the gusting wind, and she saw him wince.

"You can do this," she coaxed.

"This better be worth it."

"Trust me. One step at a time."

And that's how he did it, one step at a time toward the brink. When he finally reached her, his face broke into a smile that stole her heart.

"Woo-ho! You did it."

"I did it," he echoed.

"Congratulations. You conquered your fear of man-made heights," she murmured, and spontaneously threw her arms around him.

And then, not even realizing what she had intended on doing, she kissed him.

Caleb wrapped his arms around her as her lips sank onto his, enveloping her in his woodsy scent. The smell of him entered her nostrils, invaded her bloodstream with a heady rush of sensation.

Heaven help her, she hadn't meant to give him a real kiss. It was just supposed to be an atta-boy-I'm-darned-proud-of-you-for-conquering-your-fear kiss. But somewhere between her lips and his, the intention had become distorted, and she could not seem to control what happened next.

Blame it on Don Juan. Blame it on the full moon. Blame it on the fact that for the first time in her life she was seeing Caleb for who he was now and not for the kid next door he had once been.

He was all-man, absolutely no doubt about it.

Meggie melted against his body. She increased the pressure of the kiss, coaxing his lips apart, thrilling to her own bravery. Caleb wasn't the only one taking risks tonight. She'd never been the aggressor in romance. Had never initiated a first kiss.

Boy, when she let her guard down, she really let her guard down.

Gently, she flicked her tongue over his lips, slow and lazy, seducing him by increments. Her head spun with the realization of her own audacity as she took their first kiss deeper and deeper still.

He tasted of creamy, sweet Lunar Orbiter and strong,

dark espresso. And something else. A sweet, familiar taste she could not name.

His mouth was hot and moist against hers. The gusting wind, the tower's gentle sway, shook the very air between their bodies and sent a fog mist swirling about them like something from a fantasy.

Time out! her brain cried. *What do you think you're doing? More importantly, what message are you sending Caleb? You're giving him ideas you're not able to support. Wise up, Meggie. Wise up right now.*

With a low, throaty moan, he arched his body into hers, and when he reached out a hand and cupped the curve of her hip, Meggie's eyes flew open. He was staring at her and she knew then that she was in over her head. Startled and suddenly frightened by what she had done, Meggie pulled away.

"I—I…didn't mean to do that," she stammered. "Please don't take this the wrong way. I certainly wasn't trying to seduce you."

"You could have fooled me."

His voice was rough, abrupt. Was he angry or disappointed? She couldn't blame him for being either. She'd sort of led him on. But she hadn't meant to. It had just happened.

"I know. I'm sorry." She turned her back, unable to look him in the eyes. Oh heavens, what must he think of her? She didn't know what to think of herself.

"Sorry for kissing me?"

"I'm confused. Between getting dumped by Jesse and this whole Don Juan thing. I'm just really, really confused right now and I'm taking it out on you. That was wrong of me."

"You didn't do anything wrong."

She plastered a perky smile on her face and glanced

at her watch. "Will you look at the time? It's getting late and we've had enough excitement for one evening. What say we call it a night?"

"Meggie…" He reached out for her, but she danced away. She couldn't bear the words if he said something sweet simply to make her feel better for acting like an oversexed doxy.

"Don't worry, Caleb. Believe me, that kiss meant nothing to me, absolutely nothing."

"Nothing?"

"I've forgotten it already. Honest." She waved a hand as if she kissed men atop the Space Needle every single day of her life.

"And I suppose you want me to forget all about it, too."

"If you don't mind."

"Maybe I do mind."

"Caleb, please," she begged. "I had too much wine. That's all there is to it."

He stared at her a long moment without saying anything. He looked at her with great blue eyes gone dark in the mist. His expression made her heart lock. She felt as if she had crossed some unbreachable boundary and could never make it right, no matter what she said.

A group of rowdy revelers came up to the deck from the restaurant below, thankfully interrupting the awkward silence between them.

"I'm ready to go."

A strange mix of sadness, shame and guilt dissolved into a muddle as thick as the gathering fog. This unfortunate episode was going to not only keep her awake at night, but also cause her to flinch at the memory. She wished the damned fog would enshroud her so totally that she disappeared.

How could she have been so stupid?

In that moment, guilt, sadness and shame morphed into a stinging sense of regret. Despite that Caleb had taken her elbow to steady her on the steps, Meggie felt utterly and completely alone.

The trip to her car was heavy, weighted with a sludge of unvoiced emotion neither of them wanted to explore. After she'd unlocked the vehicle, Caleb opened the driver's door for her. She plunked down in the front seat and looked up, beseeching him with her eyes to forgive her.

"Aren't you getting in?" she asked, when he just kept standing there.

"I think I'll walk. My hotel is only a few blocks." He inclined his head east.

Tears pressed against her eyes. He didn't even want to be in the same car with her. Oh God, had she ruined everything between them? Was their friendship kaput?

"It's chilly and damp."

"I'll be all right."

She should have shut up right there and let it go, but, no, in a wretched attempt to ease her pathetic suffering, she had to push.

"Are we on for tomorrow night? I can get tickets to the Sonics game."

He shook his head. "I'm booked tomorrow night."

"How about Wednesday?"

"No can do."

Hey, idiot, buy a clue. He doesn't want to see you.

"Saturday? We could hit the aquarium. Go on a harbor cruise."

"I'm going to be pretty busy for the next couple of weeks."

"Oh."

He reached out a hand, trailed a finger down her

cheek. His touch ignited her skin. "It's not what you think."

"You're not looking to avoid me?"

"Of course not."

"Then…" She paused as a new thought popped into her head. "Oh. You've met someone."

"Something like that." His smile softened the edges of his eyes. "She's a very special lady."

How could Meggie have been so self-centered? Her kiss hadn't freaked him out in the way she'd supposed. Caleb had met someone else, and here she'd been thinking he was disgusted by her kiss. What a ninny.

"Why, that's great," she babbled. "Fabulous. I'm so happy for you."

"You are?"

"Absolutely. Sure."

"What about that kiss on the observation deck?"

"I told you, it meant nothing. Go. Enjoy your new girlfriend. You have my blessings."

CHAPTER THIRTEEN

HE CAME TO HER in a dream. Dressed entirely in black.
Gone was the flowing white shirt, replaced with a black
leather vest and nothing else.

Just leather and bare skin.

But was this a dream? Meggie wondered, her entire
body trembling in his overwhelming presence. Or a reality she was afraid to admit? From the moment she'd
met him, she'd been caught up in this seductive fantasy where reality and dream merged into something
powerfully erotic.

He stared at her, his steely blue eyes enigmatic as
always behind that mask. His jaw tightened when he
noticed she wore only a gauzy red gown.

Her fingers curled with a savage urge to explore that
masculine chin. She ached to press her tongue against
it, to taste the saltiness of his skin.

He reached for her. When his rough fingers grazed
her wrist, she hissed as if burned. His firm clasp propelled liquid heat to the soft tender flesh between her
legs.

His expression was unreadable. He did not smile. He
pulled her to him and captured her lips with a kiss so
tempestuous it took her breath.

He drove the spear of his tongue deep inside her
mouth. The taste of him filled her. His mustache grazed

her upper lip with a light tickle that launched a languid shiver down her spine.

Her skin hummed with severe pleasure. Her nipples tightened.

He made a hungry male animal noise and ground his pelvis against hers. Their bodies fit perfectly. Streamers of fiery heat flowed from him to her.

Oh, this felt so good.

She breathed hard against his mouth, taking in the scent of man and leather and sex.

"Don Juan," she whimpered.

"Yes, yes?"

"I want you inside me. I want you now."

He pushed her back onto the bed, pressing her body into the mattress. He stripped off his vest, his pants, and settled his weight over her body. With brazen fingers, he ripped the material of her nightgown, exposing her nakedness.

This was what she missed. What she wanted. His forcefulness, his boldness, his daring.

"Hurry, please hurry," she begged. "I'm wet and ready."

He drove into her. Hard, hot, powerful. Again and again and again. She felt as if all the air had been knocked from her lungs.

And then they came in one blistering moment, crying together in rough, desperate groans.

He collapsed upon her, drenched in sweat and love juices.

Slowly, slowly, they drifted back down to earth.

"Let me see your face," she whispered a few minutes later. "I must know who you are."

"How long I've waited for you to say that."

Then he raised his head, peeled off his mask along with the false mustache, unveiling himself to her.

Oh God! What had she done?

Her masked lover was Caleb!

That's when she cried out and jerked herself awake.

Meggie bolted upright in bed, her heart pounding, her body soaked in perspiration, her covers flung to the floor. The dream seemed so real. Too real. She splayed a hand over her chest.

On trembling legs she went to the bathroom and took a shower to cool her scorched skin.

Why had she dreamed Caleb was Don Juan? Fretfully, she dried her body, which strangely enough was as tender as if she actually had made love with him.

Mind in turmoil, she padded to the kitchen and poured herself a glass of tomato juice. She sat at the table and tried to decipher her dream.

Subconsciously, did she want Caleb to be Don Juan?

Meggie gnawed her bottom lip. The two men were different as night and day, even though upon reflection they did possessed similar physical characteristics. Both were tall and lean, dark-haired and blue-eyed.

But Don Juan was wickedly naughty, intrepid and brash, definitely not the sort of man you married. Caleb was sweet and kind and caring, the kind of guy you'd love to bring home to Mother. Too bad Meggie couldn't have both. The exciting lover who revved her blood and made her dare, mixed with the steady, reliable man she could always count on.

And then she had her answer. No wonder she'd dreamed that Caleb was Don Juan. She was attracted to both of them, but she had reservations about each. Caleb was too quiet, too familiar; Don Juan too wild, too reckless. Her subconscious had simply taken the two and melded them into one.

The perfect man who didn't exist.

"YOU ARE THE MOST naturally gifted dancer I have ever had the privilege to instruct," Luisa Roman told Caleb two weeks and ten salsa lessons later. "And such a determined student. I have never seen anyone pick up the tango with such ease."

"Thank you." He accepted the certification of completion she handed him.

His instructor didn't know the half of it. Over the past fourteen days, when Caleb hadn't been either giving lectures at local hospitals or attending classes here at the dance studio, he'd been in his hotel room practicing the elegant yet seductive moves.

Last week, he'd almost run into Meggie in the hallway at the studio as she came out of her belly dancing class, but he'd spotted her first and, just in the nick of time, dashed into the men's locker room. Even though it was a little cruel, he would rather have her thinking he was out with another woman than uncover his plan before he was ready.

But time was not on his side. He was leaving Seattle the following Tuesday. He had to act quickly. He was determined to impress Meggie and he intended to do it up right. Make a grand romantic gesture. Give her one thrilling night she would remember for the rest of her life.

A night they would never forget.

He was ready to push all boundaries, risk everything in order to win her over. Take a chance and grab for the brass ring. He was going to prove to her that their kiss at the top of the Space Needle had indeed meant something very special.

The lessons were finished, he'd even impressed Luisa Roman, and now he was ready.

Even though it had been pure torture, he'd resisted calling Meggie these past two weeks. He wanted her to think about him. To remember their kiss. To wonder what it meant. Yes, he was playing a mind game with her, but then he was counting on a huge payoff.

Love.

Did he have the courage to seduce her without the Don Juan mask? He would find out for certain on Saturday night, when he took her salsa dancing. He imagined the moment and his heart swelled with possibilities.

Then Luisa Roman said something that altered the trajectory of his plans. "Because you are my prize student, I will tell you of a very special place."

"Ma'am?"

She pressed a card into his palm. He glanced at the bold black lettering that said simply The Mystery Room, with an address underneath.

"The Mystery Room?" He raised an eyebrow.

"An exclusive nightclub, offering the finest in salsa dancing and a little more." Luisa's voice had gone low, suggestive.

"A little more?"

"The patrons attend in costume and masks. No bare faces allowed."

Just the thought sent a thrill rippling through his body, and Caleb knew then that he would pose as Don Juan one last time to lure Meggie to the Mystery Room.

"It is very erotic," Luisa continued. "And if you have a special lady, you might want to rent one of the rooms above the club. It's amazing what a night of mystery will do for your love life."

"No kidding."

Perfect. The pieces of his plan fit like a puzzle. He would invite Meggie to the club and dance with her all night. Afterward he would take her upstairs, make love to her and then remove his mask.

"*Hell-ooo*. MEGGIE, are you even listening to me?" Wendy's voice broke through her reverie.

"Huh?"

"I asked you twice if you thought I should shave my head and you never even blinked, much less offered an opinion. You're a gazillion miles away. What's the matter? Still mooning over that foreign guy?"

Meggie shook her head. They were in her apartment, measuring for new living room curtains. She'd decided she needed a change, but she couldn't seem to force herself to concentrate on the task at hand.

No, she wasn't mooning over Don Juan. She was thinking about Caleb. Worrying about him, actually. He was a babe in the woods when it came to city living, and she wondered about the woman he was seeing. What if she was just some gold digger looking to get at his money? What if the wench ended up breaking the poor guy's heart? Meggie gritted her teeth. If that happened, she would personally hunt the twit down and crack her skull.

The vehemence of her thoughts startled Meggie.

"Oops, there you went again. One minute you're looking me in the eye, the next minute staring off into space," Wendy said. "What gives?"

"Nothing. I'm sorry. I called you over to help me and then I get distracted on you."

"Hey, what are friends for, except to be there when you need them?"

Caleb was her friend.

Or at least he used to be.

God, why had she kissed him? Meggie cringed and dropped her face in her hands. Had she ruined their friendship for good?

She'd been agonizing over that stupid kiss for the past two weeks, wondering why Caleb hadn't phoned, but too embarrassed to pick up the phone and call him. And she'd even been too ashamed of herself to confess to Wendy what she'd done, or talk about that crazy dream where she'd wished Caleb was sexy Don Juan.

"I'm not sure, though, that I've completely forgiven you for not introducing me to your handsome Alaskan naturalist before some hussy scooped him up." Wendy pretended to pout.

"Sorry." Meggie felt a twinge of guilt and regret. If she hadn't been so selfish, if she'd introduced Caleb to Wendy, he probably wouldn't have met that other woman at all, whoever she might be. At least if he'd been with Wendy Meggie would have had a chance to see him.

The telephone jangled.

Caleb? Her hopes soared as they did every time the phone rang. But this time, for some reason, she had an overwhelming sense it was him.

She raced across the living room, stumbling over the coffee table and whacking her shin.

Ow, ow, ow.

But even pain didn't slow her down.

"'Lo," she answered, her pulse pounding wildly.

"Belladonna."

"Don Juan," she whispered.

In a second Wendy popped in front of her, eyes wide, a huge grin on her face. Meggie waved her away, her mind spinning with a thousand splintered thoughts. Just when she thought she'd put Don Juan in her past where he belonged, here he was again.

"You sound disappointed," he accused in that rich Spanish accent.

"Oh, no. I'm not disappointed. I was just expecting someone else."

"Ah. Another lover?"

"No, no. A friend."

"I have missed you," he crooned, and she felt that old helplessness weaken her knees.

"I never expected you to call me again."

"And why is that?"

"The way you left me the last time we were together, I assumed it was a one-time thing."

"Never assume. Life is too full of surprises for that."

"Are you back in Seattle on business?" she asked, unable to identify the emotions churning inside her, not knowing if she wanted him to be here or not.

"Yes. And I wish to see you again."

A shivery thrill leaped through her. *Oh no. Here we go again.*

"Are you still there?"

Meggie hesitated. "I'm still here."

"Are you busy Saturday night?"

This is a really bad idea, Meggie. Say no.

Ah, but how she wanted to see him again. She ached to run her fingers through his hair, to be kissed and caressed by him. Don Juan had given her sexual healing. Their arrangement was perfect. Not like this oddness she felt for Caleb. No personal information. No entanglements. No falling head over heels in love. No getting hurt.

And yet she fully understood that this thing with her masked fantasy man was dangerous. She was taking a big chance, walking a tenuous tightrope between just sex and something more. It was too easy to confuse love and sex.

Except that wasn't really true. Sex was pretty cut and dried. It was the excitement that confused her. The titillation. The sexual adventure that promised much more than it could ever deliver on an emotional level.

If she had one more fling with Don Juan, for the sake of her own mental health she had to keep one thing firmly planted in the forefront of her mind. *It's just a little sex. Nothing more.*

"I'm free on Saturday night," she said, dismayed at her own weakness, but riddled with lust at the thought of seeing him again.

"That is very good. You make me so happy. Now, I have a favor to ask of you."

"All right."

"I am sending over a costume. Wear it. Inside the box you will find an address for a nightclub. Meet me there. Eight o'clock on Saturday night. I will be waiting for you," he whispered, and then gently hung up.

THE MYSTERY ROOM, a dark, cozy nightclub filled with people in a variety of exotic costumes, oozed sensuality. The huge salsa band played the lambada and there was some pretty steamy stuff happening on the dance floor.

Caleb checked his watch: 8:05.

His heart hammered and he willed Meggie to appear in the doorway. He had positioned himself with his back to the far wall so he would know the minute she stepped over the threshold.

What if she didn't show? What then?

Caleb bit down on his thumbnail. She simply had to come. His need for her was all-consuming, and so intense he didn't think he could stand the disappointment if she never arrived.

And in that dread-filled moment, she appeared.

She looked breathtakingly beautiful in the red-and-black flamenco outfit he'd had delivered to apartment. Her hair was swept off her neck and decorated with a mantilla, and she wore the black leather mask he had included in the box.

Moisture sprang into his mouth and his stomach clamped tight. In that moment, he knew. He wanted to have children with her. And grandchildren. He wanted to be with Meggie Scofield for the rest of his life.

He should have seen it coming. Should have known this infatuation with her was much more than physical. He had tried to use sex as a release from his distracting fantasies. Instead of freeing him, however, making love with her had only dug him in deeper.

Without her, he was lost.

She appeared bewildered, sliding her gaze around the club, taking in the band's accomplished horn section, the clutch of colorful dancers writhing on the dance floor, the intoxicatingly exotic lighting. As Caleb stalked toward her, she nervously reached up a hand to pat her hair, making sure her mantilla was staying in place.

When she spotted him, her mouth curled up in a smile of relief, and he found himself grinning like some fool in love. She wet her lips with the tip of her tongue, and when he reached out to take her elbow in his palm, he noticed a telltale pink flush spread up her neck, and her swift intake of breath.

"You came," he exclaimed, and leaned in close to brush his mouth over hers in greeting.

He'd meant the kiss to be light, a hint of welcome, of what was to come. But the minute his flesh touched hers, it was seared. Not to taste her would have been a sin of the highest order, and apparently Meggie agreed because she returned his kiss with a ferocity that rocked him to the soles of his boots.

He thought of the rented room upstairs and his body temperature notched upward. His impulse was to scoop her into his arms, carry her up to the room and get her naked as quickly as possible.

With a great internal struggle, he denied the impulse. He was going to seduce her tonight as no man had ever seduced her, and when his mask was removed and she learned his true identity, she would not be able to deny her real feelings for him.

He would seduce her not only with the dance of love, but with all his heart and soul. Caleb was ready to lay everything on the line and take the greatest risk of his life.

"I almost didn't come," she confessed. "But I can never resist the opportunity to dance."

"Or play games?"

"Or play games." She smiled.

"Then we shall dance, belladonna. And play. Until dawn if you desire."

He signaled the band with a coded message he had worked out with them earlier. It had cost him a handsome tip, but the cue was worth it. Smoothly, the band segued from the mambo into the tango.

Caleb bowed low from the waist and offered Meggie his hand with a courtly flourish. The color riding her cheeks deepened, but she readily accepted his arm and he guided her proudly out onto the dance floor.

The hauntingly dramatic music swept over them with its hypnotic rhythm. Images of all the romantic movies he had ever seen featuring the tango swept through his head. Caleb let himself go, giving over completely to the dance, caught up in the moment when fantasy and reality merged into an idyllic blur.

Meggie inclined her head and gave him a coy smile. "You're an excellent dancer, Don Juan."

"We have only just begun."

At his inscrutable words, Meggie felt her self-control slip even future. The man knew how to charm. She shouldn't have come, but now that she was here, she was glad she had ignored the common sense that had dictated her life up until the moment she'd met Don Juan. She gave herself over to the craziness.

Living *la vida loca*.

She danced with Don Juan as she had never danced with another man. They moved in perfect unison, their bodies pressed close together, stepping in tandem with a smooth fluidity.

A heated calm seeped through her body, replacing her earlier nervousness. She experienced a blissful sense of homecoming, a wondrous peace unlike anything she'd ever known. Her confusion and doubts about coming here vanished as surely as darkness at dawn.

In that single fragment of time, she understood the mystery of creation, recognized the cosmic connection between herself and Don Juan. They were one soul, one entity, even more surely than when they'd made love. His eyes remained locked on hers and she could not look away. Nor did she want to.

Step, step, step, step. They tangoed, never missing a beat.

Everyone else had left the dance floor. The other dancers stood on the sidelines, watching in admiration. Meggie barely noticed their audience. All she focused on was Don Juan, as the scent of his sexy body dominated her senses. It seemed so utterly natural to be encircled in his arms. Even more natural to press her cheek against his and close her eyes.

Time ticked by. She heard the throb of his heart and, overlaying that, the mesmerizing tango beat.

The music and his heartbeat became one sound, strumming with a growing intensity that encompassed her mind, body and soul. The sensation leaped beyond surreal and bordered on budding rapture.

And when he dipped her, she felt her brain short-circuit. She wanted him. No matter how foolish, how stupid, how irrational it might be to sleep with this man again—especially since she was also having sensual feelings for Caleb—she simply could not resist. She had to have Don Juan one last time before she could relinquish her obsession and move on with her life.

They danced for what seemed like hours as one spicy salsa song flowed smoothly into another. From Gloria Estefan's rousing rendition of the conga to the exuberant cha-cha-cha to the sensuously flirtatious rumba, their bodies brushed, touched, seared. Their clothes grew damp with passion and perspiration.

Not once did they take their eyes off each other. Their faces were hidden by the masks, but their souls… through the simmering heat of their melded pupils, they laid their souls bare to each other.

Throb, throb, throb.

The relentless beat pushed them higher and higher.

Drums, saxophone, trumpet, keyboard. The instruments bloomed, a musical bouquet of sensual sound.

Their passion for each other escalated with each step they took, drawing them deeper and deeper into a vortex of sexual hunger.

When Meggie swirled, her skirt eddied about her legs in a wild, compelling flash of red satin and black lace. She felt the material slap at her shins, the back of her legs, saw frank desire in the eyes of the other men lining the dance floor.

She felt incredibly beautiful, and for that lofty feeling she could never repay Don Juan. He was such a splendid partner, an utterly charming companion. And she knew he made her look like a much better dancer than she was.

With him, dancing seemed effortless, magical. On and on they danced, until the band played the tango once more. As Meggie kept gazing past his mask and into those blue eyes filled with the promise to give her a night to remember, she knew she would never forget the Mystery Room, the tango or him.

When the song ended, she stopped dancing and splayed her palm over his chest. "I simply must have some water."

"But of course."

He guided her to a table at the back of the club; several of the masked and costumed patrons complimented their dancing skills as they went past.

"I will be right back," he whispered, low in her ear, and then departed for the bar.

Tilting her head, Meggie admired the swagger of his leather-clad hips as he walked away. The man had it going on. No doubt about it. His butt was even cuter than Caleb's, who definitely possessed one primo heinie.

Immediately, Meggie felt disloyal to her old friend. She shouldn't compare Caleb to Don Juan. It was like comparing Granny Smiths to Clementines. Caleb was Caleb and Don Juan was Don Juan. Complete opposites in temperament and comportment.

She wondered for a moment who Don Juan really was, but then quickly squelched the thought. She didn't want to know. Didn't want to unearth something better left buried.

Don Juan returned a few minutes later with two tall glasses of iced water. He sat beside her and took a long drink from his glass. Meggie watched him swallow and realized she was in deep when she found even that simple action incredibly stimulating.

The delicate material of his white, puffy-sleeved shirt clung damply to his masculine chest, and Meggie felt her insides slowly unravel.

His face was flushed from the heat of dancing, and a droplet of water glinted on his lower lip. She wanted to lean over and lick it off, watch the flicker of sexual arousal leap to life in his eyes.

When she realized that, without even trying, he equally mesmerized the women seated at the next table, Meggie had to curl her fingers into her palms to keep from getting jealous. Good thing he was only her temporary lover and not her boyfriend. She would have a hard time dealing with this kind of feminine adoration on a regular basis, especially since Don Juan was such a powerful flirt.

Loyalty is something you would never have to worry about with Caleb, a tiny voice whispered in the back of her mind. Now there is a one-woman man.

Meggie pushed the thought away. She still wasn't ready to deal with her budding feelings for Caleb. Those emotions scared her too much, because she knew he was a man she could actually build a life with.

But Caleb had another woman, and he'd been avoiding her with a fierce diligence ever since she'd kissed him atop the Space Needle. She sighed. She had certainly made a mess of that.

You can't expect all risks to pay off.

The most she could hope for was self-discovery, and she'd certainly found that.

Don Juan placed his hand over hers. The familiar jolt of electricity shot through her. She raised her head and met his stare.

"Is something wrong?"

"No."

"You seem unhappy. Is it me?"

"Not at all."

She smiled, trying hard to dispel the sad wisp of longing in her heart. She wasn't right for Caleb and she knew it. She was older than him. She had a life here in the city. He needed a woman his own age or younger, an earthy type who would embrace life in the wilderness.

Don Juan lifted her hand to his mouth and slowly began kissing each knuckle and then running his tongue over her skin until her fingers tingled with the fire of his masculine heat.

If Caleb could see her now, would he be shocked by her indiscretions?

Probably.

What was happening to her? Why did she keep thinking about Caleb when she was in this exotic club with a dashingly charismatic man who impressed her with his flashy dance moves? She was very confused and she knew it. But this was the last time she would see Don Juan. She'd best make the most of their final encounter.

"This club is also an inn," he murmured, low and husky, in his devastating accent. "And I have reserved us a room. Would you like to go upstairs with me now?"

CHAPTER FOURTEEN

HE LED HER UP the narrow staircase illuminated only by wall sconces holding red bulbs. When they reached their room on the second floor, Don Juan did not turn on the lamp, but the curtain was open and a soft glow from the streetlights fell across a four-poster, king-size bed with a leather upholstered headboard.

Closing the door behind them with a soft click, he pulled her into his arms and ran the tip of his tongue over her lips, gently probing the warm recesses of her mouth.

She caught his head in her palms and sank her fingers in his raven hair. She melted into his arms, offering herself to him and giving without restraint.

A deep, guttural sound of pleasure slipped from his throat, a hungry, greedy noise that raised the hairs on her arms and filled her with a deep sexual need.

This might be wrong, but heaven help her, nothing had ever felt so right.

"What game are we playing tonight?" he asked. "The choice is yours."

What game indeed?

He understood her need for fantasy. Her mind hopped from one scenario to another. Since this was absolutely the last time she was going to be with him, Meggie craved a thrill to remember—a provocative memory she could carry with her to the grave.

Her mind snagged on one idea, and when the mere thought of it caused her knees to weaken and her pulse to grow thready, she knew what she wanted.

"I want you to tell me what to do," she whispered, trembling with excitement as the new sex game unfurled in her brain.

"You want me to command you to do things to me?"

Yes. She wanted him to be in control. She needed to relinquish the reins, allow him to lead her to a place of sexual discovery where she had never dared enter.

"Tonight, I am your slave. You are my master. I must do whatever you tell me."

"Are you sure? This is a perilous game, indeed."

Meggie shivered and whispered, "I know. That's why I want it."

"You are a goddess," he murmured.

"No. I am a slave. I am here to do your bidding. What is your pleasure, master?"

"If you are certain."

"I am."

"Take off your clothes." His voice changed, grew rough, dark and demanding. The shift in him both thrilled and scared her.

With shaky hands, Meggie slowly removed her clothing.

Don Juan sat in a wooden, hard-backed chair positioned in front of the window. He said not a word, but watched her with a hard-edged gaze.

She kicked off her high-heeled shoes and fumbled with the buttons on her dress, her hands perspiring so much her fingers kept slipping.

When she was finally down to her black lace bra and thong panties, Meggie discovered she was reluctant to go further—whether from nervousness or a desire to prolong the game, she couldn't say. Probably a bit of both.

Don Juan was massively aroused, a fact his tight-fitting leather pants made clearly evident. He suddenly seemed very dangerous, and she didn't know what to expect. After all, she didn't really know the guy, had no idea what he was capable of, even though they had intimately explored each other's bodies.

She crossed her arms over her chest and cowered.

"Come here."

Meggie hesitated.

"Come here, slave. Don't make me repeat myself or there will be dire consequences."

He stared at her with such arrogant disregard, his haughty eyes enshrouded by that mask, that Meggie almost stopped the game by crying out, "Enough." But at the same time she was panicking, she felt the crotch of her panties growing decidedly moist.

"Now!"

Tentatively she inched across the room to where he sat enthroned on his chair.

"On your knees."

Slowly she slid to the floor, her pulse jackhammering in her head. Ribbons of sensation streamed through her when she saw just how turned on he was. She licked her lips.

"Now untie my pants."

No sweet croons of "belladonna." No soft murmurs, no tender touches. But she had asked for this and her body was swamped with a degree of stimulation she'd never before reached. The thick wetness in her panties seeped down her thighs.

She untied his pants and tipped her head upward to study his face. His jaw was stiff and uncompromising.

Pale lines of strain bracketed his mouth. The mask covered half his face, hiding much of his emotion.

What kind of man lurked beyond that facade?

He reached out and grazed her chin with the rough pad of his thumb. "Do I excite you, slave?"

"Yes, master. I am wet for you."

"Pull down your panties and let me see."

She hooked her thumb beneath the waistband of her panties and self-consciously edged them over her hips and down her thighs.

"Straddle me."

Trembling, she did as he commanded, placing one leg on either side of his thigh and resting her bare bottom against his leather pants. With a forefinger, he stroked between her legs, brusquely caressing her heated wetness.

Meggie tossed her head at the abruptness of the experience. His fingers curled inside her and she almost came right then and there.

"Do you want it rough?"

"You are the master. I am the slave. My only wish is to please you."

"Then kiss me."

His breath flew from his body in a smothered rush of sound as her mouth covered his. She tasted his hunger, felt his desperation. The kiss claimed them both, a whirlwind feeding on its own power.

The next moments passed in a desperate flurry as Don Juan lifted her from him, stripped off his clothes, sat back down and pulled her backward, into his lap. For the first time she realized he could see their reflection in the mirror running the length of one wall.

A fresh thrill shot through her.

His nipples were adjacent to her shoulder blades; she felt their sharp peaks jutting against her skin.

"Lean back," he demanded. "Let me play with you."

Meggie leaned back against his chest and he ran a hand up to cup her bare bottom in his palm. The sensations he aroused in her were so unbelievably exquisite that tears stung her eyes.

God, this felt so good. Magical.

While one hand kneaded her fanny, the other trailed to her bare breasts. He swept her nipples and pinched them lightly between his fingers, massaging them with the electricity of his masculine body heat. The sensation was at once delicious, sinful and sweetly familiar, like a favorite dessert eaten for the first time after a long hunger strike.

She'd missed his touch so very much. But how was that possible? She'd only been with him twice, and barely even knew him.

Meggie's body grew heavier, more languorous, until it seemed to liquefy into his. He forsook her nipples and returned to making those idle circles around her breasts, until once more he was back, pulling and plucking the straining peaks.

She writhed against him.

He circled back around her breasts.

This time she moaned through clenched teeth when he reached her nipples at last and rolled them between his rough fingers.

Her breath came out in low episodic gasps and her entire body felt swollen and achy with intense arousal. Nibbling her ear, he lifted her higher up on his thighs, her back still pressed to his chest. She felt her moisture slicken his skin.

His lips tugged on her ear. She delighted in the sensation as he began to suck on her flesh and the opal stud nestled in her lobe. She shuddered at the wetness of his tongue, the heat of his mouth.

He spread his legs and, in the process, pried hers farther apart. One hand slid down her breast and across her inner thigh. His other hand continued to gently massage her butt.

At first, she didn't realize what he was doing as he rotated both of them, spreading her thighs wider, moving closer to the mirror. And then she caught a glimpse of their reflection, the tantalizing picture of his naked flesh pressed against hers.

She gasped, scandalized, embarrassed and monumentally turned on.

She had never made love in front of a mirror. It seemed a wickedly sinful thing to do. She closed her eyes and turned her head.

His devilish laugh rang in her ears. "Look at yourself. Watch me make love to you."

And, heaven help her, watch she did.

He bent her over the dresser and she clung to the furniture for dear life, her entire body trembling. He lightly smacked her bottom.

"What an ass." He clutched her butt with both hands and sighed rhapsodically, as if having an oversize caboose was something to be proud of.

Their bodies shifted in the throes of pleasure. Sometimes she could see more of him, sometimes more of herself. The picture in the mirror was a hundred times more erotic than any dirty movie ever filmed. She lost all sense of herself, all sense of time and place.

The world tumbled, an easy glide into ecstasy. When she was quivering and oh so wet, he paused long enough to slip on a condom. He spent a few moments working her up again and then finally, *finally,* he slowly entered her from behind. She whimpered like a grateful puppy.

"You are so beautiful," he murmured, and sweetly stroked her hair.

His gentle croon, his loving caress, fueled her fervor. She tried to move, to give as good as she was getting, but he wouldn't allow it.

"No," he whispered, and held her still by tugging lightly on her hair. "If you do that, I won't last a moment."

With much difficulty, she restrained herself. And each time she was about to shoot over the edge, he shifted his body just enough so it didn't happen.

Frustration welled in her throat. "Please," she begged. "Please."

"What do you want?" he whispered roughly, pushing deeper into her. "Tell me. What do you need?"

"Please." She choked on the word, barely able to speak at all.

"More? Do you want more?"

"Yes…oh yes."

His tone was gruff and tender and thick with the same emotion that clogged her throat. "Not yet, sweetheart. Not yet."

A long, fat sob spilled from her lips as he lifted her off him. She tried to turn, to take hold of him and force him to finish what he had started, but he had stepped back.

She could see him in the mirror; the light from the street glinting in through the blinds cast him in silhouette. She saw the hard, broad thrust of his erection. Blindly she reached for him.

He caught her wrist before she could make contact.

"Wait. Please. Just a little bit longer. It will be worth it, I promise."

Then he bent, scooped her into his arms and carried her to the bed. He settled her on the covers and then stepped back. Meggie peered at him. She watched him illuminated in the light from the streetlamp outside the window, his face cloaked by the mask. If she reached out, she could easily flick that cover up and stare straight into his eyes.

"Take off my mask," he demanded. "I want you to see my face."

"No," she whispered, her pulse suddenly pounding so much she feared she might have a heart attack on the spot.

"I am your master and you are my slave. You must obey me."

"I won't."

"Then I must punish you."

"Go ahead."

Don Juan pinned her to the bed. "Take off my mask, slave."

She was on the verge of hysteria. She could not, would not, remove his mask. Her mind balked at the very idea. She did not want to know who he was. It would ruin everything, and she feared he was leading up to more than an unmasking. She worried that he was falling in love with her. She simply could not have that happening.

Meggie realized then she needed the fantasy of the unobtainable male. His games had sustained her, bolstered her self-esteem and renewed her belief in her womanhood after her divorce.

But the last thing she needed in her life was another bad boy. She'd made that mistake once. She wasn't about to do it again. Fireworks might be nice for a fantasy, but real life commitment required so much more than spice and flash. What she needed was an emotionally secure guy. A quiet, steady man. Like Caleb.

Except Caleb already had another woman.

"Take off my mask," he repeated.

"No! Enough! I won't."

"Why not?" he growled.

"Because I don't want to know who you are. Don't you get it? I don't want to see your face. I don't want to fall in love with you. I need security. I need a man who can provide for me, not some gadabout pretty boy who likes to dress up and play sex games with strangers!"

MEGGIE'S WORDS SHATTERED Caleb's world.

She wanted a man to provide for her. She didn't care about love, but security. She was no different from those women who had shown up in Bear Creek seeking to marry him because he was a millionaire.

Disappointment and a great sadness washed over him, but those emotions were quickly replaced by anger.

"Then why are you here with me?"

Meggie blinked up at him, her face obscured by her own mask. "Why, for the sex games, of course."

Sex. She wanted him for sex. He was either a wallet or a sex object.

You're one to talk, Greenleaf. You started this whole mess with the intention of living out your teenage fantasy. No sense blaming her for something that's your fault. She told you from the beginning she wasn't looking for anything serious. You're the one who messed things up.

His conscience scolded him, but his heart was aching so much he didn't want to hear anything rational.

"So it's sex you want?" His voice grated rudely in his own ears.

She nodded. Her eyes widened, looking rather frightened, but also very excited.

"Then sex is what you'll get."

He shouldn't have taken her. He was too mad and he knew it but, dammit, he couldn't help himself. This was the last time he would be intimate with her.

Caleb parted her thighs with his hands, positioned his body over hers, and then in one forceful, barbaric thrust buried himself deep within her warm wetness, in a pathetic attempt to assuage his despair.

"Oh yes!" she exclaimed, wrapping her slender arms around his neck, arching her hips upward and pulling him deeper inside her. "Yes."

Sensation, hot and solid, spread outward from the core of his belly. He might not be able to love her forever, but he could love her tonight. And she loved him back, in her way, using her hands and her mouth. Caressing him, biting him, tugging impatiently on his hair whenever he slowed.

Nothing mattered now. Not the past. Not the future. There was only this moment.

He shifted, going from long, slow thrusts to short, quick ones.

"Yes," she whimpered, her eyes squeezed tightly shut. "I like that. More. Deeper. Harder. I want you to fill me up. More…give me more."

She hugged him with her love muscles, tightening around him with each thrust and parry. His heart slammed into his chest, into his ears, into his head, swamping his body with a heat so intense he felt as if he were on fire.

He stopped moving and stared down at her.

"What's the matter?"

"Look at me."

She raised her lashes to peer up at him, and he almost stopped breathing at the expression of sweet longing in her eyes. With his gaze fastened on her like a heat-seeking missile locked on a target, he began to move again.

She surrounded him, engulfed him, absorbed him so completely that he couldn't say where he ended and she began. He'd never experienced anything like it. Not with anyone.

It wasn't her sexiness—although she certainly was sexy! It wasn't simply a testosterone dump. It wasn't the masks or the games or the mystery of the moment. And it wasn't even the notion that he would never have her again after tonight.

Rather it was the yearning in her eyes. The solid connection between them. The sensation that they were the only two people on the face of the earth.

It was too much to take. Particularly since she'd just made it clear she didn't want him for anything more than sex or money. He'd spent his entire life being loved and respected only for what he could provide, never for simply being himself.

The old pain, along with this new one, knotted his chest. It was all too much emotion, too much hurt, to contemplate. He refused to think anymore.

He broke his visual bond with her then. Closing his eyes, shutting himself off, pulling away like he did when feelings got too intense.

Caleb thrust harder, faster. Meggie growled her pleasure, sounding all the world like a she-cat. She ran her nails down his back, scratching him lightly. She wrapped her legs around his waist and clung tight. She lifted her head off the pillow and nibbled on his bottom lip.

"Almost," she cried. "Don't stop."

He was about to make her come and he'd never felt so proud, so manly. Pushing into her one last time, Caleb felt her convulse around him, just as his masculine essence shot from his body in a splurge of release.

In his blind, heady rush of energy, he cried out her name, forgetting that Don Juan was not suppose to know it. Forgetting, in fact, to use his Spanish accent. He forgot everything except that for the first and last time he and Meggie had shared the ultimate act of intimacy. He had made love to her with all his heart, mind and soul.

And the awful thing was, it hurt more excruciatingly than anything he could ever have imagined.

CHAPTER FIFTEEN

I DID IT. I took a walk on the wild side. I lived a little. I made my own adventure. I had a no-strings-attached affair and proved I'm not a dud in bed.

She'd gotten what she wanted.

Why then did her victory feel so hollow? Why was she aching for something more? And why couldn't she stop wishing that the man in the bed beside her was not this dashing, unobtainable masked stranger, but rather her dear friend and confidant, Caleb Greenleaf?

Kind, sensitive, intelligent, caring Caleb.

She had thought she had wanted mindless, feel-good sex. She had thought that proving Jesse wrong was a worthy objective. Instead, she'd discovered that revenge was never sweet, and while Don Juan had indeed satisfied her most forbidden fantasies, her real craving wasn't for adventuresome sex at all, but for true and lasting intimacy. Something she would never find through meaningless encounters with strangers.

She'd been looking for love in the wrong place, when Caleb had been right under her nose all along.

Could she be in love with Caleb?

No. That was crazy. She'd known him most of her life. If she'd been in love with him wouldn't she have realized it long before now?

Okay, then why did she keep thinking about him? Why, in the middle of having sex with Don Juan, had she kept pretending he was Caleb? Not to mention that weird dream she'd had. And why did she continue to wonder what Caleb would say if he could see her now?

He would be so disappointed that she'd been unable to resist Don Juan's seductive allure. Shame had her swinging her legs over the side of the bed and searching for her clothing in the darkened room.

Don Juan sat up. She refused to look at him.

"So you are going?"

"Yes."

"I will never see you again." It was a statement, not a question. He got up and came toward her.

"No." She shook her head, reached around to zip the back of the flamboyant flamenco dress.

"You have taken from me what you needed."

"Yes." That sounded so cruel, so cold. "You've given me a lot, Don Juan. You've given me back my femininity and I can't thank you enough for that."

"You are welcome." Gently, he touched her cheek. "I will always remember you fondly."

She slipped her feet into her shoes and then turned to go. She hesitated at the door, her hand on the knob. "Take care of yourself, okay?"

"Adios, belladonna," he whispered in the Spanish accent that no longer sent chills of desire pushing down her spine. "Adios."

MEGGIE PACED THE LENGTH of Wendy's kitchen floor, arms crossed over her chest, a thousand conflicting thoughts tumbling through her brain. She'd arrived at her friend's apartment not long after leaving Don Juan's bed, still dressed in her elaborate dancing costume. She'd desperately needed someone to talk to, but now that she was here, she didn't know how to begin.

"Whoa, girlfriend," Wendy said. "You're gonna wear out the linoleum way ahead of its time."

Pace, pace, pace. Hit the wall. Pivot. Pace, pace, pace. Repeat.

She liked the short rhythm of measuring off Wendy's small kitchen in her high-heeled shoes. It kept her focused on something other than her tumultuous feelings.

"Can you at least give me a hint at what's got you so agitated?"

Meggie opened her mouth and started to speak, but then sighed and just shook her head, not knowing how or where to start.

"What? Talk to me. How can I help if you don't tell me what's going on?"

"It's all wrong," Meggie finally said.

"What's all wrong?"

"What I'm feeling."

"You're gonna have to clue me in." Wendy's brow dipped in an expression of concern. "What are you feeling?"

"I think I've fallen in love with him."

Wendy gasped. "Oh, Meggie, I knew you were going to lose your heart. You're just not the kind of girl who can love 'em and leave 'em."

Irritated, Meggie waved a hand. "That's where you're wrong. I used Don Juan to bolster my damaged ego and I thanked him and walked away." She snapped her fingers. "Just like that."

"But I thought you said you thought you were falling in love with him."

She shook her head. "Not Don Juan."

"Then who?"

"Caleb."

"What?" Wendy looked as shocked as Meggie felt.

"I know. It's illogical, irrational, but there it is. I'm in love with him."

"Wow."

"The awful thing is, he doesn't feel the same way about me."

"How do you know?"

"I kissed him," Meggie admitted. "And he backed off. Quick. Told me he'd met someone else."

"Ouch."

Meggie bit her bottom lip to keep from crying. "I feel like such an idiot."

"Are you sure Caleb doesn't have feelings for you? If he just met this woman, surely it's not that serious. What if you told him how you felt?"

"I can't do that," Meggie wailed.

"Why not?"

Why not indeed?

Because she was afraid to put her heart on the line. Afraid of getting hurt again. How did she know that what she was feeling for Caleb was real and not some weird case of transference? But all the signs of real love were there, weren't they? Her heart skipped a beat whenever she heard his name. She'd melted when they'd kissed. She had erotic dreams about him.

He took a risk for you, Meggie. Remember that night atop the Space Needle when he dared to brave those heights? Take a chance on him. He might surprise you.

"You owe it to you both to at least go and talk to him," Wendy said. "Ask yourself this—what have you got to lose if you don't?"

Meggie eyed her friend, swallowed hard and whispered, "Everything."

"I'M SORRY, MA'AM. Mr. Greenleaf has checked out."

"Checked out?" Numbly, Meggie stared at the desk clerk. "What do you mean, checked out?"

"Mr. Greenleaf paid his bill and vacated the premises about…" the man consulted his watch "…an hour ago."

"No. There must be some mistake. He has one more lecture to give. He's not supposed to leave town until the middle of the week."

Even to her own ears her voice sounded high and desperate. The desk clerk probably thought she was a certified nutcase.

The clerk shrugged. "I'm sorry," he repeated.

"Maybe he moved to another hotel. Did he leave a number where he could be reached?" She curled her fingers around the counter and stood on tiptoes to peer over the desk, as if the paperwork stretched out in neat piles might reveal some clue about Caleb's unexpected departure.

"No. He left no forwarding number."

"Oh." Meggie let out a sigh and settled the soles of her shoes back down on the ground. She felt as if she'd just taken a swift kick to the solar plexus. Where had Caleb gone?

Perhaps he's staying with his new girlfriend. The thought hit her like a sledgehammer.

"Wait." The clerk pulled a yellow Post-it off the edge of a nearby computer screen. "Are you Meggie Scofield?"

She pressed a hand to her throat. "Yes. Yes, I am."

"It seems Mr. Greenleaf left a package for you."

"A package? For me?" she parroted.

"Just a minute. I'll get it from the back room."

"Okay."

The clerk disappeared through a door behind the

desk. Meggie glanced down at her hands and was surprised to find them trembling.

Calm down. Don't jump to conclusions.

A couple of minutes later the desk clerk returned
with a brown paper bag. "Here you are, Ms. Scofield."

Meggie took the sack and went to sit down in a plush
upholstered chair in the lobby. She set the sack on the
floor, opened it up and removed a pair of shiny, knee-
length leather boots.

What the heck?

Her pulse skipped erratically. What was this?

Next she extracted a pair of black leather drawstring
pants, a black cape and a white, puffy-sleeved pirate's
shirt. By the time she reached the bottom of the bag
and the black leather mask, Meggie literally could not
breathe.

She stared at the evidence in her hand, at first choosing not to comprehend what it meant. Then she sucked
in a shuddering breath.

Oh no! Oh no! It couldn't be!

Don Juan and Caleb, one and the same? Just like in
her dream?

Disbelief knifed her belly.

Caleb simply could not be Don Juan. No way. There
had to be another explanation. Honest, trustworthy
Caleb would never have deceived her this way.

The main question was, why?

Why had this kind, understated man gone to great
lengths to hide his real self? Why the charade? Was it
because he simply wanted an erotic adventure of his
own before finding a wife and settling down for good?
Meggie cringed to realize she had been far more than
eager to oblige.

Or was there a more deep-seated reason?

Denial is not just a river in Egypt, honey.

Meggie rubbed her fingers over the leather mask and clamped her lips closed over a deep, mournful moan. Her life was filled with lies, lies and more lies. The lies Caleb had told her. The lies she'd told herself.

She had wanted so desperately to believe in a fantasy, to relish the way he made her feel as a sexual being, that she had been too selfish to see beyond the mask to the real man beneath. In an attempt to assuage her emotional pain and bolster her self-confidence, she'd accepted Don Juan at face value. She'd gone seeking shallow pleasures, telling herself it was all in the name of living a little.

She hadn't wanted to look beyond surface appearance. Why else had she insisted they make love in the dark after the Halloween party? Why else had she refused to remove his mask last night, even after he'd begged her to?

That's when she realized the startling truth. Somewhere deep down inside her, in the part that had ached to live out her wildest fantasies, she'd secretly known all along that Don Juan was Caleb. She had wanted the pleasure without accepting the responsibility of a real relationship, so she had willingly indulged in his pretense.

And now they were both in pain. Suffering for their perilous masquerade.

She had no one to blame for this mess but herself.

CALEB SNOWSHOED THROUGH the forest. He'd gotten reports of poachers in the area, and he was checking out the sightings, but his heart wasn't in his work. He missed Meggie something fierce. Missed her and hated himself for his weakness.

It had been almost two weeks since he'd left Seattle and returned home to Bear Creek. Two weeks, and he hadn't heard a word from her. He told himself he was glad, that it was for the best. But he was lying.

For the hundred millionth time, he imagined her sitting in the lobby of the Claremont Hotel, looking through the paper bag, realizing for the first time that he was her masked lover.

His gut twisted at the thought of her pain.

She probably despised him. Probably felt pretty darn betrayed.

Well, no more than he. Caleb had thought Meggie was different. That if any woman could accept him for the man he was and not for the money he'd made, Meggie would have been the one. When she'd told him she needed security, she'd as good as turned his soul inside out and stomped on it with both feet.

Yeah? Well, buddy boy, how can you expect her to accept you for your authentic self when you deceived her? Lies don't breed trust.

How many countless times had he had this argument with himself since returning home? A thousand? Ten thousand?

He should let the whole thing go, stop poking and prodding the snafu with his mind. It was better this way. They'd had great sex. Both of them had gotten their needs met. Problem was, he'd romanticized the situation, made out their loving to be more than it was.

So why the hell couldn't he stop thinking about her— and wishing things could be different?

Caleb snorted, disgusted with himself. He'd manufactured this house of cards. He shouldn't have been surprised when it came tumbling down. Solid relationships were built on honesty and trust. They had neither. Because without honesty, how could you trust someone?

He tramped through the forest, not really noticing where he was going. The wind gusted with the waning daylight. He snuggled deeper into his parka and raised his head to see where he was. He should be getting back to the ranger station before nightfall.

That's when he saw where his subconscious had been leading him.

To the clearing in the woods. To the skaters' cabin where he and Meggie had first become intimate. He stared at the cabin, remembering, and a fresh tear rendered his heart in two.

CHAPTER SIXTEEN

THE TELEPHONE RANG.

As she'd been doing for the past three weeks every time the stupid thing jangled, Meggie jumped and made a mad dash for the receiver.

Caleb?

"Hello?"

"Meggie?"

Her hopes fractured. "Kay?"

"What's going on?" her friend demanded in a none-too-pleasant tone of voice. "Your mother just told me that you're not coming home for the holidays."

"I can't afford the time off from work," Meggie said.

It wasn't a total lie. She'd recently been promoted, so there was no problem with her job. Although she was entitled to take time off at Christmas, even after taking a leave of absence this past summer, working overtime during the holidays would go a long way toward earning her additional brownie points with her boss.

But the real reason she'd told her mother she wasn't coming home for Christmas had nothing to do with work and everything to do with Caleb. She wasn't up to facing him again. Not yet. Not now. Not until her heart had plenty of time to heal. Whenever the hell that might be.

"I've got to tell you, Meggie, Sadie is really hurt you're not coming back for their wedding."

In the tumult of her messy love life she'd forgotten all about Jake and Sadie's wedding. "I'm really sorry. Tell Sadie I'll make it up to her."

"If she's lucky a girl only gets married once," Kay chided.

"You're right. I'm a terrible friend. What can I say?"

"Just tell me what in the hell happened between you and Caleb."

"Caleb?" Meggie heard her voice rise an octave. "Who said anything happened between me and Caleb?"

"Oh, come on. The way you two were making goo-goo eyes at each other at the *Metropolitan* party, the way Caleb came home in an utterly black mood, the way he scowls whenever your name is mentioned… I'm not dumb."

Stunned, Meggie blinked. "You knew that Caleb was Don Juan?"

"Well, of course I did."

"Why didn't you say something?"

"Because you and Caleb both needed a grand romantic adventure. I don't know what happened, but you two need to make up. It's as obvious as the noses on your faces you guys were made for each other."

"It is?"

"For a smart woman you can sometimes be pretty dense, sister-in-law mine."

"You don't understand. This thing between me and Caleb is very complicated."

"Whatever. But by behaving like a spoiled brat you're hurting a lot of other people."

"Spoiled brat?" Meggie felt herself growing angry.

"Yes, spoiled brat. Just because you and Caleb aren't speaking to each other doesn't mean the rest of us should have to suffer. Your folks want to see you for the holidays. Sadie and Jake want you at the wedding. And there's something else you're needed for. *Metropolitan* found out Bear Creek's health-care needs are grossly underserved and they're planning on holding a Christmas bachelor action as a fund-raiser for a new clinic. They wanted to know if you'd serve as spokeswoman."

"They did?"

"Yes. Caleb's going to be in the auction."

Meggie gripped the receiver tighter. "That's not really an enticement."

"Okay, here it is. My big confession. I need you to come home."

"You?" Meggie laughed. Kay was the most self-contained woman she knew. "Why would you need me?"

There was a pause.

Anxiety gripped Meggie. "Kay? You and Quinn aren't having problems, are you?"

"No. Nothing like that."

"What is it then?"

"I need a nurse to assuage my fears."

"Are you sick?" Alarm swept through her at the thought her sister-in-law might be seriously ill.

"Well, not exactly."

"What then, exactly?"

"Quinn and I were going to wait for Christmas day to spill the beans, but since you won't be here, I might as well tell you now."

"For heaven's sake, Kay, tell me what?"

"I'm pregnant."

"Let's hear it for bachelor number three," Kay spoke into the microphone. "Put your hands together for the single remaining bachelor from the Bachelors of Bear

Creek *Metropolitan* ad. You know him, you love him, our own Caleb Greenleaf."

Wild applause, catcalls and whistles greeted Kay's announcement. Liam Kilstrom shone the spotlight and played a short refrain of "Bad Boys" as Caleb strutted out on stage in tight blue jeans and a red flannel shirt. He looked so handsome Meggie forgot to breathe.

Jitterbug nervous, she stood at the back of room, her heart in her throat, running her hands over her brand-new outfit. Red leather pants, red silk blouse, red cowboy boots. She had arrived a few minutes earlier, slipping through the doors and lurking among the crowd. So far only Mack—who had flown her in from Anchorage—knew she was home.

The Bear Creek community center, gaily decorated with red and green Christmas lights, was packed to the rafters with women of all shapes, ages and sizes, eager to bid on the bachelors and add to the charity coffers for the *Metropolitan* clinic fund.

Meggie's stomach knotted. She chewed her bottom lip. She was willing to spend all her savings if that's what it took to win Caleb away from the next highest bidder.

"Let's start the bidding at a hundred dollars," Kay called out. "Who's willing to fork over a hundred dollars for the pleasure of this man's company?"

Two dozen hands shot up.

Meggie cleared her throat. "Five hundred dollars."

"Goodness, ladies, you hear that? Someone is willing to shell out five hundred dollars." Kay grinned. "Do I hear five hundred and ten?"

Most of the women who'd bid earlier dropped out, all but one saucy lady that Meggie recognized as Lizzy

Magnuson, a friend of Sadie's. Lizzy had recently moved to Bear Creek from San Francisco.

Boldly, Lizzy waved a hand. "Six hundred."

"Seven hundred," Meggie exclaimed.

Kay shaded her forehead with her hand. "Okay, who's Miss Moneybags in the back of the room?"

Meggie moved closer to the stage, pushing through the crowd of women, her eyes on Caleb.

He stared at her, first with shocked surprise. Then a wide grin spread across his face and his eyes crinkled in greeting.

Meggie's heart soared. He was happy to see her!

She kept walking. People shifted, allowing her through.

"Seven-fifty," Lizzy challenged.

"Eight hundred." Meggie never dropped her gaze from Caleb's.

"Nine hundred." Lizzy was damned determined, but Meggie was even more so.

"A thousand dollars." She arrived at the edge of the stage.

Caleb took the microphone from Kay and dropped to his knees in front of Meggie. His stare drilled a hole straight through her. "Sold to the lady in red for one thousand dollars."

The crowd went nuts, laughing and talking and cheering.

Caleb tossed the microphone back to Kay, hopped down off the stage, took Meggie by the elbow and swept her out the exit and into the cloakroom.

He spun her around to face him. His intense blue eyes ate her up. "You came home."

"I came home." Now that they were alone, she felt her nervousness return.

"For Christmas? For the wedding?"

"For good."

"What? But you're a city girl. You love Seattle. Why would you move back to Bear Creek?"

"A lot of reasons."

"Yeah?" He arched a quizzical eyebrow.

"Well, *Metropolitan* offered me a job running their clinic."

"Oh they did, did they?" He pulled her into his arms. It felt so good. So right. The minute his chest touched hers everything just fell into place.

"Uh-huh. And Kay's going to need a lot of help with that baby. Did you hear? I'm going to be an aunt."

"You being a nurse will really come in handy." His lips were millimeters from hers. His rich, masculine scent filled her nostrils.

"True."

"So are those the only reasons that you decided to move back?"

"Well," she said, enjoying drawing this out, "there is one other reason."

"And that is?"

"I discovered I don't need the big city for excitement, after all."

"No?"

"Nope."

"If that's the case, then how do you plan on getting your kicks from now on?"

"I was kind of hoping you might help me answer that question."

"Me or Don Juan?"

She bit her lip, dropped her gaze. He cupped her chin in his palms, raised her face and made her look at him.

"Why did you leave me that night, Meggie?" Caleb whispered.

It hurt looking him in the eyes and seeing just how much she had wounded him. "I wasn't ready to face the truth. But then again, I wasn't the only one running away. Why did you flee Seattle? Why did you leave me the sack? Why didn't you tell me face-to-face?"

"I owe you an apology for that. I have no excuse. I was scared to death and that's the honest truth."

"What were you afraid of?"

He swallowed so hard his Adam's apple bobbed. "That you only wanted me for my money."

Meggie shook her head. "Why on earth would you think that?"

"When I tried to get you to take my mask off, to acknowledge who I was, you told me you needed security. I realize I'm apprehensive about money issues, because of the way my mother is, because of my childhood. But I was afraid you could never love me for myself."

"Caleb, I meant *emotional* security. As exciting as Don Juan was, I needed more. Great sex wasn't enough. I needed a strong, steady, reliable man."

"You thought the sex was great?"

"You're an amazing lover. An amazing man."

"Really? You don't mind a guy who'd rather commune with nature than join the rat race in pursuit of the almighty dollar?"

"I don't give a damn about your money. Give it away for all I care."

"You're serious."

"As a heart attack."

Caleb couldn't believe what he was hearing. He reached out with his index finger and pushed an inky curl from her cheek. As he stared into her upturned face, he couldn't recall ever having been moved so deeply by anything.

"I've loved you since I was fourteen years old, Meggie Scofield. But because I believed I never stood a chance with you, I convinced myself the attraction was purely physical."

She gazed up at him with a quiet acceptance in her eyes that gave him the courage to continue.

"I was a goofy kid who liked hanging out in the woods watching animals. You were older and so sophisticated. I knew you were out of my league and yet I couldn't stop fantasizing about being with you."

"You fantasized about me?"

"Babe, you have no idea."

"I never thought I was fantasy-worthy," Meggie admitted. "I mean, my butt is too big for the rest of me and I've got freckles and my face is sort of plain and—"

"Shh." He placed his finger on her lips. "I love your butt. It's perfect. I adore your freckles, and your face is most certainly not *plain.* I know you've got this idea that you're not very pretty, and my stupid stepbrother is partially to blame for your distorted sense of yourself, but I'm sorry to disillusion you, Megs. I think you're gorgeous and I always have."

"Honest?" she whispered.

"I tried to forget you. I had a few flings in college and thought I got you out of my system.

"But I never could seem to connect with anyone. Not with the level of intimacy I craved. And then when you strutted into the costume party in that Klondike Kate costume, I was a goner, even though at the time I had no idea it was you."

"I fell for Don Juan the minute I saw him, too."

"No kidding?"

"No kidding."

"When you whispered your phone number to me and I realized Klondike Kate was you I was totally rattled. After what we'd done in the skaters' cabin…" He shook his head. "I wasn't going to act on the attraction. I tried to pretend it never happened. But then I get this invitation from that committee you were on, asking me to give lectures in Seattle and I'm thinking maybe you had figured out that I was Don Juan and this was your way of asking me to come for you."

"I didn't realize you were Don Juan, at least not consciously," she admitted. "But deep down inside, I knew. That's why I didn't call. I thought I'd just been using you to get over Jesse. But I couldn't stop thinking about you. And when Kay told me how miserable you were, I knew I had to come home. I had to discover if there was a chance for us. Do we have a chance together, Caleb?"

"Do you really have to ask?"

She smiled. "I love you, Caleb Greenleaf."

"You know what, Meggie Scofield?"

"What?"

He pointed above her head. Meggie glanced up, saw she was standing under a sprig of mistletoe.

"I love you, too."

She said, "Oh," just as his mouth closed over hers and he gave her a thrill to remember.

Forever.

EPILOGUE

MEGGIE AND CALEB were married exactly one year to the day after the masked costume ball where suave Don Juan first clamped eyes on his mysterious Klondike Kate. The ceremony took place in the Tongass National Forest on the front porch of the skaters' cabin. The guest list included the entire town of Bear Creek, Meggie's friends from Seattle and the *Metropolitan* editorial staff, who'd insisted on paying for their reception as the last bachelor joined his buddies in wedded bliss.

From where she sat in the audience, Kay shifted baby Ella on her lap, leaned against Quinn's big, comforting chest and whispered, "I told you they were meant for each other."

He laughed softly. "Who am I to argue with an intuitive woman? You convinced me that I was perfect for you and you were right on the money."

"And don't you ever forget it." Kay regarded him with loving eyes.

"As if I ever could." He draped his arm across his wife's shoulder and pulled her and the baby closer to him.

Quinn gazed over the crowd and met the eyes of his buddy Mack, who was one of Caleb's groomsmen. Mack grinned and mouthed, "Look what you started with that advertisement" and nodded at his wife, Cammie Jo, who was positioned at the makeshift altar. Cammie Jo wore a chic maternity bridesmaid's dress and an expression of pure joy.

Sadie, Meggie's matron of honor, stood beside Cammie Jo. Sadie studied the blushing bride with a hitch of happiness in her throat. Meggie looked completely adorable in her white wedding gown and that red-feathered mask substituting for a veil. And Caleb was pretty darned handsome in his Don Juan outfit. Although, in Sadie's estimation, no one was as handsome as her husband, Jake.

Sadie snagged Jake's gaze. As Caleb's best man, he was positioned across from her. Sadie tipped the corners of her mouth up in a Mona Lisa smile. Jake winked. Just wait until she told him about the outcome of her recent doctor's visit. It looked as if Bear Creek was in for a real population boom, courtesy of those lusty ex-bachelors.

Sadie's attention was drawn back to the ceremony when Caleb started reciting in a deep, poetic voice the wedding vows he'd written himself.

"Darling, you are my sun, my moon, my stars, my everything. My heart lights up when you walk into a room. You've helped me to change, to grow, to become a better man. I promise to spend the rest of my life showing you exactly how much I love you." With shaky fingers Caleb took off Meggie's red-feathered mask and gazed into the sweet face he knew as intimately as his own. "The removal of our masks symbolizes that we lay bare our souls to each other and place our faith in the greatest power of all—real and unconditional love."

The audience sighed in unison.

Tears rolled down Meggie's cheek as she gazed deeply into his eyes. Caleb's heart thumped with emotion. To think this wondrous day had come at last.

Sadie handed Meggie a handkerchief and she dabbed

the tears away before raising her hand to remove his mask.

"I lay bare my soul to you, Caleb Joshua Greenleaf. From this day forward we are one. I, Megan Marie Scofield, take the…"

As she continued, Caleb was aware of nothing except his beloved bride and their bright future together. Not the crowd, nor the minister, not the majestic mountains surrounding them. He was the luckiest man on earth to have captured the heart of the woman he'd loved for half his life, and he knew it.

"I now pronounce you husband and wife," the minister announced.

Caleb's lips took possession of Meggie's in a kiss so powerful her body hummed with its impact. The crowd cheered when he deepened the kiss.

After a long, rapturous minute, he dragged his mouth from hers, pressed his lips to her ear and whispered, "You know we have an hour before the reception starts, Mrs. Greenleaf."

"What are you suggesting, Mr. Greenleaf?" she whispered back, tantalized by his bold innuendo right here in front of everyone.

When she had set her course for adventure that fateful night she'd followed Don Juan into the woods, she had never guessed she would get everything she'd bargained for and then some. Her body tingled with anticipation for what lay ahead.

Caleb took her hand and led her down the path strewn with rose petals. A saddled horse awaited as their getaway ride. The guests got to their feet and blew bubbles as they walked past.

"A game?" he whispered.

"What kind of game?" she murmured, all the while

smiling at the crowd. "Master and slave? Doctor and nurse? The Big Bad Wolf and Little Red Riding Hood?"

"You know my favorite."

"Mountain man and city girl?"

"You got it," he growled.

"In the park ranger's cabin?"

"I was thinking on horseback." He stopped beside the waiting steed.

"Caleb!" She spoke too loudly, then glanced over her shoulder to find that everyone was still watching. She ducked her head and lowered her voice. "Is that even possible?"

"Never know until you try."

His strong hands spanned her waist and he lifted her onto the saddle. The crowd cheered and applauded. Caleb climbed up behind her. He gathered the reins and urged the horse into a trot.

They quickly disappeared into the forest. His back was flush against hers, and even through the lacy material of her wedding dress, she could feel the evidence of his desire pressing hard against her fanny.

He slowed the horse to a walk and wrapped his arms around her. Meggie leaned her head into the curve of his neck and sighed deeply. Her mind expanded with the erotic logistics of making love in the saddle.

Caleb growled low in his throat. "You are the sexiest woman in the world. Do you have any idea what you do to me?"

"Mmm." She turned her head and flicked out her tongue, licking a hot, wet trail along his jaw as she slipped her hands behind her back and undid the string ties on his leather pants.

"What...what are you doing?" he asked in a gravelly voice.

"Following up on your fantasy. If we're clever we might not even have to take our clothes off. Oh, by the way, I forgot to mention I'm not wearing any underwear."

His chuckle was low and seductive. "Neither am I, babe. Neither am I."

"I love playing games with you."

"There's no one else on the face of the earth I want to play games with."

Her nimble fingers separated the leather material at his fly, and Caleb's now-exposed rock-hard shaft burgeoned in her hand, letting her know just how much he wanted her.

"Ah, woman, see what your naughty games do to me?"

Meggie trembled with excitement as the man she loved slid his hands beneath her dress, cupped her bare bottom in his palms and lifted her off the saddle.

As he eased her down over his erection, Meggie hissed in her breath and whispered, "Let the games begin."

* * * * *

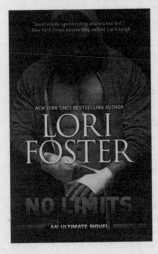

REQUEST YOUR
FREE BOOKS!

2 FREE NOVELS
FROM THE ROMANCE COLLECTION
PLUS 2 FREE GIFTS!

YES! Please send me 2 FREE novels from the Romance Collection and my 2 FREE gifts (gifts are worth about $10). After receiving them, if I don't wish to receive any more books, I can return the shipping statement marked "cancel." If I don't cancel, I will receive 4 brand-new novels every month and be billed just $6.24 per book in the U.S. or $6.74 per book in Canada. That's a savings of at least 22% off the cover price. It's quite a bargain! Shipping and handling is just 50¢ per book in the U.S. and 75¢ per book in Canada.* I understand that accepting the 2 free books and gifts places me under no obligation to buy anything. I can always return a shipment and cancel at any time. Even if I never buy another book, the two free books and gifts are mine to keep forever.

194/394 MDN F4XY

Name	(PLEASE PRINT)

Address	Apt. #

City	State/Prov.	Zip/Postal Code

Signature (if under 18, a parent or guardian must sign)

Mail to the Harlequin® Reader Service:
IN U.S.A.: P.O. Box 1867, Buffalo, NY 14240-1867
IN CANADA: P.O. Box 609, Fort Erie, Ontario L2A 5X3

Want to try two free books from another line?
Call 1-800-873-8635 or visit www.ReaderService.com.

* Terms and prices subject to change without notice. Prices do not include applicable taxes. Sales tax applicable in N.Y. Canadian residents will be charged applicable taxes. Offer not valid in Quebec. This offer is limited to one order per household. Not valid for current subscribers to the Romance Collection or the Romance/Suspense Collection. All orders subject to credit approval. Credit or debit balances in a customer's account(s) may be offset by any other outstanding balance owed by or to the customer. Please allow 4 to 6 weeks for delivery. Offer available while quantities last.

Your Privacy—The Harlequin® Reader Service is committed to protecting your privacy. Our Privacy Policy is available online at www.ReaderService.com or upon request from the Harlequin Reader Service.

We make a portion of our mailing list available to reputable third parties that offer products we believe may interest you. If you prefer that we not exchange your name with third parties, or if you wish to clarify or modify your communication preferences, please visit us at www.ReaderService.com/consumerchoice or write to us at Harlequin Reader Service Preference Service, P.O. Box 9062, Buffalo, NY 14269. Include your complete name and address.

ROM13R

New York Times bestselling author
DIANA PALMER

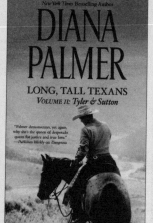

TYLER

If a man took only a cursory glance at Nell Regan, he could easily miss the beauty in her shy face, or the sexy figure hidden beneath her shapeless clothes. Nell has learned the hard way that she doesn't have anything to offer a man. Her future is here in Arizona, running her dude ranch by herself...until Tyler Jacobs arrives. But Nell's not about to mistake kindness for love. Not again. Yet could denying her own desire destroy her one chance for happiness?

SUTTON

With one glance of his piercing black eyes, rancher Quinn Sutton makes an indelible mark on Amanda Callaway, and she finds herself increasingly fascinated by her new neighbor. She quickly learns that the gruff single father isn't only devastatingly handsome, but he also insists on having *his* ranch run according to *his* rules—it's Sutton's way or the highway. But Amanda has her own secrets and plans to keep her distance. If only she weren't falling for her unlikely hero....

Available now wherever books are sold!

Be sure to connect with us at:

Harlequin.com/Newsletters

Facebook.com/HarlequinBooks

Twitter.com/HarlequinBooks

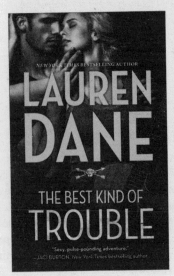